THE POSTMEN'S HOUSE

By the same author

The Bridge
Stop House Blues

THE POSTMEN'S HOUSE

Maggie Hemingway

SINCLAIR-STEVENSON

First published in Great Britain by
Sinclair-Stevenson Limited
7/8 Kendrick Mews
London sw7 3hg, England

British Library Cataloguing in Publication Data

Hemingway, Maggie
    The postmen's house.
    I. Title
    823.914

    isbn 1-85619-009-9

Typeset by Rowland Phototypesetting Limited,
Bury St Edmunds, Suffolk
Printed and bound in Great Britain by Richard Clay Limited,
Bungay, Suffolk

DICKENS, DARWIN, DOSTOEVSKY – that's what we've got painted on our door in large red letters. Walking down the street for the first time and catching sight of it, it stopped me in my tracks: the artlessness, the boldness, the reckless freedom of it. I remember I gasped and laughed all in one breath. Then, out of habit, I glanced quickly over my shoulder to see if anyone was watching me. But the road was deserted; it lay disinterested and silent in the late morning sun and there, not twenty yards away, at the end where it formed a cul de sac, was the House. It looked out of place in the crumbling bow-fronted terrace. It seemed to nestle back into its draperies of creeper and ivy with a comfort felt nowhere else on the street, a curious battlemented tower rising above its gothic-arched doorway. And the door. A double door with yellow painted panels, bright yellow like the door of a child's playhouse, or a progressive kindergarten. Van Gogh yellow. And on one of them the words – Dickens, Darwin, Dostoevsky – a rhyme for precocious children, a mnemonic for life. I walked up to it and put my hand out, gingerly, to push open the unlatched half of the door. I was so close I could see the brush strokes and the way that the paint had run into little splinters. I brushed my fingertips across the words, and laughed softly, but they did not disappear.

Inside the door, when I got to know people well enough to talk to, nobody seemed to set much store by the words. Nobody knew what it was supposed to mean. When I asked people about it, they would stare at it as though at something strange but harmless. 'Ah, yes,' they would say and smile bemusedly. To others the mere mention of it would make them angry. These people, I thought to myself, either already know what it means and find it at odds with their own ethics, or know that they will never know what it means and therefore despise it. No one could remember when it first appeared on the door, or who had done it. No one seemed to take any notice of it at all. But I became obsessed by it. It was like a secret that I could not now unlock, but whose presence, even in its unsolved state, filled me with reassurance. The sight of it as I left each day would send me off whistling and when I returned to it again as dawn broke every morning I was always full of apprehension that it might have been painted out in my absence. But it never was. And that was strange, perhaps the most curious thing of all, because our building was an official one. Postmen's House, District 17.

Now that I am an inmate of the House it is difficult to describe it with any objectivity. It is. And I am. And all I want is for the being and the belonging to go on and on. To pass in through that yellow door, past Dickens and Darwin and Dostoevsky, and be absorbed into the world beyond. It was pure chance that I was assigned to District 17 – the random hovering of a pencil over the grids of an official map in Head Office.

'We got a vacancy in 3 and we got another in 17. What's it going to be?'

The pencil darted into a tangled mass of black streets, paused for a second, then, extricating itself, lunged against a small white space. I stared at the map, at

London spread out before me like a vast landmass, an unknown continent demarcated by red lines into countries. Their borders fitted neatly against each other like jigsaw pieces drawn with a ruler. Some of them made strange incursions into each other, small squared-off, half-inch forays, or curious triangular invasions. Across my imagination flitted images of pitched battles for a street or square and I wondered briefly what property they might possess to make them so coveted. But to a stateless person any country may be a refuge. All are equally unknown. I could distinguish nothing familiar on this map except its river which snaked and wormed its way through the great city towards the sea, as though trying to evade capture by any district bordering on its shores.

'What's your lucky number then, 17 or 3?'

I smiled and shook my head.

'Nine.'

'Well then, where d'you live? Where's your mum? Or your auntie?'

My mother was on every street corner, in every shop window I passed. And my father's sister lived in a small room over a tobacconist in an alley off Gregor Mendel Square, in one of the inner districts of Prague. But this was not relevant to the present inquiry. I cleared my throat:

'We've got lodgings in Victoria.'

The pencil tapped its point briskly against the small white space, as if its speed of thought was swifter than the man's who held it.

'Right! That's 17 then, isn't it. Cross the river, follow your nose and you're there. Oudenard Road. Number 63. Ask for Mr Harry. Send him my best and tell him he still owes me for the one that came out of the trap backwards. Very hot on the dogs is Mr Harry. And if Mr Harry's not available, you see Sid.'

With a crackling of duplicate and triplicate carbon

papers a docket was made out, separated, stamped, signed and pushed across the desk towards me.

'Don't lose it. You'll need it when you get there. You can tell them we've sent you, but they won't let you in unless you got proof. Stickler for the book is Mr Harry.'

To meet Mr Harry is a deceptive experience. And you will meet Mr Harry if you go to the Postmen's House. You can push open the yellow door without a creak and tiptoe across the gloom of the concreted entrance hall, but he will hear you. You will look up from your concentrated tiptoeing and he will be there waiting quietly for you in a doorway. Even when he is not there, he will know that you have been. He will say to Sid, when he returns, not looking at him directly, but at some notice pinned upon the wall, some paper lying on a table:

'Had any Inquirers, Sid, while I've been away?'

He has a very gentle voice, Mr Harry. A very pleasant voice; low but clear. He never has to speak twice. The words roll out softly, swiftly into the silence one after another. You almost think his lips aren't moving, though you can see they are; you almost think that you are making up in your head the words you hear. But there is Mr Harry, waiting for an answer, looking as if he knows it already and is in fact thinking about something more pressing, but is just checking to make sure you know it too. It would be impossible to lie to Mr Harry. Not even Sid could bring himself to do that. Sid least of all. Sid cannot hide anything from Mr Harry. As Court Chamberlain to Mr Harry's King it wouldn't be right. But, position apart, it couldn't, psychologically, be done.

He is quite small, Mr Harry, so is Sid; and old – late fifties at least – and so is Sid. But Sid is younger. We've never been able to work out how much younger, whether days are involved, or years, but younger, certainly. Though Mr Harry is the dominant character, Sid takes upon himself the role of his protector. Should Mr Harry go to see about an Inquirer or a delivery or some unusual noise that has caught his fine ear, Sid will be unable to let him out of his sight for more than a quarter of a minute. He will be drawn after him. I have watched him. Whatever he is doing will not exactly cease but will continue in a long movement which involves him being drawn out after Mr Harry, hovering at his shoulder, assuring himself that he requires no assistance and moving back to his work again all in a kind of effortless glide like a sleepwalker, letters or documents still in his hands. And the movement in which he was involved before the interruption will then be completed. Sometimes Mr Harry will turn and involve Sid in the Inquiry. But in the presence of Mr Harry and a stranger Sid generally doesn't say much. His mild face appears a few inches behind Mr Harry's, a slight tension in the brown eyes, a slight shyness mixed with deferentiality keeping him back in the shadows. He has a high-domed forehead and less hair than Mr Harry and this gives his face a certain lugubriousness in comparison. Mr Harry is all of a neatness. Small-boned and open-faced with wise eyes changeable as the colour of water. And a manner that draws conversation out of you. You tell him all he wants to know and then, later, it is difficult to recall exactly what he said. They are quite different characters, Mr Harry and Sid, and yet in one's mind they become inseparable, linked by invisible threads, so that you cannot form the image of one without, soon, having the other materialise beside them. They are never hurried, but they are always busy, never without an envelope or two in their hands. They are Lettermen to their fingertips. Not Walkers, like us, but senior members of the hierarchy who have won the right to remain in the House all day, and no longer brave the wind or the rain or the uncertain darkness of a winter morning. Mr Sid 'n' 'Arry Jack calls them – out of earshot. Jack works next to me in the Big Room. There's just the Big Room and the Back Room in the Postmen's House. And the Tower, but none of us Walkers is allowed up there. I haven't come across anyone yet who's been in it.

'Go up there, mate,' Jack says, 'you might never get down. Bread and water job. Don't touch it.'

I would have liked to have met the architect who designed our building. I would have liked to have known the exact wording of his brief and heard from his own lips the account of the discussions he must have had with the directors of the General Post Office. But unless he obtained his commission as a very young man and has lived into his nineties, he will have been dead for some time. For the Postmen's House was completed in 1902. There is a lozenge above the door incised with the date and surmounted with the King's arms: E.R. and trailing stone leaves. All we needed was a large room. But to those top-hatted gentlemen such meagre provision was unthinkable. It was an age of pomp, largesse, expansiveness and pleasure, even in the Post Office. Never had there been so many collections and so many deliveries of letters and telegraphic communications. There was pride to think of and the glory of the King and the bottomless coffer of Treasury for the embellishment of Industry. I can imagine we were industrious then, working double the shifts on a fraction of the pay and proud of the steady job and the polished badge – servant of the Crown. So they gave us a castle. A folly.

Every man's house is his castle, so they say in England. But I can't decide whether our architect was a man in a bushy handlebar moustache with an Edwardian fondness for practical jokes, or whether he was lean and serious. Whether his commission was for one new Postmen's House, or a batch of six all to have different facades, and plans to be delivered for approval by the next quarter day. Did he just fling at us battlements and at another Dutch gables? Or did he come out to the site at the bottom of Oudenard Road and walk down the brand new bay-fronted terrace while a smile curled up into the

shadow of the handlebars at the smug, proscribed awful-
ness of it. I incline to the latter. I think he was a man who
knew how to please all his masters – and himself. He
knew of the Postmaster General's pride and the King's
honour and the postmen's weary feet. He studied the
postal service schedules and visualised the huge sacks of
mail going in and the small sacks of mail trudging out. He
walked around the site and looked up at the solid dreariness of Oudenard Road and wondered what he could do
to enliven it. While on the corner of an envelope, almost
without his noticing it, his pencil began to sketch a
driveway wide enough for the heaviest of His Majesty's
Post Waggons. Along one side of the driveway he blackened in a wall with deep, meditative strokes and topped
it with a tower and crenellated battlements picked out in
white stone. Then, leaping a space for a gateway, his
pencil flourished out into a semi-circular courtyard
around the rear perimeter of the site. He cross-hatched
iron spikes along the top of its wall and thought of the
sacks of mail unloading into the courtyard, the horses
steaming and shaking their heads to make their bridles
ring. He thought of the work to come next, while his
pencil waited, rounding off gate-posts with urns and
swags and plaster leaves, marking out loading bays. He
saw the sacks untied, the contents spilled out on long
tables lined with sorters. Four walls and a roof, he
murmured to himself and saw nimble fingers darting
among the spillage. Abdale Road, Bedford Place,
Caernarvon Crescent, Dunloe Mews. 1 comes before 2, 2
comes before 3, 3 . . .

He designed us a schoolroom. A large airy room with
arched windows set high in the walls, close to the roof,
too tall for us ever to be able to see out and be distracted
from our work. Instead of desks we have sets of open
boxes, like lockers. Each box represents a street and each
set a man's territory. You can mark out the whole district
just looking around the room from man to man. My

territory is in between Mr Finch's on my left and Jack's on my right. There is, in the early hours of the morning, a trance-like quality to the atmosphere of the room. There is a constant soft thudding sound, like a barrage of heavy paper darts, as envelopes are thrown into boxes, a murmur rising every now and then into a curse as somebody drops a letter. But nobody turns, nobody starts at the noise, and it dies away quickly into the low surf-like rumbling that washes about the room like the random, unconnected sub-sounds of a dream. It is a strangely comfortable place to be. It smells of paper and dust and men. It slips for seconds in the timelessness of dawn into recollections of early morning classrooms. The same feeling of ragged sleepiness, our clothes heavy and unfamiliar upon us, the surprise of the cold and the softness of our mothers' kisses still on our cheeks. It is the best time for sorting letters, before the brain is fully awake to interfere. Sorting letters requires a delicate balance between hand and brain in which the hand has to dominate. The brain needs only to be sufficiently awake to decipher numbers and addresses. You acquire a facility to be able to regulate the power of the brain, like a furnace. You discover a dial which you can turn at will until the flame burns very low, until you feel that thought is scarcely moving and only a tiny portion of the brain, the millimetre required for reading envelopes, glows.

I have come to like this twilight world of thought. It has brought, because of its reduced capacities, a great simplicity to my life. A slow contentment. The contentment of just being. My pleasures now come from the most ordinary things, the smallest events. When I first came to England I was like a person who has been ill for a long time, who has floated in a grey world tossed back and forth between life and death by forces he can neither see nor touch, imprisoned day after day within the four walls of his room, their very familiarity shot through with menace. A person who, when the unfathomable waves of pain recede, and consciousness creeps back distrustful of every sound, flinches as the curtains are drawn open and sunlight streams in. At first I stared at the bars of light across my fingers, incredulous that there was ever a world beyond my world – my 'room' – that continued to be governed by laws of logic and benevolence, in which grass grew and spring turned into summer and one particle of earth sat solidly upon another. I am a convalescent of a sort and the Postmen's House is my convalescent home. Its slow tempo suits me; its acceptance and its undemandingness.

My greatest pleasure in those first days in England was to sit on the steps of the Postmen's House in the sun. Between the morning shift and the later one, or at the end of the afternoon's work. To sit with my back against the peeling paint of the door. The door on which are painted the words Dickens, Darwin, Dostoevsky. My words. My back hid them, kept them safe, though I knew there was no need. Not here. Not in England. Here we are all safe. In ones and twos my colleagues would come down the sun-warmed steps. We nodded and smiled; open English faces, shy English smiles. 'Bye Arthur.' 'Bye Fred.' 'See you, Jack.' 'Bye.' But I sat on, in the sun, in the quiet of the drowsing street. I ran the dry, dusty gravel through my fingers, staring at the grains as they dropped, handful after mesmerising handful. Even the dust was different here; the scent of it, the colour – darker somehow. English dust, I whispered to myself, rolling the pleasure of the words round in my head. Or I gazed, sun-blinded, at the leaves of the low plants that grew around the black wrought-iron railings at the gateway. Staring into the dappling of light and shade. Watching a butterfly alight suddenly on a head of groundsel. I know the names of many English butterflies. I can reel them all off, visualising them against a pale blue sky, being chased across green downs by a boy in neat socks and laced-up shoes, waving a butterfly net.

It was not me that child, though the same kind of shoes lay in my cupboard. He was some composite English child. A poster on my nursery wall. Foreign-boned, foreign-eyed, a foreign frankness to his perfect grin. We did not smile like that. In the shimmering insistence of heat my eyes would close and I would lean more heavily against the door of the Postmen's House. I would roll a stone between my fingers and the sun would beat blood-red against my eyelids. Meadow Brown, Common Blue, Purple Emperor . . .

You taught me well, darling Mama, for I have forgotten nothing. It is all just as you said it would be. Nothing that I have encountered so far is alarming, nothing is strange. Each object, each person I meet is like a clue in a treasure hunt leading me back to you, to the safe world of childhood. That world of make-believe and dressing up and recitation and charade. That private world you created for me which was always filled with the scent of English soap and Earl Grey tea. Where clothes with labels that had English writing on were folded away into the top drawer of my wardrobe, and English toys and storybooks arrived in brown paper parcels from London at Christmas and became the pride of the nursery. But of all the stories, the ones you made up were the best. I remember long afternoons and winter evenings on the sofa in front of the fire or wrapped up in your bed, drowsing against your shoulder, while you wove your endless tales of England. Until it became a magic land whose inhabitants and customs, cities and hills I knew by heart. It was your home, this magical place and therefore, you said, by extension, mine. I had a whole other family there: grandparents, cousins and aunts who became more real to me than my father's relations living round the corner in Podolska Street. I could trace with my finger their faded smiles and stare into their blinking eyes. I knew my way round their houses and the best places to play in their gardens; I learned of their feasts and their feuds.

When my father went away on business you used to keep me home from school, pleading my illness, or yours. You used to teach me English kings and queens and poetry, and march me round the flat visiting Hampton Court Palace or London Zoo. You even used to make up parcels of sandwiches in greaseproof paper and tie a silk scarf over your hair and bring in the bench from the kitchen, laughing all the time. And we would pretend we were taking a steamer trip down the Thames, or a red double-decker bus ride, and call out to each other, between mouthfuls of sandwich, the names of the sights we passed, describing each minutely. We used to play at English Tea, with digestive biscuits and thin pieces of bread and butter. And six o'clock drinks. You taught me how to pour a perfect gin and tonic and how to drop in the ice without splashing from the claws of the silver tongs. I learned to sit at your feet and sip my lemonade without making a noise while we listened to the news from London on the world service. The world service was our favourite radio station, the only one we ever deigned to listen to. 'Uncle' Grigor had given you a special radio set so you could hear it without difficulty and which was so precious you kept it locked away in a cupboard. Uncle Grigor was a friend of my father's who used to work in one of the embassies. He used to come in occasionally for six o'clock drinks, and the news, and I would have to pour him a whisky.

'Just a finger, darling, in one of the square ones.'

I can still see my finger, white against the deep facets of the glass, and the solemn wavering stream of brown liquid that made a distorted pool in the bottom. Some-times, I remember, my father would be there too, smiling indulgently and drinking vodka.

They were games for life, I see that now. Games that were meant to make sure I never forgot what it was you were preparing me for. You gave me the inheritance of your blood, but as if you knew it would not be enough, you taught me all you could remember of that foreign land to which you were sure that I would travel. For suddenly, in the midst of our play-acting, your bright eyes would brim over and you would seize me by the shoulders.

'You will go, darling, you will! You will go to England.'

Frightened by your intensity, your fingers digging into my small arms, I would feel my own eyes prickle and swim. And then, seeing my tears, you used to shake your head and laugh – a low-throated gasp – and lean your forehead against mine and whisper:

'You will.'

And we used to sit there, hugging each other; sobbing and laughing all at once, like doomed lovers. I would have thrown myself to the lions for you, but there were no lions in our country. Only hyenas, earth-striped and low-bellied, licking their lips.

I used to wonder, after your last illness, where, precisely, you had gone. For everything else seemed to go with you. The games, the English food, the wireless, my special crate of lemonade. Even Uncle Grigor, who had, in some convoluted way I did not then understand, been responsible for supplying us with all these things, never came to see us any more. It was as though I found myself on a bare stage, just my father and I sitting in our accustomed armchairs with the lights out and the painted gauzes you had hung about me torn down. I did not believe you were in the dismal, wet cemetery beyond the railway bridge, nor in the stifling gloom of the baroque church next to the market – we never went to any of those places, you and I. And so life became just something that had to be done. Without you. But now I know. It was as I always suspected. You came here. When I sit very still, like this, I can feel you close: hovering behind my shoulder, whispering in my head. However new the situation I find myself in, or strange the people I encounter, there is always something about it that seems familiar. Day by day I fit another piece of reality beside the image I hold in my memory and see with pleasure how they dovetail, how the colours slide together and are indistinguishable. I can stare for hours at rain on roofs, at dust along the floor and, even acknowledging the wetness or the dreariness of them, gaze at them with slow smiling pleasure seeing them as romantic, almost exotic. The secret of their enchantment is perhaps that I have come at last to this land of fable and make-believe – and discover it to be real.

I find it difficult to explain my pleasure, my contentment, to my wife. I haven't wanted to tell her all that I feel because I know she does not share it. She would not even understand. I don't know why, but my wife – my wife refuses to accept that England is now her home. Give her time, I tell myself, give her time. For the harsh images of memory to lose their vivid colour. For her to find her own contentment. She resists, my wife. She refuses. She will not allow the smallest trace of contentment to undermine all the defences she has thrown up. She will not surrender to its power. It has great power. It has the power not only to turn fable into reality, but reality into fable. The acrid taste of fear, the dry mouth and the shivering skin, the rank suffocation under tarpaulins, the slow swaying through the night, the dragging footsteps that cannot run – these are transformed into a tale of flight from an ogre. Escape from a dark wood, from whose borderland you burst free into sunlight, or else are caught by the fear that races dog-like at your heels. Once out of the wood you cannot believe there was anywhere but this safe place of sunlight, of warm stone steps and soft dust filtering through your fingers. But my wife . . . my wife. My wife is still trapped. The reality of the brambles, the dog . . .

My uncle just thinks that I am malingering, here in the Postmen's House. He does not understand that such a thing is necessary for a time, my solid, English uncle. He is head, now, of all that mythical tribe of English relations my mother used to tell me about. In his essential kind-heartedness he could not refuse my request for help. But I know that I am an embarrassment to him. I have always been an embarrassment to him. Ever since I phoned from Paris. There was a hitch. Our papers turned out to have been insufficiently prepared to take us any further. The organisation manning the Paris end of the escape route were irritated and dismissive. It was not their fault if papers had been made up with reference to out-of-date regulations; it was Prague's fault, it was nothing to do with Paris. They turned on us, suddenly hostile, wanting to dump us. They sent us across the street to a bar while they conferred. It was from there I rang my uncle. It was pure chance he had not moved house since my last address for him; luck that he happened to be in. My poor uncle. It had not been possible to warn him of our arrival. Such plans could not be written down or spoken over the telephone; we scarcely dared to discuss them ourselves, Eliska and I. When we wanted to talk we went out into the forest. All that spring we paced between the silent trees, our low, urgent words falling without sound into the beds of moss beneath our feet, slipping between the dead pine needles that lay in drifts on the forest floor.

'There is some trouble with our papers,' I shouted down the crackling line, and then, alarmed at the sound of my own voice, glanced over my shoulder. But no one had moved in the small shadowed bar, no head had turned, no eye met mine, not even Eliska's. She was huddled at a back table away from the window. 'Some irregularity . . .' I yelled. I thought I heard my uncle groan, his breath catch in a sob. But it must have been the bad line. His questions when they came seemed irrelevant, the staccato croaking of a robot. Where was my father? What nationality was my wife? Why were we coming to England? How could I prove I was who I said I was?

'I have to ring again at six,' I said to Eliska.

The organisers of the escape route took pity on us, grudgingly. They had a vacant room, they said, in a safe house which we could have for three days; then we were on our own. One of them took us out to St Denis, out to where the Metro ended and a wide boulevard began. We walked past a flea market and then block after block of tall rooming houses. At that time of day the street was almost deserted. We felt like slowly moving targets, the noise of our heels on the pavement unbearable. At the corner of every block I had to force myself not to break into a run and by the time we arrived Eliska was shaking uncontrollably. The man led us up two flights of dark stairs, on the third landing he pointed to a door: 'Lavabo'. Two paces on was another door. He unlocked it. Inside was a room with a sink, two chairs, a bed without linen and a table nailed to the floor; he threw the key onto the table. 'Trois jours.' He jerked his head scornfully towards Eliska. 'Stay inside.'

It was from there that I went out to phone my uncle again as pre-arranged that afternoon. It was from there that I went on his instruction two days later to be interviewed by the British Consul-General. I expected to be seized as I approached the embassy door. Paris swam about me and my head buzzed. The duty officer looked at me knowingly as I gave my name and showed me to a waiting room. I thought he pushed me inside, but on reflection I noticed a loose join in the carpet that I might have tripped over. I waited. And waited. For two men in familiar mud-grey uniforms with black attaché cases to appear. But instead a woman came, a woman in a grey-striped blouse and a red skirt.

'This way, Mr Remek.'

I followed her up wide, curving marble stairs and down a corridor. Finally she knocked lightly at a door and pushed it open. That was when I first felt I had reached England. When I walked into that room. It had a curious familiarity: the smell of it, the slight gloom towards the back of it, the light that fell between the draped curtains and the expected objects on the desk. The click of the closing door was like the clap of a conjuror's hands. I clutched at the edge of the desk, but it did not slide away, the walls did not fall in on themselves to reveal a concrete room, a low swinging light. Instead the man writing at the desk looked up and smiled with surprised politeness.

'Won't you sit down Mr Remek?'

I waited for the interrogation to begin. But it did not. He remarked on the weather and gazed out of the window. He began to talk about London, and Highgate in particular, he even knew the street my mother had lived in. But he mustn't have been there for a long time for he got a lot wrong. I had to correct him over tiny details, even though, as I pointed out to him, this was only what my mother had told me, things might have changed in thirty years.

'Some things, Mr Remek,' he said, smiling, 'essential things, never change.' He stood up. 'Brought your passports, have you? Good man.' He held out a slip of paper and opened the door for me. 'Give them this downstairs and they'll stamp your documents for two weeks.'

I shook my head, he seemed to have understood nothing. He hadn't asked me any of the necessary questions. But somehow he had already manoeuvred me out onto the landing and was retreating into his office, one hand on the doorknob blocking my way. I tried to take a stand, head back. But he just stood there firmly, smiling his amiable smile.

'Given your uncle a bit of legwork in the past forty-eight hours, haven't you? We've had to request he meet you at Dover for final verification, so he might not be too pleased. Civil servants don't like irregularity, you know.' He wrinkled his nose in a pretence of confidentiality. 'Next time you go away on holiday, make sure they give you the right visa.'

'But we are not holiday! We . . . we are . . .'

'Goodbye, Mr Remek. Downstairs. Second window you come to. Can't miss it.'

When the young Caesar came to conquer England he wrote how, wild with excitement, he stayed at the prow of the ship throughout the crossing, straining his eyes for the first sight of land. Of how he felt the waves danced around the ship and the wind rushed them on, of how he saw dolphins leaping and rolling with lazy smiles. And he knew that nothing, *nothing* would stand in his way. So I watched. My hands, numb and wet with spray, clasped the rail of the ferry. The sea slid away below me in vast troughs; in the grey sky gulls floated giving hoarse cries. Eliska came out on deck, looked at the heaving sea, and went below again. I stared and stared into the greyness where sea met sky watching for the fabled white cliffs. But there was nothing. The sea went on stretching away before and behind and on either side, limitless. And then, slowly, negligently, as though it was merely a line of wave, as if it was nothing but a gently rising crest of foam, a white mass lifted itself lazily above the horizon. As I watched it grew, slowly at first, diffidently, and then, as we drew closer it suddenly reared up, towering and majestic all along the shore. I tried to call out for Eliska to come and see. There were bays and identations, a glimpse of green fields rolling away behind, a castle outlined against the sky, a town huddled beneath it. But I could only whisper.

It was an uneasy meeting with my uncle.

He stood in a glass-fronted anteroom flanked by officials. We stood outside in a corridor and looked at each other through the glass. I do not resemble my mother at all. I have a certain Englishness in my face, a soft-contoured, fair-haired, pale-skinnedness about me that many of my countrymen have. But they are not my mother's looks. Nor are they my uncle's. My poor uncle. He looked so anxious, so uncomfortable staring out at me, I had to smile. That did it – the smile. Laura's smile. I saw him make a sign to the men with us and they led us then, through into the glass room. Anyone could have got hold of my papers, learned my history, but only his sister's son could reproduce exactly that unique sequence of muscle spasms. When I see it in the mirror – that flutter across the muscles of the brow, the wrinkling of the eyes, the wry downward curve of the mouth that is over in a moment, I feel myself hollowed suddenly into a great cold pit. I stare into the emptiness after it, blank-eyed, and am overwhelmed by the vastness of infinity billowing out before me in which time and space are dissolved in the blackness. And I marvel that among all the important things that one generation tries to pass on to another, like little glittering bridges thrown out across space, my mother's smile should have been preserved. That its pattern and intensity of muscular activity should have been so perfectly encoded and reproduced in me. I see her smile and glimpse in that split second both the fleetingness of mankind and the stubborn fragility of its humanity.

My uncle drove us to London in a car that purred. I will never forget the sound of the soundlessness of that car. I laid my ear to the polished wood dashboard and bent my head to the carpeted floor and laughed in disbelief. And my uncle smiled for the first time, at my pleasure in his car. We passed through a countryside of unbelievably small fields and green trees drowsy in the dusk and drove through towns ablaze with lights, each one of which I expected to be London. But when we finally did arrive, the vastness of the city exceeded all my dreams. My uncle left us at a small hotel, promising to be back at nine the next morning.

'Sleep,' he said wanly. 'Sleep. You've had a wearying time. We'll talk in the morning.'

But it was he who looked the most exhausted of us all. We forgot our tiredness and our surprise that he did not take us home with him in the bright street lights and the noise, the crush of people and the smell of frying food.

He came the next morning at nine. We were waiting for him in the bar of our hotel, a television whispering in the corner, our papers spread out on a low table before us. The morning sun penetrated the barrage of grime and the net curtains at the window, sharpened the garish colours of the room and cut through the haze of dust and beer and smoke and disinfectant that hung around us. In its uncompromising light my uncle sat uneasily, his briefcase on his knees. We were strangers pretending to be close relations. My exuberance and my perfect English unnerved him as much as my wife's silence. It was not what he had expected. He exhibited a curious kind of helpfulness mixed with anxiety – the anxiety of being involved with us at all. He shuffled uncomfortably on his plastic banquette, pulling the jacket of his pin-striped suit ever more tightly round himself. It was as if he feared to catch some disease either from us or from the atmosphere of the room; some germ which would worm its way into his life and destroy it. Some irregularity – poverty, statelessness, homelessness. He talked rapidly of job centres and evening papers and the necessity of taking anything, anything that seemed at all possible, just to begin. He would sort out the immigration details. He kept picking up my documents from the table, turning them over and over, peering first at them then at me. Looking at me as if waiting for something. I knew what it was. The smile; the only tangible proof he had that I was not an impostor. Laura's smile. It gave him reassurance. But only for a second. Fear followed swiftly on, a different kind of fear. I could see it in his eyes: a vague gnawing worry that if I was Laura's son then I might expect something of him; that he, through some accident of birth, might be construed to be financially responsible for me. I smiled again to reassure him that I had no such thoughts in my head. But, of course, it only alarmed him further. He advised us on finding a cheaper place to live and free language classes for my wife. He apologised for having to rush back to his office, and then for having to go away on a conference for a couple of days and left us hastily with an invitation to dinner at the end of the week.

My wife was outraged.

'Dinner!' She swept the papers from the table to the floor. 'Dinner!' Her throat was so constricted with rage it came out only as a whisper. 'You are his nephew – his sister's son!'

'Eliska, it's . . . it's difficult for him.' I took her hand and tried to uncurl the tight fingers. 'I can see how he feels. Here we are out of the blue, no letter, no warning; it's all – very unconventional.' I nuzzled my nose into her cheek. 'The English don't like that. It makes him suspicious. He can't even quite believe I am who I say I am. He has his comfortable little life and suddenly a stranger turns up claiming to be a long lost nephew – with a wife!'

'You are his family, he should have taken us to his house. Instead of leaving us in this . . . this . . . dump!'

'You heard him. It's only a small flat. There's just his and his wife's room, and his son's.'

Eliska leapt to her feet.

'His son is married. And lives in *Cam*bridge!'

'Eliska . . .'

'I'm not going!'

We did go. We walked up from the garishness of the quarter round our hotel into streets of white icing-cake houses, roses clambering along their walls and small trees planted into their pavements. It was an evening in early summer. One of those evenings where day lingers on into night and the sun continues to shine, until, very slowly, the sky arches into paler and paler blue, into an almost whiteness that subsides into green and rose. Against the softness of this light the sodium glare of street lamps is reduced to ineffectuality, the power of the city dwarfed by the immensity of the sky. Heat reverberates up out of streets, and the warmth and light seems to hang there for ever until, at last, creeping in from the edges, night comes. I loved those evenings, when the sun shone all day and day continued all night. They seemed constructed entirely to mirror the endless lightness of heart I felt at that time. All boundaries were rendered meaningless here, and, like darkness at midnight, fear was for the first time absent. There was only this lightness, this ease in which everything clicked into place; this absurd delight in everything which even the most banal object seemed to radiate back.

'I've got a surprise for you,' I announced to my uncle as he opened the door to us. His face fell, his glance darting swiftly beyond us as though he looked for something behind us in the hall. Even the smile in his wife's eyes faded and for a second the manicured hair, the painted finger nails, the elegantly sober silk dress were disembodied. What did they fear to see? Suitcases? We did not possess suitcases.

'I've got a job.'

I can still hear the silence and then the burst of laughter. They drew us in, all welcoming arms.

'Well done my boy . . . I never thought . . . Eliska dear, come in, come in . . . Four days he's been here, Maud. Four days! . . . I know! It's wonderful, Jan. Congratulations!'

We had champagne. French champagne. Dry as powdered snow. Dry as the dusty scent of elderflowers.

'To the postman!'

Even Eliska was laughing as we all clinked glasses. My aunt wrinkled her nose.

'Oh Harry!' She made a little moue with her mouth and smiled at us with her eyes. 'It's warm!'

'Well, dear, I didn't expect . . .' He beamed at me.

'I'll go and get the bucket.' He scurried out and she followed him half-way across the room calling out instructions about ice.

I bent my head towards Eliska and linked my wrist around hers. Her long, spade-shaped fingers with their bitten nails curled around the flutes of her glass as she bent her own wrist back to forge the link. We lifted our glasses.

'To you, Eliska,' I whispered. She smiled.

'To England.'

'England.'

Our lips were so close we could have imprinted words on each other rather than spoken them.

'Here we are, here we are!'

My uncle bustled back, shaking a silvered bucket at us. It was ornamented with bunches of silver grapes and little round handles too small to hold that rattled against the sides. He seized the champagne bottle by the neck and crashed it among the ice cubes, burying it deep. His wife pressed warm, salted almonds on us and olives stuffed with anchovies.

It was only after dinner, towards the end of the evening, that their uncertainty returned. My uncle had got up to fetch the brandy bottle when he paused, his hand hovering over a drawer in the side-board, and glanced, as if for support, at his wife who was pouring coffee for us.

'We found some old photographs of you the other day. Pictures of you when you were small that your mother sent over. We've been looking at them . . .'

They laid them out on the table between us, spreading them beneath their palms, face up like playing cards. Faded images of a small face with dark, inquiring eyes. Eliska picked one up and laughed.

'Look at you here!'

But my aunt and uncle were very still. They looked from me to the photographs and back to me again, taut and silent, darting hurried glances. I could imagine them sorting through the pictures alone together, silently handing each other images of their unknown nephew. Wondering. Some children have in their faces the imprint of their adult looks from birth; you can see them already middle-aged, old. They have been born with the map of their lives etched into their features. They must have hoped for confirmation, but I could give them none. From my tenth year onwards my looks began to change till I resembled my father; even my hair lightened till, particularly in the summer, I was almost fair. It was my aunt who recovered her good humour first. She took up another picture and held it out to Eliska.

'Look at this one. Isn't he sweet, swinging on a swing.' She shook her head: 'It looks another world away.' And smiled at the grainy image as though thinking of her own childhood, not mine.

It was not long before my uncle was dissatisfied with my status of postman. It was his own fault. I watched, over the next few weeks, how his pleasure declined rapidly into disappointment, into a vague feeling of unease. Perhaps it was an habitual flaw in my uncle's character, this vacillating state of mind. Perhaps he slid from optimism to unease and back to stability again like a lens always slipping in and out of focus. The trouble was that he insisted on taking us into his family circle. Not in any positive sense, or one that made us feel taken up, suddenly beloved. But rather in the sense that he felt constrained to talk about us to other people. There is a way that certain English people appear to feel a kind of aggrandisement, a defining of their own personality or perhaps their relationship to society as a whole, by talking about their relatives. They will do this even to comparative strangers, introducing sons and cousins by name. Name first, that was what was so curious about it, as though you were expected to know them. He could not help himself, my poor uncle. He was compelled to drag us in. We took our place somewhere after his wife and son and daughter-in-law. 'Jan, my nephew, you know . . .' And then, of course, any kudos he might gain by the possession of a nephew would be immediately lost when his acquaintance politely inquired further. It would come out. The terrible admission. Almost as if it were my uncle who had to confess to having been reduced to a trudging postman; to being without his warm, silent car with the mahogany dashboard, without the icing-cake house, its huge vases of flowers and its chintz sofas. He would squirm and blink and hasten to wave it away with a plump hand '. . . only temporary of course.' And then, like Sid confiding a runner in the 3.45, would add in a low voice: 'Brilliant brain . . .' I've seen him do it. I've been there, standing next to him, his arm round my shoulder often as not. His compulsion insisted that we be invited to his cocktail parties, too. I don't know why he couldn't just have left us alone, he would have been happier and so would we. As it was we were an embarrassment to him: Eliska, silent, in unsuitable clothes, following me around the room like a nervous shadow. And myself, the nephew – the postman. Perfectly happy with his lot. Irritatingly happy, no doubt. So it was that my uncle became impatient. Not for my sake, but for his own. He wanted to be able to talk about his nephew, the barrister, his nephew, the stockbroker, even his nephew the computer programmer.

Survival is not only the deep-seated will to live, it is the ability to breast waves of ephemera, incomprehensible trivia, and not to drown. Cultures are made up of thousands of tiny strands which weave together to make up a picture of the whole. Looking back, I realise that each one of these strands must have been alien to Eliska.

She said very little, directly. But to begin with she never left my side. She tried, in those first few days, to stay in our hotel room for as long as possible. She would delay by all manner of means our getting up. Some of my first recollections of England are of making love in that ugly room. Having to open my eyes on that stained wallpaper, torn and rubbed where the coupling of others had forced the bed-head against the wall in exactly the same spot as we had. Rolling over onto my back, I would blink at the light striking sharply through the space between the thin, gaudy curtains. And Eliska, feeling my spirits sink, would twine her arms round my shoulders and stroke my neck, whispering in my ear. She would have had me stay there all day, safe within the perimeter of that room. Her known world. When finally I would disentangle myself from her, she would continue to lie there, her body loose, the covers thrown back where I had left them, her neck arched slightly, so that her head drooped against the slant of the pillow and her upraised mouth became the most prominent part of her profile. Until all I could see was her mouth. Washing, dressing, all I wanted was to sink back into it. When at last I bent over her, her heavy eyes smiled up at me a victor's smile. I would kiss her lightly.

'Come on, Liski, it's getting late.'

'Can't you bring breakfast in?'

One of the first things Eliska learned about England was take-away food. Around the hotel was a mushrooming of kiosks, everything was portable.

'They don't like it in the rooms.'

'They don't offer it.'

'You're supposed to go out.'

'Not even just coffee?'

The only thing that would get her up was my threatening to set off without her and to meet her later in the day.

'No, no, I can't get there on my own!'

Swiftly she would dress. Glaring at herself in the

mirror she would draw on her lipstick and blacken her eyebrows. It was her armour. Fragile and inadequate.

We went everywhere with a map in those first few days, tracing journeys on little creased and folded squares of paper. Stopping often to check our position. It was then that I would see the others, mirror-images of ourselves. I would look up for a landmark and across the street another head would lift itself from the flapping corner of a map and our eyes would meet. Sometimes they were older than ourselves, these couples, sometimes younger. But always when I saw them I felt a bursting of pride. I felt it fizz out of my finger ends and lift my shoulders. I would smile across at my 'reflection' and sometimes he would smile back, a wry, comradely smile. We became, at such moments, tourists, Eliska and I, counted in among that band of travellers who wander foreign cities for pleasure, in the innocent luxury of curiosity. For whom the freedom to come and go was a given, so taken for granted that it was never even considered. In that split second we had no other care in the world save the identification of some colonnaded portico and finding a good dinner in a cheap restaurant. The elation of this new identity was overwhelming. I would excitedly turn to Eliska, who stared solidly in front of her.

'Look.' I nudged her. 'That man over there . . .'

Her gaze did not follow my pointing finger. Instead she grabbed my arm. Her feet seemed to trip over themselves as she stepped backwards and sideways, falling against me. Her fingers dug into me with terror.

'Where?'

'Liski!'

'Where!'

'That man – next to the post-box over there.'

'Who is he?'

'I don't know.'

'What's he doing!'

'Looking . . . looking at his map. Like us. Like that couple at the far side of the square and the others in that doorway. We're all – tourists!' In the silence the word didn't sound so lighthearted as it had before. Eliska's eyes had become like small stones:

'You think that we are tourists? That when we have looked around this quaint old city and bought some souvenirs that we are going *home*!'

I bent down and picked up the fallen map. I drew her stiff arm through mine.

'Come on, Liska,' I whispered.

Her gaze slid away, slowly, distrustfully, back to the street. Back to the endless stream of people who pushed past her, the drifts of wastepaper blowing at her feet, the tightly packed cars that roared dangerously close to the edge of the pavement and the brilliantly lit shops from whose doorways waves of heat and noise leapt out at her.

'These people – how do you know they are not following us?'

'Eliska, this is England. Anyway, we are not of interest to such people any more.'

A couple of days later I started at the Postmen's House and Eliska was left alone. I never really knew what she did while I was away. I would leave her at dawn so heavily asleep that her eyelids scarcely flickered as I crept out of bed. And when I returned early in the afternoon, there she would be waiting for me, cross-legged on the bed, licking her finger to flip languorously through the pages of a cheap magazine. Or sitting, knees hunched up to her chin, on the window sill gazing through the open space in the half-drawn curtains. The room always had a somnolence to it, as if it was deep under the sea. The constant noise of traffic muffled as though far away. I had the increasing feeling that in my absence she never left the room. To my questions she was vague, resentful.

'I don't know where I went. I just walked about . . .'

'Don't you take the map?'

'I can't be bothered.'

'Eliska! What if you get lost?'

'Lost?' She stared at me scornfully. 'I am lost all the time.'

'*All* the time?'

'Every day. Every day,' she murmured, hunching one shoulder and hanging her head, 'when I am out, I walk, and I recognise this shop or that house and then, suddenly, between one moment and the next, between crossing from one side of the road to another – I am lost. It just comes down, like a blanket. Cutting me off from wherever I am.'

I put my arms round her and buried my nose in her hair.

'Liski, you must always take care. You must always take the map with you.' But for some reason even as I spoke, I was no longer thinking of her; my mind had started running once again on a possible venture that had been preoccupying me for several days.

'You know, Liski,' I whispered, 'you shouldn't be alone all the time like this. You should have something to do, somewhere of your own to live. It's high time we moved out of here. Why don't you find us a pretty little flat, Liski? Go house-hunting. Mmmm?'

It was Jack who had put the idea into my head. He had been explaining to me about Cockneys.

'A Cockney, my son, is someone who was born within the sound of Bow Bells. Ain't that right, Sid?'

'What?'

'Cockney.' Jack winked. 'Bow Bells.'

'Oh, yeah. Once a Cockney always a Cockney.' Sid turned to me with a slow almost inquiring smile. 'Once they heard those bells they ain't happy nowhere else. They might move on, leave the area, better theirselves, but they won't never be really happy. Not till they gets back.'

We were standing in the sun on the top step of the House and Sid was talking to us from the hallway. Jack shook a cigarette from a packet and stuck it in the corner of his mouth. He cupped his hands and lit a match.

'Remember Stan, Sid?'

Sid nodded.

Jack blew a stream of smoke up into the air.

'Then there was George.'

Sid tapped the side of his head and grinned at me. 'Gets 'em all.' He wandered off into the gloom winding a length of string round a packet that had become unsealed.

I turned to Jack. 'Is it true?'

Jack smiled off into the distance. 'Well, it could be.'

'But is it?'

'You heard Sid.' He loped off down the steps. 'What I do know is it's time for a kip. See you, old son.'

I went on standing on the top step gazing out up Oudenard Road, the fingertips of one hand pressed lightly against the door and moving absent-mindedly across the warm wood, tracing over the familiar ridges of paint. Across one word and down to the next. It had become like a nervous tic, a guilty habit. I couldn't keep my fingers away from them, as though I sought constant reassurance of their existence. Out of the corner of my eye I watched Jack disappear along the street. I thought of Bow Bells. What was it that they rang to draw the faithful home? 'Di-ckens, Dar-win, Dos-toe-yev-sky' I sang under my breath. They fitted exactly! It was possible, it was going to become possible. I was sure of it, now. The street was empty. Jack had gone. Behind me the Postmen's House was silent. I ran down the steps and out of the gate. Di-ckens, Dar-win, Dos-toe-yev-sky jangled in my head and the red-painted words danced up and down in front of my eyes. I crossed to the right-hand pavement of Oudenard Road and began to run backwards up it, keeping my eyes on the painted door. The words rang in a breathless peal, faster and faster: Di-ckens-Dar-win-Dos-toe-yev-sky. And the words on the door swayed and bounced as I ran, growing smaller and smaller. They blurred into indistinct lines and then to a red square. Here! I clapped my hand onto a low garden wall beside me. With a sudden hissing and yowling a cat shot out from beneath its shadow and fled away down the area steps. This would be the boundary of my country, the outer radius of sight of my words. I walked into the middle of the road and stood there; the writing was still just legible. I crossed to the far pavement and, grinning, began to walk back to the Postmen's House. This would be my little city, this half-street and I would not, like Stan or George, live anywhere else. I looked at the upper storeys of the houses that I passed. From any one of them I would be within sight of the door of the Postmen's House. Always.

Every day after that I walked up and down the same portion of Oudenard Road after work, looking for signs in windows that might say Rooms To Let. There were only twenty-three houses that would serve my purpose, but I did not let that daunt me. I read all the notices stuck in the display case in the newsagent's near the Underground, and the cards that hung in the stationer's further down the High Street. I searched in the local paper. But I did not mention any of this to Eliska. She had unwillingly begun house-hunting round Victoria. Each afternoon when I returned she would complain about the impossibility of her task: the exorbitant rents demanded for decent places, and the squalid rooms which appeared to be the only thing we could afford. And I would console her. I would stroke her hair and kiss her neck and uncurl the fingers that twisted in her lap. And she would look at me with heavy, sullen eyes. I knew that it was hopeless; I had intended it to be so. I simply wanted to preoccupy her till I had found what it was I was looking for. It would not take much longer, I was sure of that.

I do not know why I was unable to bring myself to tell Eliska about Dickens, Darwin and Dostoevsky – and Oudenard Road – but I could not. I had intended to. From the very moment I saw it. My first thought had even been to bring her to see it too, this astounding phenomenon, this unique example of freedom of expression. Not just what it was, but where it was. At least to tell her about it. But I did not. It got, somehow, overlaid by the excitement of getting the job, starting work, going to bed early and remembering to wake at dawn. By the time I saw it again, it had already become my private obsession. And I could not. It was stupid. I knew it was stupid! All obsessions run the danger of falling into absurdity. But the more I realised how disregarded it was in the House, the more I hugged it to me. The more I realised that only someone like myself, who had lived another life in which the freedom to say such words in public was denied, could understand its importance, the more I wanted it to belong only to me. So I became secretive about it, even from Eliska. Most of all from Eliska – which was unfair. And yet I did not understand it. I think that was part of my reluctance to talk about it, because I did not know what it meant. I believed in the words, rather than being able to decipher them. It was an act of faith. The personalities involved in the words were so illustrious, their ideas so vast and the juxtaposition of those ideas upon each other so unexpected that it was impossible not to believe it had meaning. It was partly in this certainty – that I would discover the answer, that in the end it would be revealed to me – that my obsession with it lay. It could not possibly be only random graffiti. It did not come from a spray can. It did not lurch defiantly across the door of the Postmen's House. It had been painted with surprisingly neat brush strokes. It was intended as a clue, a sign: its solution would give meaning to the world. Once I understood it I would hold the key to all of life. But in my temporary state of unknowing all I could do, until I had worked it out, was to believe. Perhaps the comfort I took from it was irrational. Perhaps in its mystery I expected more than I would find. It was even possible that its present illogicality would never resolve into logic, into connectable certainties. It could be nothing more than a false trail laid by a madman. But I had made it the centre of my life and I could not bear to have it challenged. So I kept silent.

We never read your letters. That is not permitted. We are never allowed to open letters. We would scorn to do such a thing. There is no need. The envelope always tells us everything we want to know. We sometimes, among ourselves, wonder why you bother to put letters inside them at all. To the trained eye the envelope gives everything away. You write your little private words on sheets of paper and then you hide them, folding the paper twice or even three times upon itself – end to middle and middle to end. The very paranoid even fold them again, side to middle. You slide them into the envelope, seal it and consider the operation complete. But for us it is just about to begin. Your caution gone, your defences relaxed, you scribble the address, toss the letter to one side and put the whole business out of your mind. And into ours. Our minds are trained to very delicate conjecture. With a logic quite possibly beyond you we know how to discover the minutest nuances of meaning. From the smallest shreds of evidence we can reconstruct not only a face, but a whole character and even, beyond that, a life. We may not be able to tell you the size of the bill you receive, but we could tell you to a degree the depth of passion of your lover. We could almost tell you whether they have fair hair or brown eyes. It is all on the envelope

– on the size of it, the shape, the texture, the bulkiness, the colour, the scent, even, of it. You get a feel for paper. The sensory receptors on the fingers of a sorter become refined to a degree unimaginable to anyone outside the trade. The eyes, despite their dull glaze, miss nothing. There is the method of sealing the envelope. Have you licked it, glued it, stamped it with sealing wax, plastered it with layers of adhesive tape? Or merely tucked the flap inside? Then we come to the writing. Ah, the writing! One could fill volumes with the writing; whole treatises on the psychology of communication. Typing? Typing will not hide your secrets from us. I sometimes think that typing only makes them more plain. The desire to hide always reveals more than the openly displayed.

It is, of course, not in the initial sorting that we are able to chart so accurately the progression of your life. That happens too quickly. We merely note outstanding features for closer perusal when we re-sort each street's letters into numerical order for delivery. It is then that the pattern emerges more clearly. It is then that your fortunes spread themselves out before us. Two final demands for number 4, no mail again for number 6, another letter from her mother for number 8, the four-teenth postcard of Greece in a week from Jerry to Kath in number 10. We get blasé, punchdrunk with our own omnipotence, our exceeding cleverness. At first it is exciting, vicariously thrilling to sniff out other people's secrets, piece together their lives. Then follows a kind of boredom, the satiation of a sweet-shop worker whose jadedness of palate borders on nausea. We long for something new to deliver – a summons, a telegram, or a battered letter with a stamp from Outer Mongolia – something new to get our brains working on.

I am not yet in this class of jadedness. I am still a student. My mother's careful preparation fits me for life in England but not for life in sufficient detail to excel in this field. I received my training for this elsewhere. I learned, under duress, in the grey streets of a small town sunk in the depths of a dark wooded valley. And our senses were not sharpened for academic amusement, as they are here. Oh, do not mistake me, I am as fast as most of the men around me; Mr Harry would not have me in the House if I were not. It is only now and then that I falter. That in spite of myself the old fear returns and I feel my lungs become squeezed by a pressure so intense I can hardly breathe. And yet, if I turned and handed the envelope I knew it was my duty to single out for closer investigation to Mr Harry, he would have stared at me as if I had gone mad. He had no manilla folder to slide it into, no Method of Closer Perusal to follow. No report to make on it. No visit to instigate. And yet it still returned, the old alarm. It happened one morning, I remember, suddenly, invading the warmth and security of the room, isolating me beyond help from Jack or Sid, or even Mr Harry. Drops of ice began to trickle down my spine. Despite my bent head and my wide-open eyes, I could not bring myself to look at the envelope in my hands. Because I had seen it already. Word chasing word across the surface of the paper, thick-nibbed and careless with the speed of thought, the thoughtlessness of vision. I could see the man who wrote it could stare into his clear gaze – a frankness of regard that alone would damn him. My fingers closed over his incriminating hand, but the letters laced out beyond my finger ends, looping and spilling beyond containment.

'Got a looker, have you, Jan?'

Beneath the careful wiping hands of memory the dark woods faded. My lungs filled with air.

'Come on, mate, move away. Give us a shufty.'

Jack's bright lascivious eyes peered over my shoulder. His elbow jogged my paralysed arm. And my fingers parted.

'Nah, that's not a looker. That's a bloke's writing! You losing your touch, or you going funny? Here, I tell you where there is a looker on your patch. You know half-way down Northfield Road there's that mews . . .'

Jack's life was one long search for lookers. There was warm beer for consolation and cars for sublimation, but if he could get all three to coincide his joy was unconfinable.

'You want to know where the lookers are, mate, come down the Nag dinner-time.'

He tied the last bundle of letters, packed it into his sack and swung the sack onto his shoulder.

By the time I pushed open the door of The Running Nag it was almost two o'clock. In the sudden darkness, the closeness of red velvet and beer-wet mahogany and the unfamiliar faces that turned slowly to see what had caused the unwelcome burst of daylight, I could distinguish nothing. A terrier waddled officiously out from behind the bar and snuffled around my ankles. Across the drifts of cigarette smoke and noise, the room seemed to lengthen and lighten. Alcoves and small round tables pushed back into recesses; faces detached themselves from the gloom. A man moved away from a table balancing a clutch of glasses in his hands. A woman turned to call after him. And beyond the curve of her body I saw Jack. He was leaning back in a window seat, eyes half-closed, legs stretched out in front of him. As I approached him, the eyes did not flicker and the trail of smoke from the cigarette lodged in the corner of his mouth scarcely dipped. He merely lifted his glass a few inches from the table with a gesture of great weariness.

'Mine's a pint of best, mate.'

When I got back to the table the crowd round it had thinned and there was a vacant chair next to Jack. He took his new pint and ranged it reverently next to his half-empty glass.

'That's it Jan, line 'em up!'

He squinted across the wisp of cigarette smoke.

'How you doing, mate? Finding your way round all right?'

'It's falling into place.' I took a pull at my beer. 'It's quite a good patch. Lots of big houses split into flats.'

'Nah!' Jack screwed up his face. 'That's a desert.'

'It's a better desert than a lot of other rounds I've had. You can half-empty your sack in just one of those streets.'

'Oh yeah, it's all right for the letters. That's a doddle for letters. That's what I thought to begin with; an' I thought a bit more. I had my eye on that patch year and a half. I used to work the bit down the hill: all little houses and council property and shops. And old Jimmy Vye used to do where you are now. Wasted on him. I used to go up onto his patch round about eight o'clock in the morning, walk up and down like it was my beat, watching all the little lookers coming out of their doors, all going for the Underground. Lovely they was. And there was Jimmy Vye sixty-five, well, sixty-four then. Talk about waste – criminal! I put in for a transfer to Mr Harry, contingent on the retiral of Brother Vye. Didn't say anything, Mr Harry; just smiled like he knew what was in me mind. I reckon he knew a lot more, too, sly bastard. Drink up and we can just get another in before they call closing. Anyway, Vye retired and I moved in. I ain't never worked so hard on a patch. I had the brain going fit to bust in the House, and the soles of me boots wore out on site, getting them all worked out. Then I got going on the action – singles early in the morning and the marrieds on the second post. I never worked so hard.' Jack paused to drain his glass. He shook his head and laughed. 'I had my pockets stuffed with blank recorded delivery slips. Couple of fake parcels in my sack. I was ready with all the usual never-fail openers. "Would you sign here, please Miss." Or "Parcel for Miss Trott. Oh, you ain't got no Miss Trott. How strange! You ain't expecting no Miss Trott?" I never had so many bleeding doors slammed in my face, Jan, I tell you. I kept it up six weeks. And then a mate of mine, Corker Lawrence, said in here one lunchtime he were packing in the mail, going down to Devon where his wife's family had a business. I said I was so pissed off I'd go with him. So it all come out. Anyway, long and short of it was he not only arranged with Mr Harry for me to take over his patch, but he give me a couple of introductions, in person. Lovely girls.' He winked. 'Friendly. Corker come up to your patch one morning, take a look. Shook his head soon as he'd seen half a dozen. "Wrong material, Jack," he said. I don't know what you're going to do Jan, my son, to make water flow in the desert. Still, bit of continental charm might do the trick. You got a batch of slips in your pocket – recordeds and specials and pay on deliverys and such like, have you? You know the wrong parcel delivery trick and letter-through-the-wrong-box? Course they might go for the intellectual approach. That gets some of them. Glasses. Never seen it myself. Still. You got some glasses?'

I grinned across the top of my beer. 'No, but I've got a wife.'

He laughed.

'Well, she ain't going to pull them for you, that's for sure!' He puffed out a sudden cloud of smoke from the dangling cigarette, behind it the smile still hung around his half-closed eyes. 'You got anyone special lined up yet?'

I shook my head.

'Don't give up. You keep your bag of tricks handy and you want any advice, you come to Uncle Jack. She foreign, too, your wife?'

I nodded. We fell silent for a while.

'Don't mind my asking, mate, but what're you doing in a job like this?' He crossed one leg over the other and leant across the table to crush out his cigarette. 'First time you come down the House, I thought to myself: what they doing giving us another bloody student, it ain't Christmas in July.'

'Back home it's Christmas all year round.'

'Come again?'

'Half of Prague University has been transferred to the postal service.'

'What for – ain't they got no jobs?'

'Keep us out of trouble.'

'You been in trouble?' His eyes gleamed.

'Depends what you mean by trouble.'

He shifted eagerly on his seat. 'Well . . . ?'

'Well, back home we have two sorts of trouble. One's simple. It's like yours. Everyone knows what it is – throwing a brick through a jeweller's window, robbing a bank. You know where it begins and ends, you choose whether or not you're going to go in for it. There's a kind of relief about it because it's definable. But the other – the other comes looking for you. It doesn't follow any law, or even any sense. Because it has no logic, you can't evade it. You can try. People spend their lives in fear of it, not doing anything, not saying anything that might attract its attention. Even then you're not safe. It's like a kind of fog drifting around, but you don't know where it begins or ends. One day you're walking around in the normal world and then the next you find you've committed some crime, like having the wrong father, or the wrong friends, or an envious neighbour. And suddenly the fog has come down. And you find everything sliding away in the mist, all the landmarks of ordinary life – job, flat, friends – until you find yourself alone in a kind of blank silence.' I shrugged my shoulders and picked up my beer. 'You know what fog's like.'

It was out of this fog that Eliska had come, stumbling out of nowhere. A human body, shivering, wet and frozen. Tangible and heavy in that endless white nothingness and we had clung to each other, numb and shaking, simply to have something to cling on to.

'Rather you than me, mate.' Jack's voice cut in. 'There was a time we used to have fogs round here. Notorious for it, it was. You'd get lost crossing your own street. Then they passed a law, couldn't have fires. That did it.'

Outside the pub the day seemed pale and wasted. Real life was back there among the dog-ends and empty glasses, in the luxurious folds of artificial velvet.

'Hang on a tic, I want to get some fags.'

Almost next door to the pub was a newsagent. I waited outside it, leaning against the plate-glass window, running my eye absently over the cards taped to the inside. 'Child's tricycle . . .', 'French lessons . . .', 'Microwave oven . . .', The unwanted paraphernalia of lives, 'Rooms to let . . .' Suddenly alert, I peered at the small card. 'Rooms to let share bath, suit couple no pets no children, £35.00 pw, Oudenard Road. 600 7419'. I fumbled through my pockets for a pencil. Jack lurched out of the shop.

'You ready for the tube?'

'No, I forgot. I've got to make this phone call.'

'Right.' He nodded. 'See you.'

The telephone rang for a long time. It rang into a space that I could not quite imagine; with a sound surprisingly close and clear, as if it was ringing into a box. And when at last it was answered I had the distinct impression not that the person had been hurrying towards it from some far part of the house, but that they had been standing silently beside it, listening, for quite a time.

'Yes.'

The voice was not a voice that liked telephones. It was a woman's voice, an oldish voice and it seemed to be pressed very near to the mouthpiece because I could hear the dryness of her lips and the slightly obstructed wheeze of regular breathing.

'I'm ringing about the rooms.'

'Ohhh! Yes?'

'I – I'd like to come and see them.'

'Oh, I think they're gone.'

'Gone?'

'I had a couple lunch-time. Very keen.'

'They've taken them?'

'Ringing back tonight. After six.'

'If they're still free I'd like to view them this afternoon.'

'You want to come and have a look?'

The more doubt the voice expressed, the more anxious I became.

'I'm – I'm just round the corner.' In desperation I waved my hand in a wide sweep as if, by peering down the mouthpiece of her telephone, she could see for herself the street in which I stood, the shuttered pub, the newspapers blowing in the dusty gutter. 'I could be there in ten minutes.'

I didn't wait till the ten minutes should have passed, I went straight away to Oudenard Road and walked anxiously up it counting off the numbers. According to my calculations 42 should be just within sight of the writing on the Postmen's House. I deliberately approached it from the far end of the road. For a time the numbers on the houses seemed to mount swiftly, then half-way along they dawdled. At number 36 the door of the House was just a smudged yellow. But by 40 lines began to clarify across its surface. I paused in front of 42, my hand on the gate, looking down the street. The red lines danced before my eyes and set up some kind of correspondence inside me. A buzzing grew in my head, the slow sequence of thought suddenly quickened producing a strange lightness in which, in fact, all thought dissolved save one – that something might happen to thwart my desire. I hardly noticed the appearance of the house at all, I was only afraid that it would be empty, locked against me, or that the other couple would have already rung back to take the rooms. As I reached the front door I glimpsed a shadow move across the dark bay window. A dog started barking wildly in the hall. The door opened and a terrier, identical to the one in the pub, rushed past me and skidded to a halt in front of the gate. A small woman stood on the doorstep wrapped in a large cardigan. She screwed up her eyes against the sun so that the wrinkles fanned together hiding her expression, and nodded at the dog.

'It ain't you. He's gone soft in the head. It's the tom across the street's done it. He drapes hisself across the garden wall and just lies there. Course the sight of him drives Monty wild. You the one who rang?' I nodded and she led the way inside. 'I spoken to his owner, but she can't do nothing neither. You can't do nothing with pets can you? The rooms is up here.'

There were two rooms. Unremarkable, unlived-in rooms. And I wondered fleetingly whether the woman had ever had lodgers. The bedroom was small and had a stuffed appearance. But there was a morose bareness to the living room despite the ill-assorted relics from deaths or sale rooms: a sofa, a table, a couple of dining chairs. Ignoring them I made straight for the window, parted the net curtains and craned my head backwards. From this particular angle you got a clear view of the Postmen's House, although it had to be admitted that the words on the door were scarcely legible. But they were there, they could be seen: a red block of colour on the yellow door. The buzzing in my head, which had become intense, quieted itself a little at this. I looked down at the window sill and ran my hand along it; it was wide enough to sit on fairly comfortably.

'All very strong built, these houses,' said the woman uncertainly from the centre of the room.

But I was thinking of long, light evenings sitting on the window sill gazing down the street. Or, if not the window sill, then one of the straight-backed dining chairs could be brought over; though then one would not be so high, so well placed to . . .

'And here's the kitchen.'

She drew aside a flowered curtain and I turned from the window reluctantly. A sink had been set into a narrow shelf covered with plastic cloth; above it on other shelves were stacked a small pile of china, a kettle and an electric cooking ring. We stood and stared at the cubbyhole.

'Very compact,' I said. She screwed her face into a knowing grimace.

'You don't want a kitchen you have to be walking round all day.'

In a curious way we were not interested in the rooms at all, the woman and I. We acknowledged them but we skirted round them, bent on private preoccupations of our own.

'Very nice indeed,' I said. 'It's all – very nice.' I looked around the room, seeking a particular feature to praise. The woman watched me closely.

'I thought,' she said, 'on the telephone, I thought you might be foreign.' She made a display of pulling down the sleeves of her cardigan and folding her arms. I had the sensation of ice sliding quickly down my spine and collecting in a pool in my stomach, of a tingling in my arms and the helpless emptiness of my hands hanging numbly at my sides.

'I wouldn't have no foreigners. I got nothing against them,' she added quickly, 'you ain't allowed to have nothing against them. But of course, now I see you . . .' She smiled. And even her smile now looked like a trap. 'You Welsh?'

'No, no.' I shook my head, I knew my face would not betray me but my accent might. 'My mother was a Londoner, from Highgate.'

'Oh.' She drew the flowered curtain sharply along its plastic runner so that the hooks jangled against each other. 'Funny. You remind me of a friend my Les had, Stav Bronsky; he come from Cardiff. She gone, your mum?' she asked in quite another tone of voice.

'Yes.'

'And your dad?'

Without hesitating, I nodded. And she nodded too, in sympathy.

'My Les went nine year ago, in October.'

I inclined my head gravely and let the silence deepen. Two minutes silence for Les. But I was aware all the time that I must press her, press her quickly while I had the advantage. Not let the silence fade into doubt.

'These people who saw the rooms today . . .'

'Oh, yes, them.' She shrugged and I doubted that they had ever existed at all. 'People always say they'll phone back, don't they?'

'I would like to take the rooms,' I said firmly. 'I know my wife will like them as much as I do.'

'Oh, your wife! You didn't say . . .'

'Yes, she couldn't come this afternoon. But she was very anxious I should. We both admire Oudenard Road.'

'Oh yes, it's very handy, Oudeynarde Road.'

'Yes. I – I work at the Postmen's House, just down . . .'

'Down the House, well, that is handy! Nice regular work, and no travelling. She work?'

'No.'

'I don't like a wife as works. They can't make no home. She'll make a nice little home for you here.' She patted the back of the pock-marked sofa.

The further away that I got from 42 Oudenard Road, the more the memory of it glowed in my head. My fingers curled around the key in my pocket. I thought of my new landlady, Mrs Bartholomew, and I smiled. I thought of the two rooms with their ill-assorted pieces of furniture and I smiled even more. I walked down Queenstown Road grinning like a fool. They were unique those rooms. If I had been set the task of designing and furnishing two rooms for let I should not have managed nearly so well as Mrs B. She had the touch, the flair, the intimate understanding – Eliska would . . . I walked more quickly, pushing away the thought of Eliska. I marched over Chelsea Bridge. The charm of them was their Englishness, Eliska would come to see that. The English liked old things. They preferred the comfort of old clothes, old houses, the habitual, the known, the therefore safe. 'Tried and tested' my mother used to say as a joke. Everything had to be tried and tested. The furniture in those empty rooms had been tried and tested so often by so many people that it had become old very quickly. It would not, I knew, ever qualify to be antique. Still, it was more English to have old furniture like that than brand-new matchstick stuff. I saw the rooms again more clearly than I had when I had been standing in them, my mind's eye flickering over each abandoned piece as if I was checking off an inventory, noting with proprietorial pleasure their informal dilapidation. Eliska could have the sofa. I the chair. The chair could be pushed into the window bay, the sofa turned slightly away. It was not, after all, Eliska I wanted to look at. The net curtains would have to be removed – some excuse found for the landlady – the windows kept open. Always. And I would sit there, always. In the evenings, the long, light evenings. Watching. Till the light faded. Smoking. I could start smoking, and the smoke would curl out into the still evening air. Watching till the words painted on the door blurred and smudged; until finally even the yellow door was enclosed by darkness. I would take the words then, hold them tightly in my head. And in sleep uncurl them, unravel the meaning that they guarded. I turned the key over and over. Acquisition of the flat had been vital. But it was only a means to an end. The end in itself was solution – that was inherent in the very nature of ends.

I dropped down into Pimlico and came into a little cluster of shops not far from our hotel. At the end of the row, where I turned right into Braceguard Street, was a small café, the kind of place that was never full. The kind of place that had a desiccated fern and a lopsided cardboard bottle of Pepsi-Cola in its fly-blown window, and where stiff-legged chairs seem to take up all the room. Where beyond the glass all animation seemed suspended and people sat silent, without moving. As I passed I looked in out of habit, as one might into a small aquarium, not out of interest at the gaping mouths and expressionless eyes. And there, to my surprise, among the fish-like bodies, sat Eliska. I halted. But I was already past her. Her eyes, glassy as her neighbour's, had not flickered. Her hunched shoulders had remained immobile. I . . . I did not turn back, I walked on. I almost ran. And the further away from the café I got, the more convincingly I managed to persuade myself that that drooping body had not been Eliska. By the time I got to the Miramar Hotel I half-believed that I should find her, as I used to, waiting for me in our room. I pushed through the narrow hall and, seizing the banister, began taking the stairs two at a time.

'Mr Remink!'

I stared down into the steep well of the hall where the reception desk was. There was no sign of anyone. All round the pigeon holes at the back of the desk were various doors and cupboards and hatches, all painted a different shade of cream as each had been added. From any one of them the voice might have issued. I waited, but none of them flew open. I shrugged my shoulders and climbed another two steps.

'*Mister Remink!*'

From the gloom of the basement a figure emerged, its hands writhing in the folds of a dish towel, its head twisting and craning upwards to see where I was. I backed down the stairs and it caught sight of me, acknowledging the fact by coming to rest, nodding its head and smiling. It was the proprietor's wife. She folded the dish towel and placed one ringed hand on the lowest edge of the banister.

'It's about your wife.' She paused. Her stare passed rapidly across my face, delving into every line, peering into every crevice, knowing already in the way that hotel servants always know. 'She's givin' Jess trouble on account she don't go out, Mr Remink. Jess go in there all hours, but your wife's still layin' in bed, or in 'er dezabble, or I don't know what. Jess can't clean with them still in their rooms. I've spoke to 'er myself, but it don't go in.'

'My wife is in our room now?'

'Oh no, Mr Remink.' She smiled and smoothed the folded cloth against the banister, picking at a loose thread with her nails. 'You come 'ome two-thirty. She's always out by two o'clock; two-ten latest.'

Eliska did not come back for nearly an hour. At first I lay on the bed, brooding, turning the key over and over in my fingers. I had had it in my pocket back there on the stairs, I could have given notice immediately. I could have said . . . But even then it would have sounded lame, placatory. I could still hear in my head the gloating voice of the proprietor's wife. Her ferret-eyes squinted at me from behind the faded flowers on the wallpaper, glinted from the scarred depths of the mirror. Wherever I turned my gaze she was there before me. I went and sat on the window sill, pushing aside one half of the filthy net curtain with my knee and stared out at the windows of the building back to back with ours. Our fire escapes almost joined; our almost-touching window ledges were like stepping stones. I thought of the other lifeless rooms behind those windows and the figures that sat in them. Whatever I said, however I worded it when I gave notice of our departure to the proprietor's wife, now it would sound as though we were creeping out like unwanted foreigners leaving at her complaint. We had not comported ourselves like proper English even by the standards of that woman. We would be the people who would never become English. We would join that large band of travellers who never arrive, who move from country to country, from room to room, sinking down among the lost places of cities with their cooking pots and their gaudy mementoes, never finding a home, never being a part. They had left their homes behind in another country, but in their hearts they wanted no other and travelled only to find it again. They lived in complaint and dissatisfaction, never able to admit to themselves that they had lost it for ever. You saw them arriving daily, such people, in this part of London; here they lodged for a while and then moved on. You saw their puzzled, disorientated faces in the crowd and then one day they were gone and another had taken their place. These were the hunched shapes I had seen in the café. These were the shadows I passed on the stairs. Foreign faces. I leapt down from the window sill and glared at myself in the mirror. My face was not foreign, it was not! I ran my hands through my hair raking it with my fingers making a parting to one side, Englishmen always parted their hair to one side. The more I stared, the more the feeling of panic increased. I dragged my fingers down the sides of my face pulling the skin tight over the cheekbones: this was an English face, I had been told it was. It was, it was, I whispered, and my troubled eyes looked back at me out of the glass knowing the truth. And Eliska, Eliska could look English, if she tried. Mrs Bartholomew had thought I was Welsh! I let my hands drop. But the proprietor's wife knew better. I began to pull out the drawers of the dressing table, hurling our possessions onto the floor. I would pack. We would leave. It was dangerous to stay here any longer in this place with that woman spying, listening. Here we would never be regarded as anything more than strangers.

I did not hear the door open. I caught sight of her in the

mirror first, standing in the doorway watching me, her face pale, her eyes listless, just as I had seen her in the café.

'What are you doing?'

'We are going. We are leaving!'

'Why?'

'We are going!' I turned back to the drawers slamming them shut one by one.

'Where?' There was a sudden light in her eyes, a lifting of her voice that at the time I scarcely noticed. I heard only the sound of wood thudding on wood and it was this sharp sound that brought me back to my senses. I thought of the proprietor's wife, listening. It was important that Eliska did not become stubborn, it was important that there was not a scene, a scene was not English. I looked up twisting my mouth into a smile.

'Because I have found us somewhere else to live.' I tried to make my voice light and playful, but the words sounded as if I was grinding them between my teeth. 'I have found us a flat. Look.' I turned round and held up the key.

'Where have you found us a flat?'

'You don't believe me? This is the key to 42A Oudenard Road.' I took a step backwards and threw it at her. I intended her to catch it but she was too stupid and slow. It hit her on the wrist and fell to the floor. 'Bedroom, living room, little kitchen attached and share bathroom; I knew right away that you'd like it. And it's very near where I work.'

'You have been lent the key so that I can come and see it too?'

'I've taken it, Liski. I had to, there were so many other people after it.'

She didn't bend down and pick up the key and neither did I, it stayed on the carpet all night. But I scarcely took my eyes off it. I refused to go out; I said I was tired. So we ate in. We did that sometimes, eating cold food with our fingers out of little plastic containers that Eliska bought in a supermarket. Drinking water from the tap of the handbasin in our room, out of a paper cup that she had saved. She didn't speak again all that evening, just sat on the bed looking at old magazines, free magazines that were given away on the street and which she kept. And I sat and stared at the key. Sometimes it stood out clearly against the lozenges of brown and purple on the carpet, sometimes it vanished completely beneath them. My concentration would waver for a moment and it would be gone and I would have to screw up my eyes and move my head this way and that to catch the glint of metal again. Things would be all right when we were in Oudenard. Road. Everything would come together. Life would begin properly then. This was just – just a false start. This was a place of transition and that would be a permanence. I thought of Dickens, Darwin and Dostoevsky staring out from their doorway up the quiet lamp-lit street. Tomorrow night I would be there with them. When I got my wages tomorrow afternoon I would come back here, pay off the hotel, collect Eliska – and then we would be gone. When Eliska went out to have a bath, I brushed my teeth, peed into the handbasin and climbed into bed. I lay there looking at the floor, marking the position of the key. When she came back she got into bed without a word and I turned off the light. Curiously, the key was easier to see in the dark, it lay exactly where the street light came in through the gap in the curtains, gleaming like a silver coin. I waited till I was sure Eliska was asleep and then I crept out of bed, snatched up the key and slipped it into my trouser pocket.

The first few weeks in Oudenard Road I woke constantly, the swift, excited wakening of a child counting the hours till Christmas morning and then dropping back into the warmth of sleep again. I listened to the incessant rumbling of traffic like waves washing around the shore of my small country, protective, lulling. I heard Eliska whispering in her sleep, a low murmur rising and falling, cracked with sighs and broken into harsh silences until, with a jerk of her body, words twisted out of her again. I gazed into her lifeless face. I touched a strand of her hair that lay along the sheet. Where had she gone? Into what caverns did she stumble, the thread of her life paid out behind her along the dusty floors of endless passageways, searching in the roaring darkness for the whispering of forests, the scent of wild raspberries and narrow white roads lined with rowan trees. I saw the light of the street lamp fall in rippled bars across the curtain and throw vague shadows against the far wall. In the breathing darkness I could make out the shapes of furniture, scattered clothes, a picture in a gilt frame, the gilt blackened, the covering glass whitened to blankness. Beyond the door a cliff of shadow. Dreams. Three men, their features indistinct, their movements slow like movements under water. Silver and black. Silent. Beyond, in the living room, they sit on the hard armchair. Run their hands over the worn back of the sofa, see the cigarette burns gaping on its arms. They stand before the chipped, tiled fireplace looking about them musing, wondering. At the five books on the empty bookshelf, the glass candlestick, the brass ashtray, the pictorial vase with views of Clacton painted on its billowing sides. At apples on a plate. They turn in the dark air, gesturing. They vanish. But their names were on my door. In red letters. In a looping hand I had not seen before. From every loop long drips of red had trickled down. Some nights it appeared on the inside of the door to our flat. At other times the panels of the door were bare, touched only by moonlight and street light and shadowed crevices. Then I knew the writing was on the outside of our bedroom door. I did not see it, not even in my dreams could I see through a solid door. But I knew it was there. I knew it. Like I knew that beyond the window dark houses stood sentinel two by two all the way down the silent street to the Postmen's House.

I CLOSE MY EYES but I do not sleep. Jan sleeps. I hear him. First there is the silence, round and hard and studded with tiny points of quiet, like an orange studded with cloves. It is a conscious thing, this silence. He makes it. He holds it to himself, like a talisman, willing sleep to come. And sleep always comes. It slides its fingers over his but he does not feel it. He does not feel his tight-willed silence slip its shape as it slips his grasp. Spreading like milk from the first drop till it covers him entirely. Deep in its milky depths he stirs. The first small sounds. His breath comes in a long shuddering sigh; his lips part and settle again. He is gone. And I am left. With my own silence. My silence does not sit in the palm of my hand but on the exact point at the base of my neck, on the precise vertebra between my shoulders, where Atlas's burden sat. My silence weighs on me with the weight of a whole world. My fear is that the boundaries of that world will dissolve and engulf me. That the voices I hear clamouring faintly from within it will burst into sound. That is why I lie here, my eyes open on the dark. I am afraid to sleep. For when I sleep I wake. Suddenly. There is no drift into forgetfulness. There is only the remembering. Endless, tireless remembering. Sometimes it starts with a single whisper, then the first voice is joined by another and another. Sometimes it erupts in my head with a great crashing noise. The sudden clamour of shouting, the harsh crack of a tarpaulin being thrown back, the splintered glass sound of my own screaming. The cold stone taste of fear in my mouth. And then, so late it seems always too late to save me, the involuntary jack-knifing of my body. In the beginning I woke Jan too. I would burst, gasping, into unfamiliar darkness beating away his arms that tried to surround me, as if they were a stranger's. Sleep-numbed hands fumbling for my own. Dry-mouthed whispering of my name. I have learned to be still. As the fear explodes and the nightmare shatters, at the very moment that my limbs kick out, I clench them in again. My body convulses in a small contorted spasm. That is all. Even the shriek is silenced before it can leave my throat. Jan scarcely stirs, now, in his sleep. I hold myself rigid, silent, staring out into the neon-tinted darkness. I hear his breathing break its rhythm, stop, and then ease back into itself again.

Cliffs of shadow loom out from the walls. What is this place? This place in which I find myself. This place in which – I am not. This was the place to which I longed to come. For which I defied everything. I have crossed its border. I live within its city. As the dead live. Between it and me there is a veil, a thin opaque skin. It is as though my body has arrived but not its animator – not my heart. Or else my heart has arrived too, but finds itself baffled. It finds no correspondence, only difference. It finds itself in such strange circumstances that its accustomed mechanics of beating seem to have no effect. The oxygen that I expect to be in the air is absent. Yet everyone else in this place lives. Generations of being in this place have modified their bodies to acclimatise to this – deficiency. I move among them without purpose, without sense of a reality. Everything that I hear them say or do is alien to me. Though I was accustomed to say and do similar things, yet they were – different. And in this small difference lay their wealth of purpose. I see objects and I know what they are. I learn that they have names in a different language. I sit on the chair. I lean on the table. I turn the small key in the wardrobe door, and the door swings open. But it is as though there was nothing beneath my touch.

Nothing . . . Is it I who am now the ghost? Or is it all the others – the living, who people these objects? It is only when I look back that the film of glass slides away. I hear, I see, I touch, I smell in a great vibrancy of connection, the whole intermeshing with piercing clarity. It is difficult to believe that they are only memories. There was fear. And deprivation. And constraint. But we were used to it, we had had it always. We had grown up with it. It was as much a part of life as the wind or the rain. You could not fight it to make it go away. It was not wise; it was not sensible. Instead you learned to live with it. This is the winter, they told you when you were small, and you were wrapped up in layers of clothing. I remember being wrapped up like that: my own clothes close to me and bigger garments – other people's cast-offs – on top of those, the whole lot tied with string. I hated it. I screamed and kicked. The ignominy of the string. The smell of the clothes of other people. I would turn and twist between my mother's bundling, buttoning arms and run out before she could get another layer on me. Run out into the garden. Out into the waiting jaws of the cold that seized me pinning me to the spot with shock and fright. The bands of ice that snapped round my lungs. Stopping my breath. Freezing my blood. Nipping the ends of my fingers and toes with little pointed teeth. I learned to submit to the tying of baler twine. I learned to snatch up a potato sack from the pile behind the kitchen door to drape over my head when I was sent out into the rain. And after a while it was not strange. It took on the appearance of wisdom. These things, after all, were all we had to protect ourselves. Simple, everyday measures of precaution. Things that everybody else did. Peering out from under my sack I came to see that there were other deformed tortoise-like shapes moving along the village street. Small bodies like mine shoved into carapaces not their own. Old bodies and young bodies contorted out of shape, until we all looked alike. We all huddled against the biting cold. We all had the appearance of being bent double under our sacks. Buffeted by the wind, we wove strange meandering paths along the street, like demented insects who can no longer walk in a straight line because of damage to one of their antennae. A whole community of demented insects. But all we were doing was trying to avoid the deep puddles that filled the potholes in the road whenever it rained. You might have thought it looked strange, but we knew that in our situation it was wisdom. It was self-protection. It was the approved pattern of behaviour. If one of us had been offered an umbrella, we would not have taken it. We would not have dared to make ourselves different. If you had held out to one of our children a pretty, child-sized umbrella printed with flowers, frilled with plastic ribbon, though she might have desired it more than anything she had so far encountered in her small life, I can guarantee absolutely that she would have shrunk from your hand.

From what did such fear grow? The fear of strangers. The insidious fear, deeper-biting, of each other. How did it happen? There was a day, my grandmother told me, before I was born, when they came with bulldozers to knock down all the stone barns in the village. Did it come then? Did it come in the scream and whine of gears as they spied out another pig-sty, another cow-byre and ploughed over gardens and through hedges to get to it? Was it born in the terrible second of stillness before walls topple? There was to be a new direction to our lives, they told us. New plans. The old memories were to be forgotten. There was to be a new future. Was it then that we became afraid? Was it then that the silence fell upon the village? When no one dared protest. Not even to his neighbour. We had seen what happened to those who complained.

In place of our farms and smallholdings they built us a new farm. They sited it on the shoulder of the hill, just above the village. So we could all look up to it. So we could all see it wherever we were. This is for you, they said. But we were not fooled. We knew that now we had nothing. They made it of corrugated iron. Barns. And grain silos. And a silage tower. Right in the path of the prevailing wind. Every winter one or other of the roofs blew off. But they were always slow to send us replacements. We were not of interest to them any more. The silage tower was as poorly contructed as everything else. For some reason the vents could not be closed properly. The fit of the slats was imperfect. Perhaps they did it on purpose to remind us.

But that was a long time ago. When I came on the scene attitudes were already in place. These things had happened, life had changed and in order to survive people had allowed themselves to be changed with it. No one spoke of these things. No one spoke of the fear. But we picked it up. Young children are the most adept survivors of all. Soft-limbed. Liquid of mind. Chameleon. We saw it in the eyes of the adults around us. Heard it in the sudden breaking off of conversations as we entered rooms. Felt it in their anxious, pushing arms. If they pushed us towards something they did not believe in, the only clue to their private doubt was this – anxiety. Their fear was not only for us. But for themselves. That we, in our innocence, might let fall something that might lead to their betrayal. So they stood close behind us, ready with excuses for us. Ready to laugh it off, scold it away. Cover it up. 'They are too little,' they would have said. 'They don't know what they are doing.' But we knew – without ever knowing exactly what it was that we knew. We knew from very young what is permitted and what is not. You got a sense for it. We understood complicated ideology without ever thinking about it. We were of an age for it. The age of pencils in straight lines and dresses that mustn't have a crease. The age of joining and excluding. Of smugness and small tight faces and finding a victim to denounce. Of whispering in corners. And having a new best friend every week. We were ripe for political affiliation. It was tailor-made for minds like ours. I accepted it willingly. I was even eager for it. Another belonging to belong to. Another tribe. Another family. Another school class. I wanted them all to love me. So I scurried about clutching my paper flag, or my drooping posy of flowers. Drilling. Marching. Smiling my huge little girl's smile in all the group photographs. I can still hear the songs we used to sing. They were recorded indelibly into my brain – as they were meant to be. Without meaning. Senseless. And yet, hearing them in my head as I lie here in the darkness, memory flows stronger than ever.

We sang them in the classroom. Little shrill voices floating up with the heat from the stove to the high ceiling. And we sang them in the summer out on the playground. Below the school ran the river and the drone of the sawmill. Above straggled the village and the road to Opecno. And around the cluster of cottages lay the fields which belonged to no one anymore. I sang to my peg dolls as I put them to bed endlessly in eggboxes and got them up again. I sang as I tramped around the packed earth of the hen run with a handkerchief tied to a stick and a shawlful of apples on my back. I was the little patriot who conquered all the world. Beneath my feet the hens ran away squawking and flapping, their heads bobbing from side to side. Sometimes I stared down into the mud as I tramped to make myself dizzy, singing louder and louder. To make it feel as if my steps lengthened into furlongs and miles. To imagine that I strode over hills and mountains. Leapt across rivers. I liked the hen run. I like the small confined safeness of it. The silly, fluttering hens. In the hot afternoons, when they slept in the shade of the plum tree that overhung their run, I would creep up on them. Catch them and hold them tight to stop them struggling, one hand around their necks. I would bury my nose in their warm feathers that smelled of dust and grain. I would listen to the agitated rolling, clucking sound in their throats. Poor hens. They would hold themselves stiff and still, their eyes almost closed with fright, though they could have struggled easily out of my grasp. Beyond the hen run was the plum tree. That was where I sat to shell peas for my mother. Beyond the plum tree were the redcurrant and black-currant bushes. I was not allowed to approach them. They spent the summer with torn curtain netting draped over them like washing hung out to dry. Like aunts sleeping in the sun under handkerchiefs. Beyond the currant bushes the stubbly scythed grass of our garden squeezed under the lowest strand of the wire fence and was transformed into the willowy grass of the meadow, dotted with speedwell and Mary Bells and campion. And beyond the slope of the meadow hung the valley, shimmering in the heat haze as if it was held in water. Hills. And hills beyond that. Forests dipping down to little coloured fields and the broken threads of twisting white roads. The real world, into which I never ventured. A land as well-known yet as distant to me as that of fairy tales. I could stand on the meadow slope with the circle of hills all around me and recite the names of everything I saw. Everything had a name. Everything. The corner of a field, a tree, an outcrop of stone. To an outsider these things were nothing. But for us they had significance. They gave us reference and place. The history of one was bound up with the history of another. They were like code-words. You only had to say them and between you and your listener spread out well-known stories of love or greed or death or magic. The whole story in one word. They were our morality tales. Our heroes. The names of places kept being changed by the authorities. Changed to official words like dates, or Party leaders. People found them hard to remember. They became confused as to which was current and, fearing mistakes, dropped them from their conversation altogether. It was as if the more recent history of the nation was never able to stabilise into myth. Because of its own doubt. Its own uncertainty. If they had not kept changing things . . .

As the old names of places were dropped, so some of the romance, some of the decoration of our lives was lost. They became as unadorned as the thick white bowls and plates that were made at the porcelain factory in the next village. You could find them in all our houses. As our painted plates broke, these thick white plates were all there were to replace them. And sometimes not even those were available. And so, little by little, small vital things, things not practically but spiritually necessary to our lives, were lost.

Lost.

What is – lost?

Is something lost if it ceases to be?

Is it lost if it is never performed? Never re-created? Never transmitted?

What if it is thought, only? If it is remembered, kept in the memory. Then it is not entirely lost. But then it is in danger. For what happens when all those who hold it in their memory die one by one, silently, without having communicated that memory? Then it is as lost as if truth were lost. If truth were known, but not spoken . . . If people kept silent, merely holding it in their minds, never exercising it, truth would slip out of our lives. Slowly, but certainly. Fading from neglect. And one by one the people who had known of it would die. And then, finally, it would be lost. When truth has been lost entirely from a nation it is difficult to reintroduce.

Against loss I have only memory. I look back – and there I find myself. There I have being. I can trace it. Touch it almost. The taste of buttermilk. The powdery smell of dried clay thrown up in ruts by tractor wheels. Coded sensations to a whole life. My life. My being. They are Vinja's Oak and Marenka's Stone. They are all the names I used to recite from my hill-top. Why did I never go to see them? Why did I not store up more memories? Why could I not foresee a day when I might have – nothing else?

How could I have known? When you are small, you do not know such things. I could not even have imagined that I would ever leave the village boundary. It was not our custom. Not – our habit. There was no mark to tell us, but we knew, each of us by a kind of intuition, where the village ended. We felt the sudden strangeness of the road. A certain coldness to the air. The hedges began to crowd unnaturally close, the leaves of the trees lining the roadside rustled with a sound unfamiliar to us. The difference provoked unease and few of us tempted it. We were cautious. But perhaps we had good reason. My grandmother would not even leave the perimeter of her garden. 'Why should I?' she would demand, jutting out her chin. 'Why should I?' But you could see beyond the defiance the fear. The fear of loss, the fear of the bull-dozers returning. Her house was all that she had left. The house, and the patch of garden that it was my duty to weed. Weeding was a time-consuming business. It involved learning all the names of the plants. And with the names would come the inevitable stories. We spent a long time, my grandmother and I, weeding. And yet, in my memory, her garden is wild. Convolvulus twines along the paths, goose grass climbs into the trees and hangs there like green spiders' webs. Her house was dark and small. It had a smell like boiled milk hanging about it, and the curious sensation of time suspended. Between the picking up of a cup and its putting down again, would pass, in my grandmother's house, not one second or two, but minutes, hours, lives. It was as if, as a reward for her extreme old age, her long endurance of time, time had granted her knowledge of its true nature. Of its timelessness. Its illusion of constancy. She was allowed to play with time. To juggle it. To unwind it, and roll it in again. For her own amusement. And mine. Inside my grandmother's house I would only have to point to an object on a shelf, pick something up out of a drawer, for the slipping of time, the unleashing of stories to begin. We would find that it might take a whole afternoon just to walk past the dresser in the kitchen. Or, sitting down on the bench outside the back door, it might take us several hours to stand up again. Anyone looking in on us would see us held in strange arrested motion. A small silver teaspoon upraised in the hand of one person. A scrap of cloth, perhaps, clutched by the other. It was as if we were bewitched. But there would come a time when the flow of words would cease and a small cunning smile would creep out from the corners of my grandmother's mouth. Her eyes would hood themselves as if closing, like the eyes of a fortune teller who 'sees' no longer. 'You'd best get back,' she'd say. '*She*'ll be wondering.' Beyond the window the daylight would be pale. Uncertain. I could not tell how much time had passed. And I would walk out, reluctant, bemused, into a strangely flattened world.

My mother and my grandmother referred to each other always as She or Her. I used to wonder sometimes what happened when they met. They must have done so. But I cannot recall it. Was there confusion? Silence? Or were their names dragged out like best linen from some deep drawer? Mouthed stiffly. Unwillingly. My grandmother was not my mother's mother. She was my father's mother. My mother was sharp-eyed and quick-tongued. She saw every lump of mud not scraped off my boots. Every slip of my coloured pencil from the paper onto the kitchen table. My father was silence. Silences that I followed eagerly, waiting for them to break. Waiting for the warm, quiet words. My father was slow, a measured stillness. The calm of wisdom, deep-seated. It was, I realise now, the stillness of the countryman. He worked with the other men of the village on the communal farm. My mother worked in the kitchen when she was not needed at harvest or when they were short-handed. The kitchen was her room – living room, dining room, scullery all rolled into one. Along one wall was a porcelain sink, along another the range, under the window a table and on the other wall a dresser. Within this space she moved, ceaselessly. Her long quick fingers prodding, wet and reddened; darting, with a dexterity I knew I would never match. In the heat of the stove and her constant exertions wisps of hair would uncurl and droop over her face pulling at her features like weights. She was the law-giver. Such people cannot smile often. And yet, out of the kitchen she seemed to feel herself vulnerable. If I suprised her in the cool darkness of the family bedroom bending over an open drawer or a pile of linen, she would start, and snap at me suddenly, without reason.

My mother did not like to see me idle. Such is the way of very busy people. I would try to escape her by playing outside, but even there she would call to me to run this errand or that. It was the way of all our mothers. We tolerated it up to a point, it was their right after all, and then, beyond that, we rebelled. Silently. Slipping away quickly through hedges and along walls to those places on the edge of the village which were beyond our mothers' call. There we would congregate in little sidling bands, drifting and gossiping until hunger or obligation drove us home again. The other way to avoid my mother's tasks was to be playing with Katia and Marie. Katia and Marie were the daughters of my mother's brother. They were much praised by her. There was in her attitude a curious unspoken implication that they were of the right family and I – was not. Katia. And Marie. Just whispering their names, even now, makes a small knot tighten in my stomach. One was older than me and one was younger. One had small eyes that narrowed every time she spoke, and the mouth of the other was thin, the lower lip curving in a sulky line. In my memory they slide in and out of each other like two parts of a whole. You never saw one without the other. They had a habit of preening one another. Of fussing with plaits. Re-tying ribbons. Rubbing grass stains off skirts with licked fingers. Where the rest of us were complained over by our mothers, they were held up as models of virtue. Faced with a muddy path or a wet field they would stop, their identical snub noses would flatten themselves even further with distaste. They would shake their heads so that the tight plaits bounced and swung and one of them, generally the elder one, would say: 'We mustn't get our feet wet.' Or 'We mustn't make our socks dirty.' Such statements seemed to me nonsensical. What was a bit of water to a sturdy foot? And what were socks but irrelevant nuisances much prized by mothers? But they would already have turned back and I would be left to go on alone or follow them. What they liked was to sit in the meadow threading chains of daisies and buttercups. Talking. I would sit uneasily beside them. As if I sat within striking distance of two lazily curled vipers. There is a Katia and Marie in every school playground, whose bite paralyses instantly and whose look is the marking out for death. Even I, their cousin, was not granted immunity. Their talk was not of marbles or the best places for blackberries. They traded reputations and indiscretions, bending forward to each other, nodding their sleek heads for emphasis. In the silences that fell, ominous and still in the bright sunshine, I would let drop the crumpled daisy I had been twisting in my stubby fingers, searching, baffled, for stories to equal theirs. I would offer up the small sins of my school-friends. Imperfectly understood fragments overheard from my parents' conversations. I can still see the slow kindling of derision in their eyes. Still see the impatient gesture as they shook out their lengthening daisy chains, each flower a severed head. Hear the smug sing-song of their voices as they took up their chant once more, statement and response, turn and turn about. It used to puzzle me where they got their information, how they discovered our secrets. It made us all afraid of them. Afraid as we all were of the pointed finger. The whispered word. We learned to tread warily, on tiptoe as it were, without even being consciously aware that we did so.

We are a nation of tightrope walkers. So they say, those who walk on the ground. Walking is a sober, serious thing to do and if performed carefully, one foot after the other, you can go on for ever. Or at least for as long as you want to. It is not dangerous. It is not dangerous, really, to walk a tightrope; once you become accustomed to it. You can see very little children doing it with apparently no effort; those who were born to it. All it needs is practice, a cool head and expressionless eyes. After all, there is always the net. We, too, have nets spread out below us. Taut, knotted, square-eyed with watching, with looking up our skirts. The net waits to catch us. But you don't look down at it. That's rule number one for tightrope-walkers. You look at the net even for one second and you are drawn to it, and it to you. Somewhere in mid-air, in a no-man's-land, beyond help of any kind, suddenly you find yourself tangled in its ropes. Hopelessly enmeshed. No, you never look down. Nor up. Straight ahead is best. Only the tight-rope dancers look up, into the bright lights. The lights that flood their eyes and dazzle their senses till they hear nothing, see nothing and scarcely feel the wire beneath their feet. Till for them the tent of the circus dissolves thread by ragged thread, tearing apart to reveal an infinity of stars.

I had a friend and she was a dancer. All her life she was a dancer. All the time that we were growing up together and later when we went away to college. Her name was Magdalena. Magdalena Vosporova.

I can remember the precise day we became friends. A day in midsummer. Hot and windless. A day of restlessness. A day of edging round my mother's elbow. Of waiting. Circling. Refusing to go out.

'Why don't you take your father's lunch up to the field?'

'Why don't you go and play with Katia and Marie?'

'Why don't you pick the blackcurrants for me?'

'Why don't you . . .'

But it was none of those things I wanted. Curious the slide between inertia and purposefulness. The sudden brightness of sunlight after the darkness of the small kitchen. The resoluteness of brown toes in red sandals scrambling over banks of dried clay, pushing through grass, dust-brown moths fluttering up from my feet. The high-pitched frenzy of cicadas and the scrabbling of tiny startled lizards, small grains of earth dislodged and rolling away under their claws. The wide sky and valley floor falling away below me as I climbed.

You know when you are getting near the forest. The grass dwindles and the flowers stop. Then suddenly it rises up before you. Black against the sun. You can scarcely hear any more the shrilling of the sunlit world behind you. You gaze into its depths and shafts of sunlight slide down the trunks of the trees turning them pink and brown, shadowing them with violet and falling onto the bed of pine needles beneath. High above the silence of the forest, the tops of the trees creak and sway together like masts of ships. A breeze ruffles them and a sigh passes through them like waves on the sea. All at once I came out onto a dried mud bank. Beside it a white road ran on between the trees, shadowed to a point and was lost. After a few yards the bank dropped suddenly and I jumped down. There, sitting on the opposite side of the road, was Magdalena. It was as if she was waiting for me. As if she had known that I was coming. She grinned and held out a cupped hand, the fingers curled over something in her palm. I went towards her trying to peer over her fingers, but when I got close enough to see she drew in her hand. Smiling to herself she poked about in it and then thrust a raspberry at me. She held it out between thumb and forefinger. I can see it still. The tiny hairs on it. The bead of juice trickling down. I stretched out my hand for it. But she didn't give it to me. Instead she turned it over, slowly. Out of the hole where the stalk had been crawled a maggot. And then another. Three. Four. Their white heads questing and burrowing. I stepped back quickly. Magdalena laughed and flicked the raspberry away over her head. She picked out another and offered it to me, turning it over and over so that I could see it. Cautiously, I approached.

'It's good,' she said softly, nodding her head to reassure me.

I inspected it carefully and put it in my mouth. I can still remember the taste of it. The first sharp bite and then the sweetness later. She threw another couple in the dust. I crouched down beside her on the bank. And we sat there in silence, the warmth and the half-light and the creaking of the forest all around us, eating raspberries turn and turn about from the pile in her lap. When they were gone we didn't pick any more. I don't know why. We just got up and wandered back into the village. From that day we became inseparable and I accepted Magdalena's judgement in everything.

My mother tried to forbid me to play with Magdalena.

She tightened her lips and hooded her eyes. She clashed pans together on the stove.

'You stay with your own kind.'

People in the village called Magdalena a gipsy, though they knew this was not so. Magdalena's father had been a schoolteacher. He had come to the village, so the story went, married Magdalena's mother and then had been reposted. Five years later Magdalena's mother reappeared with a child in her arms. The child was Magdalena. Her husband had died, she said, in a street accident. It was regarded as an unconvincing tale. In those suspicious days there were other, more likely, reasons for disappearance. She was accepted grudgingly back into the village, moving in with Magdalena to the kitchen of her mother's house. She was given a job at the porcelain factory in the next village, getting up at five each morning. Magdalena was left to her grandmother, but the little girl was too much for the old lady. She ran wild, watched by the other women of the village. These same women who now clustered round my mother, condoling with her. These women with narrow faces and watching eyes. They whispered to my mother, so I couldn't hear what it was they said. They whispered, as their daughters whispered in the corners of the school playground. As they had whispered all their lives, spinning webs to entrap each other. They said that she led me. They said it to each other over and over again, nodding their heads, until they had convinced each other that it was true. Perhaps it was true. There is always one who leads. And one who follows. But so long as what you think that you are doing is walking side by side, then that's all right. And that is where I see us. When I look back. Side by side. Two little girls straggling along white gravel roads. Out to the perimeter of our known world and back again in faded cotton dresses and unravelling plaits. Heads together. Talking. Talking. What was it we talked about? I don't know . . . The scratch of serge? The nauseous taste of skin on boiled milk? The green smell of high grass when you lay face down in it? I don't know any more. With Magdalena nothing else mattered – except being with Magdalena. Everything else slid away. Beyond our frame of vision everything shrank, everything became pale and colourless, reduced to monochrome. Beyond the sound of our voices there was nothing but a low murmur that rose and fell and dwindled into silence. Like crowds in dreams. The words indistinguishable. Without meaning. We saw, as we wandered through the village, people whose arms gestured and whose lips moved, but if there was sound it did not penetrate our world. We moved as if held in a bubble. If it was an enchantment, this absorption, this – apartness from the world, then like all enchantments there was a price.

Perhaps it would have been better if I had stayed with Katia and Marie. I would be there still. I would have gone to work on the collective farm. Or at the porcelain factory in the next village. I would have married one of the lank-haired moustachioed boys who hung around the pond on summer evenings. And lived in the back room at my mother's, until we were allotted a house by the commune. I would have had babies and my voice would have grown shrill. I would have become dulled and bitter. But I would not have known. After Magdalena such a thing was not possible. I would always have known what we all sensed without wanting to know it. Without ever openly admitting it. We guessed at the poverty of our lives. Out there, in the country, the freezing over of a puddle, the easing of the wind – these were big events. Subjects of conversation. Not serious conversation. We were not that stupid. You heard the irony in grown-ups' voices, saw the jaded smile. A slow hunching of the shoulders. When they discussed the formation of ice they laughed. Short, barking laughs.

Laughing at ourselves. At the absurd situation we found ourselves in. The emptiness of it. The pettiness of it. Laughing because there was nothing else to do. Except cry at the pain of the nothingness. We talked of the wind and the cold because they were our life. They were what had been allotted to us. They were the experiences we were permitted to have. And we accepted them. Accepted them ruefully, without much thought of doing anything to alter them. That was how it was.

But Magdalena would not accept. Magdalena would not accept that there was only one way to bake bread. She would not accept that winter vests could not be taken off till May had passed. She would not allow herself to be taught to knit by her mother. And when her mother then refused to knit anything more for her, she went about stubbornly in jerseys till their sleeves scarcely covered her elbows and her chest was so tightly constricted she said she could hardly breathe. Every time she giggled we expected filaments of wool to snap. I used to hover in the doorway of Magdalena's mother's kitchen nervously picking at splinters of wood, making myself as unobtrusive as possible, watching. Listening. To Magdalena and her mother. To the endless battles that raged across the kitchen table. To the stubbornness of these two women, closeted together year after year, that battered itself into echoes against the smoke-stained walls. And then into uneasy silence strung taut with pride. While I hung, caught between fear and admiration, swinging on the door.

Magdalena would not even accept the wind and the rain. Trudging home from school in the dark winter afternoons under our potato sacks, Magdalena would refuse to shuffle bent double. In a lull of wind she would suddenly whirl her sack above her head and run shrieking up the road till the next gust pushed her back down the hill. She would seize my arm. My shivering numb arm. She would peer under the tent of my sack at my glazed eyes and my chattering teeth and my runny nose. 'Come on!' She would tug me after her. 'Come *on*! If you run you will be warm.' Run? No one could run in the icy gales that roared around our valley. Not even Magdalena. But when the wind beat her back she just laughed. She would let her wet sack hang on her head like a shawl, her unprotected face streaming with rain so that she glistened in the dark like a marble statue.

'Sing,' she commanded.

She never sang the songs they taught us. Even in school I never heard her, I only saw her lips move. At the corner of my lane we would part. She would battle on up the road, the words of one of her grandmother's old songs tumbling back to me. But I always stood too long watching her go. For when I turned at last for home, the cold and the dark and the ice needles of the wind had descended on me again.

What was it that she knew and I did not? What was it that she saw when there was nothing else visible beyond the minuteness of the present? I watched her in the playground. And in unguarded moments when we were alone together. I repeated her gestures and whispered her words in secret, hoping to discover some trick of mannerism, some key to her. I made my mother knit me a yellow jersey like the one she wore. I stood on tiptoe and stared at myself in the gloom of the mirror on top of the chest of drawers. My pale, thin face stared back at me, puzzled. I pulled at its mousy hair to make it look longer. I bit its lips to make them flush suddenly red. I smudged soot under its eyes to make them look blacker. But the essence of Magdalena still eluded me. When she flung herself in a rage into the long grass of the meadow, she would pull flower heads savagely from their stalks and mutter:

'This place – this *stupid* place!'

And I would sit beside her, arms clasped round my knees, staring down into the valley shimmering below me in a heat haze. I could trace every tree, every bend in the road. What other place *was* there?

There was Opecno. When we were fourteen we were sent on to Opecno to school. It was a new plan for our region. And we were the first group chosen. We were regarded as very fortunate. Privileged. We were looked upon with awe and envy. Some foresaw great futures for us all, new chances at lives they themselves could only have dreamed of. Others predicted ruin. My mother was one of these. Though she didn't go so far as to speak of ruin, she complained of the possible expense and the pointlessness of such an exercise. This attitude ensured the response from her friends of a mixture of commiseration and condolence which they all relished. But I knew that it was the continued presence of Magdalena at my side that really troubled her. Without Magdalena I doubt that I would have had the courage to face even the school bus. Five miles of shrieking and jolting as we lurched from village to village, the bus driver oblivious to everything in an impenetrable cloud of cigarette smoke. And then Opecno. Paved streets, a church, four shops. I hung at Magdalena's shoulder, bemused, overawed. The vastness of the town. The vastness of the school. They have dwindled now. To insignificance. I think of them with a twinge of shame. I think of them and in my mind shutters close, hurriedly. It was in my awe of Opecno that my provincialism lay. Not in the dumb unknowing of my village. Opecno was nothing, scarcely big enough to be called a town. But it was there, I remember, that the fear first struck me that Magdalena might leave me behind. I felt her step forward from my side. Like a swimmer entering a pool. I felt her lift her arms and take in a deep breath of this new air. I saw her smile. A slow, curving smile that was for herself alone. Doubt seeped into the invulnerability of our friendship. The ease of it had been almost like flying. There had been a sense of being far above everything else, of being beyond the tethering of life, of being weightless almost. Without her I could not sustain it. I felt myself floating lower. Without Magdalena I had no belief in my ability to fly. I glimpsed the blackness of the void below me. In it moved dim figures, playmates from my childhood. Katia. And Marie. Others. For a time the void became a nightly part of my dreams. But Opecno was a puddle. One stride took Magdalena across it. She walked through it. And around it. And then she came back to me. As though she had never been away. It was not then that I lost Magdalena. It was later. When I deliberately turned my back on her. Why? To punish her for the fear at Opecno? All the times that I turned away from Magdalena I was the one who suffered, not her. What compelled me? Was it the pernicious desire to subvert the simple course of my life? Was it the private acknowledgement that I could never be Magdalena that made me snatch the reins into my own hands? To show her. To show everyone.

Only fleeting images remain in my memory of those last few years of school at Opecno. Long evenings. Lamp-light falling on dog-eared exercise books. The pervasive smell of kerosene. The drudgery of pushing away the stones in my brain. Magdalena close, confiding, inky-fingered, dishevelled. My mother watching, a small figure now, tight-lipped and begrudging. And the last summer, when we were chosen for summer camp at Lake Valcha. Lake Valcha. We talked of nothing else for a month. In our mouths the name curled, sinuous, with all the luxury, all the exoticness of foreign travel. No one we knew had ever been away on holiday.

'It will be like the sea,' said Magdalena. 'It will be so vast, it will be impossible to see from one side to the other.'

I nodded, seeing it all, all that we had never seen – golden sand, blue sea, the lap of waves.

It was true. You looked out over the water, and at the place where the horizon should have been, water and sky just dissolved in a mist. In a curious long cloud that was tinged a heavy copper colour at its edges. The camp was in a field next to the lake, on the edge of a small holiday settlement of old wooden cabins. There was a general store selling mainly fishing tackle and tinned fruit, a café and a pier. That was where the road stopped, at the pier. It petered out under the pale feathery branches of low pines at the edge of the water, lost in its own dust. In front of the café were chairs and two wooden tables. Late in the afternoons the radio would play dance music, and couples would get up from their beer and shuffle slowly and solemnly in the white dust. From the pier Magdalena and I would watch them with envy. All our free time was spent on the pier. It fascinated us, this creaking wooden edifice, this road that ran out over the water – and then stopped dead. I loved the feel of the warm splintered boards beneath my bare feet. I would sit staring down through its cracks at the glinting water below, mesmerised. The small brown wavelets broke with a little curl of reddish foam against the crumbling clay banks of the lake. There was no beach. In some places along the shore there were small muddy inlets. Here the fishermen sat, still as statues, hunch-shouldered. As daylight waned and we sat in camp after supper, listening to our leader, we could still hear the radio playing. It wafted over us in snatches with the smell of frying, distracting our thoughts with its promise of life to come. As dusk fell, the lights strung along the pier and fixed haphazardly to the front of the small café would come on. In the evening wind the small bulbs swung backwards and forwards, twinkling on and off. Now some, now others, now all together. By nine o'clock the faltering power system gave up completely and the whole settlement was plunged in darkness. Early to bed, early to rise. But Magdalena didn't believe that, like she didn't believe anything else she was told. She insisted that we creep out of the camp, when everyone was asleep, down to the shore. At night Lake Valcha was transformed. Darkness hid the strings of shanty settlements along its shore. But the factories glowed with arc lamps colouring the sulphurous clouds that hung above them green and orange. Every now and then, from their long chimneys, tongues of flame would shoot high into the sky. Along the shore the fishermen sat under black umbrellas. Night after night. Yet there was no rain. Night after night we crept down to stare at them. Some had lights in jars that wavered beside them on the bank, throwing strange shadows on their immobile faces. An oil lamp would suddenly flare as men bent over a catch, or leant into the light to bait a hook. But we never dared approach them.

I can still feel the sun of Lake Valcha on my back and the softened planks of the pier under my heels. I can still smell the dry cement-dust smell that always hung in the air. There are two fried onion rings still left in the greasy cone of paper that lies between us. And your shoulder is still firm against mine, the imprint of it as strong as if it still pressed against me. The faint pain of it reconstructing instantly in the muscles of my arm. Like the remembered weight of a dismembered limb. Magdalena.

It was not I alone who turned against you. Things were made difficult for me. I was bemused. Uncertain. Led. Besides, in the student teachers' dormitory for women at Ludovice dormitories were allotted strictly by alphabetical order, by surname. It was not in my hands. We would have been parted anyway. Once allotted to a dormitory . . . You remember those dormitories, Magdalena? Those white iron beds, all the paint chipped off. The green walls. The cold linoleum floors. The flurry of excited girls. The eyes. Watching. The heads bent together. The voices low, fading into whispers . . . Magdalena?

From the high windows of the Postmen's House early morning sunlight filters down through motes of dust into the warm murmuring of the room. Outside the streets are silent, stalked by cats and the fluttering of birds. And while you sleep we rearrange your lives. We are the dealers of fate, wielding the power of life and death over our small territories. The millimetre of brain glows, the hands flick out, slick as a card-sharper's dealing, splicing, shuffling. The envelopes fan wide and with a jerk from the wrist are sent flying one after the other into their boxes. With dreamers' eyes and slow smile we deal out the Hanged Man and the Queen of Love.

Jack was usually the first to leave the House. Mr Finch and I, because we worked at more or less the same pace and had adjacent territories, generally left together, later. To begin with I welcomed Mr Finch's company, I liked the slow deliberation of his stride and his amiable silence. He was the perfect early morning companion. But latterly I have begun to resent his presence. I have begun to resent anything which drags me away from the Postmen's House. I long to become one of those loitering boys, those men who stand in doorways hour after hour, slack-eyed, loose-limbed, staring into space. They are despised, such men, if they are noticed at all, and yet perhaps they stand as guardians to something of private importance. Perhaps they have found a vantage point from which they can glimpse infinity. I have begun to see them everywhere. And they have begun to see me. Sometimes as I pass one his eyes will flicker from vacancy for a second to engage mine in a dull stare. I have become recognisable. Eligible. But they are mistaken. I am not quite as they are; I have a clear purpose, an identifiable responsibility. I look into their doorways and their corners and I see nothing to suggest why they have chosen this particular place to stand. Whereas if I were to take up their calling, I would stand beside the door of the Postmen's House. And everyone who glanced at my slouched figure would see immediately why I was there.

Some mornings it is worse than others, this reluctance to leave. As the moment approaches, it can get so bad I almost believe that if I went over to Mr Harry and told him that what I ought to do was stay behind and stand guard over the writing on the door instead of going out with the letters, he would agree with me. He would see that the preservation of such freedom of expression should be undertaken as a matter of national importance. That particular morning it was worse than usual. I longed to call out to Mr Finch, waiting for me on the path:

'Go ahead!'

But I lacked the courage. I pointed myself at the steps and let myself fall, my legs buckling, my feet thudding one after the other onto the path, back into life.

'Think it'll stay fine, Mr Finch?'

He turned from his contemplation of the sky.

'Could do, Jan. Could do. Glass was very steady last night.'

We turned out of the gate and made for the common by a series of side streets. On reaching it, we avoided the diagonal path across it and took to the grass. To a Walker grass is pure joy. Coming to grass after pavements is like walking on cotton wool after treading barefoot over nails. I even dream about grass. In my dreams it grows over the edge of the common, across the road, over the pavement and even up the front paths of houses. I push open doors into blocks of flats and there it is growing silently up the stairs and away into the darkness of passages, smelling as if it has just been mown.

We picked our way through strutting clusters of starlings who clicked their beaks with irritation, and passed young blackbirds casting uncertainly for worms, round-eyed at the newness of the world. The sky was a pale cloudless blue as it had been all week and the stand of trees at the far end of the common away to our right already shimmered in a light heat haze. I had the curious sensation, walking beneath the trees, of catching sight of leaves turning on their stems as if of their own volition, and the sense of life millennia ago before man. All around the common streets ran away in varying directions looking like lifeless stage sets. Cars had been set out on them and houses. Lamp standards had been erected to give light when the inevitable darkness should fall. But man himself had not yet appeared. Mr Finch and I crossed the road at the edge of the common, nodded to each other and, turning away into our separate territories, slid into the sleeping streets.

It is here in the unexpectedness of early morning that we meet – messenger and victim. It is here, out in our territory, that we can complete our speculations about you. We may never encounter each other face to face, but your life spreads out around you. It seeps out beyond your control imprinting your image on everything connected with you – your front door, your doorstep, the abject abandonment of your garden, even your hungry cat. Just turning into your street can settle for us fundamental questions as to the nature of your existence. A glimpse of the colour of your curtains, or the state of the paint on your front door builds swiftly for us essential details of identification as individual as eyes or nose. It is here on your doorstep that we fill in the missing clues to your life. The sound of your letters dropping onto the floor beneath your letter-box is like the comforting click of jigsaw pieces fitting neatly into place. Letters always fit their recipients, however ill-matched they may seem at first. The fault – the discrepancy – has usually been in our judgement: a laziness of diagnosis, a picture too hastily drawn without sufficiently perceptive observation. The usual temptations. There is a feeling among some Lettermen that it is better for us not to meet. But I am always surprised how, when we do, you do not see us. However sleepy we may be, you appear to be sleepier still. Wrapped in your sleep the familiar figure with his badge and sack is as unseen as the furniture in your bedroom. You seem to be negotiated past us by automatic impulses and not woken till you aproach a patch of ice, or need to be warned of traffic. This is, we should admit, how we prefer to see you, if we see you at all: transparent, struggling towards consciousness, all your efforts directed towards attaining wakefulness, leaving for these few minutes your self unguarded, all innocent trust, like a sleepy child. For this is the time before the mask sets, when we can check our speculations. When the mask is clamped tight, we should beware of looking at you, for unless we are strong, unless we are experienced, we will see what you want us to see and be distracted from the truth of you. If you talk to the old hands, to the real Lettermen who live for nothing else, who know the ramifications of their clients' lives better than they do themselves, they will admit they'd really rather not see any of you at all. You never quite measure up, they say. There's always something, well – disappointing – about seeing you face to face.

And yet – I am curious. I am curious to see you and to see the inside of your houses. I am, in relation to those hard-bitten Lettermen, like one of the young blackbirds on the common, still round-eyed at the newness of the world. And this particular morning had such a lapping stillness to it. It was as if the normal world had been dissolved in the night and replaced by a new one in which anything could happen. In the soft shimmering of the early morning air the tall houses set back slightly from the wide road seemed to be made of some insubstantial material. I could see them and beyond them to the backs of other houses, which proved that they were solid and three-dimensional, but their colours appeared muted, the roughness of the bricks smoothed out. I felt that if I touched them they might give slightly, like rubber, under my finger. Walking up garden paths and pushing letters through letter-boxes, I was seized with the desire to peer in after them. I wanted to see the halls into which they dropped. I wanted to glimpse figures in dressing gowns sitting dreaming at kitchen tables. I wanted to knock softly at front doors and wander through the sunlit rooms of these sleeping houses. I found myself pushing unnecessarily hard against letter-boxes, as if I hoped that some of the doors might have weak catches. I fanned through the envelopes in my hand, looking for a registered delivery, or a letter owing postage. I searched inside my sack for a parcel; for any excuse to knock on a door. There was nothing. I shuffled through the letters again. What about wrong delivery? What about posting Mr Grant, 23, into Mrs Ames, 25? And ringing the bell. I slid the two letters back and forth across each other. Perhaps it should be the other way round. My knowledge of Mr Grant was sketchy, but Mrs Ames's dossier was even emptier. There was a Mr Ames, I knew that. There were two Mr Ameses, in fact. A Mr A. Ames and a Mr F. Two husbands? Two sons? One husband and one son? Two brothers-in-law? Various theories of relationship splayed out enticingly around me. I fingered Mr Grant's letter as nervously as if I was shoplifting it and turned up Mrs Ames's steps. What would I say and how would she reply? What would she be like? In the insubstantiality of the morning anything seemed suddenly possible.

'Beg pardon, madam,' I could say pointing at the envelopes on the hall floor, 'pushed in someone else's by mistake. New round here. Jan Remek.'

Would she slam the door in my face, or would she hesitate on the doorstep, nonplussed? Would she – ask me in? It happened. I knew. The others joked about it in the House when Mr Harry was out of earshot. What if she let me in and led me, without a word, to the stairs? How could I then explain to her that all I wanted was to sit in her kitchen and drink tea with her, meet her husband, see the debris of their last night's supper and the ornaments she kept on her mantelpiece. Immerse myself for a moment in the Englishness of her life. Breathe it in and savour it.

'Arthur! There's a bloke here from the Post Office. Says he wants to come in. Have a cup of tea . . .'

I paused, one foot on her lowest step.

My colleagues at the House would be outraged if they got to hear of it – knocking on doors, telling them we know their business, giving away secrets of the trade! The cat would be out of the bag then: servants revealed as masters. The apple cart upset. Little red solidities up-ended and rolling about the floor. Mr Harry wouldn't like it and Sid would be distraught. Even Jack would be uneasy.

'Phew, mate, you shouldn't have done that!'

Better not then, I thought, taking my foot off the step. And then it was that I had the curious sensation of being bumped and jostled, of a crowding at my shoulder.

'I don't know . . .' said a bright voice inside my ear. 'Arthur and Mrs Ames . . . tea . . .' It was wistfully enthusiastic. I stopped, but I didn't turn round. I knew there was no one to see. I stood staring at the bunch of letters in my shaking hand. I felt if I moved, I would shatter the images that coalesced and clarified, swinging into vision with the random whirling movement of objects lost in space, crowding together and then turning slightly away from each other half-smiling self-absorbed smiles like shyly animated frontispieces. Dickens, Darwin, and Dostoevsky – released from behind the blistering paint on the door of the Postmen's House. Of course! Dickens would have got us invited into the Ames's house. Ever a good man at a party, never mind the hour. Mrs Ames would have opened wide her door for him.

''Ere, *Arthur!'*

The voice would have been quite different: low, incredulous. We would have crowded down the hall. Dickens next to his hostess, already making her laugh. Then Darwin, discussing animatedly with Arthur the cross-breeding of pigeons. While Dostoevsky and I could have skulked in the background watching and listening. Foreigners. Included but excluded from the undercurrents of known reference and inference which sparked like synapses, connecting the others, drawing them into a whole.

Why not! I took a step forward, full of determination.

'Good morning,' I rehearsed under my breath. 'I am Jan Remek, your new postman.'

And in that instant I sensed that they were gone. I looked behind me. There was only the warm, silent morning and the empty street. Slowly I went back down onto the pavement. I had a curious lost feeling and at the same time a feeling of re-entering the known world.

The plateau on which the common is situated runs level for a time and then drops in a long incline towards the river a couple of miles away. The street drops with it, the houses sliding down the hill, their basements bracing themselves against the slope. I have discovered there is a particular point a few yards down this hill at which the surrounding houses fall back and before the lower buildings rise up to obscure the view, where suddenly the vast, sleeping city opens up before you in a breath-taking panorama. That morning the unusually clear air seemed to distort distance. I stood there gazing out at it. Mile upon mile of clustering roofs and close-pressed blocks of houses twisted and turned and pushed against each other. Like a dark line of shadow the river snaked among them, darting out now and then into a flash of silver. Rows of windows blinked in the early morning sun, and back to back others turned sharply away. Smokeless chimney pots huddled together tracing out streets and squares in wavering lines, whose grimy bricks merged in a haze of soot. In between the concrete monoliths and glass towers I could see the spires and pinnacles of ancient landmarks. Away to the east stood St Paul's, with St Bride's appearing to nestle under the shoulder of its dome.

You should have stayed a little longer, I found myself whispering in my head. You could have seen your city. It is not quite as you left it, but you would still have recognised it – the vastness of it, the closeness, the submissiveness of it – lying sleeping below us, as though laid out for conquest along the river plain.

In between my daydreams and the city the jerky figures of sleepwalkers began to advance. In ones and twos they fumbled with keys, stumbled down steps and disappeared over the top of the hill in the direction of the rising roar of traffic. I swung my sack from one shoulder to the other, glanced at the topmost letter in my hand and went on with my round.

Mr Finch's tale is not long, nor is it very strange, but it has a certain haunting quality to it of something irreparably lost. It struck me all the more forcibly when I heard it because of his habitual reticence, his old-fashioned politeness of not putting himself forward in conversation. It is quite possible that I might never have heard it if I had not been sitting as usual after work on the steps of the Postmen's House. One by one the others had all left and I was listening to the sounds of the House returning to silence. The creak of a board, the whisper of a swing door, the buzzing of a fly. And the silence itself. Mr Harry and Sid were still there, pottering quietly, waiting for the House to become something other: the House that only they see. When we are gone and the safety of silence returns, then the House takes up its own private life again. It uncurls. Chairs inch closer together as if drawn into soundless conversation, shadows move. A piece of paper will detach itself suddenly from one pile and drift down from the table in slow eddies to another pile on the floor; and though no breeze stirs, the cord at the window swings to and fro, to and fro. I have not seen these things – I would not presume to intrude – but I can sense the metamorphosis. From my corner, where the door meets the warm bricks of the wall, I can smell it. I can smell the settling dust and the cavernous coolness of the hall. I can taste the silence. And see the emptiness of that busy room. But my place is here. Out here, in the lazy heat of early afternoon, I can smell the paint cracking in the warmth and the asphalt bubbling in the sun. I keep watch through half-closed eyelids. And if there is any time more propitious than another to the unravelling of the words on the door of the Postmen's House, then it is now.

I whisper them to myself in the warm buzzing silence. Dickens, Darwin, Dostoevsky. I reverse their order, jumble their position, seek out their connection, their relation. But it will not come, it will not fall true: three pat in a line, like the jackpot on the fruit machine at The Running Nag. Whatever cohesion I try to force on them, always one escapes, and each time a different one. Two

Englishmen and a Russian. Two men of letters – and a scientist. Two Charleses and a Fyodor . . .

A cat slinks up the road keeping to the shadow of the low stone walls and privet hedges and vanishes suddenly into a garden. Twenty yards beyond it is my house and within it my flat and within that my wife . . . my wife who sits brooding. Why do I not go home? I do go home, but not yet. I . . . wait for a while. I sit. I revel in – just sitting. If I had gone home like everybody else, I would never have seen Mr Finch. He took me by surprise. I was watching a caterpillar climb one of the stems of grass in the clump that grows by the gate, my eyes almost closed in the attempt to focus on such a small thing at such a distance. The translucent green body squeezed itself up the blade of grass. Just as it neared the top, just as the blade was about to bend under the caterpillar's weight, a huge boot swung through the gate. I looked up. Leaning heavily on the ornamental gate post was Mr Finch, he was still wearing his postman's jacket, and an empty sack drooped from one hand. His other leg seemed to drag behind him. He limped up the path and lowered himself onto the step beside me.

'You're back late, Mr Finch.'

'I done my leg in, Jan. Turned my ankle on a stone.' He began rolling his sock down, inch over inch, glancing up at me, eyes full of surprise as though at some betrayal. 'A silly stone.'

The skin that was revealed was very white; small dark hairs lay close against it, in places it was mottled blue. This was an Englishman's leg, a private part not normally exposed. I stared at it almost with reverence. I wanted to put my finger out and touch it, like an icon. Over the bone of the ankle the flesh swelled, a small red and blue balloon puffing itself up. Mr Finch's hands dropped away quickly.

'Well, that's it then.' There was almost a choking

disappointment in his voice and a despair in his eyes that I never thought to see. 'Can't walk on that!'

'Oh, they won't expect you to, Mr Finch. Not as bad as that. They'll get someone else in for a bit. Or . . . they'll split it up among the rest of us.'

'That's very good of you, Jan, very good of you,' he murmured. But he was not comforted. His gaze moved distractedly about, from the steps to the path to the elder bush sagging over the fence. He gave a short embarrassed laugh. 'It's not *that* walking.' He glanced at me, eyes narrowed, and instantly his gaze swung away from me again, searching along the empty road, passing sightlessly over the blind windows of the houses, up into the sky. Then suddenly it swung back. 'It's walking the roofs.'

I stared at him.

'The roofs!'

'Yes,' he nodded vigorously. 'The roofs. Oh, wonderful it is Jan. Mile after mile you can go. Different every night if you want. Not so good in the rain. But on a fine night . . .' He shook his head.

'What about the height, Mr Finch; you don't mind being . . . ?'

'I was a builder, Jan; a builder – years ago, before this. Up in Norfolk. Little country town, pretty place it was. My uncle was a builder there and I went to him as apprentice straight from school like it was the most natural thing to do. And so it turned out to be, I liked the feel of wood in my hands and the smell of a new-plastered wall. I learned fast, though you were taught slow and proper in those days, roofs an' all. I *was* scared first time I was sent up a roof; I remember. Thought I'd never get down to dry land again all in one piece. But I got used to it. It was the pride at overcoming that fear, I think, that started it. I got bolder. Then I got a taste for it. And it was just as well. My uncle was getting past roof work. Couple of years later he died and the business came to me. I did well. In time I acquired a wife and then a small child. We became famous for roof work, Finch & Son. But it weren't just my work; it were my hobby. On a Saturday afternoon where another man might stroll down to the cricket pitch to see the batting, or walk along the river bank to watch the fishermen, I'd be up on the roofs. In that little town they were stepped and piled and laid against one another. Walking was easy. I could do it blindfold. From house to house, street to street; eaves jutted across alleyways, arches spanned narrow lanes. You could go all round the town without touching ground. It was another world up there, Jan; a private quiet world. After the first couple of roofs I used to forget about the town below me. I was lost in that roof world, walking through centuries, back through generations of builders. They'd all left their mark, done their finest work where they knew probably only another builder would ever see it. I stepped so lightly, no one below ever heard me. I didn't pry, Jan, I admired. I'd run my thumb down the fine cut of chiselled stone, admire a spread of perfectly overlapping tiles all cut and pegged and the colours blending just so, scrolled chimneys and faced parapets. I was always finding something new in a hidden corner. I was never happier than those hours up there; like another town it was that no one else ever knew about.

'I don't know how the pleasure died, Jan. What turned it sour on itself. But one day when I got to the outer edge of the old town I paused between a cluster of Victorian chimneys to look out over the flat fields and when I turned to look back across the town it just looked – dead. Small and confined, in a way I'd never noticed before. I was looking out over the same patchwork of roofs but the beauty of them had gone. I got down quick as I could and went home. I didn't know what to do. I didn't know anything else. Come the next Saturday, I went up there again, but I just sat with my back against a chimney stack, staring out over the meadows. When my usual time for walking was up, I climbed down and went home. But I felt like a stranger in my own town. Like I had some knowledge of it that the others, who lived there, didn't. It went on all that summer. Till one day when I was asked to go up to London by a customer to look at some property he had there as needed renovation. I did as he asked. I worked my way through the house, making notes of this and that, till finally I pushed my way up through a trapdoor onto the roof. What I saw around me took my breath away, Jan. Mile after mile in every direction, such a clustering and a stepping. There was no end to it. I gazed and gazed. And my heart was racing – I wanted to laugh out loud. It was the old thrill back inside me again. I went home to Norfolk and sold everything up, lock, stock and barrel. Within a month I was back in London with my wife and my child and Finch & Son. But – things never went right, Jan. Too many calls on my capital at once, too many bad debts, too much competition – I don't know what finally done for it. In the end I lost the business. And I come here. But the roofs have never failed me. That's gone on from strength to strength, that's never dimmed. You'd never believe the life up there: wild flowers, little creatures. That's what keeps me going, Jan, I reckon.'

'I'm not very good at heights, Mr Finch.'

'Ah, you'd get used of it, Jan. Get used of almost anything you can.'

He leant down and lifted his leg with both hands into a more comfortable position, the foot trailed after it like a broken wing.

'How are you going to get home?'

'I'll get Sid to call me a cab. Go home in style. It's not far – Streatham Hill.'

'Do you know Gad's Hill?'

'Don't believe I do. That where you live?'

'No, no.' I pushed some stray pebbles back onto the

path with my foot. 'I thought . . .' I rolled the peculiarly English phrase round on my tongue, and looked up at him. 'I'd take the wife out there for the day. It's . . . it's where Dickens used to live.'

'Ohh.'

It was like a gap opening up between two roofs. A very small gulf. He lowered his eyes and turned away his head. Slowly. I should not have said it. I had miscalculated. I had – offended him. It was their phrase 'the wife' and I had taken it, without permission. Though permission could never have been sought, nor granted. I had rolled it round on my tongue. I had practised until I knew I had the intonation and the pacing of it, the dismissive possessive swagger of it. But my ear was not theirs, instinctively tuned, it would always be the ear of a stranger, imitating. And it had failed. There was a sudden cold fear in the realisation of its failure; like the wrong answer in class, the slip during interrogation. One such miscalculation and the safe world you have constructed around you falls away as though it had never been. I glanced across at Mr Finch. He brooded in an awkward silence over his swollen foot. *Had* I miscalculated the phrase – or was it something else? Was it – Dickens? Mr Finch would not look at me. It was not just that he did not, he kept his head stiffly bent and he would not bring himself to raise it. And yet a moment ago he had been all confidence. He had told me of his aspirations and his private pleasures. I had hinted at mine. And it was there, there between the two, that he had suddenly perceived – an abyss. It was so unexpected, that I couldn't think of anything to say. Calm, reflective Mr Finch. I had not meant . . . Why, I could imagine him reading Dickens as clearly as I could see the fingers of my hand. I could imagine him having a complete set of Dickens bound in fake leather proudly displayed in a glass-fronted cabinet of ornamental teak in his living room. I had almost expected him to tell me who his favourite characters were, quote me a passage by heart. Instead there was – this silence. I did not see how it could be broken. I could not allude to the abyss, so I could not push a plank across it. There were rules to this English game, but they were not written down. You learn them like a gambler learns, by losing often. But the price the gambler pays for an unlucky spin of the wheel is petty in comparison to the small death exacted for each mistake in the English game. Winning is not a positive thing, it is merely not losing. And not losing is achieved not just by the careful avoidance of known mistakes, but by being aware of potential mistakes. The most delicate things collude to form a mistake, like tiny, drifting molecules: the tone of voice, the placing of words in a sentence, the mood a person is in, the other people in the room, the room itself, what is outside the room. The clouds, the sky, the weather. The weather. The weather could stand as symbol of the arbiter of the English game. The vagaries of weather match exactly the shifting elusiveness of structure and position in the English game. Perhaps there is after all significance and not dullness of intellect in the Englishman's obsession with the weather. Perhaps it is not just idle chat. Perhaps with each person he meets he is working out form with subtle questions, laying odds on his likely success in the day's game. Perhaps . . . Perhaps I knew nothing. I got to my feet.

'I'll go and get Sid,' I muttered.

The next day Mr Finch was absent and I had completely recovered from my social gaffe of the day before, there was after all a new sun in the sky. I was determined to try it out again. On Jack. Jack had undertaken to sort Mr Finch's streets and Perce, who worked on Mr Finch's right, and I had agreed to split the delivery between us. Jack, sorter-king of the Postmen's House, stood in front of Mr Finch's boxes feet apart, body angled slightly backwards from the hips to give a swing to his throw, eyes half-closed, whistling beneath his teeth the intricate rhythms of a love song. The letters thudded into their boxes.

''Nother nice day, Jack.'

'Going to stay fine right over the weekend an' all, wireless said this morning.'

'You been to Gad's Hill?'

The letters flew out from his fingers like darts. He paused, frowning slightly.

'That's not motors.' The letters began again. 'That horses?'

'Dickens.'

'What?'

'Dickens lived there. You know, Dickens, the . . .'

'Yeah, I know, mate. I know Dickens. I seen the film. Great . . . whatever it was. You going there 'cause Dickens lived there?'

'Yes. I think you can go round his house, see his books and his desk and things.' I cleared my throat. 'Thought I'd take the wife.'

Jack laughed.

'You want to come down Balham, old son. For a ten bob note I'll let you look in my place. Pick up the mug I has my tea in, read my girlie magazines!'

Finally, I tried it out on my wife.

'Let's go out to Gad's Hill on Saturday.'

'What's Gad's Hill?'

'It's a house out in the country where Dickens lived.'

'I promised to meet Rinka on Saturday.'

'Well, let's go tomorrow afternoon.'

'OK.' She pushed her chair back from the table. 'You want some coffee?'

'No, let's have tea.'

She laughed.

'Do you think if we drink enough tea we will become English?'

I smiled sheepishly and stood up.

'I like it.' I began collecting our plates. 'I'll go and make it.'

'You know that you will only become a certain sort of English if you drink so much tea?' she called after me. I banged the plates down into the sink in the cubby-hole. Above the small porcelain sink were shelves, the tins and packets that stood on these shelves were all English, but there was something about the arrangement of this cubby-hole that reminded me always of other, darker cupboard-kitchens. 'The sophisticated English drink more coffee than the poor English, who drink tea all the time. Even for breakfast the sophisticated English drink coffee. You have seen Breakfast Tea in packets with gold lettering, in the shops? That is just for tourists and old colonels and ladies in boarding houses. If you drink too much tea, Jan, you will become a poor English instead of a rich one.'

Where had she learned all this? I turned the tap on full as I filled the kettle to drown out her words. I crashed it onto the hob and lit the gas.

'Janek,' she caught my hand as I began clearing the rest of the table. 'Make me a small, strong, black coffee.'

'Where did you hear all this rubbish?'

'Oh,' she shrugged her shoulders. 'Here and there. Magazines. You know, all the magazines have advertisements in them for powdered coffee in little paper bags. Not – proper coffee. Not – tea.' She looked up at me through half-closed eyes.

It was not magazines. I knew exactly where she got it all. It came from Rinka. Rinka was her Hungarian friend whom she had met at language classes. Her one and only friend. Frequently she would bring her back to the flat in the evening after class. I would hear Eliska's key in the door, a second of silence and then Rinka's husky cracked voice speaking its broken English out in the hall and my skin would prickle with dislike. They were forced to talk

English to each other, there was no other way they could communicate. Rinka could not speak Czech and Eliska couldn't speak Hungarian. So there they would sit, over coffee, fingernails rapping out their impatience on the table-top, compelled to speak the language of the despised. And Rinka despised everything English with a loathing bordering on hate. Every now and then she would look over to where I sat in the armchair by the window watching the fading light behind the chimney pots or pretending to read the paper. She would run a hand through her bleached hair that stuck out from her head like bits of straw and lick her lips quickly, like a lizard flickering its tongue. 'Mmm . . .' she would begin, collecting words together in her head. I can still hear that delicate little moue of sound she used to make, see the chipped varnish on her nails. And then the bitter invective pouring out. We conducted a war of scowling glances, Rinka and I, though we rarely spoke directly to each other. For hours after her visits the flat would stink of her cheap perfume, stale sweat and American cigarettes.

'Is Rinka coming here on Saturday?' I asked Eliska.

'No, we're going shopping; she wants me to help her buy a dress. She's been asked to a dance by some man at work.'

'Well, well; some – *English* man?'

Eliska shrugged, letting go my hand sharply. As I turned away with the rest of the things from the table, I saw her face fall and the old sadness creep back into the corners of her eyes. From the cubby-hole I heard the scrape of her chair and, glancing quickly over my shoulder, saw her walk towards the window and lean against it. And then I turned away to reach for the coffee.

WINDOWS ARE LIKE the eyes of a house. All down this street pairs of eyes stare back at me. Like the eyes of birds, sleeping. Drawn down over each of them a filmy opaque gauze of net curtain. When birds sleep an opalescent membrane of skin drops down over the eye like a blind, a third eyelid. The nictitating membrane. These houses stand like birds, dozing, in the dull light of late afternoon. Eyes open, sight closed. Into this street Jan gazes hour after hour. What does he see? What does he look for? The stirring of life behind these closed eyelids? The parting of curtains at a window? What else is there? People say eyes are windows to the soul; that what is in our hearts cannot be hidden but shows clearly in our expression. As if the pupil of the iris was a pinprick hole to the darkness of our souls. As if by peering into the eyes you could see, with concentration, down into the winding spirals of a thread-like tube. Down. Down. Perhaps it is so for the English. But not for us. With us such a thing would be impossible. You could not look into our eyes to see our hearts. For we have learned to hide them. Concealment has become our only weapon, our last defence. You would not find us in our houses, either; they have become just places to be inhabited.

Search them. Tip out our papers. Trample our match-stick furniture. You will see no more than we intend. We have gone to ground. To earth. We live out our eternity of winter on the memory of spring. Only in our gardens is there a wild flowering, an exuberance of spirit we cannot bring ourselves to restrain. 'They are just flowers,' we say if anyone remarks on them, shrugging our shoulders. But they are not. They are – ourselves. The remnants of a nation. On the edges of towns and in forgotten pockets of cities they flourish, these gardens. Wherever there is a patch of ground and someone to tend it. Tucked away in small streets. Clustering around the crumbling walls of dilapidated houses. They spring up. A burgeoning of life. A bursting of colour. Defiant with a strength we have almost forgotten.

From where I stand I can look down over half the gardens in Oudenard Road. They are abandoned places. Ignored. Some are just dusty patches of earth. Some have stiff plants in rows standing beside the path and round past the bow-fronted window. Others have been buried entirely under concrete. Plastic dustbins stand about on them. Waste paper lies in the shadow of their walls, or whirls slowly in the empty concrete space, caught in some unseen wind. Nobody has a real garden. They are indifferent, the inhabitants of Oudenard Road. Sometimes I think they are indifferent to life. But maybe it is just that they do not need to have gardens the way we do. They are at liberty to do what they like and say what they like and go where they like. So they do nothing. Perhaps freedom dulls the senses. Perhaps contentment has a double edge, like a wish in a fairy tale.

The woman in the house opposite shakes a duster out of an upstairs window. One of the 'eyes' has opened. In Ludovice I don't ever remember seeing an open window. Not even in summer. Ludovice was the first big town I had ever been in. My first city. Its streets, its trams, its streams of people, they all – overwhelmed me.

Perhaps it was just a rainy autumn that year, perhaps winter followed unseasonably quickly, but my first impression of Ludovice was of an overall greyness. Heavy blocks of streets. New buildings and old buildings pressed together, all of them crumbling. Where sections of plaster had fallen off walls it was like flesh torn off bone. You could see down to the lathe structure beneath, the bare ribs of the house. Fragments of stone balconies still clung, high up, to the fronts of some of the houses. Garlanded urns balanced with a kind of drunken obstinacy at the corners of gables. But it was the rows and rows of windows covered in a thick layer of dust which struck me most. It was not just the dust of summer, that dust. It was the dust of years, left, to accumulate. It was as if a plague had fallen over the city some time ago and the inhabitants had sealed themselves behind these high windows. You could see nothing through this dust. No sign of life. Not a pot of flowers on a window sill. Or a cat. Or the head of a person looking out. It was as if sealed windows had become a habit, a measure of safety. As if life had been withdrawn to cover actions in the far corners of hidden rooms.

It was the same in university buildings, too. At one time the University of Ludovice used to stand in a massive four-square campus on the top of a small conical hill in one of the city's central districts. From wherever you looked up in Ludovice you could see it. It was renowned throughout the country as one of the great centres of learning. But at some point in the city's recent history, a point about which people were always evasive, the campus had been turned into a vast military academy. The University was disbanded. Dispersed down into the streets. Broken up, faculty by faculty, and squeezed into disused buildings. You would come across them quite by chance, in the most ordinary streets. A length of wall would suddenly strike you as unnaturally long, unbroken either by apartment house entrances or small shop windows. And then, beside you, would appear a modest double doorway. Often the upper panels would be of glass, but so encrusted over that you could scarcely make out the gloomy hall that lay inside. Such buildings seemed deserted, cobwebbed over with silence. The only clue to their identity was chiselled into the blackened stone above the door in letters so small and plain that they seemed to be trying to efface themselves following some disgrace. Faculty of Law. Faculty of Electrical Engineering. Faculty of Applied Mathematics. All through my time in Ludovice I kept coming across new faculties in strange out of the way places. Our lectures, too, were spread about the town in mausoleums like these. It was inconvenient and irrational. Much time was wasted between classes scurrying from faculty to faculty. But such, we had observed, was the pattern of the grown-up world. It made us feel sophisticated to be part of the irrationality, to be put upon, to grumble. And to accept. For we could count ourselves now as part of that adult world. We had already taken our places, Sonia told us. We were to be the teachers of tomorrow. The guardians-elect of a new generation. Everything Sonia told us we believed, in those early days. Was it 'believed'? Or was it just an instinctive response to agree. A measure of self-protection. To murmur. To nod our heads. To smile at each other that half-smile of people in meetings as we shifted position, clustered together on the end beds of Dormitory 5.

Sonia, our group leader, had eyes so pale they were almost colourless. They were like mirrors in which we saw only reflections of our anxious faces. We never knew for sure when she watched us, or when her gaze had passed to someone else. It was unnerving. Unsettling. It made us all wary. So that though we might have wanted to confide our anxiety to one of the others, we did not dare. She bound us together. And then she fragmented us. Sonia came after the matron of the Residence for Student Teachers. After I had been ticked off on a clipboard and directed towards bed number 10. After I had been ordered to put my things in the small locker beside my pillow and my empty case under the bed. After the matron's stout shoes had squeaked in a sharp half-circle on the linoleum floor and marched off down the corridor with Magdalena. But not immediately. There was time for me to lift onto the bed the battered cardboard suitcase that my mother had borrowed unwillingly from a neighbour. In our village, daughters only left home to get married. Time for the interrupted conversations to begin again. Lower now, with longer silences; so I knew they were watching me. The rusted catches of the locks stuck, I remember. The wet cardboard tearing a little round their edges. As I lifted the lid, the familiar scent of my mother's house rose from the case. The smell of damp. And cheap household soap. There had been no trip to Opecno to buy linen. No crowding in of neighbours. No new clothes. As I reluctantly laid out on the bed my washed-out jerseys and home-made skirts, I knew that the watching eyes saw it all, too. The dark communal bedroom at home, the heavy ungainly furniture, the crocheted woollen bedspreads. And beyond the window the flat fields that fell away behind the patch of garden. It was then that Sonia came, with Mira on her left and Zdena on her right. Her best friends. Her – lieutenants. Not everyone was invited to join her group, I discovered. But no one refused. Do you refuse? When you have just arrived in a strange city for the first time? When you find yourself assigned to a dormitory among thirteen other girls who stare at you, without smiling, from cold blank faces? Thirteen strangers. We were all new girls. All alone. No, we none of us refused Sonia's offer of comradeship.

When the bell went for supper and we linked arms six abreast along the corridor, bumping into everyone who did not get out of our way, even the shyest of us felt our reserve, our newness, vanish. We became dizzy with speed and laughter. Drunk on the power of those strong arms. When, in the refectory, we took up the whole of one end of a long table and, at Sonia's urging, made so much noise that people turned to look at us, we felt dazed by our own daring. And when, back in the dormitory, she announced that rules should be drawn up for everyone in the group, we all agreed. We nodded and murmured. It was sensible, we said. It was needed. We knew about rules. They gave us security. They limited the perplexing vastness of infinity. We were the architects of the loss of our own freedom. All that I learned from you, Magdalena, gone, the minute you left my side. Perhaps I had learned nothing. Perhaps I had just gone along with you. As now, eagerly, I went along with my new friends. I had not looked for you. I had not thought of you all evening. If you had seen me – if you had called out as we went past in the corridor. If you had waved across the crowded refectory, it had been lost. Without even being consciously aware of what I did, I had moved allegiance. If you had questioned me, I probably would not even have hung my head. I might have shrugged my shoulders. I might have said: situations change. I might have even said something about survival. But probably not. By the end of that first evening we had, by inference, agreed to a loyalty that excluded everyone outside the group. To rules which dispelled all home sickness by the tightness of their security. We left no room for uncertainty. We regulated the length of our hems. The set of our stockings. The cut of our hair. Permissible subjects for conversation. Even the correct intonation to a giggle.

You could see several groups like ours. Perhaps potential leaders were placed in every dormitory. We scurried in little flocks from one lecture to another. We kept together, clustering shoulder to shoulder in refectories and at the obligatory meetings of the Socialist Union of Young People to which, of course, we all belonged. We wore little wool hats and carefully darned stockings. We giggled and shrieked thin high-pitched girlish shrieks. For all that Sonia told us how we were the ones whose task it would be to form the new generation of our glorious socialist society, how we would help these children push back frontiers, march at their head into the twenty-first century, we were curiously old-fashioned. Archaic. The image that we presented was of an earlier age, one of innocent girlhood that was outdated even then. But we were diligent students. It was our duty, Sonia said, and we agreed. The state paid, at vast expense, for our education and we owed it diligence. But it was not true learning. We did not explore new thought, unfamiliar ideas. Perhaps that was not expected of us. Not even wanted. We learned what was set before us without questioning it, as we had at school. We went out to our literature classes and read in our Dostoevsky: 'liberty is not for feeble souls'. But we did not stop to think what it might mean. We went home again to Dormitory 5 and laid down more rules for the group. We had got to the stage of reinforcing these by recounting at such meetings all the gossip we had heard about other girls in our year who did not behave as we did. Petty, insignificant trifles. But it became a mania with us. A disease. A gorging that we could not stop. We found ourselves condemning others for exuberance and life. For the very experimentation we should have tried. Which one of us secretly did not want to curl her hair? Or talk to boys?

At our Political Theory lecture, the lecturer grasped the sides of the reading stand and leant down towards us. 'Socialism,' he announced in a hushed tone, 'is a child's smile.' We stared at him for a second in the silence that followed, bewitched, though we had heard the slogan many times before. And then swiftly bent our heads to write it in our notebooks in careful, looping hands. We had moved on by then. Condemning those outside our group who did not behave as we did had become a stale pastime. So we turned on each other. It seemed – required. Sonia expected constant proof from us. Of our allegiance. Daily expressions of loyalty. It was a pressure that was felt, constantly, by all of us. A pressure that increased the more that it was fed. I don't remember how the denunciations started. Or with whom. It was like a ball, rolling. As soon as one fell, we were all doomed. As soon as one person caved in . . . One turning in fear on another to avert from themselves the intolerable weight, the unbearable pain of this pressure. That other turning, in surprise – in self-defence, swiftly on a third. And that third . . . There is no point blaming the weakness of individuals. It was a thing common enough in life. And what was our education for, but to train us for life.

The relief from fear for those who denounce is very short. It gets shorter with each denunciation. First a week. Then a day. Then an hour. A minute. And finally only the second it takes for your master to turn away his head with a sneer when you have finished speaking. You cannot buy relief from fear. You cannot buy security. No one can. Not even the innocent. Someone can always be found to make up something about you. For a threat. Or a promise. In the end Sonia got us all. One way or another. Whenever we saw one of our group hurrying after Sonia in the corridor. Or loitering behind everyone else in the communal bathroom at the head of the stairs, we knew what was taking place. The person who brushed her teeth with extra care till one by one we had all filed out. Who dried herself after a shower with unusual slowness and thoroughness. We knew whom she waited for. No one chose to linger in that bathroom. The concrete floor always seemed to be wet. The single light bulb kept the room in permanent half-light, like being already underwater. In the shadowed darkness of the furthest shower stalls the walls were stained where the taps leaked and the ridged floors were always slippery.

What was my crime? Sometimes my crime was vanity – I had been seen to spend too long brushing my hair – such a thing denoted un-seriousness. Or I was accused of irresponsibility. Someone had seen me in the reading room passing notes and giggling with one of my class-mates. Disturbing other people when we should have been studying. But mostly my crime was knowing Magdalena. When we met, she and I, as we did some-times by chance in the corridors of the residence, or waiting to be let in to lectures, it was like the uneasy meeting of estranged sisters who, hard as they might try, cannot pretend that a vast commonality does not exist between them. Though we saw no more of each other than that, the association rankled with Sonia. It was a taint I could never lose. It made me unreliable. It made me a target. However dismissively I might shrug my shoulders when the accusation came up again. However candidly I might reply – Vosporova? Of course I knew her, she lived in my village, I couldn't avoid knowing her! It did me no good. The accusation stuck with me even after Magdalena had left our faculty. Even her departure, in some obscure way, was held against me. None of us saw her go. We did not generally look in her direction, it was part of our ostracism of those we did not approve of. She just slipped away between one term and the next. Transferring, it was discovered, to the Faculty of Art History. Next to Philosophy, Art History was one of the most degenerate subjects our group could think of. Magdalena had already stopped going back to the village during vacations and so, for a time, I lost touch with her. I did not feel sad. I felt relief. When she is forgotten, I thought to myself, Sonia will forget my association with her and her suspicions will be dropped.

That was before the letter came. The letter from the Bursar's office. I knew as soon as I saw the grainy envelope, the indistinct typing of the address, that it was an official letter. But by then it was too late to hide it. Other people had seen it. By that stage, anyway, nothing could be hidden from the group. Letters were to be read aloud. Parcels shared. The letter summoned me to attend the Bursary. I was to bring all my papers. An irregularity had been found. Permission was given for a morning off classes. I showed the letter to my professors. And then, that evening, to Sonia. The news hushed the low buzz of gossip among the group. They all fell silent, shifting uneasily. I became aware of a prickling feeling in the air, as though they were drawing themselves back from me. From contact with the air that I touched, the oxygen that I had breathed. Only Sonia leant forward. In her pale eyes there was a sudden gleam, like winter sunlight striking icy water. 'Irregularity?' she said.

It is perhaps difficult to understand what fear can be conjured up by the enunciation of that single word: irregularity. For all the spikiness of its syllables it is a word made slippery with over-use, so that it slides out of our grasp. Into meaninglessness. The fear that it conjures up is the fear of the unknown, the unspoken. Irregularity can mean anything. From the greatest crime of treason to the mis-spelling of a word in a document. A necessary signature not procured, or placed on the wrong line. It is a cloud on the horizon, your horizon, which, once formed, never dissolves and drifts away. Sometimes the irregularity does not even need to exist. The word is just dropped, a small explosion of sound, into the calm of your life, to shatter it. Like the word 'fire' whispered into a sleeper's ear.

In the waiting room of the Bursary there were hard chairs all round the perimeter of the room. In one corner a paraffin stove sighed over its wavering circle of low blue flame. I sat and stared at the dust between the cracks of the floorboards, staring down as though I could see my future laid out in miniature among those fragments. There was no irregularity I could think of – nothing. Nothing misplaced. Nothing omitted. Nothing unusual in the history of my family or myself. It was two hours before they brought my documents back. It did not need two hours to look through those few papers. They are not so diligent, our officials. There was not that much to read. The two hours was not for their purpose. It was for mine. It was to allow sufficient time for the conviction of innocence to erode itself. Into confusion. Uncertainty. Alone in that room I began to think that perhaps there was something wrong. Some – error. Something I had said. Something I had done. Something, even, that I had . . . thought.

I can see myself quite clearly, but with a feeling of such distance that continents and centuries might separate myself now and myself then. It was early spring, along Beresova the chestnut trees were just beginning to break tips of green from their tight buds. But in that room it was always winter. Where your stomach turned to ice water. And the palms of your hands burned as if with frostbite. I looked even younger than my eighteen years, huddled on that chair, in those shabby clothes. What can a child like that do with such fear, but turn it upon itself. Now, standing looking out at the blandness of Oudenard Road, I cannot believe that anyone would fall for such cheap tricks. I cannot believe that we – believed them! All it would have taken was one person. To laugh at them behind their backs, these bureaucratic tyrants. One person. And then another. And then, hearing the laughter of the other two, a third. But it is difficult to start. To be that one person. It is difficult even to think such things might be possible. Here, from a distance, from within safety, you can see the illogicality we were forced to live under. Perhaps it was that very absence of logic that made everything so unstable. Perhaps it was that instability which generated an undercurrent of fear in a whole nation. Among those who are afraid, it is not wise to laugh out loud. Now I can laugh. And now it is too late.

When the Bursary official came back, finally, into the waiting room with my papers, I stood up stiffly. Jerked to my feet without being aware that I was going to rise. Like a puppet pulled by strings. She thrust my documents into hands that stretched themselves out obediently. That trembled so much that one of the documents fluttered to the floor.

'You may go now,' she announced, turning on her heel.

'What – what was it? Was it – an error?' I asked.

But she did not pause. She did not look back. Or speak. I heard the sound of her heavy shoes clatter out into the hall and climb stairs somewhere, out of sight. A door opened far above me. There was the clicking of typewriters, the ringing of a telephone bell, the sound of voices. Then the noise was shut off. And there was just silence. I bent down to pick up the sheet of paper that had fallen to the floor. I knew what my future was now. In my file, for ever, would be the mark of a suspected irregularity. And the date of its investigation. In time, to other eyes, it would take on a significance it had never had. I wished, as I shuffled together the documents and slid them into my folder, that I had anyone else's papers. *Anyone.*

'What was it?' demanded Sonia that evening.

'It was . . . nothing.' I shrugged my shoulders.

'Nothing!'

'They didn't say.'

'Ah . . .'

They drew breath then. All of them. Glancing at each other knowingly. Not saying meant no exoneration. Not saying left a question mark beside my name. A door ajar.

A door that could be pushed open at any time. 'Nothing' was a void, an indictment of its own. Voids were there to be filled. They were untidy spaces. They could, if they tried, think of something. Sonia looked round the group, from bed to bed. She knew no one would speak before she did. I waited helplessly, sitting on the end of a bed, a little apart from the others, my hands folded in my lap, staring at the beginnings of a ladder in one of my stockings.

I think I started going out with Grigor to get away from Sonia's tyranny. It is difficult to remember now exactly where I met him. It was unlikely to have been the Students' Union. Our group only went there once. It was not for timid creatures like ourselves. We were out of our depths, deterred even by the dark wooden staircase that led to the second-floor room. Inside it was full of noise and cigarette smoke. Ignored, we pushed through the crowd and squeezed ourselves round a small table in the corner. Talking was impossible, we could not hear what anyone said. Conversation became a game of Chinese Whispers, gossip relayed from ear to ear. Between the backs of people we glimpsed, now and then, girls from our own year raising glasses of what looked like wine to suspiciously red lips. We stayed only long enough to drink warm orangeade through straws from bottles and then, still ignored, we left. I might have met Grigor in the central reading room. It was, curiously enough, a favourite place for assignations. Even though you were not permitted to speak, there was always an opportunity at the main desk, when you were ordering books, to glance. To smile. For the stubby pencils on long strings attached to the desk with which you filled out the slips of paper to become tangled. In each other. To murmur: excuse me. To blush. To touch fingers, inadvertently, during the untangling process. Or I might have met him at one of the student societies we went to. The film club.

The Socialist Union of Young People – it ran all kinds of things.

In my mind the image of Grigor waxes as Sonia's seems to wane. He was the first boyfriend I had had. But he was not the sharp memory of passion. The sudden fibrillation deep within of pleasure remembered. The slow smile that curves unconsciously along the lips. Grigor just became. He became someone who telephoned me on the students' telephone, my name shouted out across the common room, heads turning to look in my direction. He became someone who sat in the visitors' waiting room in a round collar and a thin tie. While upstairs in the dormitory, I unrolled my best stockings and took out my woollen gloves, and saw in the spotted mirror the shadowed, envious glances of Sonia's group at the far end of the room. Clustered, as always, on the ends of beds. Sitting, waiting. For their turn to come.

Grigor was an engineering student. 'Civil' he used to say, with a mock bow. It was his joke. His only joke. He was quiet in company and we saw each other mainly in the company of others. So that I never really noticed, till later, how silent he was. He was formal as, in a way, we all were, then. But it was a curious formality. There was something – lopsided – about it. Like a dog dressed up in clothes in order to attend a feast. There was a sense of manners learned unwillingly and grudgingly performed. A kind of – lumbering in his walk. He had a widowed mother in Prague. And his life all mapped out, ready, before him. A single-minded ambition that was not thought, only, as with the rest of us. Conjecture. It was not even the exertion of will. It was a kind of bodily force almost beyond his control that flared up from deep within him and had to be snatched back again before it exploded. You could see it lurking in his sullen eyes, feel its presence behind the heavy bone-structure of his face. When he talked of engineering, he spoke of pulverising rocks, levelling hillsides, cutting through valleys, bull-dozing villages. He would bend close towards me, his breath suddenly heavy. His small black eyes bright and sharp, darting quickly over my face, searching like lecherous fingers for my complicity. And when he saw distaste in my expression instead of eagerness, he would draw sharply back, covering his awkwardness with a harsh laugh.

If these were faults, it did not occur to me to take them seriously. If ever I weighed them in the balance against the envy of my friends and the gradual silencing of Sonia's tongue, they were – insignificant. We all dreamed of love. In spite of Sonia. We dreamed of love without really knowing what to dream of. It was a phenomenon of hearsay, to us. A confusion of old wives' tales and private longings. It was . . . like imagining the taste of pineapple. None of us had ever seen a pineapple, let alone eaten one. Such exotic fruit were not to be found in our country any more. It was difficult enough to buy apples or pears that were worth eating. When the rumours of a consignment of oranges ran round the city, people would present themselves at dawn outside the designated shop only to be informed, when it opened, that such a rumour was false. We live in hope. Though we scarcely believe any more in its fulfilment. But there was a time when you could get pineapples. Some of the old people still remembered it. Pineapples, melons, any-thing you wanted. And falling in love, they remembered that too. Over in Vienna you could eat pineapple, we knew that. Scarcely thirty miles away, over the border, people were eating pineapple and being in love all the time. Couples no older than ourselves could go to res-taurants whose walls were lined with long, gilt-framed mirrors and sit at tables with starched linen tablecloths and eat fresh pineapple with silver spoons out of tall, delicately fluted glasses. It was as impossible for us to get permission to go to Vienna to eat pineapple as it was for us to fly. And perhaps it was as difficult for most of us to fall in love. Really in love. The kind where you gave your heart without restraint. How could we do that? Taught from our earliest years to be wary, to hide our private thoughts behind public conformity. How could we suddenly abandon ourselves to another person. How could we – give – ourselves. It was too much to expect. Distrust had made us all misers.

It is not difficult to understand, in our situation, how great the longing for security was. Perhaps romantic love, the love we heard about from our grandmothers and read of in old novels was . . . too uncertain. Too demanding. Such love overwhelmed the heart, enslaved the body. It filled our dreams. But it was for dreams only. There was in place, in current circulation, another kind of love. One that could have been devised especially for a generation such as ours. You saw it portrayed on posters. Filling the pages of contemporary novels. The subject of the latest films. It was the new way. It had a seriousness that was much admired. These lovers were level-headed. Pragmatic. Theirs was a public association rather than a private coupling. They remained within the regulatory eye of their peers as objects of admiration, symbols of a future to which we all aspired. Their energy was not frittered away on passion, but put to sober use. Following their pattern we could delude ourselves that we were lovers without having to expend any of the effort of love. It was safe. It held out to us the promise, the possibility of security. And the comfort of another. If you have never seen a real pineapple . . . If you have never tasted love . . . It is easy to see, now, how simple it was for us to be palmed off with an ersatz substitute. Especially if it came with official approval. Approval was something always promised to us: if you do this, if you do that. A carrot on a stick held always a little way ahead of us. But for it to be given. To feel approval encircle us. And remain there. The temptation was too strong. There was, I think, scarcely any hesitation. Or any thought. As I slid into the pre-cast mould of my new role even the shadow of the irregularity in my file receded. It had always been nothing, I told myself, and now its nothingness, seen against my new favour, was eclipsed.

We were easy to pick out among our fellow students. We had a look of couples long married. A staid, old-fashioned look. We did not display affection in public. Or even very much to each other. No holding of hands. Or kissing. Or getting lost in one another's gaze. We thought our manner bold and cool. In fact we were timid, uncertain. Shy. Beyond this initial role lay others, carefully tailored, deftly presented to us. They stretched out before us, a life-time of orderly progression. We could not refuse one without refusing them all. And if we did that, then, we knew, we could expect nothing from life. We did not refuse, Grigor and I. It was not just that we were not strong enough. It never occurred to us to do so. My dreams changed swiftly. Unconsciously. I no longer dreamt of passion. I dreamt of marriage. I no longer walked anywhere. I scurried. I did not think up my own opinions, I repeated those which accorded with my new position.

Back home, my mother repeated among her friends the gossip from my letters. My Eliska this, my Eliska that. She showed around the photograph of Grigor I had given her. 'An engineering student,' she would say proudly. They looked at the bland face and the tweed jacket handed down from his uncle and the pipe he had taken to smoking in his last year, and nodded with approval. In my final year, when I went back for the vacations, she seemed to have grown smaller than ever. Yet the thin lips that I remembered from my childhood were now no longer taut with disapproval, but with pride. The possibility of marriage began to be hinted at. 'An engineer!' murmured her friends to each other. But when exactly was this marriage proposed? Perhaps in our enlightened modernism, such romantic, backward-looking formalities had been abolished. All I remember is that between one unknown day and the next it became – understood. Though I understood nothing of what it was, or what it would become. We quarrelled about where the ceremony should take place. Our first real quarrel. We argued bitterly. Grigor wanted us to be married in Prague, not some nonentity of a village. But I held out. That village which I had long ago grown out of suddenly meant more to me than he did. I was of its stones, its hills and its forest. They had their respect due to them. Their ritual. If Grigor had insisted, it is possible I might have thrown him over. But he did not. I wrote to my mother. And then, after a week of hesitation, I wrote a note to Magdalena and dropped it into the Faculty of Art History. A single line. Without explanation. How could I explain all that had happened.

Magdalena's reply said simply: 'Come.' I had it folded and folded over again on itself in my pocket as I climbed up through the old streets of the town. My fingers tight around it. Afraid that if I lost it I would lose her again, too. Such a small object. Such a precious object. Following her directions, I climbed higher and higher. This was a part of the city to which we never came. We were directed to look to the future. Out to the suburbs, to the stacks of bricks and frames of scaffolding. To new houses, new schools, new generations. While the old heart of the city, abandoned, crumbled slowly in on itself. Beneath my feet the potholed tarmacadam gave way to smooth round cobblestones. In the early evening sunlight the buildings on either side took on a softness, a beauty, that masked their decay. I passed lanes arched with shadows. Balconied courtyards suspended in silence. Beside the cathedral steps, I came upon The Turk's Head. I drew my shawl tightly round my shoulders and pushed open the door. After the sunlight the long narrow room seemed like a tunnel, deep below ground. I must have paused. I remember tables. And candles stuck into the necks of bottles. Table after table appearing out of the gloom as my eyes became accustomed to the light. And a familiar figure with long dark hair rising from one of them. Coming forward to meet me. Laughing. Among all those empty tables. Arms spread wide. But I could not speak. I could not begin. It was as if I had come from a funeral. Slowly I advanced towards her, lifting the shawl from my shoulders, placing it over my head to hide my hair completely. It was a gesture known to everyone from our village. The gesture made by a young bride as she leaves her mother's house for the last time to go to her wedding. Magdalena's eyes glistened with tears. 'Liski!' She put her hands on my shoulders and shook them, gently. 'Liski?' The lines of the room wavered and her face blurred. I tried to tell her Grigor's name, but only a noise between a sob and a hiccough came out. Laughing and crying we hugged each other.

'Come,' Magdalena said, 'we must have wine to celebrate.'

'No' I croaked. 'Really, I don't want . . . we never . . .'

'No wine!' She lifted the lopsided shawl from my head and arranged it round my shoulders. She smoothed back my hair. 'No wine!' she murmured clucking her tongue and shaking her head at me.

We sat down at her table, one on either side.

'You will come?' I blurted out. 'You will be there? You will keep me company on the night before my wedding, like we always promised? You will watch with me for the moon to rise. And be the teller of the wedding-night stories?'

Magdalena smiled.

'The Golden Bird and The Silver Rose? The lovers who would defy all for their beloved? The length of white silk that can be fitted into a walnut shell? The riddles that cannot be solved without love? All those?'

'Yes, yes!' I nodded. 'All of them.'

She laced her fingers and pressed the tips down onto the lacquered surface of the table trying to make them all touch at once.

'Liski . . .' When she looked up at me the corners of her mouth were lifted in the familiar wry smile. 'Liski, I don't go back there any more. You know that. My mother . . . has become . . . difficult.'

'But for one night? One night that you would spend in our house. For – old times' sake?'

She hunched one shoulder and then the other.

'If I come, my mother has to be invited. If my mother is invited, it will only add to her torment. She must sit in your mother's kitchen, where she knows she is not welcome. She will deliberately refuse the food your mother will offer her and sip with distaste at the obligatory glass of wine. And before her eyes always will be the gold lettering of your new teacher's diploma and the scrubbed face of your new husband. Things she will never have in her own house.'

'Of course she will! She will have your degree diploma.'

'I left university a year ago,' she said softly. 'I was not allowed to continue.'

I stared at her.

'Why not?' I whispered.

'I did not pass the ideology exam.'

'But you can re-sit.'

'I did. But said the same things in the re-sit.'

'What – things?'

'What things do you think! What things can be said to such questions? Do you believe, do you really believe what you had to say to pass that exam year after year? Or would you have said anything not to have been thrown out?'

Behind Magdalena a plump, bald-headed man began to waddle between the tables towards us. The pointed ends of his greasy waistcoat bumped against his vast belly. His flat slippers slapped on the stone floor. I touched Magdalena's hand quickly to warn her of his approach.

'Wine, Ahmed,' she said, glancing round, and then, without waiting for him to pass out of earshot, she went on. 'So, all my mother has is all she thinks she has ever had from me – irresponsibility and trouble. What is intellectual honesty to her but something dangerous and alien. And what is love, to mothers, without a marriage certificate to prove it.'

'Love?' I murmured.

'I stay on in Ludovice only to be with my lover, Liski. There is no other reason to remain here. It is,' she waved her hand, 'an affair of complications. He is on the academic staff. I was his student. It is still a little difficult for us in Ludovice. But this summer he has been given permission to begin an archaeological dig on an interesting site in the north of the country. Near Vibrov. In Vibrov, Liski, we can at last have time together, uninterrupted. This time is very important to us.' She reached across the table to lay her hand over mine. 'You understand that, don't you, Liski?'

Ahmed's slippers flapped towards us again. In one hand he held a white jug and in the other two glass tumblers. Magdalena leaned back to smile up at him.

'This is the friend of my childhood,' she announced, 'who is about to be married!'

He glanced at me briefly from small, heavy-lidded eyes and dropped a glass from between his fingers in front of each of us. His face, lapped in folds of flesh, remained expressionless. He watched the dark wine flow out of the white jug that he held above my glass. And he clicked his tongue softly and shook his head.

'May Allah be there,' he murmured, 'to catch your soul.'

So they came, out to our village, Grigor and his

mother. For a day and a night. That was all it took. Out to the wind and the bare hills and the stink of manure. They came one day and left the next. Taking me with them.

To GET TO Gad's Hill you had to take the train to Rochester and walk.

'This is how Dickens used to do it,' I told Eliska. 'He used to walk up here from Chatham with his father when he was a little boy. But I should think it was all different then.'

The outskirts of Rochester were low and bleak. We walked across the great iron bridge and looked down into the wide, muddy river. It slipped slowly between the piers of the bridge in a fat, slovenly way. One or two freighters were held at anchor mid-stream lower down; at their bows the water parted thickly, with scarcely a ripple; and slid on. We walked up the hill through clusters of shops and past a garage forecourt full of second-hand chairs tied together with ropes. The windows of all the shops we passed were plastered so thickly with small posters offering bargains that we could not even see inside. In the stone gardens of bungalows straggling up the hill blackbirds sat on twigs, so still and unblinking they looked like toy birds. Lorries roared past us belching out diesel fumes, shaking and dancing their articulated loads. Eliska unknotted the scarf from her neck and held it over her nose and mouth.

'Dickens . . .' I shouted, but she couldn't hear.

At the first plateau of the long hill we did not even turn and look back at Rochester far below us; ahead we could already see trees rising up beyond the farthest houses. The road dropped a little, the bungalows ended, fields ran on beside us, then, round a bend in the road Gad's Hill rose up, a line of houses in silhouette along its crest.

'Which one is it?' yelled Eliska over the noise of the traffic.

'It's too far away to see.'

We trudged on. There was no Palladian mansion gazing gracefully out over the valley, there was only a genteel cluster of large suburban houses obscured by trees. Was this all it was? Was this how all pilgrimages ended, not in ecstasy but in disappointment; the earthly embodiment of one's goal never matching the grail of one's imagination? Were all such pilgrimages best conducted in the mind so that one begins and ends in illusion which is never tarnished by petrol fumes or signs saying 'no dumping'? Eliska lagged further and further behind me panting in the heat. We reached the first of the houses and she sank onto a low garden wall.

'I'll go on,' I said, 'and find it.'

There was the feeling of having come a very long way and ending up in the wrong place. Or of having carried in one's head a vision of something through much adversity only to discover that it was erroneous. 'And then I'll come back for you.'

'No, no.' Eliska levered herself up. 'I'll come with you now.'

I felt her sudden distrust of me as sharply as I felt a sense of my own betrayal. I had been tricked into belief by the desire to believe. In my head the words painted on the door of the Postmen's House floated off, separating as easily as though there had never been any association between them and I saw them all at once as random words that had by chance been placed together and on which I had tried to superimpose meaning. I wished I was alone. I stared fixedly at the toecaps of my shoes swinging mesmerically forward on the asphalt path, scuffed and dusty. I wished I had not brought Eliska. All this meant nothing to her, she just followed blindly; her heart was not . . .

'Jan, look, that's it! Gad's Hill Place! Palladian? Is this Palladian?'

'Small Palladian.' I smiled.

It was – smaller than I had expected. Quite modest. I walked along the fence staring in. Nevertheless this was it; there were the steps leading down from the front garden through a tunnel under the road to a shrubbery on the other side. I turned back to Eliska and hugged her.

'Clever girl.'

'It's what you expected?'

'Nothing's ever quite what you expect.'

'It's a school now, did you notice?'

'Yes, it's a shame we can't go in.'

We stood in one of the gateways of the circular gravel drive that ran in from the road at one gate, swept past the front of the house and out onto the road at another gate.

'You know it was his dream house when he was a little boy. He and his father probably stood just here gazing in at it, and his father would say: "Charles, if you are very diligent, one day you could live in this house." And Dickens always remembered how he used to quiver with longing and excitement at the impossibility of ever living in such a mansion.' I squeezed Eliska's shoulder. 'I suppose to a little boy it must have seemed enormous and grand in comparison with his own lodging. Anyway, in the end his dream came true.'

She smiled. 'And did he live happily ever after?'

A great clamour broke out from the house, sounds of doors banging and voices shouting.

'No,' I whispered.

But Eliska had already turned to see what the noise

was. The front doors had been thrown open and a jumble of little girls poured down the steps and swirled out onto the gravel. They wore tiny maroon blazers over short maroon and white check dresses showing a lot of brown summer knees, and swung straw boaters from elastic straps. They eddied and shrieked in a skittering of gravel then fell into silence at the appearance of two young women on the front steps. Hats were snapped into place, they were marshalled into pairs and, led by one of the young women, they marched solemnly out towards us.

'Do you think they know?' whispered Eliska.

'Where they are? Who . . . ?'

The woman at their head drew level with us, stared through us and passed on. Two by two the little girls hurried after her in a wavering crocodile, their boisterousness swiftly compressed behind small closed lips. Stray giggles burst out and were suppressed into silence as they passed us. They passed so quickly. I remember the gunfire sound of gravel beneath their shoes. And the sudden exploding realisation that not only did they know, but that they somehow were a clue to the words on the door of the Postmen's House. It was so irrational a conviction, so frantic and so real, and still they went on passing with the swiftness of flickering shadows. And none of them would speak to me and I could not speak to them. And then they were gone. Not all we know is learned. Perhaps the real part, the best part, is not learned at all.

I looked at the scuff-marks in the gravel and I looked at the house. Through those rooms Dickens had wandered. He would have gazed in a daydream out through those windows at those very trees. He would have climbed the central staircase of the house, sliding his hand inch by inch up the banister; he might even have paused on the stair that creaked at the turn of the flight and gazed down at the chequered flagstones of the hall, watching the sunlight move across the patterned floor, while thought clarified, faded and resolved itself again in his head. And now these little girls lived in his house. Their small feet trod in the same hollows of the flagstones, they climbed the same stairs. They could put their hands exactly where he had put his. They could look up from their history books and watch, in a daydream, robins fighting over territory on the far lawn, as robins had fought for generations, and gaze up into the trees . . . those very trees. And if, at the same time that their minds floated loose and receptive, it occurred to them that Mr Dickens might have seen the very same thing, what might they not . . . But this was Darwin's territory, too. These little bright-eyed creatures all potential survivors. He had a blueprint for survival, Darwin, he had an ideal man: quick, bright, perceptive, adaptable – sinuously adaptable – with a litheness of mind and body that could accommodate himself to any conditions. He might have lived all his life on maize meal porridge and then suddenly been transported by a quirk of nature or the warring of man to a place where strange fruits grew on strange trees and unfamiliar animals howled in an unknown darkness. But the survivor would not huddle against a rock bemoaning his fate. He would not poke among the curious bushes for maize and finding none slowly starve to death. He would take a look around, rub his hands, wink one of his bright eyes at no one in particular and say: 'Just the werry thing, the *werry* thing.' So, in a less extreme way, it was with these schoolchildren removed from their homes to Dickens's house. They could spend their time there in a blunted misery of longing for their life at home, they could discount entirely the stories they would be told of how the great Charles Dickens had lived in this very place and, looking about him at these very walls, had written some of his finest novels. Such information would go in one ear and out the other. But one child, or more than one child, would grasp an understanding of the treasure of this new place. It might, when it knew itself to be alone, climb up the stairs to where the top one squeaked and whisper to itself: just here. And place its hand carefully finger by finger on the banister and in a sudden rush of bravery seize it tight and feel . . . and feel . . . a great surge of excitement that Dickens too had touched . . . and now they did. It was the force of imagination that brought this surge to the heart as if an intangible power was being transferred. As if by touching that worn wood the starter motor of some generator of potential had been tripped into action, the sound of whose humming spread silently across the shadowed hall, through the door, across the garden, out . . . out . . . As long as they remembered, it would hum in their ears. You could see the ones who remembered, the ones who knew. The little girls who had come marching out of the gate had all been taught not to look at strangers, the strangers who would come to stare at the house. Some of them were too bound up in themselves to even notice our presence, others were too obedient or too shy to look up at us. And then there were the others. They knew why we were there and they could not resist looking at us, taking our stares almost as their due, gazing back at us with bright bold eyes and then removing their gaze before their teachers could catch them. We know why you are here, their eyes said, but Mr Dickens is dead. We are the queens here now; we are the possessors of the kingdom. Seeing them, these little schoolgirls, I had almost felt myself smiling. Dickens and Darwin . . . It was Darwin, of course, who gave a significance to the other two. Darwin who had spent his whole life trying to chart the progression and development of man's body. Were not the others evolutionists of a kind, too? Did there not have to be a progression of the soul? And the heart – for man to love his fellow human beings?

'They're gone.'

It was a whisper, almost a sigh, but it cut across the threads of thought that would not quite join, pulling them out of my grasp. Eliska appeared through a haze of other images, all for a split second seeming insubstantial.

'What?'

She waved her hand up the street. A dark smudge bobbed and swayed, and then disappeared round a corner. The street was empty, for a moment there was even a lull in the traffic, in the silence we could hear birds and the droning of a light plane.

'Well?' Eliska lifted her arms and let them drop against her sides. Her voice was scarcely more than a gasp.

'You miss your schoolchildren, Liski?'

I had broken one of our taboos. As if from a cracked jar despair came flooding out, Eliska's eyes filled with tears.

'What am I going to do!' she gasped. 'What am I going to do here, Jan? Am I just going to sit in that room while you walk about all day with letters!'

Letters, letters! She doesn't under*stand* about letters. She glances with the dismissive eye of the completely – ignorant! What does she know? Perceive. Comprehend. See . . . think . . . hear . . . taste . . . smell? Nothing! I swept up another sheaf of envelopes and took aim again at the sorting boxes. She thinks that this is nothing – this fellowship, this brotherhood. This ritual of early morning; the silence; the coughing; the shuffling now and then of feet, the click of an envelope falling to the floor. The intricacies of knowledge which we possess of which she knows – nothing! My hands were shaking so much that I dropped some of the letters, but I didn't notice. I splayed them out in my fingers to be sure one didn't stick to another. And what does she do while I do this – nothing? I scowled into the stack of pigeon holes, un-aware of the movement of my hands, so that the en-velopes seemed to fly by themselves like paper darts. She sits . . . in that room . . . and broods. She goes out.

Comes back. She paces. Round. And round. Caged . . . lost . . . remembering. Forget! My hands were empty again. I scooped up another pile of letters and turned them this way and that. I was aware that my lips moved. I pretended to myself that I was reading the addresses, but in my head I heard only rage. White rage like a swarm of electric bees buzzing. They drowned out coherent thought, singing like high wires, so high, so loud. I knew that everyone else in the room could hear them, so I looked neither to right nor left but stared stiffly ahead. The high room was cool with the clear water-light of early morning, but the palms of my hands were slippery with sweat.

She despised what she did not know. She condemned this place without ever having set foot in it. She had never seen . . . never felt . . . She had never asked to see it. Yet she behaved as if I denied her something. As if she was waiting to begin, waiting for some missing part of machinery without which she could not start. She was silent. That was her reproach. When I held her to me I felt as if I pressed against me joined parts of a body: breasts, stomach, limp arms. I kissed her and she moved her head from side to side slowly, heavily, as if tethered unwillingly. Sometimes her skin tasted of salt. I entered her and she fled away from me down a long tunnel.

'There you are, mate.'

Bundles of letters tied with string dropped onto the table beside me. Mr Finch's letters.

It was strange to cross the common on my own. I left the darkened row of shops that wound around the edge and passed the drinking fountain that dribbled in its solitude, an ever-flowing spring. About me were heavy-leafed trees. In the distance a mist was dissolving in the sunshine; thread by thread it shrivelled away revealing more trees, drifts of green like an endless landscape unfolding before me. I half-expected that out of that mist would come the tall chimneys of a great house. I waited for grey stone to appear and small tame cows to wander towards me across the parkland. But instead, in the mist, I saw Eliska's face, sleep-soft, the mouth opening . . . To speak? To kiss? I felt my body soften out of its rage, all my limbs suddenly heavy with the same sleep, the same warm nakedness. I dropped onto a bench unaware of what I did. It is forbidden to sit down during the exercise of our duties. It is not permitted, a rule of the House: resting is forbidden. But I felt only that I turned against the light resistance of sheets, smelt the heavy scent of sleep, sensed arms lifting and other arms . . . Oh Liski, Liski. There was a time, Liski, there was, when we clung together and could not bear to be parted. Now you seem no more than a wraith among the trees, a speck in the mist. You drift, you turn, without orientation. You see, you touch, you speak, but it is all unfamiliar. I have brought you to freedom but you are wary of it. I have spread out a feast for you, but you will not try its dishes. You sit at the table with tears in your eyes and hunger in your belly.

I bowed my head. Beneath my hands the wooden slats of the park bench came into focus as something apart from the heaviness of my thought. They were weathered grey, small patches of green algae grew along their edges and one slat was missing, torn out, probably, by vandals. It made sitting on the bench uncomfortable. Sitting! I leapt up, seizing my sack. Resting was forbidden. I did not glance over my shoulder to see whether anyone had seen me. Never admit to error. Never behave as if you are guilty. Where everyone is suspected, then everyone is under surveillance, and the slightest manifestation of guilt is seized upon as evidence of some crime as yet undiscovered. I marched along the path that led straight across the common and into my territory. I strode in long swift strides and looked neither to left nor right. I fixed my gaze on the first house of the street. And I listened all the time for the sound of footsteps hurrying behind me. But I knew I would not hear them. When they come for you, they come in silence, soft-soled.

It took only half a street to calm me. The measured dropping of envelopes onto empty hall floors, the security of sequence and sameness: 2,4,6,8. Dusty buddleias, paved areas, stained glass fanlights gradually soothed me. At the legitimate turn at the end of the street, I could at last look back. I crossed the road staring up it at emptiness, silence; testing the shadows for deception. Listening, but hearing only the sound of my own footsteps. At the opposite side of the road I paused. I swung down my sack and held it a few inches above the pavement, wanting to feel the weight of it, the sag of it biting into the muscles of my hand. I let it down and it subsided with a puff of canvas. This was reality, safe, anchored reality. But when it slipped it could slip quickly without warning, the same logic constructing menace where a second before it had directed order. I thought myself safe, but perhaps I, too, was still on the borderland, still within range. But it passed. It passed. As the morning passed and the houses passed and cats trotting out of garden gates passed, and then one by one the occupants of the houses, hurrying into long streams. The district woke and bustled and fell silent again. I got to the end of my own streets and I started on Mr Finch's. They were not vastly different, but their novelty gave me new energy.

It was in one of the mansion blocks that I first saw the card. I was untying a new bundle of letters, walking from the first floor to the second, and it fell out as I pulled the string free. I scarcely noticed it drop, the light on the stairs was so poor, I just caught a glimpse of the flickering colours of a picture turning over and over. I went back and picked it up. It was a picture of a castle rising above a sea of roofs on a hill. It was . . . There is only one castle and only one hill that look like that. The stairs, the house, the whole world seemed to drop away. The picture blurred for a moment, the image doubled and then realigned itself. The other letters dropped out of my hand, I could feel them flutter away. My breath came in gasps, like hoarse whispers, a muttering inside my head that got louder and louder. The words bursting out in spite of me, a gabbling of names. And with them, from the darkness of the shadowed hall, there seemed to be a looming of buildings. A lopsided moving past me of . . . streets. Such – familiar streets. The flash of a stretch of wide river and the swift narrowing in of small houses. Squares lurched past me and reeled into alleyways with carved lintels and grinning stone faces. And all the while the names, their names, were torn out of me like precious secrets that I was being forced to confess. What was this power, this force that had taken hold of me and held me entirely at its will? I stared down at my shaking hand. At the piece of card that trembled in its tense grasp. At the card that trembled my hand; that made my whole body tremble. The postcard was the power-house for this surge of longing, this betrayal of my new life. With a great effort of will, I moved one hand towards the other. I heard the card rip. I saw coloured fragments flutter to the floor.

'Oh, God,' I whispered. 'I have torn it up!'

I crashed down onto my knees, my sack tumbling against the apartment door in front of me with a thud. I scrabbled among the envelopes for the coloured pieces and as I did so the door in front of me opened. My fingers went numb, my nails scratched once or twice ineffectively at the carpet. I was discovered. I was going to be denounced. To the postmaster general of Great Britain. To Mr Harry and Sid and Jack and Mr Finch. 'I beg pardon,' I said in a hoarse whisper, still staring at the carpet. Something was wrong with the words, with the way they came out, but in my numbness I couldn't tell what it was. 'I am – very sorry.'

The feet standing in the doorway were bare and

brown. Their toes were painted bright pink. And then the toes were obscured by a voluminous blue skirt, brown hands reached out to pick up the letters.

'These all for us?'

I looked up slowly.

'Did you trip? I heard voices and a thud.' The girl grinned. 'I thought it might be a fight?'

'You open the door – to a fight?'

Her smile faded, she was looking at me now as if she suspected something wrong.

'You all right?'

She had picked up so many letters that soon she could not fail to notice the pieces of card.

'There is a card that has torn itself.'

'Ah! I see.' She bit her lip, but her eyes were full of laughter. So, it was a joke over here to denounce. It gave her pleasure to think that now she could pick up the telephone and . . . But she didn't get to her feet. She put down the envelopes in a pile beside her and began to piece together the card.

'It's . . . it's . . .' I clenched and unclenched my fists.

'Prague,' she said quietly. She looked up at me. 'Don't you like Prague?'

'I am from Prague,' I said, my voice as low as hers. 'But I will never go back.'

'Marietta!'

I stumbled to my feet seizing my sack. She jumped up too and laid her hand on my arm, small strong fingers.

'No, no.' She shook her head. 'There's nothing to worry about. That card, that's – not important. Doesn't matter. Marietta!' she called again. 'Marietta is a friend,' she whispered, 'she's in – sympathy. She's very interested in Russia and everything.'

'We are not Russia!'

'No, but you know . . . *Marietta!* . . . She's reading Eastern European literature – at evening classes: Kafka, Dostoevsky . . . Oh, Marietta there you are.'

I don't know whether it was the mention of Dosto-evsky or the sight of Marietta grave-faced, pushing dark hair back from her forehead that calmed me, brought me back to myself. I took in as if I was only seeing them for the first time the pile of letters in the open doorway, the fragments of card, the pattern of the carpet on which they lay, the girls close together, talking in low voices, smiling, pointing – at me, at the card. The girl called Marietta scooped up the pieces.

'Was this for us?'

'I didn't see.'

She turned them over in her fingers.

'No, it doesn't look . . . from these fragments, no, it's for 24. Miles up at the top; I don't even know them. Linda, do you know?'

'Who?' Linda peered over her shoulder as she laid the pieces out on a small table in the hall. 'No.' She began to giggle. 'Marietta, we can't give it to them like that. What are we going to say happened to it?'

I stepped into the hall.

'It is my fault.'

'I am going to burn it.' Marietta stood up very straight. 'We must destroy the evidence. Not in the fireplace, in – in a saucer. That is how you would do it, wouldn't you? We haven't got an ashtray because neither of us smokes.'

'Well, I'm going to leave you to your pyrotechnics.' Linda picked up a bag from the floor. 'I've got to be going.'

'I'll just get some matches.'

Alone in the hall I stared out at the internal well of the building, narrow, white-tiled like a cell.

When Marietta tried to open the box of matches at first it stuck. The movements of her hands were jerky, her fingers seemed to tremble slightly. But they were nice hands, English hands. The nails were neatly filed and polished with a clear polish leaving the little childish half-moons free.

'What do you do?' I asked.

The box flew open and some of the matches fell out. She piled them swiftly back in again.

'I'm a secretary.'

'You don't look like a secretary.'

'I'm not supposed to be one. My parents think I'm wasting my time. All that school and university and then – just typing. But I don't want to tie myself down to a job. I don't want to do the same thing every day in the same place. What if I wanted to go away all of a sudden; what if,' she glanced up at me, 'it was – necessary. I do temporary secretarial. A week here and a week there. I just work till I've got enough money and then I stop for a while.' She began striking matches, but the pieces of card were reluctant to take fire.

'It's the lousy paper we have over there.'

'Linda says you can't go back.'

'No.'

A fragment flared. Then another.

'I'm sorry.' She touched my wrist.

I think of that finger on my wrist. And when I do I see sometimes the serious arch of that slender neck, the shadow cast by the chin. The dark hair. And the dark eyes. I think of the light-boned skulls of birds, rain-whitened, sun-bleached, held between finger and thumb, so delicate that all it needs is for the other fingers to be brought round and squeezed and squeezed for first one bone to snap and then, swiftly, all the rest, breaking and falling in on themselves. Thumb and forefinger sliding along the chin, the skin so – soft. These thoughts come at the most unexpected moments, fragments slipping across consciousness with such clarity they could have been real. But I laugh them away.

Mr Finch was absent for a week. Jack went on sorting his mail and Perce and I went on splitting the delivery. I explained to Eliska that I would probably be coming home late every afternoon. I told her right away. That first night. In bed. I slid my arm round her and drew her in against the angle of my neck. I ran one hand up over the curve of her shoulder and down again rolling with it the strap of the slip she always wore to bed. The silky material slid down over her breast and was drawn back up again by my caressing hand. I gazed at the reflection of the curtain in the glass of the picture. The half-darkness had an orange glow to it from the sodium street light outside our bedroom window so that it was never entirely dark. It had to me the comfort of a nightlight but Eliska disliked it, she thought it was ugly. We went to bed early because I got up early, but she never complained, she seemed to welcome the return of sleep.

'What are your dreams, Liski?' I whispered into her hair.

She shook her head and shut her eyes.

'Everyone has dreams, Liski.'

In the shadow of the cavern made by our bodies and the bedclothes Eliska's breast appeared tantalisingly pale as it was uncovered and re-covered. All I had to do was move my hand over . . .

'There is a man at work whose dream is to walk from end to end of London over the roofs.'

She had drawn back her head and opened her eyes and was listening intently.

'Mr Finch.'

She pulled down the corners of her mouth – '"Mr *Fitch!*"'

'No, Finch. Once upon a time Mr Finch was a builder in a small Norfolk town . . .'

The pale half-moon of breast rose and fell, was obscured and then revealed. I unfolded the story for her but I didn't hear the words, I was alert only to the pulse of my own desire. My hand slid lower and lower down her shoulder with each stroke. At one point the words were lost entirely in a buzzing of blood. I pressed myself closer to her, all sequence of thought gone, flooded out. She shifted irritably as the words flagged and pressed her lips together in impatience.

'. . . and then, yesterday, Mr Finch slipped and twisted his ankle. He can't go in to work. Or up on the roofs. He is a man separated from his dreams – from his desires.'

Eliska looked away, but I caught her mouth as it turned and held it with my own while I pushed my tongue against her lips until they softened and separated.

Later, in the silence, in the warm, sodium-tinted darkness, listening to the steadying of our breathing, I remembered why I had begun to tell her Mr Finch's tale. I straightened the sheets solicitously over her shoulders and pulled up the counterpane, but hovering over it came the stale scent of sweat and with a quick movement of her hands she pushed it away.

'And so, Liski, we are having to share Mr Finch's work. Jack is doing all his sorting,' I could see in the shadow her lips tightening; anything to do with the House exasperated her these days, 'and Perce and I are doing the extra delivery. It's going to mean I'll be home late. For some time. Till Mr Finch's well.'

'Don't expect me to be here!' she hissed and flung herself over onto her other side.

Where would she go? I gazed idly at the back of her head. She had nowhere to go. I turned on my back and watched the slow ripple of the curtain against a faint night breeze. On the far side of the common an arched neck lay against a white pillow in a cloud of dark hair. Somewhere along the street a cat yowled and another answered it. From the main road came a sudden screech of car horns. I closed my eyes. In the great sorting offices of the metropolis there were neither pillows nor sleep. There was light and noise and an insistent thudding rising over all like the beat of a great heart. The sorters at work. In long trains running north to south and south to north they stood, splay-legged, swaying like sailors, envelopes in their hands. Flicker, flicker. Flicker, flicker. Never an error. Never.

S UNLIGHT MOVES ACROSS the floor. Nothing else in this room moves. The apples sit on the plate. The precise distance apart from each other that they were this morning. And yesterday morning. From the wall hangs a plywood bookcase supported by an ornamental metal frame. On it are five books upright and one lying on its side. If I close my eyes . . . until lines waver and colours merge, I can make them disappear. Make the pattern of the wallpaper smudge dizzyingly over them. Against the floor squat the sofa and the chairs, smug and over-stuffed. Loose, torn, stained and spreadeagled, waiting to take us in their greasy embrace. The only thing that moves in this room is the light. It is full of light. Un-hindered. When I went to live in Grigor's mother's flat in Prague, that was one thing I could not get used to. How dark it was. Here . . . it is all light. In the light motes of dust dance up and down, up and . . . It is because there are no curtains. Jan has taken them away. So he can look out of the window. Everyone looks out of the window in Oudenard Road. But not as Jan does. They look from behind their curtains. You see them twitch. You see a hazy shadow move. A corner drawn back. 'Jan likes to look out of the window,' I told Mrs Bartholomew when she came up to see what we had done with her 'nets'. 'He likes to have light in the room.' She stood jingling money in the pocket of her apron. Behind her snuffled her dog, sniffing eagerly in corners and under chairs. Running about. The dog whose brain, Jan says, has been turned by a cat. I kept my eye on it, that dog. It looked untrustworthy to me. As if it was going to piss on something. And out of the corner of my eye I caught sight of the old woman. Watching me with the same expression.

When I cannot bear any longer to sit in this room, and I go out into the street, I know that from behind every window I am watched. There is a flurry of movement so minute you might not notice it. If you did not know to look for it. I know. I know it is there. I turn out of Oudenard Road into Warrender Street. At the top of Warrender Street is the High Street. Here, among the disinterest of strangers, among all the foreign faces, I am hidden. I move with them. I push. I eddy. I stop. I am drawn into shops, their doors wide open to the street, full of light and noise. Music plays from loudspeakers. Children cry. A purposelessness descends on me. A melancholy that numbs my brain. On the shelves of these shops are all the things I might ever want to buy. I wander past row after row. But I cannot even lift my hand to pick something out. There is nothing of this that I want. What I long for is a small dimly-lit shop with half-empty shelves and 'Potraviny' – Grocer – painted in faded letters above the door. I want to ask for cheese and be told there is none. I want to ask for a cabbage and have only a dusty jar of pickled cabbage banged down on the counter in front of me. I want to ask for bread. And be told I am too late. Such a thing is perverse, I know it. I am perverse. I have been told it, often. So what, I shrug, I am a woman, what else do you expect? Funny what you miss when you can't have it any more. Funny the things that mean home to you. Not the good things, always, about the life you had, but the things that grated on you –

the difficulties. The things that ground in to you till they lay embedded beneath your skin so you could never forget them. Back home we longed for shops like these. We would even dream about them. We knew they existed. We knew from gossip and travellers' tales and unjammed western radio stations and Austrian television which could be received by many of our television sets in the border region of the country. And how we longed for them. For orgies of possession. Feasts of long-forgotten delicacies. Clothes that did not have to be home-made. And now . . . Now I can scarcely be bothered to eat at all. You don't eat enough to feed a sparrow, Liski, Jan says. So what. The food that is here turns my stomach these days.

Grigor's mother had a delicate stomach, that was what she said, that was why she insisted on doing all the cooking. But I soon saw the real reason. I saw it in the gloating expression with which she set down each plate of food before her son, the superciliousness with which she motioned me to clear it away, the pride with which she accepted his dutiful compliments. 'Be conciliatory,' my mother had warned me. And I had nodded. 'Remember it is her house.' My mother knew of what she spoke and I did not. My mother spoke with earnestness, a low seriousness that was intended to penetrate my day-dreaming. But I only smiled and nodded and thought of my marriage to come. Of my new life. That's how I was then. Sure of everything, knowing nothing. It was only when we returned to Grigor's mother's house after the wedding, when we climbed the stairs and she unlocked the door to her apartment, when we stood at last in her living room squeezed in between the furniture and I saw how small it was. When I saw how Grigor's mother's mouth drew itself down and Grigor turned his face away as, almost unwillingly, he led me into the bedroom, the only bedroom, that was now ours. And when, with slow fingers, I opened the door of the wardrobe that loomed above the foot of the bed and saw on half the rack his mother's clothes, and next to them Grigor's, smelt the faint scent of her sweat, the close, mothball smell of closets. Then I knew that there was in place another marriage of a kind. A wedding of habit. In the narrow bedroom and the small living room beyond it the furniture was packed so tightly nothing could ever be moved. Nothing changed. When I went back into the living room Grigor and his mother were already seated at the dining table that took up all the central floor space. She looked up sharply above half-empty teacups. 'I've *made* tea,' she said.

It was the pattern of many young marriages, I knew that. But knowing it was little consolation. There we were, Grigor's mother and I, the old mother and the young wife shut in together all day in two rooms, four floors up. She could scarcely bring herself to cede any of her territory to me. She did not want another hand to press her son's shirts or polish her furniture. 'You keep your room,' she said, brushing small crumbs from the dining table and straightening the crocheted doily that sat in the centre, 'and I'll look after this one.' I took a duster into my room every morning after breakfast and sat there, on the edge of the bed, staring out at the windows and chimney pots of the apartment house behind us. Wondering if tomorrow there would be a letter in the post offering me a teaching job. It will not be long, I told myself. It cannot be long. But I had already been warned how difficult it might be to get a teaching post in Prague. In the living room I could hear Grigor's mother bustling around, making much of her housework. 'My work' she would call it solemnly. Everything she clutched to her with the same possessiveness: my Grigor, my Martin – that had been her husband – my ironing, my dizzy spells. But I could not stay in my room all morning. Any more than we could sit in the over-stuffed living room face to face because there was nowhere else to sit. That was why, perhaps, unwillingly, she eventually delegated to me her shopping.

Down the ill-lit stairs, through the heavy swing door lay Prague. For these banal little excursions I would shut myself in the tiny bathroom, brush my hair first to one side and then another, arrange a cotton scarf round my neck, lick my eyebrows into a shape they did not normally possess. I ignored the sneer in Grigor's mother's eyes as they took in my careful preparations; the pursing-up of her moustached mouth. Out on the street the massive grey stone apartment buildings constructed at the turn of the century rose heavily on either side of me. I would pause for a moment on the doorstep, looking down the wide street that ran from our suburb in a series of undulating levels straight to the heart of the city. And always there would be that same catch of breath in my throat, the same sensation as if pent-up blood had suddenly been set free in my veins. Though you could not see the castle or the river from Grigor's mother's apartment, though in some way the city rose up to obscure them, I knew they were there. 'I am in Prague!' I would whisper to myself. And I would clutch my handbag tighter to my side and the tattered string shopping bag that Grigor's mother would have given me, and in a peculiar, mincing step that I only ever used on these occasions I would set off. I think I thought it was the step of the wife of an engineer. I think I thought it was the way all sophisticated women walked. I would lift my chin so high into the air that I rarely saw the pavement beneath my feet or even what went on around me. I was only aware of cars passing, the particular whistling noise their tyres made on the uneven surface of the road. Of people, now and then, walking by me. I imagined myself the object of admiring glances. Sometimes I almost believed I could hear at my ear the indrawing of breath as some exotic stranger prepared to introduce himself. And I would raise my head even higher and hurry on. I would be impervious to such advances, I told myself, while my fingers shook with excitement at the thought of them. Faithful. To Grigor. It was some weeks before I lowered my chin sufficiently to see how empty the pavement always was, how dirty and run-down the buildings that I passed.

It is absurd now to think that the objects of these exciting expeditions were two shops. They were little more than cabins let into the facade of a building, side by side. A grocer and a chemist. There was always a low pyramid of tins of potatoes set out on faded crepe paper in one window. And in the other, in front of a poster of mountains, a single bottle of cough mixture and a placard from the Department of Health on the benefit of eating oranges. The woman who ran the grocery shop was impatient. Sharp with a city quickness. I was no match for her. Hers was the kind of shop where the shelves were always half-empty and you knew the goods were all in the back. Frequently when I asked her for a packet of this or that she would begin shaking her head even before the words were completely out of my mouth; her hands all the while moving things on the counter with swift scraping sounds. It developed into a kind of battle. A siege, almost. In the end I was reduced to buying only those goods that I could see on her shelves. Things whose existence she could not deny. The chemist, on the other hand, was a mild-looking man in a patched and carefully mended white coat. Soft-faced. Quiet-voiced. If you asked him for something he had not got, he would start as if accused. 'No, no,' he would whisper. Then swiftly he would raise his head. 'Next week!' And you knew he was lying. I used to go there to get Grigor's mother's medicines for her.

'Next week,' I would repeat to her when I got back to the flat empty-handed.

'Next week! What does he think – that I will still be alive next week?'

'I could go down to the centre of town . . .' I would offer. But she would turn on me.

'And waste a tram fare! Who else will have it if there is shortage?' And then, quickly remembering herself: 'This is the price that it is necessary to pay. Shortage in some things one week, for plenty in the future.'

It was our habit to console ourselves thus with such slogans. To wrap ourselves in such lies. One was never enough to warm you, they were such thin things. And so we wound ourselves in more and more. But none of us had ever seen such futures come.

Grigor's mother took pills for rheumatism, powders for indigestion and a strange brown liquid for insomnia. She had given up her bed to us. Every morning she complained of her sleepless night and the stiffness in her joints. Every night I lay awake listening to the squeaking of the springs of the sofa as she turned. And turned again. In the ancient bed in the small stuffy bedroom Grigor and I lay still, stiff as boards, scarcely touching one another. The slightest movement made the mattress groan. At any heavier movement the wooden frame of the bed creaked. We did not consummate our marriage for three weeks. Three weeks of lying awake, wondering. The scent of his pyjamaed body sharp and close in my nostrils. Near. Suddenly, frighteningly near. And always the tossing and turning in the next room. The dry cough breaking the silence that we had thought signified sleep. Until we fell asleep ourselves. There had been no honeymoon. There was no money for such a thing, no time. Grigor had already started work in the drawing offices of the state engineering company. It had not even been discussed as a possibility. I was proud of our seriousness; proud of Grigor's job. It was evidence, I thought, that we were a modern couple, part of the new society to which we were all directed to aspire. Besides, I said to myself, living in Prague, the wife of an engineer, will be better than any honeymoon. I did not think of the difficulties. Or how the relentlessness of small things repeated day after day can become unbearable. How constraint binds tighter and tighter. And how, never speaking of these things, finally we fall silent. And by this silence – accept.

When, finally, we made love it was tense and fleeting, like the mating of dogs. Wordless, without pre-arrangement or fondness. We coupled with the minimum of movement and separated quickly afterwards as though nothing had happened. It became the pattern of our love-making. Part of the larger pattern of our life in which, for some reason, Grigor drew himself away from me. Instead of coming closer. He seemed, more and more, to hold himself apart. Alone. In that space reserved in some households for men – for husbands and sons. Such aloneness was a kind of power. The power to push away. I was his now to keep at arm's length or to hold close. And charting my confusion, he could calculate the strength of his power over me. I did not see it then so clearly, it did not come to me till long afterwards. At the time I felt baffled, only. Lost, suddenly. Uncertain. I could not speak of it to anyone. There was only Grigor's mother and she would not have listened to me. She encouraged him. I was unprepared for the intensity with which she tended him. It was the severe devotion of black-shawled women before icons, and against it I was powerless to compete. Beside her I was little more than a stumbling acolyte.

Grigor was tired when he came home in the afternoons. He was tired when he came back from work at midday on Saturdays. And on Sundays all he wanted to do was sleep and drink beer and read the paper. He did not want to show me Prague.

'I've seen it all before,' he would say. 'It's nothing to me, I grew up here.'

'You don't want to go down there,' his mother would add, shaking her head vigorously. 'All those crowds.'

And when my expression remained stubbornly forlorn, she might add: 'There was that museum, Grigor, we went to once. That Palace of the People's Achievement, that was nice. That's very instructive. If she hasn't seen that, you could take her there.'

Grigor would smile at me, the smile of the cunning, his lips drawn back over his teeth, the small muscle at the corner of the mouth twitching. 'Well,' he said, 'if it rains . . .'

All that August it never rained. The days dragged on in a kind of lifeless heat, a kind of airlessness in which the dust on the streets of our district seemed drawn up into the empty space where the air had been, to hang there. When I stared down our street to where the heart of the city should have been, it seemed blotted out entirely by a haze that buzzed and shimmered. Pent-up in the tiny apartment, I waited and waited. But still no letter came from the Department of Education offering me a job. In the evenings I would lay my arms along the window sill and press my forehead against the cool glass and look out into the light night. At the corner of our block ran a wider cross street. Here trams passed. Even from behind the tightly shut windows of Grigor's mother's apartment you could hear the running of their wheels along the rails. Sense their swaying motion in the waves of sound that came up to us. Hear, faintly, the clumsy jangling of their bell. Into the silence they approached. And then receded. Like the wind on a winter's night. Wind gusting through canyons and dropping away suddenly into stillness again. Behind me, in the room, Grigor slumped in the only armchair and across the hearthrug his mother would swiftly draw her own high-backed chair close to him. As he loosened his tie and undid the top button of his shirt she would lean forward eagerly. It was the same every night. I would turn my face so that my cheek lay along the glass, and watch them. 'Tell me your day, Grigor,' she would urge.

Our conversations were rarely about anything but Grigor's office. At first I found them difficult to follow. They sounded in my ears like the intonation of dirges. Catechisms of dreariness. They consisted of names I did not know, imagined slights I could not, in my innocence, believe anyone could take seriously. But I learned quickly. I learned the appropriate responses: when to genuflect and when to bow my head. I learned to talk of suspicious whispers in corners. Looks exchanged between colleagues. The deliberate spoiling of his letters by malicious secretaries. Dust left on purpose on his desk by disrespectful cleaners. The continual disappearance of small items of office property – paper clips, pencils – whose loss we feared might be blamed on him if anyone wanted to make things look bad for him. But that was not all. It continued, this battle that it was necessary to wage, even outside in the street. There were the hostile crowds at the tram stop who pushed him. And the umbrella whose mechanism failed him, constantly. I learned to talk of all this. And as we discussed these things night after night, I saw that I had been mistaken when I thought of my husband going off every day to his office, to a room in which he worked. I had thought just of this office – and the work – and the man, bent over it. In fact, it seemed to me as I listened, that the office was instead a vast construct, a towering edifice of girders and scaffolding. Floor after floor stretched up into the sky. On the upper levels were beings so elevated they were no longer mortal, no longer flesh and blood. Eyes merely, that saw all without being seen. Voices only, that gave commands. Gods never glimpsed, of such potency that they could not be named, at least not by Grigor and his mother. And then there were the lower regions to which Grigor and his mother had a constant fear that he might be demoted. It was to the upper levels that Grigor had to progress. Not, it appeared, by the simple method of climbing stairs. There were none. But by being granted access to the hidden ladder concealed within the tangled mass of this structure. There was such a ladder in each one of our enterprises, large or small. We all knew that. They led straight, these ladders. But only those who were chosen might set foot on them. It was for such election that Grigor and his mother waited, fervently, with an anguish barely concealed. And so, it seemed, did everyone else on Grigor's floor. They sat poised at their desks, ears straining for the slightest whisper, eyes glancing nervously around them, watching each other, while their hands passed over the papers on their desks with a sort of feverish abstraction as though they were not the real reason they sat there, but were merely objects with which they toyed as a distraction to alleviate the unbearable business of waiting.

We sat, too. Each evening. In the living room of Grigor's mother's apartment. Each evening, going over the same ground. Shuffling, delving, pulling quickly from the storehouses in our heads the same pieces of information. Laying them out swiftly in front of each other. Pushing at them, squeezing them. Placing them in different sequences. Seizing on any new scrap thrown up by the day. If we could not tell exactly how much was needed to place Grigor's foot on the first rung of that magical ladder, we knew that the slightest mark against him could debar him from it for ever. It was of this that we thought as we finally lapsed into silence. It was this – unimaginable – possibility that was broached hesitantly in low, anxious voices and then dropped quickly, as though even to speak of it would bring bad luck. But in the silence I knew, increasingly, they thought of me. At first it remained unspoken in their minds as a potential source of worry. Then as the weeks went by and still no teaching post was offered to me, they began to perceive it as a real danger. I could not blame them. It was illegal not to work if you were fit and without children. You had to take any job, anything, rather than remain unemployed beyond a certain length of time. I saw their anxiety. But I knew their fear was not for me, it was for Grigor. And his prospects. Grigor had thought that he was marrying a teacher. A teacher had status. A street cleaner did not.

At the end of such evenings Grigor would shift in his chair irritably. He would stretch his legs out straight in front of him and fold his arms behind his head. I knew what was coming. I would look away into the shadowed folds of the curtain. Or down into the coloured squares of the tablecloth.

'What do you think I'm going to say at work, Eliska, when they ask? And they're going to start asking soon. Personnel. You're down in their file on me as a teacher – without a school. They've been patient. So have I. But we all know when term starts again and then they're going to want to know where you teach. They're going to call me in – think how bad that will look! Or worse, they're going to come down to my floor. In public. Sit on my desk asking questions that everyone else can hear. What do I tell them then, Eliska?'

All through such recitations Grigor's mother would poke her head forward in my direction and nod it anxiously, the sharp chin jerking up and down to emphasise Grigor's words. I had stopped trying to answer him. What was there to say? What else was there for me to do? The custom was that you were allotted jobs by the Ministry of Education. Because I was married and my husband had been posted to Prague, I had requested employment there. Because of my husband necessitating me to be in Prague, I should have a prior claim. But everyone wanted to live in Prague. As the weeks went by with nothing, I wrote to remind the Ministry of my case. Sometimes I had a grey printed slip back thanking me for my letter. Sometimes I did not. I wrote off for jobs advertised in the papers. Strictly speaking, it was not necessary to do this, such advertisements were placed in the papers by the Ministry itself. But it got me out of the flat. It was possible to spend a whole morning walking the couple of miles down to the branch library, waiting among the old men in the public reading section, to look at the daily paper.

One evening it was decided I should wait in silence no longer. Perhaps my letters were not getting through to the right department. Perhaps they did not understand the urgency of the matter. It was decided that Grigor's mother should approach her neighbour, who was known to have a telephone, to ask if I might use it to telephone the Ministry. Such a thing was not chanced on lightly. It was a momentous decision. An action almost of despair, an admission, almost, of defeat. In blocks like ours, people were careful not to speak to each other. We kept ourselves to ourselves believing it was safer that way. I was instructed by Grigor's mother, when I went out, to open the door of the apartment quietly. To pause on the threshold listening for sounds of movement higher up on the stairs or lower down. If I heard a noise, I was to come back in and shut the door. If I heard nothing, I could venture out. Grigor's mother had never before sought a favour of her neighbour. To ask to use the telephone meant some explanation of the emergency requiring such unprecedented action had to be given. Family secrets opened up. The admission made that I had no job. Such knowledge, Grigor and his mother feared, would place us in her power from that moment on.

The next afternoon Grigor's mother took me across the landing to her neighbour. In one hand I clutched my sheaf of papers. In the other, two coins were pressed deep into the flesh of my palm. 'This is my son's wife,' said Grigor's mother. The woman nodded, gravely, and stood back from her door sufficiently for us to enter. Behind her a heavy curtain hid the rest of her living room from sight, making a dim lobby next to the door. She drew the curtain aside a fraction, passing beyond it. And

Grigor's mother followed her, leaving me alone. On a low table beside the front door was the telephone. There in the gloom I knelt, feeling their eyes watch me from the gap in the curtain. Hearing the listening in the slight wheeze of their breath. The telephone rang for a long time in the Department of Employment of Teachers. This is a formality observed by both parties in such telephone conversations. We do not put the phone down. And they do not pick it up. Sometimes, however long we hold on, they never pick it up. But I was lucky. That time. I was referred and referred again from section to section. In between each there were also long waits. Sometimes the sound of ringing would cease. There would come on the line a crackling and buzzing. And then silence. Into this silence it was important not to speak the word 'Hello?' too many times. It was demeaning. Worse than that it could cause irritation. To the listener. For we were never sure that there was not a listener in those long silences. They were a test of faith, a swearing of belief. Without faith they could not be endured. And someone had to listen to make sure we were still there. Besides, often out of these silences, at the moment when we were about to give up all hope, would come a clear cold voice, usually female, speaking our name. Our correct name, just like that out of the blue, and sometimes our address, phrased as a question. The necessary reply to this was 'Yes'. But sometimes it was not possible to make a clear reply. We had been waiting, mute, for so long. Unsuspected amounts of phlegm often built up in our throats preventing us from producing more than a croak. This was the dangerous moment. If a clear reply was not given immediately the phone would be slammed down. I was lucky that day, my throat did not fail me, the line at no point went dead. 'We are looking into your situation,' I was told finally. 'We will be in touch when we find something suitable. There is no necessity for you to ring again.' In the half-darkness I replaced the receiver and tried to uncurl my stiffened legs. In my ears a buzzing still rang. My fingers were numb with gripping the receiver. Beyond the curtain the two women shuffled impatiently, waiting with their questions. I pulled the damp coins away from the skin of my palm and laid them beside the phone.

It was that night, as I lay awake, that my memory of the irregularity returned. It just – slid – into my mind with such ease. I wondered that I had not thought of it before. It was clear. The Bursar's office at Ludovice must have informed the Ministry of Education in Prague of my – offence. And that was why I had not been allocated a post. But what offence? What was it I had done? Or said? Or not said? Or thought . . . There are always small sins that one can find. The inference of guilt takes hold, quickly. In the dark imagined spectres grow. From nothing. Nothing. And yet I must be guilty. An irregularity had been found. They had said so. And I believed them. With faith like ours belief is almost automatic. Unswerving. The errors, the guilt, are all ours. It must be so. How else could it be? I turned in the darkness to look at the bulky shape of Grigor sleeping beside me. There had been, at first, no need to tell him. It was not something to admit. Not . . . Besides, I had thought it had all been cleared up after my visit to the Bursar's office. 'You may go,' she had said, something like that. But I should have known, such things are never cleared up. I stared at the hump of Grigor's shoulder beneath the bedclothes, the dark line that fell away, descending like hills, to the end of the bed. It had the hardness of rock. The immovability of earth. Hills rose and fell away again. In summer they are covered with grass and thistles, in winter they are covered with snow. They would not level themselves for the wish of those who lived in their shadow, or grow corn or fruit trees on their flanks. Such things did not happen, I knew that. It was not possible to put my hand out to Grigor, to wake him in the darkness. It was not possible to tell him I was afraid. It was not possible to tell him there was something, some error that had occurred, some small mistake – some *thing* that was not really there at all but which yet appeared to be hanging over me. Some question mark that perhaps . . . He did not believe in nothingness. He dealt in certainties. If I spoke this – fear – it would then become a certainty. And he would not have held me close, laughed it away. He would not have stroked my hair and said: 'But Liski, you know how they like to tease, how they like to hold these little terrors over us, flimsy as ghosts. It happens to everyone. Every-one.' He would not have been capable of such an ex-pression of tenderness. Instead he would have seized on the irregularity. Held it up. As though between finger and thumb. With an indrawing of breath – both their breaths, his and mother's. I could imagine the second of silence, the stunned outrage of those who believed themselves betrayed. They had calculated, between them, all manner of possible betrayals that could befall Grigor and they had thought up plans to evade them all. Except this one. The danger they had thought I posed was one of error: a bureaucratic mistake, merely. They had not thought that I . . . It had not crossed their minds. They would turn to me where I sat. I could see their heads turning slowly on their necks; slow, unnaturally slow as in a nightmare, the contorted mouths still silent, their eyes bulging with disbelief, the thin membrane containing the watery globes stretched almost to bursting point. And then the un-leashing of words pounding like hailstones, the splinter-flashes of anger. I would be from then on the enemy within. I would be trapped within the daily circle of their suspicion and distrust. Imprisoned. Within the narrow bedroom and the dark, crowded living room and the cubby-hole of the kitchen. No, it was not possible to speak. But because it had entered my head I became afraid that it would not take them long to see it there. Or guess. Our logic never led to clarity of thought, only to the clouding of suspicion.

I ran, the next morning, almost all the way down to the branch library. I was so out of breath I could scarcely speak.

'Is there no other paper, no other periodical in which jobs for teachers are advertised?'

The librarian looked at me with a mixture of curiosity and disinterest. She pursed her lips and shrugged her shoulders. She had perceived my distress and in the manner of officials prepared herself to give only the minimum of help.

'There is the weekly teachers' journal. But you will have to go to the Central Library for that. We have nothing like that here.'

My desperation made me bold.

'It is necessary for me to go into the Central Library,' I announced that night. 'There is a journal there especially for teachers. In it every single job is advertised. The newspaper cannot print everything, there is not space. It has to select.' I looked from one to the other. 'To show that I am sufficiently concerned to consult this journal could impress the authorities.'

They did not try to stop me. Their desperation was as acute as mine, but for different reasons. The next morning I set off early. Grigor's mother watched my preparations without speaking. I flourished my writing pad and envelopes with deliberate ostentation. Her eyes followed my every movement to report them to her son.

The tram did not turn right at our street or the next to run downhill towards the centre of Prague. A thing that at first surprised me. Until I came to learn that the heart of Prague could only be reached by circumvention. By stealth. By a slow wriggling through the undergrowth of streets that wound lower and lower towards the river. By subterfuge. By pretending to go in one direction and then doubling back quickly along a parallel street. By appearing to abandon your journey and climb back up one of the foothills, only to dart into a side street and slide quickly down another slope unperceived. In such a way you arrived always at your destination without being quite sure how you had done it. But there you were, standing a little dazed at, say, the tram stop on the embankment of the river between Charles Bridge and the National Theatre, while the tram rattled imperviously away. That was my stop, the embankment. Behind me, I knew, lay a proliferation of narrow, twisting streets leading to the vast cobbled space of the Old Town Square. In front of me across the river were the pinnacles of the gateway of the Charles Bridge and above them crowded the roofs of the Little Quarter. And hanging over all, high on its rock, the castle, its granite face turned to its city, the spire of its cathedral rising above its shoulder.

The library was in a side street scarcely five minutes' walk from the embankment. Down Anenska, along Retezova and left at Husova. Up three marble steps and in through the revolving doors. It was hushed inside, high ceilinged, warm with the close, almost vanilla-like scent of row after row of books. High up on the wall ran a tracery of leaves and flowers painted in gold. The librarian was kind, I remember.

'Ah yes,' she said in that low clear voice that librarians have been trained to, that voice that disturbs no one and is audible only to its listener.

'The teachers' journal. We keep it behind the desk because it is of specialisation. You are a teacher?' I explained. 'You have applied through central channels? Of course you have.' She smiled at me. 'You know all that. The jobs are at the back. Good luck.'

I copied down the details of every job for junior teachers, seated at one of the long tables. Then I wrote out the application letters, each one identical, absurd. At midday I went out. Into Prague. For what felt like the first time. In one of the side streets near the library I bought a roll. I wandered on through narrow curving lanes looking for the way back to the river. In this part of the old city nearly all the walls of the houses had been decorated. Some were ornamented with stone carving, some showed traces of having been painted – half-obliterated patterns of black and white and red ochre. Faded writing in a large, square, antique script: texts from the Bible, exhortations to goodness. Each house was different. In height, in shape, in the number of perching chimney pots. Some leaned forward and others drew back shyly almost, into the shadow of their neighbours. I found myself, as if by chance, out on the embankment at last, not noticing how I had got there. Leaning against the low wall I ate my poppyseed roll. Around me sparrows hopped anxiously at arm's length on the parapet, marking where every crumb and every seed fell, waiting impatiently for me to be gone. Across the river the castle curved around its rock like all the photographs of it that I had ever seen. I threw the end of my roll to the sparrows and set off. All afternoon I wandered the old streets that wound up to the castle. Drawn on by – by a disbelief, almost, in the substantiality of this new world. This small close world of cobblestones and hidden corners. Of scrolled archways and glimpsed courtyards. Of the hill climbing steeply ahead of me. And the castle, the object of my journey, which instead of looming larger above the rooftops to my right had unnervingly vanished from sight even though every step should have been taking me closer to it. I put my hand out frequently to touch the fronts of the houses as I passed, to stop and catch my breath. And always I was – surprised – at their solidity. The warmth of their stone. I paused at the head of flights of stairs cut into the rock of the hillside as inviting as the running of water. I stared down into the shadows where the steps disappeared between tiers of tall houses clinging to the contour of the hill. Old-fashioned street lamps with glass panels and delicately-wrought iron brackets were fixed to the walls of these houses, and stood at the head of the steps. They were for lighting people in wigs and cloaks; beyond their pools of light would be the whisper of intrigue, stifled laughter in darkness. To run down those steps would be to enter such a world. My foot hesitated on the top step. I do not have time, I said to myself and trudged on.

It was already mid-afternoon by the time the road emerged onto the wide sweep before the castle. At its gates I hesitated. There were sentries, with rifles. Beyond the high iron railings men in the familiar grey-green uniform crossed and re-crossed the courtyard going in and out of doorways. What was it that I thought? That they would see my guilt? Trained to look for weakness in those of us who offend and therefore are guilty, did I think that their eyes would be even sharper than those of Grigor and his mother? I turned away to sit in the shadow of the castle rock on a low stone wall beside the pavement, looking out over the wide sweep of the city. On a clear day you can see right to the outskirts, to where the bare concrete blocks rise in clusters. That day the endless roofs and buildings lost themselves in a haze that blotted out the horizon, making the city seem endless. Across there was our district, where identical grey apartment houses marched up identical wide deserted streets. In one of them I was consigned to live. The bafflement, the intangible sense of being somehow lost, spread out in a kind of inky blackness inside me and then, just as quickly, contracted again to nothing. I had not known how marriage would be. So how could I tell whether my marriage was according to custom or not? We dreamed of love, despite our pragmatism. And perhaps this belonging, this appropriation of one person by another was love. But then, many things are done under the pretence of love – which are not love. Perhaps love was just for dreams. Something in constant short-age like cars and pineapples. There were other things, more important things Grigor and I worked for. Perhaps when I had a job . . . Perhaps when we had a flat . . . Beyond our prescribed institutions there is nothing. A frightening emptiness. A state of being cast out. Back in our village I knew my mother bragged of me. I thought of the narrow white roads, of the gloating smiles of Katia and Marie. It was not possible to admit anything. You cannot go back, so they say; you must go on.

That evening I told them it was necessary for me to return to the library the next day.

'They could not let me have the journal for more than ten minutes,' I lied. 'There were too many other people waiting to see it.'

That night as I lay beside Grigor in the space between wakefulness and sleep, there floated in my head swags of stone flowers beneath window sills. Across the incised lintel of a doorway putti giggled at each other, their chubby arms blackened and pitted with time, their laughter loud in the silence of the night. At us? Who think such embellishment unnecessary to our lives, dangerous even. Such anachronistic gestures are not permitted to our architects. And yet, in the decadence of our souls, we yearn for such small comfort.

I began going to the library three, sometimes four, times a week. Grigor and his mother did not try to prevent me. They might have begrudged the tram fare, the crown for the poppyseed roll, but they said nothing. It was difficult to tell which displeased Grigor's mother less: going out or staying in, under her feet. When term started again in the schools all over the country there was a taut silence in the apartment like the silences that used to hang over our valley before storms, when even the birds did not sing for fear of bringing the rage down out of the sky. I crept about feeling my guilt wrapped round my shoulders like a shawl that had stuck to my skin and trailed, whispering, behind me across the floor. It seemed to me as the days went by, that they turned, Grigor and his mother, more and more frequently to each other, repeating each time, as though it was newly acquired information, that they could not understand how it was that I was not offered a post. How there was talk, that everyone knew, that classes were overcrowded and more teachers constantly needed. And then they would turn to stare at me as though I was some strange phenomenon. And I would look away. Shrugging my shoulders and hunching my body over to hide the truth which day by day seemed to me to become more obvious. One day, they would swivel in their chairs and they would look and they would see. I found myself more and more uneasy in the apartment. As if I had begun to develop some phobia of being indoors that made my heart race and a curious shaking deep inside my arms and legs start to manifest itself. I trembled inwardly and found it increasingly difficult to sit in one place. But when I boarded the tram in the cross street below our block I felt my heart lift again. With the shaking and jolting of the carriage my oppression seemed to drop away little by little, like an insubstantial thing, clinging to the surface only, which I could have picked off myself. If only I had known how.

September passed into October. I went on writing letters of application. Letters that seemed increasingly pointless. Slowly the replies came back to me: 'Your application has been unsuccessful.' 'Your application has been . . .' Over and over. They are not designed to give us hope, our official communications. The curious grey-brown spongy paper. The almost illegible typing that has usually been cyclostyled so often that all that remains is a blurred shadow. To these ghosts of words, these scraps of rag paper we are expected to attach all our aspirations.

And so we do. Because we have nothing else. These offices of state are our highest court of appeal. They are, we have been told from birth, our guardians. There is nothing more. Nowhere else to go.

In early October the days were blue and clear.

Outside the pubs, signs advertising the new wine appeared. In the Jewish cemetery at the corner of the twisted street close to the river the leaves began to fall. I kicked them up in drifts and let them flutter back burying my shoes. I wandered between the narrow rows of graves, packed tight, strewn higgledy-piggledy. I stared at the lopsided headstones and the broken monuments.

'You are looking for someone?' The young man who appeared at my elbow had dark insistent eyes. I shook my head. 'I can help you? There is something . . . ?'

I began to run awkwardly down the gravel path towards the street, the silly way that young girls run in high heels. From the safety of the pavement I glanced back between the railings as I hurried away up the empty street. He was still standing there, quite motionless, among the graves.

In the library the librarian reached behind her for the journal as she saw me enter.

'Still nothing?' she asked. 'You are later today. I thought perhaps you had been successful.'

'No,' I whispered, the word so reluctant to be spoken it was hardly audible.

'Do you think?' she said quietly, 'that now the school year has begun nothing will change? That you have no chance? Do you not know that people can fall ill? Husbands can be posted outside Prague. Women can find themselves unexpectedly pregnant. Life changes always, it is only we who think it must be the same for ever. If you don't believe me go down and look at the river. Go onto Slovansky Island. Walk up to Charles Bridge and stand in the centre of it. It is the Vltava always, but watch how it eddies and swirls and its colours run dark and light, shifting constantly.' An old man shuffled up to the desk with a request slip in his hand and the librarian prepared to move away. She put her hand on the journal, pushing it towards me. 'And if you still don't believe me,' she smiled, 'well, the air and the walk at least will have done you good.'

On Charles Bridge a cold wind ran down the river rippling its surface. People walked quickly. There seemed, now the season of tourists was over, to be fewer vendors out on the bridge. The gusting breeze made the plastic covers on their folding tables flap, and plucked at the state licence pinned to the table top, or the base of their pedlar's tray. Their eyes were sharp and cold, restlessly moving among the passers-by. But it was not for custom that they looked. I did not stand, as the librarian had suggested, in the centre of the bridge, instead I walked on over it. Near the end the crowd bunched suddenly and then parted to let pass two work-men carrying a wide section of hardboard. I moved back against the parapet and, standing for a moment next to one of these hawkers, stared down into the tray of wooden toys she carried. Among small carved bears and rocking horses and dolls in tiny cradles were minute wooden apples, each with a stalk and a leaf, the whole thing scarcely bigger than the ball of my thumb. I stared at them as the crowd cleared and vanished. And as I stared I heard again the voice of Magdalena counting off the wedding-night stories; I saw her chin cupped in her hand and the faint, wry smile. The hawker tried to turn her tray away from me irritably.

'How much are they?'

She did not want to sell and I should not have bought from her, and once I had the toy I could not think why I had done it. I had used housekeeping money to buy it and if I took it back to Grigor's mother's apartment they would see what I had done. Just before the arch at the end of Charles Bridge on the castle side, the parapet widens out. From here you look down on the clustered roofs of the Little District, pretty curving streets of tall, colour-washed houses running up from the river. You can see children playing sometimes, a solitary cat stalking in the shadows. I sat on the parapet staring down at the houses, turning the apple over and over in my pocket. It had been for Magdalena, the apple. I had bought it to give to her. Knowing I – could not give it to her. In my handbag was an envelope with two sheets of paper in it, folded carefully, in case it was necessary to write a letter at the library. I wrapped the apple in one sheet of paper and smoothed out the creases in the other. What could I say to her? And what could she do? Slowly I rolled the apple in the second sheet of paper and sealed the envelope. What could she do, if she came? I sat for a long time. Just staring at the bumpy surface of the envelope. At the porous weave of the paper, at the grey tinge of it that was supposed to be white, 'Magdalena . . .' I wrote finally. It was difficult writing over the apple. The formation of some of the letters was not clear. I paused again. There was nowhere I could send it. To her mother's house? To Ludovice? But where in Ludovice now? I walked back along the bridge to where it led out over the river, placed my hand on the parapet and let the envelope flutter out of my fingers. It whirled white as a snowflake and then was gone. No one saw, I think; I saw no head turn. There was a moment of panic, as though I should have tried to catch it up again. But I did not look down to see if it had floated or sunk. I stared straight out before me. At the island and the weir and the bridges in the distance with traffic on them. I did not feel the consolation promised me by the librarian. I shivered in the wind.

When you pass under the gateway of Charles Bridge on the castle side, you pass through a small dark gatehouse, like a little room open at both sides. You can smell the dankness of its stones, feel the weight of its age. If you pause too long in this strange 'room' you will be blinded for a moment to the street outside. In the brightness of its sudden light you will see nothing but black shapes and dazzle. It was like that that morning. For ten seconds perhaps. In which I blinked and saw, among all the others, one particular black shape, moving with them. The back of a head, suddenly familiar. The profile of a face as it leant down to open the driver's door of a small delivery van. There was a sudden starting forward by my feet, almost without my knowledge. And then the blindness left me. Everything fell into light again. The van had gone. Scanning the street I caught a glimpse of it again far up ahead turning right, not black now but grey, streaked with mud, vanishing finally into the stream of traffic. The blaze of certainty faded into impossibility. I stared into the crowd searching quickly among the faces. I crossed to the other pavement and peered into the shops near where the van had been. There was a stamp dealer's shuttered and locked. A florist's. I pushed open the door. Two women were bending over long brown cardboard flower boxes at the far end of the shop. They moved together, protectively almost, the lifting of their heads was sharp, abrupt, as if I had startled them.

'Yes?' said the elder woman stepping towards me, scowling.

I glanced past her into the wooden partitioned workroom with its sink and rolls of coloured paper ribbon. It was empty save for more boxes. And the faint, light scent of carnations.

'I – I thought . . . I was looking for a friend.'

Out in the street again a sense of silence, of foolishness, overtook me. The feeling of having been taken in. What if I had called out? Waved my arms! I did not look up from the cobblestones as I walked the rest of the way up the street and turned into the square around the church of St Nicholas. I did not look up until I had crossed behind the church and begun climbing the shallow steps that wound up to the castle.

A letter came. I knew as soon as I slit the envelope that it was different. The sheet of paper inside was larger than usual. The typing had not the blur of having been cyclostyled many times, the metal letters of the type-writer had bitten deep into the rag paper. 'A vacancy has occurred . . .' they wrote. I scarcely bothered to read the rest of the letter. What did I care which district the Suslova primary school was in? What interest was it to me how many crowns my salary would be? Or what extra-curricular duties I might have.

There was no celebration, no praise that I remember. Only a kind of exhalation of breath by Grigor and his mother. Only the sudden understanding cutting in to my own elation of how close I had been to an abyss.

'Took long enough,' commented Grigor's mother emerging from the kitchen. Grigor put down his newspaper.

'When did you apply for it, Liska?' His face was tightened into a rare expression of generosity, the lips pressed so firmly together you thought of a miser's purse being squeezed unwillingly open.

'This – this is not one of the ones I applied for.'

Grigor's mother stopped beside his chair, folding a tea towel into a smaller and smaller square.

'You hear that, Grigor. They had it all this time. They knew about it all along.'

Grigor compressed his lips even further and shook his head.

'Keep children without a teacher? A teacher without a job?'

'Mistake,' countered his mother. 'Error. That's a big organisation, that teachers' one. Does teachers for all over the country.'

'We have no reason to think of error, mother,' said Grigor quietly.

'No,' agreed his mother swiftly. 'No, that's right.'

'Emergency of some kind.'

'Yes, someone wasn't – suitable.' She seized the letter that had been lying on the table all day and read it for what must have been the tenth time. 'Not going to be easy to get to,' she said. 'Outer Stresovice district, Grigor.'

'Mmm.'

'Stresovice and border of Dejvice. She'll have to change tram at least once. Twice, wouldn't you think, Grigor?'

'Opposite direction to the one I go in,' replied Grigor, crossing his legs.

I did not care. All I thought was – now everything will come right. Everything will fall into place. There is nothing missing now. I will be happy.

WE RARELY TALK of women in the Postmen's House but when we do we smile. Slow, knowing smiles that make words almost unnecessary. The first thing to learn is the smile, it is better than speaking. If you speak you invariably give too much away, you define too precisely your position and your relation to women. The smile, however, camouflages a whole ocean of floundering, it can encompass both the initiated and the uninitiated, those with and those without. The smile unites us all in a brotherhood. But you have to be careful. A false smile brands you immediately as a woman-less man and however well you perfect it later it is first impressions which count and which are remembered; you will always be seen later as a hanger-on in such discussions and your eligibility will be discounted. It is better to stay silent. Better to stand with your head slightly turned away or bent to the task you are engaged in, merely allowing a non-committal rippling of the facial muscles to flutter across your face, while you watch the expressions of the others. Watch. And remember. Practise it alone until you are certain you have perfected it. Then, when the talk turns, when one man looks up, a glint in his eye, a slow curl along his mouth; when the smile is smiled and no words said, *then* you can catch it and turn to the next man with the same sharp gleam in your eye. So we pass it like a loving cup, like a can of beer on a hot day, swiftly between us. We think of women and we cannot help but smile. And in our smile is mirrored all their soft, scented, warm breathing illogicality that always is trapped by the same snares into high-pitched, sharp-faced, sullen submission. We smile because this mastery is not taught us by other men; it is given to us by women. We learn this – management – at our mother's knee. One disappointed generation of women selling out the next. You would think they would make sure it would never happen again. But, on the contrary, it is they who take us in their arms and teach us our rights to kingship, give us all our power. They seem to take no thought of the women who will be our subjects, women like themselves with dreams and aspirations. And there is no question but that they will be our subjects. No man in the House would admit to being run by a woman, or even allowing her equality. The younger men, the unattached men, they will sometimes admit to difficulties, they will come in with hang-dog faces and rueful grins. But this is par for the course, you have to expect it: a bit of playing up, a bit of assertiveness till they're hooked and landed.

'Give 'em enough rope, my son,' says Jack paternally. 'They always hangs theirselves.'

And we all smile.

There's a hard core of boys in the House who are always having Bother.

'How y' doing, Ted?'

The face will be screwed into an endearing grimace, the kind that immediately elicits sympathy, the breath will be sucked in.

'Having a spot of bother, mate.'

We smile.

Nob has spots of bother with Marlene, a plump wilful girl. Kevin's involved in a permanent juggling act, always something new in the hand and too many up in the air. Frequently everything crashes. 'Are you surprised, my son?' Jack admonishes him. 'You want to make it easier on yourself; limit it a bit. Know what I mean?' But Kevin only purses his lips and shakes his head. 'They was none of them right, mate. There's a nice little one just moved in next my mum, though.' Terry's having bother with Elaine, but they're getting married in six weeks' time so that'll soon put a stop to that. Vic, forced some time ago into simultaneous engagements with his two women, has just taken the plunge and dropped them both and is going about offering us fake diamond rings half-price. Over in Rasco's corner it's like intensive care; we move quietly and talk in low voices offering him cigarettes, promises of pints, paper cups of tea. His wife, a mean-spirited woman, has just found out about his bit on the side, and life in the Postmen's House is, for the moment, calmer than life at home. They don't ask me about my wife. Or whether I have girls. We don't ask each other such questions, we give that kind of information of our own accord. But I don't talk about Eliska. What could I say? I don't know what to say about Eliska. Sometimes I don't know what to say *to* Eliska. So I say nothing. I wait. The others probably think because I am foreign I won't do such things as they do – that we don't do such thing. But we do, we do. If anything it's worse: our mothers are worse, our sons are more spoiled. We grow up little princes and turn into little kings – kings without land or riches, the only arena of power we have left is the small space behind our front door. So I smiled along with the others; I knew how to do that. And I thought at such times of Marietta and wondered whether to slip in a word about her when everyone else was laughing. But it hadn't really been an Encounter. Besides it would have meant I would have to tell about the card and that was not possible.

I began to think there might never be a subsequent

meeting. When I delivered letters I used to make as much noise as I could outside her flat and along her landing, but she never opened the door and I could think of no excuse to knock on it. I used to stare at it, wondering what to say if she appeared. And the longer I stared at it the more I wondered whether I really did want it to open. The longer I stood there the more I began to wonder what I wanted at all. If you come out, I used to say in my head to the figure I imagined sitting waiting for me beyond the door, if you come out, well, here I am re-tying a bundle of letters or readjusting the weight of my sack. And if you don't come out, well, that's another day gone.

After a couple of weeks I had to stop delivering to her building altogether. Mr Finch came back. I didn't say anything to Eliska. Instead I took to going for walks after work. Funny, wasn't it? You'd think I'd be walked off my feet all that delivering all morning. And so I was; but this was different. There was a strange kind of urgency about it, a compulsiveness. I didn't hang round the Postmen's House anymore. As soon as I'd handed in my empty sack and brushed my fingers for luck across the words painted on the door, I was off: over the common, across to the duck pond, marching round the perimeter of the football pitches. Walking, walking; pushing myself forward. Perhaps it was the benefits of my convalescence that were making me restless. Perhaps it was the niggling of my uncle and the discontent of Eliska. Perhaps it was my frustration at not being able to solve the riddle of the words on the door. But I had the feeling that my new life, having at first progressed so swiftly, was now slumped in a hiatus. What I wanted was to feel in it again some movement. My uncle would have seized on this restlessness as evidence that it was time I moved on to a more illustrious profession. He longed to immure me in a bank or an academy or some other place more fitting for one of his relatives. But I was determined not to leave the Postmen's House till I knew the answer to the words on its door. With that knowledge in my possession, I knew that the whole world would then be open to me. And so – I walked. Often I had the craving to take bus rides or go on the Underground and get off at unfamiliar stations. Sometimes I did. But I was careful never to stay away for more than a couple of hours so that Eliska would not suspect anything.

That was how I bumped into Marietta, or rather she bumped into me. I didn't recognise her at first. It had been raining earlier and she was still wearing a headscarf which hid the dark hair and obscured her arching neck. She had to say hello twice. Curious how slipshod memory can be sometimes, when on other matters it is so painfully accurate. For as far back as I can recall I have always had difficulty recognising the women to whom I am drawn. It is a flaw, a lapse, which I have been unable to cure myself of and which has vastly increased the trials of love. It has led to my being called cold-hearted and inattentive. In an effort to combat this I perfected an expression of welcome bland enough to wear as I stood at an appointed trysting place turning my face hopefully towards each girl who approached, and soft enough to have meaning to one who sought it. But I was then accused of being flirtatious and ogling every girl who passed. This was unjust and inconsiderate. My girl-friends took no account of the panic which beset me when I realised there was a vast gulf between my remembered image of them and their reality. In my adoring mind I smoothed away their imperfections till no trace of them remained in my memory. Sometimes the strength of my passion was such that I even managed to turn brown hair blonde or chestnut. It was not surprising that frequently I was unable to recognise them when they approached me. In love a moment's hesitation can be fatal. To stare blankly, even for a second, at the face of the adored is never tolerated. It is regarded as one of the gravest insults. I knew all this but it did not help me out of my predicament. My teens were filled with doubt and rejected love. It was only later that I learned to protect myself with excuses – never with the truth, the truth would have angered them even more. I used to blame my eyes chiefly, an inherited defect, I said, somewhere between long and short sight which affected sometimes one and sometimes the other. They would peer suspiciously into my face but they never challenged me, they were not sure enough of their ground. Eyes can be tricky things, deceptive. There are even some kinds of blindness in which, to a casual observer, the eyes continue to look quite clear; there is just a certain deadness to their centre.

I did not explain about the eyes to Marietta. I did not want to appear before her with any faults. I was aware that I was not putting on a very impressive performance, but I had been suddenly struck by the thought that I had never once failed to recognise Eliska. This observation should have flashed across my brain, been logged and then vanished. But it did not. It blew itself up and elaborated itself. It was not recognition in the visual sense, it informed me, but something much deeper, a recognition of the senses like smell or the feeling of warmth or cold. I *knew* when Eliska was near. This thought entirely monopolised my brain, while Marietta stood in front of me swinging her shopping bag backwards and forwards against her legs and moving her weight from one foot to the other, stepping backwards and forwards and sideways like a bee dancing. I began to unroll and re-roll the sleeves of my shirt, flicking the material at every turn to draw her attention to the suntan on my arms. I have always been very proud of my arms. But she seemed too agitated to notice. She darted sentences at me and fell into silences. She tugged at her headscarf till it fell in soft folds about her neck. Most of the time she kept her head turned away from me, but when she did look at me I was overwhelmed by the darkness of her eyes and the steadiness of their regard. When she looked at me, then I was sure of everything. When she looked away we were both plunged into incapability. We would stare together at something happening on the far side of the common, glancing at each other to make sure the other was looking too. Trying to force some communion into the looking, as if it could be taken for conversation. While all the time the unsatisfactoriness of our silence lay between us.

Finally Marietta tossed her head so that the curtain of hair fell down again over her eyes, swung her bag against her legs and turned to go.

'Well, I'd better get back,' she said without enthusiasm. Her eyes, in the shadow of her hair, looked larger and more appealing than ever. I smiled wanly and bent my head in acknowledgement of my disappointment.

'What are you going to do?'

I shrugged my shoulders.

'Go home too, I suppose?'

'If it's on your way,' she murmured, 'why don't you come and have a cup of tea?'

As if we had only been waiting for such a line to be spoken out into the air we turned, both together, and began to walk quickly away from the duckpond. Almost at a run we crossed the common by a quite different path to the one I usually took home. Moving at such high speed, Marietta's grace became ungainly, almost awkward; she kept her head bent and the upper half of her body tilted forward and the veil of hair between us as if she was now ashamed of what she had done. My spirits, however, had entirely returned. Our speed produced an exhilarating sensation of breathlessness and I could feel the blood racing round my body in a way it had not done for a long time. Even the strangeness of the path was exciting, the private knowledge that it was not the way home. It was only when we arrived at her mansion block that I began to feel uneasy. What if someone saw me and recognised me as the postman and wondered what I was doing back there in the middle of the afternoon in civilian clothes? But even that unease disappeared as I climbed the stairs. In the dimness and silence of the interior there was only the hasty shushing sound of our shoes on the stair carpet, and in my head only the thought of when, exactly, I should kiss her. The door of her flat, however, refused to open. Or rather Marietta could not make the key turn. She appeared to have lost the strength to grip it. As I stepped forward to do it for her I felt a rush of pride: she was not only surrendering her key to me, but with it her domain and even herself and stood there at my shoulder, waiting, her head modestly bent, a slight flush in her cheeks. But when I touched the key my fingers slid off, too. It was wet. And warm. It had a repulsive slipperiness to it, like sweat. It was a severe setback, a sobering surprise. Could I love someone with sweaty palms? It was not something to admit in the House. I made myself grasp the key and with great effort managed to turn it. The door swung open and Marietta darted through. Surreptitiously I wiped my wet fingers on the seat of my trousers, but in that moment she looked back over her shoulder and I am sure she saw. When I came up behind her in the small kitchen she waved me out again as if it was she who did not want me near her. I suppose I should have put my arms round her then and kissed her, but instead I went through into the living room.

It was a large room with a high ceiling, very light after the hallway, with tall windows all along the far wall. I threaded my way slowly across the room between an assortment of chairs covered in faded velvet and scuffed chintz. Below the window was a chaise longue with tufts of horsehair hanging beneath it. Next to it in the corner stood a large oval table covered with books and papers and glasses and tea-cups and one or two small plates with the remains of food on them. I pressed my finger into some crumbs on one and licked them off. They had gone dry and stale in the sun and had a sharp, clinging taste. I leant against the table and looked around the room at the vases of dead flowers, elegant even in their deadness, at the clusters of photographs at one end of a bookcase, at the bleached watercolours and the darkened prints. I was relieved that Marietta would never see my room.

'Where are you going to sit?' she said coming in suddenly with two mugs of tea in her hands.

I lowered myself into the nearest chair, but as I did so I heard distinctly a faint click and felt the angle of the back tilt and the arms move slightly and the seat slide, almost, under me. I held myself rigidly still, the mug of tea at arm's length, waiting for the chair to collapse around me. It seemed to be connected by a series of hidden mechanisms that one might release unwittingly by pressure on certain parts.

'Have some cake,' said Marietta returning from the kitchen with a plate. She did not seem to notice how reluctantly I moved my hand to take the plate, or the curiously stiff position of my back. She settled herself on the floor at my feet, leaning against a low velvet chair.

'It's nettle,' she said blowing steam off her tea. 'It's a new one I wanted to try from the delicatessen next to where I do yoga. I hope you don't mind.'

'Ah, nettle,' I replied. 'I'm very fond of nettle. My grandmother always made nettle tea.'

She watched me closely. I sniffed at it, but it had no smell. I drank and felt I was drinking dusty leaves swept up from someone's floor. My grandmother's tea had burst like spring in the mouth, like the green blossoming of early summer, a thing transformed, not dry and prickly as you might expect. The scent of it was the covered bowl of strawberries on the kitchen table, the small eager flames in the black stove that leapt up each time she fed them another stick, the end-less meadow that waited for me beyond the open door.

'Is your grandmother dead?' she asked.

I nodded. My grandmother had always seemed to me unbelievably old, it was in the nature of things . . .

'And your relatives, too?'

I stared at her in surprise, it was such a strange question, but she was hunched towards me, watching me intently, waiting. My conversation with Mrs Bartholomew suddenly flashed into my mind. Perhaps English women liked death, perhaps it . . . Her lips were parted, wet from the tea.

'No, I don't think they're all dead.'

'Prison?' she whispered.

Her eyes over the rim of the mug had become large and troubled and as I gazed, her right eyebrow lifted itself infinitesimally out of its alignment. But I was speechless. Staring at the quivering eyebrow. It was with difficulty that I brought my upstanding uncles and aunts to mind at all, never mind visualising them in prison. I shook my head. Perhaps I should kiss her now. I put my plate in my lap and tried to shift my weight on the chair to lean forward. She stretched out a tentative forefinger. Hurriedly I disengaged my hand from the handle of the mug. But her finger had already reached my chair and was sliding slowly up and down the slender carved balustrades that supported the armrest. It bumped up over lozenges, glided across the veined flutes of columns and slipped back down again. I could not move, I could not breathe and my hand hung in mid-air paralysed. Her finger paused at the top of a column.

'Labour camp?' she breathed.

I let my breath out all in a rush, in a wave of angry disappointment. She retreated back across the floor. I thought of trying to catch hold of her wrist, but she was too quick for me. Her expression was not one of alarm, but renewed eagerness.

'I wasn't trying to pry, really. You don't have to tell me anything you don't want to; anything you can't.' She leapt up, clutching the mug of tea. 'I don't want to place you, or anyone connected with you in – in *danger*!' She paced to the window and looked swiftly up and down the street. 'It must be terrible for you,' she went on, turning quickly round. 'It must be awful, what you have to endure. I mean, I could tell right away that you weren't really a postman.'

I stared at her. Not a postman! What did she mean – not a postman? Mr Harry could put her right, Sid could tell her. I felt as stunned as if my whole life had been called into question. I made some inarticulate gargle of protest, but she took no notice. She moved over to the table and swept a hand abstractedly across it, picking up one of the books as if out of habit and standing it on its end.

'I won't tell anybody.' She looked up. 'I haven't told any . . . well, Linda; we've talked about you a bit but she won't . . .' Still clutching the book she came over and sat on the low chair facing me. Placing the book on her knees she leant forward. 'Are you part of a cell?' she whispered. 'Are you over here to recruit? To raise sympathy?'

I think I must have gone very pale. I had overwhelming visions of my permit of residence being withdrawn, of deportation. I struggled in my chair as though she had bound me to it by ropes. She laid a hand on my arm, no doubt to calm my distress. Obediently I sank back.

'You mustn't think that I would breathe a word. I shouldn't even have asked you what I did. I know the rule is never to ask questions like that, and never to talk about – about *it*. Although here,' she gripped my arm, 'we are quite safe. I just wanted you to know that I *sympathise*.' She relaxed her grip and smiled sheepishly through the veil of hair that had fallen across her face.

'And if there is anything that I can do . . . you know . . .' Her voice trailed away.

She was so close; she was so near, that suddenly it was very easy. I put my hand on her hand and she did not draw it away. I reached up and laid the tips of my fingers on the nape of her neck and pulled her towards me. The book tumbled to the floor. Just as my lips were about to touch hers she sprang away.

'Ow!' she gasped. 'The tea.'

My mug of tea lay on its side, sprawled across it was her book and around them both a stain of dark liquid. We do not talk, in the Postmen's House, of shocks like these that numb the brain and leave the body hollow, eviscerated. Marietta picked up the book by one corner and it dripped tea onto her skirt.

'Poor book,' she whispered and giggled into her hair.

Somehow my brain remembered the handkerchief in my pocket; somehow it pushed my other hand towards the book.

'Here,' I heard myself croak. 'I'll dry it with this.' Patting at the book with my handkerchief was like patting the real world back into place. As I turned the volume over I caught sight of the title. '*Dead Souls*! What are you . . . ?'

'Oh that's just something I've got to read. I'm doing an evening class in Eastern European Literature. This week it's Gogol, next week it's Dostoevsky. Do you want some more tea?'

'Dostoevsky?'

'Yes.' She grimaced. 'But Dostoevsky's not the problem, it's Dickens.'

I felt my heart stop. I felt the breath rush into my mouth and choke my lungs. I felt myself stopped short on the edge of a ravine, teetering. But I did not fall.

'Dickens?' I said and was amazed at the calmness of my voice. 'What has Dickens to do with Dostoevsky?'

I was going to have at last the key to the words on the

door of the Postmen's House in my hands. I had even held it momentarily in my arms. I had thought that it was its kisses that I wanted, but I had been misled. She was going to sit there, my pretty canary, perched on the edge of her velvet chair, and sing. She was going to tell me everything I wanted to know. And with that key . . .

But she only laughed. 'You tell me!' she said. 'You should know.'

I knew that I should know; I *knew* that! I had been thinking of nothing else for the past two months. But it was unbearable to be taunted by her with failure. If I was to get anything from her I could not admit to the truth. I spread my hands and shrugged my shoulders and drew what I hoped was an enigmatic smile across my face.

'Ah.' She narrowed her eyes. 'Then it's not true! Our tutor's been telling us that Dickens is admired in Russia for being the English equivalent of Dostoevsky. He's even set us an essay: Dostoevsky, the Russian Dickens. Discuss. He says there are a couple of studies on the subject we can look up, but even so. I mean, I've never read any of Dickens – only half of *Hard Times*.'

'You've never read Dickens?' This was a serious setback.

'No. When we were just starting him I got shunted up to school in Scotland and there we had to do Sir Walter Scott.'

'Never?'

She shook her head. 'I've dipped into a couple, but I always get stuck at the beginnings, he's – he's too long-winded, too excessive.'

I was appalled. 'What about Dostoevsky?'

'Well, *Crime and Punishment* of course, and *Underground Letters*.'

'Yes, yes; *Letters from the Underworld*,' I said tersely. 'What else?'

'Nothing much.'

'When's your essay due?'

—172—

'Ten days.' She looked suddenly forlorn.

'Listen. I will read Dickens for you. You go on with Dostoevsky and draft your essay and then, if you like, I will come round and we can discuss your draft and add in the Dickens.'

'But you don't have to read the books for something like that, you only need read the studies.'

'Marietta,' I said quickly, coming up very close to her, 'it is essential that you read the books.'

'But what about you? You have far more important work to do, as well as being a postman, and . . .'

'It is my pleasure, Marietta.'

I thought for a second she was going to kiss me. Instead we walked out into the hall. There I thought she swayed slightly towards me. I thought I moved towards her. But it was dark in the hall after the light of the room and now I'm not so sure. There was a feeling of being overwhelmed, of a sudden searching for the door in that dimness, the right door among all those that simultaneously presented themselves to me. Of being entangled briefly among coats on a rack.

'Next week, then,' I think I murmured. But it may only have been in my head – next week, next week I will.

I ran down the stairs of her apartment block as if I was running from the scene of a crime, an unspecified crime, a crime of a sort so pervasive that it did not have to have been physically performed for it to have been commit-ted. A crime that seemed to pursue me, rather than I it; if I looked behind me, there it would be. If I stopped for a moment, it might overtake me and pass from the im-agined to the real. Out on the street I tried to regulate my pace to the rhythmical lope of a jogger; I pumped my arms and puffed out my breath as I had seen runners do. In this way I went through the side streets and crossed the common without anybody giving me a second glance. By the time I reached the bottom of Oudenard Road I slowed into a walk. I was out of breath. Besides, no one in Oudenard Road jogged. In the enclosed warmth and dust of the street with its broken front walls and shabby bay windows I felt at last safe. I craned my neck to see our window staring from its row out across the street, stiff-necked and blind, its glass dull with dust, its painted struts blistering. 'Liski,' I whispered, catching sight of it, and at once the panic subsided. I wished that I had flowers for her, but I never bought her flowers. I pulled a piece of flowering privet from a hedge to give to her, but in my hands it looked a scrappy, desiccated thing and I threw it away.

The house was silent when I entered it, there was no sound from Mrs Bartholomew's radio in the back room, nor the familiar snuffling of Monty under the kitchen door. I tiptoed up the stairs. I wanted to surprise Eliska. I wanted to catch her unawares. See her turn, watch her smile her slow, sad smile of recognition. I put my hand on the door knob, turned it with a little click and pushed the door open. The room was empty. I stared at it for some time, unable to believe it. She was always there. Waiting. But there was nothing to see except dust falling slowly through the shafts of sunlight between the ugly chairs. I crossed the room and peered round the bed-room door. The smell of sleep was still trapped between its claustrophobic walls, but it, too, was empty. I prowled around the living room and peered at the kitchen shelves looking for a note to explain her absence. I slumped into the armchair and stared sullenly into the gloom of the kitchen cubby-hole, listening to the silence of the house. I waited for the sound of her key turning in the downstairs door, or footsteps on the stairs. But there was only silence and the peculiar waiting stillness of empty rooms. The fear grew that perhaps she had seen Marietta and me out on the common and followed us back to her flat. It was impossible, I told myself, shifting uncomfortably on the chair. Impossible! She'd gone out when she knew I would be coming home as deliberate provocation, that was all. That was why she'd left the door unlocked. Anyone might have got in – Mrs Bartholomew, the dog – there was my new shirt in the wardrobe and the transistor radio we'd bought from the market. She'd done it on purpose. That was why there was no note. There was nothing to say because she had nowhere to go.

It was nearly seven o'clock by the time Eliska finally returned. I pretended not to notice the opening of the door or the dropping of her handbag on the sofa or her passage through into the bedroom. I was immersed in my book, anyway. Pacing round the room earlier in the evening I had stopped in front of the hanging wall-shelf to read for the hundredth time the titles of the five books that stood there, and I did what I had always meant to do. I picked up the sixth book which had always lain on its side propping the others up. I turned it over and discovered it was one of Dickens's novels. It had been here all the time, under my eyes – like the words on the door of the Postmen's House – but hidden. I forgot Eliska. I carried it back to the chair and began to read. I read all through supper, the book beside my plate. I grunted whenever Eliska tried to speak to me and soon she left me alone. I didn't even bother to ask her where she'd been. I was absorbed in *The Mystery of Edwin Drood*. I read all night, but the mystery remained unsolved. The next day I went to the library and borrowed another. It was called *Little Dorrit*.

MEMORY IS LIKE a long corridor. A long corridor broken by a series of mirrored swing doors. I glimpse myself fleetingly as these doors blow open one by one and sigh shut again. Myself at various stages of my life. I glimpse both the image of myself as I was at a particular time and then, in that image, the reflection of myself to be. I look down through those doors at the busily moving figures of myself and I think – Why did I not do this? Why did I not see that? How was I . . . ? It seems so obvious now. And all that time – like wasted time. But nothing is wasted, so they say. Nothing. I used to look, in idle moments, at the faces of the children in my class. I could see in each of them their adult looks and character. The signs were all there. Imprinted, ready. I could even tell, though I had never met their parents, which one they most resembled. Yet I could not help myself. When I looked in the mirror, I could not read my future. I saw only the present. The rest was invisible.

The Suslova primary school was not new. And yet it had a raw look to it, as though it was still unfinished. It had been constructed beside one of the main arterial roads into Prague, to serve the surrounding housing blocks. A concrete box one storey high divided into narrow rooms by plasterboard walls. Behind it was a playground fenced in with ten-foot high wire mesh. Tacked onto one end a couple of shops – small concrete cabins. It was the standard plan, the modern concept of social facilities. In theory and on paper it looked good. In practice it was always inadequate. But – inadequate – was a comment we rarely bothered to make any more. Everything was inadequate. It was the general state of being. It was the plane on which we were forced to operate, on which we coped. It was like walking forward over trails of disused barbed wire; it tore a little at our ankles here and there, but a thing like that was to be expected. Such grazes healed. And others were made. Inadequate. It was not how I thought of the school my first day there. It was how I thought of myself. Everything, everyone seemed to know better than I what should be done. It was not just the children of my class who called out 'Miss, Miss!' It was the cupboard that held the books I needed, the clock whose hands moved erratically above the door. The desk drawer that knew in which corner of itself the chalk for the blackboard lay hidden. Though I did not. Even the thin sallow-faced girl who was the other junior teacher, whose limp fingers scarcely touched my palm as we shook hands, even she appeared to me more competent than I would ever be.

I was completely confused for several days by the semi-circle of green-painted doors at the end of the corridor. One was Mrs Ostrova's, the headmistress's, classroom, one was a walk-in store cupboard that was always locked, two were washrooms. I could never remember the order. My hand landed inevitably on the doorknob of the locked store cupboard when what I wanted was the girls' washroom. The last room was a small office with a desk, a telephone and two hard wooden chairs. This room was always kept locked, too. On rare occasions the telephone would ring inside it. You would hear a flurry of noise from Mrs Ostrova's classroom, a jangling of keys and then the bursting out of insistent ringing as she got the door open and rushed inside. Mrs Ostrova was proud of her school. 'My little school', she would say, beaming. She wore a copper bracelet for rheumatism on her wrist and brightly coloured scarves knotted at her neck into which the heavy folds of her jaw sank, and were concealed. She loved her children, I am sure. She wanted only to guide them onto the right path. 'My little eyes and ears' she would call them, ruffling a blond head as a child trotted past her in the corridor, or bending to turn back a collar neatly. And they would grin up at her, these little confederates, and scurry on. I was proud too, of my school. I had a title, a position in life. I had something to talk of. An importance to pretend. I could leave the flat in the dark and the cold of those winter mornings, so early that I hardly noticed Grigor's mother's complaints. And when I got back home I had a reason to be tired, too. For a time, at least, the hollow spaces were filled. The bewilderment blunted.

My classroom faced onto the road. Even with the window closed the noise sometimes was deafening as heavy lorries churned their way up the hill in low gear. Often the whole building would shake. My words would be drowned out. And the chanting of the class. We would have to stop. Begin again. Sometimes they giggled at such interruptions. Mostly they sat, patiently waiting. One or two would glance up, round-eyed, at the rattling window. The others took no notice. They just accepted it. The starting, the stopping; the shaking, the roaring. Like they accepted that some days there was no heating. 'Coats on today' we would call out as they trooped into school early in the morning. There was no need to explain that the quota of coal was late, or had run out prematurely. Or that the janitor had not turned up to stoke the boiler. They were used to such things. We all just sat there, in our coats, carrying on with whatever the programme was for that day. Our movements were a little slower, that was all. More clumsy. Our arms restricted in heavy sleeves. The corners of books would get caught in coat cuffs and pencils would be knocked from desks. Small pieces of jigsaw would be swept off skittering along the floor, and have to be retrieved. The greatest nuisance was the dust. It lay over everything. It seemed to leach in between the joins in the plasterboard, to drift in through the cracks around the window. We never opened the window all the time I was there. Summer or winter. Helena Skalnik, the other junior teacher, was allergic to dust, so she said. I had never heard of such a thing. I stared at the sallow skin that flushed red along her arms and the backs of her hands, and the weals that came up in bands around her neck. I would hear her coughing from the next classroom, a dry tickle that turned into endless racking coughs. The reflex once started, unstoppable.

'Ask for a transfer,' I suggested.

She smiled. 'To somewhere where there is no dust?'

It was her husband who was ill, she explained. Not her. No one could tell what it was, she said proudly. He was thin, so thin, and she would shake her head. 'He eats, all there is, but he never seems to put on any weight, never seems to get any strength. He goes from clinic to clinic and in between he gets what jobs he can.' He came to meet her at the school, once or twice. A face white as paper and a straggly black moustache. He was so skinny his clothes hung off him awkwardly and his constant grin was foolish and lopsided. He held on to my hand with long bony fingers when Helena introduced him to me, leering out of small red-rimmed eyes. Making stupid innuendoes in a rush of spittle. Until his wife blushed and tugged him away.

I thought back often, at this time, to my own village school clamped to the side of another hill, a very different hill. But they were not so different, the schools. The same patriotic songs were sung, the same marching performed. The same holidays were observed. Little paper flags brought out and handed round and packed away again in the same kind of battered cardboard box tied with string. Only now – I was the teacher. I led the singing. I told the stories, the myths of our re-born country. And all of a sudden it seemed – so easy.

One afternoon as I was about to leave, Mrs Ostrova called me over.

'Eliska, dear. Staff meeting tomorrow. Won't take long, half an hour after school.'

'What happens at the staff meeting?' I asked Helena as we stood watching the children gather in the playground the next morning. Helena had wound her scarf over her nose and mouth, against the cold. She stared at me over the top of it.

'What staff meeting?' she mumbled through the folds.

Mrs Ostrova came bustling over to us. Her head and shoulders were swathed in a pale blue shawl of soft, fluffy wool that we had not seen before and a strong scent of violets hung about her.

'Roll call! Get your children into lines, girls. Line up, children!' she called. 'Come on, girls.' She placed a hand under Helena's elbow to steer her away. 'Staff meeting this afternoon, dear.'

'I . . . I . . . have to go to the clinic. I promised to meet Jiri . . .'

'Jiri can manage on his own,' cut in Mrs Ostrova, 'for half an hour.'

I caught a glimpse of Mrs Ostrova's expression as they moved forward out of earshot, the eyes black and cold. I saw Helena's head droop.

Her cough seemed worse that day. It was a day, I would have thought, when even the dust might have been frozen into stillness. But the coughing went on and on. At lunch-time Mrs Ostrova took Helena's place supervising in the playground.

'I told her to stay inside,' she said, settling down on the bench beside me, 'her cough seems worse.' A group of little girls sidled up to us and asked to stroke Mrs Ostrova's shawl. She put her arm round one of them.

'Now my Katinka, how's your mother these days; she better?' The little girl nodded. 'And that big, grown-up brother of yours, has he been back to see you?' She shook her head, her gaze fixed on one of the ends of Mrs Ostrova's shawl that dangled below the bench. Though Mrs Ostrova's arm was round her shoulders, the child steadied itself with a hand on my knee. 'Tell me Katinka,' went on Mrs Ostrova and her voice purred as if it was not Mrs Ostrova who spoke but a warm, blue, furry cat to whom all secrets could be confided, 'whose is that green car I see parked outside your block sometimes in the afternoon?'

The little fingers tightened on my leg and without thinking I slid my hand over hers, hiding it completely.

'I don't know, Miss,' whispered the child.

'Miss! Miss!' clamoured some of the older girls eagerly. But Mrs Ostrova ignored them.

'It's such a smart car I thought it must have come to visit your flat.' The child shook its head. 'You've never seen the driver on your stairs? You've never watched out of the window?'

'We have, Miss, we've seen him. It's a man, Miss!'

The child was very still, its fingers like pincers in my knee, its gaze fixed on the end of Mrs Ostrova's shawl.

'Katinka.' Mrs Ostrova gave her a little shake and released her. 'Eyes and ears, remember! Eyes and ears all the time.'

Just before classes were due to end that afternoon I heard the front door open and footsteps approach up the corridor. It must be the janitor, I thought. I heard a key turn in a door, the door open and close. There was a moment of silence and then Mrs Ostrova's class burst from their room. The noise in the corridor drowned out everything else. It fractured the silent concentration of my pupils.

'Miss, Miss, it's time!'

'No,' I said, pointing to the clock. 'It isn't.'

The front door banged open and shut, open and shut. The noise was now in the playground, the corridor was almost silent. Perhaps classes left early on the day of staff meetings, I thought.

'Miss, Miss!'

'Go!' I said.

When the classroom was empty I wandered out after them. At the end of the corridor Mrs Ostrova was ushering Helena in to the office. She saw me in the same moment I saw her. And as I turned, smiling, to join them, she seemed to push Helena in to the room and pull the door quickly shut behind her.

'Ah, Eliska, put on your coat, dear, and go and supervise the ones waiting for late mothers. See they don't run out on the road. We'll call you in ten minutes. Helena's talking to the Inspector first, she's in a hurry to get to the hospital.'

'Inspector?' I felt something catch in my throat, so that the word hardly came out; some speck of dust, of fear.

'Yes, dear, hurry along.'

We call our school inspectors 'Major', but they do not wear a uniform. Uniforms alarm. And there is no cause for alarm. We are all devoted to the same end. To the education and proper upbringing of the nation's children. I smiled and nodded as he told me this, Major Jezek. We had had such lectures all through college. But in my left knee there was an unaccountable slight pain, like pincers digging in, a stiffening of the muscle that distracted me from his words. He had to repeat some of his questions twice, and even then I did not see the point of them.

'I don't know what is wrong with Mrs Skalnik's husband. Surely she can tell you better than I.'

'We are interested in your opinion of his – undiagnosable – illness.' He smiled, rolling his pencil back and forth across the desk. It clicked faintly against the wooden surface in the silence. 'Your husband, on the other hand, has good prospects. Your husband is ambitious?'

I shrugged cautiously, I could not see why we were talking about husbands and not the scholastic performance of our schoolchildren. 'My husband is proud of his work. He . . . he is keen to do well.'

'Yes,' he nodded, 'yes. And that is right. And you,' he paused, 'you are there to help him. In any way,' he picked up the pencil with a sudden deft movement, 'you can. Mrs Ostrova is a good headteacher, do you think?'

I felt my mouth go dry. This was another unexpected question. Who was I to comment on my seniors. 'She – she is very good,' I managed to say. He nodded, an expectant look in his eyes. He was quite young for a major, hardly more than thirty. Nodding. Waiting. Not smiling anymore. 'She is very –' I spread my hands, '*encouraging* with the children.'

'Encouraging!' he broke in quickly. 'Encouraging. That is right. That is the way, with young children. We wish that all our headteachers were as satisfactory as Mrs Ostrova. We are very pleased with her results. You would do well, Mrs Vaculik, to take her as your model.' He turned a page of the open file before him. 'This is your first appointment, no?' He gestured to the crowding walls around him, leaning back awkwardly on the hard schoolroom chair. 'This is a charming little school, but it is a very junior school. It is in a district far out from where you live. A long journey on these dark mornings, is it not?' I made some noise of deprecation, some gesture – shrugging my shoulder, half-shaking my head, I did not wish him to think that I . . . 'You wish for something better.' He had to raise his voice to speak across me. I was suddenly aware of it reverberating off the walls, like an argument. It could be heard no doubt in all the school. 'You wish one day to be a headteacher, too!' I fell silent, a foolish grin on my face, as if he had unmasked some secret. 'Of course you do,' he said softly, smiling. 'Let us talk again about Mrs Skalnik. That cough of hers. That husband. We are concerned.'

I have never forgotten that conversation. Word for word I remember it. More than all the others that followed later. I remember the fear. The tensing of the muscles of my stomach, the drying of my mouth, the not daring to lick my lips. And then the quick rushing of thought. The justifications that elbowed their way in. That this . . . that this . . . was right! That this was how we should behave. Co-operating, helping each other. 'You can talk to me in strictest confidence,' he had said, 'at any time.' And stretched across the desk to hand me his card. We could not look each other in the eye the next morning, Helena and I; we knew that each had been asked to talk about the other. We spoke only of children and lessons in rapid bursts of conversation and uneasy waiting silences in which crowded all the questions we could no longer ask.

I was so late home that evening even Grigor was back before me. When I came in they stared at me suspiciously. Each staring in his own way. Grigor over by the table turning the pages of a newspaper and his mother coming out from the kitchen for a moment to stand in its doorway as I moved into the room, unbuttoning my coat.

'You're late,' said Grigor, looking up briefly.

And they waited, both of them there, for an answer. What other life, they insinuated, did I think there was for me beyond the walls of my classroom and the walls of this apartment? In my pocket I ran my index finger back and forth along the edge of Major Jezek's card, as I had done all the way home in the tram. I worked the sharp point of one of its cardboard angles under my fingernail.

'I was at a staff meeting,' I said, and drove the point hard between the skin and the nail.

Grigor's mother looked sharply across at her son, but he did not turn his head. She went back into the kitchen and he continued to leaf through the paper.

'They fired you yet?' he drawled.

I did not answer.

I will not tell you about Major Jezek, I whispered at him in my head as I went past him into the bedroom. And covertly I slipped the small white card from the pocket of my coat to the pocket of my skirt. All evening I kept my finger on the edge of it, or poked tentatively with one corner of it at the tear under my nail. All evening I did not mention once Major Jezek. I do not know now why I did not. It would have brought us closer. I would have told them and then, when I had finished, we would have smiled at each other. Slow, creeping salacious smiles of complicity and expectation. And pleasure. I would have been one of them, for that moment. But I did not.

It rained all that evening. Listening to the incessant sound of water falling, I thought of the cold and the dark and the wet outside and I tried to be grateful for the warm room. To feel fortunate. When you catch a drop of rain in your hand it has no colour, no smell, no shape even. It runs away between your fingers. Emptiness was like that – without smell or taste or form. Yet you could drown, too, in emptiness. And nothing would save you. I thought again, as I often did, hopelessly, of the small wooden apple floating away down the Vltava in its blank white envelope to find Magdalena. Wondering how long it had taken for the waterlogged paper to sink and drag it under.

We had staff meetings every three months. More or less. Every three months the same questions. They were never announced in advance, these meetings. Mrs Ostrova was too clever for that. We might not have turned up – we might have found ourselves ill on that day. Had news that our mothers were dying. When you are afraid, anything will do, any excuse to push away the numbness; the dazed staring at the thing you cannot bear to see. What made it worse was that there was no reason for fear. Such meetings were for good! For everybody's good. Our children. Ourselves. If we searched in our minds there was nothing to explain such fear. They were just regular meetings between our superiors and ourselves. Friendly, informal meetings in which we were encouraged to speak our minds freely. The good society is self-regulating, self-balancing. We were merely helping this regulation. The information we provided was a check on the running of the great machine. Information came in from all quarters, all angles. From it an overall picture could be built up. Deductions made. Decisions taken. Such helpful individuals, where possible, receive the grateful thanks of the nation. Not all of them, but enough to make the others try harder. I knew all this. Why then was there this small reluctance that wormed and twisted itself into a knot in my stomach? Why was it that Helena and I could never discuss these meetings? Why did we not earnestly relate the helpful things we had said, pool observations? Or the reverse, why did we never laugh and say: 'Well, what did they want from you this time?' Some such thing. We did not dare. What if one of us had said that and the other received it with a stony face. The laugh alone would have been enough to denounce us. So also we did not dare become friends. In circumstances such as these how could we confide one in the other? Yet there were things in both our lives, though Helena might not have suspected it, that could at least have made us, if not friends, then commiserators. But – it was no longer possible. That's what our society does. It turns us inward, away from each other with distrust. and in this distrust run little trails of fear, like fire. Zigzags of slow-running flame burning out then flaring up again. Helena was afraid, for her worthless husband. Malingerers are not tolerated. I could see, in the way that her eyes avoided mine for several days after our staff meetings, that she had given information about me. Out of the fear that I would give information about her. I knew it. From the way she always got in first to see Major Jezek. I used to wonder sometimes why Mrs Ostrova let her go first. It was Mrs Ostrova who was in charge of such things with, perhaps, the consultation of Major Jezek. Why did they show such favouritism to Helena? Except that I knew it was not favouritism. It was cunning. In denunciation it is important to get in first. Counter-denunciation does not have nearly the same weight about it, the same authenticity. It does not feel – so believable, there is something slightly lame about it. It does not give the same pleasure. I remembered this from my days in Sonia's group.

Major Jezek took to ringing me at the school. Mrs Ostrova would have to come and call me out of my classroom. My heart would beat against the cavity of my ribs so loud I thought he would hear it at the other end of the line. I could scarcely open my mouth to speak. His voice was teasing, friendly.

'Eliska, you never ring me! Why is that? What have I done? You said you would and yet day after day goes by. I don't believe you have nothing to tell me. You have a class of thirty children. Thirty families. Do all of them do nothing? What a dull life, Eliska!'

And so on. On and on. After such telephone calls I used to get a kind of neuralgia in my leg. A painful stiffness in my knee. I would go back to the classroom and look at all those faces, watching me expectantly. The phone rang so rarely at school that in their minds it never rang and no one was ever called out of class to take a call. They stared up at me, grinning some of them, expecting at least the news of a death in my family. I said nothing of the telephone. I just carried on with the lesson, but my voice trembled a little and the reflection of my face in the glass of the bookcase was pale. I sat at my desk and let my eyes wander from head to bent head. Where should I guide them? They had already been guided well. They had already learned their lessons. They came to me of their own accord, Katias and Maries some of them already, with their own tales. 'Miss, Miss!' I listened seriously to what they had to say. And I responded, in the correct manner. We knew the words, both of us, they and I. The right formulae. What other children in the world, of six years old, have such extensive vocabularies to prattle about subversive tendencies, unpatriotism and anti-socialist behaviour. Where else are tellers of tales praised and their victims publicly arraigned. There is a natural spite often in children of this age, particularly in girls, which can easily be trained. Built upon. But such facility is a two-edged sword. These children can become without allegiance. I knew that if I did not answer them properly, if I did not mete out the 'justice' they expected, they would have no hesitation in denouncing me to Mrs Ostrova.

Major Jezek's phone calls terrified Helena even more than me. No doubt she thought that I was making a further report on her. But we never spoke of them. We never even alluded to the phone that rang unexpectedly in the middle of the day. It was not that she did not hear them. Such events were impossible to ignore. They were of the classic type. They had all the hallmarks. No adult hearing the phone that never rang ringing in such a place and at such a time would have any doubts about who had dialled our number. If we had picked up the receiver and heard instead the rough voice of the coal supplier apologising for a late delivery of coal we would have had hysterics of panic and disbelief. That is how we are. We fear the worst always. And, inevitably, the worst always comes – to reassure us that we are not insane.

From that point on I stopped asking Helena any questions about her husband, to try to set her mind at rest. To try, perhaps, to prove my innocence to her. If I knew nothing I could say nothing. But it meant that then I could not talk to her about Grigor. About – about – what? What could I have said to her? I could not even define it to myself. There was just a small sadness inside me, that sometimes I thought was large. So large I could not see it because it was all of me. And then it would shrink to a tiny dot, so that I thought it was nothing after all. Just normal life. Everyday, practical life.

Once they get hold of you they do not let go. Over the months Major Jezek became persistent, tenacious. If I would not sing of my own accord, like Helena, then I would have to be given songs, forcefed.

'Hello. Eliska? Eliska, there is a child in your class, Martin Strasnik. We are concerned about what his father does. Where he goes, who his friends are, how much he drinks, that kind of thing. We are concerned, you understand, on behalf of the little boy. It is thought, perhaps, things are not – as they should be – in his home. We do not want even one of our lambs to stray. And you are their shepherd, Eliska. Remember that.'

The line went dead. It clicked into silence. And I was left, still holding the receiver to my ear, staring at the uneven surface of the painted wall, where the green paint had chipped away to show the grey plaster beneath. Into that crevice the name of the child just – slid. For a moment fragments of it remained visible, memorable. Syllables which might recall the whole. And then it vanished. The wall became smooth. And in my mind there was . . . nothing. I heard my breath drawn in sharply like a gasp, and felt my body jolt awake as if out of a trance. I jiggled the rest of the telephone receiver frantically.

'Major Jezek. Major Jezek,' I whispered, almost

sobbing. Without the name of the child, what could I do? And then I put the receiver down very slowly, very deliberately. I sat for a while, I do not think it was long, on the edge of the desk, gazing out of the window. At the concrete yard and the concrete housing blocks and the thin wire lattice of the fence. What happened to you if you refused to report? Why did I ask? I knew already the answer. But what did it matter, I was doomed anyway. They knew what to expect of me. There was an irregularity already marked in my file. Major Jezek had never mentioned it. It was not from politeness, though Major Jezek was always polite; he had not needed to. The fear bites deepest when you have something to hide, when day by day you expect exposure. You will do anything then to stave it off. Anything. He knew that. I was no braver than anyone else. I did not have the courage to admit I could not remember the child's name. So I feigned stupidity, vagueness. The little boy, I said, did not seem to understand my questions. His father – he had nothing to say about his father – he worked, he slept. What else could one think of to say about a father? But, I reported, the child seemed quite happy. No different to the other children in his class.

They sent another Inspector to see us the following staff meeting. Autumn had come round again and lengthened into winter. We had the first frost the day he came. He had a leather overcoat with a fur collar and wore a brown suit that smelled of stale sweat. He was impatient, intolerant of fools. He stared at me across the desk with small unblinking eyes. From such scrutiny nothing can be hidden. At the end of our interview he snapped my file shut.

'I suggest you take your job more seriously, Mrs Vaculik,' he said.

I think it was from that time that the sleeplessness started. That time, or in the weeks before. It became, slowly, like Helena's cough, an entrenched habit. A way of life. A life of half-darkness, inhabited by no one but me, which began to seem preferable to the life of day. Began to seem as if it was life. It took on defined periods of activity. As each night began and the noises in the apartment and beyond in the street were gradually extinguished; as the bedroom became first dark and then, by degrees, lighter as my eyes accustomed themselves, I felt not the panic of the sleepless who long for sleep and cannot achieve it, I felt myself wake. Felt myself surface from hours of sleepwalking through grey, almost subterranean streets, hours of sitting in stuffy rooms with low sounds rising and falling around me in the inarticulate manner of dreams. Now that it was night everything took on clarity. The folds of the curtains stood out as if they moved; as if they had just moved, and momentarily stood still again. I gazed into the deep clefts between them, expecting always something to leap out. Some small bright thing like a magician's trick to jump out of the dark fold and hang there, its head cocked to one side. Sometimes I would laugh, quietly, into the darkness, convinced it was there, hiding, playing a game with me. As the night progressed the sense of alertness increased. I could have heard a feather drop from a chair to the floor. A particle of dust fall against another. It was then the restlessness would start. In the dark I would lift my arms, stretch my fingers. Beside me Grigor's body lay inert, heavy. Even from his mother, beyond in the next room, there was silence. It was as if they were gone. At last. And I was alone. The sensation came like the lifting of cloud, the blowing in from somewhere of cool air. Intoxicating. I would slide out of bed. Walk around the room. Pass my fingers over the objects on the top of the chest of drawers. Run them across the polished surface of the wardrobe. Drawing aside the curtain a centimetre and holding it close to my face so that no light should enter the room, I would gaze out, often for a long floating time at the empty street. But always, eventually, I would gravitate towards the door of the bedroom. I would try sometimes, at this point, to steer myself back into bed. Out in the dark living room, I knew, the euphoria always drained away. Scratchings of fear returned, like the scrabblings of claws over stones. Running, stopping, starting up again. The slightest noise would wake Grigor's mother. The smallest creak of a floorboard would make her eyes flick open. And then she would see me, standing there, without purpose. So I would hover in the doorway until compulsion pushed me forward in a kind of tiptoeing rush towards the bathroom.

It was in the bathroom that the third stage of the night began. The stage that had to have light to take place. For this was the time when despair flooded back. In the flatness of light reality could no longer be ignored. To turn on the light in the bathroom always made a noise. I used to hold my breath. I used to expect the springs of the sofa to creak. To hear the dry cough of Grigor's mother. The cord of the switch clicked loudly as you pulled it. The lozenge-shaped electric bulb made a tinkling, crackling sound as it heated. But if I did not turn on the light I could not see the beetles. They were always caught unawares in the middle of small journeys across the linoleum floor. Always paralysed for a moment by the sudden brightness of the light. Then they would rush for the nearest crevice. I would sit on the edge of the bath and watch them, these small, shining, hard-carapaced creatures. I came to think of them as my only friends. I used to smile miserably at them, a twisting up of unsteady lips. I used to call softly to them under my breath, mournful endearments and childhood names, like a drunk. As well as shiny black beetles there were grey wood-lice with segmented shells and little wiry wormlike creatures with so many feet they looked like feathered fronds. They made no sound as they scuttled over the floor. Sometimes I would hold my toe out over one of them, low, so that its shadow fell across the beetle's path and it would turn instantly and run the other way. I did not do it out of malice. I did it – for companionship. When the floor was empty a curious loneliness descended on me. The more I stared at it, the more it began to resemble a deserted playground. Sometimes, if I sat for long enough, a few of the braver beetles would come back, edging out of the shadows to continue their forays. Like children returning to an empty playground. Playing alone, absorbed in their intense, private games. Unaware, innocent of danger. But where were all the others? The edges of thought grew dark, cold like stone. I think now and then I drifted in and out of sleep, periods of timelessness. For I would suddenly be aware that I was shivering or that my shoulder was aching and stiff from leaning too long in one position against the wall. And then the ritual would end as sharply as it had begun, cold and sleep would overcome me and I would creep back to bed.

They gave me another assignment. This time, I knew, I had to produce facts. This time I heard the child's name clearly.

'Iva Myslbek,' I repeated mechanically.

'That is correct,' replied Major Jezek and his voice, on the telephone, sounded very close.

From that moment on I could not bring myself to speak to the child. I never asked her another question in class. I never chose her to read aloud. When her hand shot up among all the others to give the answer to a sum, or the correct spelling of a word, I could not even point at her. Out in the playground when she danced towards me, weaving in and out of the groups of children, I would back away, stumbling, without even realising what I was doing. Yet once she moved off again I would not be able to take my eyes off her. I watched her skipping rope, or whispering in a huddle of friends. I watched, and in my head I rehearsed the words to call out to her. But I could not do it. Why could I not? One child more or less. One question more or less. It was nothing. I thought of my own schooldays. There had been questions then. We had been proud to answer them. To contribute, reciting our ridiculous bits of information in voices squeaky with sudden importance. In desperation I set the whole class to writing essays. Laboured sketches. 'My Brother.' 'My Uncle.' 'My Home.' 'The Visit.' 'May Day.' Thirty traps laid for one victim. The air in the classroom would be dense with concentration, low bursts of whispering and dropped pencils, stretches of heavy-breathing silence. I used to call them out one by one to see their work and help them forward. Asking them questions to draw out for them the details needed to complete their stories. One by one. She came, in her turn. There was no need to speak her name. When her neighbour returned from my desk she knew she had to stand up. She wrote in a guarded flat way, as though she suspected something. But when she answered my questions she was lively. Spontaneous in a disarmingly intimate manner. She would lean her elbow on my desk, prop her chin in her small cupped hand and gaze out at the grey sky beyond the tall windows. Sometimes she would even laugh softly as she recalled events. She did not look at me and I did not look at her. I kept my head bent to the careful rounded childish words on the page of her exercise book as though in shame. Sometimes I saw, from the corner of my eye, her forefinger stretch hesitantly out to touch my pen where it lay on the desk. Sometimes she would even roll it gently backwards and forwards as she talked. I can remember still her voice, the sing-song cadence of it. The low, confiding childishness. All else was a grey haze. Out of it floated the pressing insistence of Major Jezek. The watching eyes of Grigor's mother, narrowed with some new suspicion I could not pinpoint. And the mocking stare of Grigor for whom I had become no more than an inanimate possession. So my life passed, at that time, in a kind of numbness. My feet moved, as though they slid along the grooves of rails, round and round, day after day.

It was at New Year that it was decided that the school should have a special prize-giving ceremony to celebrate its tenth anniversary. We set the children to gluing paper chains and painting flags in streamers. Mrs Ostrova ordered the prize books; their titles still the same as in my schooldays. The occasion was so grand we were allowed to use a community hall nearby, our school was too small for such an event. It was the kind of hall which, all over Prague, was being lent out each night at Christmas and New Year to enterprise after enterprise for functions and dances. Each morning, in such halls, cleaners hurled empty beer bottles into crates. They pushed their brooms across rough wooden floors rolling debris before them: cigarette ends, bits of coloured paper, bottle caps. On the day of the prize-giving Mrs Ostrova appeared in a lilac wool costume and a bright pink jumper. The scent of violets that trailed after her was so strong it was almost overpowering. This was her day. The day of her school. All morning she fussed from classroom to classroom. By lunch-time she was beside herself with unaccustomed anxiety. My head ached with sleeplessness and her constant, bustling interruptions.

'Eliska, I want you to take the decorations over during the lunch break. The caretaker is supposed to be setting out chairs. Make sure that he does it properly. I can't go, dear,' she dropped her voice to a loud whisper and nodded at the locked door of the office, 'because of the books. I'll send Helena over in mid-afternoon to relieve you.'

The hall smelled of stale air and the cloying sweetness of beer spilt on floorboards. At the back of the room chairs in stacks of three were being carried in from the yard outside by an old man. He had long arms and a short body and staggered as though the weight of his burden was too much for him.

'I am one of the teachers,' I announced.

He paused by the last stack of chairs and squinted up at me from heavy-lidded eyes. His breath came in sharp grunts. Then he staggered forward, counting paces in a low growl, dropped his stack of chairs to the floor and shuffled out again.

I climbed up the shallow steps leading onto the stage. This was where the favoured pupils would mount to the obedient applause required at such occasions.

'Lenka Plachy,' I chanted under my breath. 'For information.' 'Otokar Rusek,' I bowed to the long table that had been set up on the stage, behind which Mrs Ostrova, Helena and I would sit. 'For information.'

I dropped the boxes of decorations onto the table, pulled a chair towards me and slumped down onto it. I wrapped my coat more tightly around me against the chill air and stared down the hall. There had been a dance for Grigor's office in a hall just like this before Christmas. Except that it had been bigger. The paper chains had been of red and gold paper and the fluttering strings of flags looped against the walls had been made from real material. The old man dropped another stack of chairs and I felt my eyelids closing. This happened often, my eyelids closing, during the day, when I sat down in such places as the tram, or during my off-duty lunch-break. They just closed without my even knowing it had happened. Without even feeling the transition, without being aware that I had crossed the border between one state of being and another. I was disappointed, I remember, that the dance was not held in Grigor's office itself, in the structure of girders and scaffolding. I wanted to see it. We had gone down into Prague on the tram, into the darkness and the flickering lights. And the cold had been sharp all around us. I can remember the prickling of goosebumps along my arm between the thin material of my dress and the rough sleeve of my coat. The brightness of the hall as we entered. Above the crush of people a band playing; remote, sedate, in dark suits. Between the long trestle table with clusters of wine bottles and beer bottles along one wall and the small round tables at which people sat, down the other, was a dance floor. Self-conscious couples gliding. Slow waltzes. Prim foxtrots. I had watched them, their eyes far away, looking at no one. Their faces serious with the strain of official pleasure. All those summer dresses in mid-winter. The light skirts floating, lifting slightly and falling with the movement. After each dance everyone had clapped politely. The dancers and the watchers, the men standing at the bar and the women gossiping in bunches. Everyone glancing covertly at their neighbour to see whether they are applauding. It is a particular sound, this regulation applause of ours. It is without emotion, without meaning. Hypocritical. Afraid. Even there at that dance, beneath our best clothes and our party smiles there was fear. The restrained clapping of our hands had been like the sound of dry leaves clattering against each other in a late autumn wood when a wind rises suddenly. And dies away again. I had danced, now and then. With some of Grigor's colleagues. Sweat and beer fumes and large, soft hands. Towards the end of the evening they began to give prizes to certain lucky pairs of dancers – the oldest, the youngest, the best . . . Each time the same pretty girl had come out onto the floor and presented a carnation to the woman and kissed the man on both cheeks. Everyone had clapped. And smiled. The carnations had been tied with fluttering ribbons. I had leant back against the arm of the latest of Grigor's colleagues round and round. Lights had whirled. Before us the other couples had parted. I had longed to win a carnation. In front of all these people. In front of Grigor.

From the far end of the room came a low murmuring, scarcely breaking into my dream. Something too far away to concern me. The crash of another stack of chairs. I tried to lift myself through sleep and sank back again.

'Flowers, Mrs Vaculik,' someone said, a long way off. 'Flowers.'

I thought I heard a light clapping sound, I thought I saw people turning in my direction, smiling, nodding. I thought I disengaged myself from a man's arm, felt myself move forward, smiling too, into the centre of white light to receive my prize from the dance hostess, now just a shadow beyond the circle of light. I thought I stretched out my hand. But the light was so bright I could see nothing. I blinked to focus my gaze – and saw in front of me only the drab walls of the community centre. No spotlight, no flags, no crowding of light summer dresses. At the back of the room the old man was kicking chairs into line. My mouth felt stale and dry. The hall cold. I half-turned in my chair to pull my coat back round my shoulders. It was only then that I saw the figure in dungarees sitting on the end of the table, swinging its legs and smiling at me. The muddy boots, the dungarees, the outsize woollen jersey were all unfamiliar to me. But the face . . . The face was Magdalena's! I stared at it. I think – I think I must have frowned at it, waiting for it, too, to dissolve and slide away. But it did not. It only smiled more and slid a long brown cardboard box onto my lap.

'For you,' she said and the voice was unmistakable.

'Magdalena,' I whispered. 'Magdalena!'

The box, without support, began to slip towards the floor. Magdalena moved to catch it in the same moment that I did, so that our hands came round it together. The image of the envelope with the small wooden apple inside floating away down the river flashed into my mind. It must have found her! In extremes of hopelessness or despair, all there is left is magic. Or the intervention of heaven.

'What are you doing here?'

She laughed, fishing for something in the breast pocket of her dungarees.

'Delivering flowers!' She unfolded a sheet of flimsy yellow paper and smoothed it out across the top of the box. 'You are the Suslova primary school, aren't you?'

'Well, yes.' I shrugged my shoulders.

'Then sign here.' She produced a blunt pencil from another pocket. 'And here.'

'They are for us?'

'That's what it says, on the delivery note – I'm just the driver.'

'They are flowers?'

'Yes. *Flowers.* As ordered. Didn't they tell you?'

She lifted the lid of the box. Inside lay single stems of yellow and orange carnations, each tied with a bow of red, white and blue striped ribbon. The colours of our national flag. They have no scent, these official carnations of ours. But as the lid was lifted there was a burst of freshness, a clouded memory of other flowers.

'You really work . . .' I peered at the docket '. . . for the Pretin Nursery?'

Magdalena grinned.

'Yes, really.'

'But – what about the archaeologist?'

'Oh,' she pursed her lips and then smiled ruefully. 'The usual story, Liski.' She dropped into the chair beside me, crossing her legs and folding her arms behind her head, as though she had lived in that hall all her life. 'There was a wife, who found out. Perhaps we had become careless. Perhaps a mutual friend had dropped a word in her ear. She came up to the dig. Unexpectedly. And I was sent packing. Back to Ludovice. But all doors, it seemed, were now closed to me. Regretfully. You know how it is. The money began to run out. So I joined the fruit-picking gangs, taken out by lorry at dawn to different orchards just beyond the town. One week it was greengages, the next week it was plums, the week after it was something else. In one of the plum orchards, I became friendly with a girl who knew someone who had an uncle who had a half-brother who ran a carnation nursery near Prague. The usual route. So here I am.'

'You are a gardener? You grow carnations?'

She laughed.

'No, no. I was no good. I was the wrong material for such work. Too impatient. You need to be calm for flowers. Meditative. Absorbed. We have such people. One is an historian, one a philosopher. My recklessness was obvious. So I was made the driver of the delivery van. And you? Is all well?'

'Yes.' For some reason it came out as a whisper. I tried to smile, but my face twisted up, tears prickled in my eyes. I passed a hand roughly across my forehead. 'I – I am just tired at the moment.'

She nodded gently, watching me with a grave expression.

'Come and see us out at Pretin, Liski.'

I did not think of the pleasure of such an outing, I thought only of the difficulty. How could I get there? I shrugged my shoulders.

'I will take you. Come on Saturday, I have to drive into Prague with some deliveries in the morning.'

'I . . . I don't think . . .'

'You are not free on Saturday? You teach?'

'No, but I . . .'

'You have another engagement?'

'No, it's not that.' I twisted my fingers round one of the buttons of my coat and stared down the hall at the rows of chairs. 'It's just – difficult, Magdalena.'

'Difficult?'

I could have told her everything, then. In my mind I leant forward to it. But something shut off the breath that I was about to take. The voice that spoke quickly, breaking in on my intention, was like someone else's voice. And the laugh that I tried to give sounded more like an exhalation of pain.

'No, nothing really. But – this Saturday will be busy.' I lied. 'I will not have time to go out into the country with you. Let's just meet and talk; catch up on news.'

'All right. We can go another day to Pretin. Where shall we meet? My deliveries are all in central Prague – the Old Town and just over the bridge. What place do you know?'

'The main library?' It was my landmark, my safe haven. 'There are some things I could look up.' It was not true. But in my head I was already rehearsing my speech for Grigor and his mother.

'The library!'

'Inside,' I added quickly. 'I will be there before.' I tried to make my voice sound as firm and light as hers. 'Reading.'

'OK, the library, Liski. Ten-thirty.'

All the rest of that week I thought about the meeting to come. The interminable waking hours of the night became imaginary conversations with Magdalena in which I confessed all. But each morning the shutters of pride, of fear, fell again, locking me inside. I was surprised at the disinterest with which Grigor and his mother received my announcement that I had to spend Saturday morning in the Central Library researching a project for school. I was surprised that, without a hitch, Magdalena slid into the chair opposite me in the reading room at exactly half-past ten.

'Come on, Liski,' she whispered. 'It's a glorious day, let's go for a walk.'

I followed her obediently out into the winter sunshine. I let her link her arm in mine and march me off around Old Town Square. She craned her neck upwards as we walked.

'Look at the paintings on the fronts of these houses!'

she exclaimed. And I tilted my head back to look where she pointed.

'See down that alley!' She dragged me to a halt. 'Through the arch, those pretty houses – and the tiny courts that lead off it.'

And I peered, nodding, after her, in silence, into the sunlit lane. We walked across Charles Bridge. The stepped roofs climbed away in front of us up to the crag of the castle. The bare branches of the trees along the river were etched like silverpoint against the water. The sky was blue and limitless.

'Isn't it wonderful!' Magdalena squeezed my arm. 'Who would ever have thought, all those years ago, that here we'd be, in Prague. Together.'

And I smiled woodenly at her. We climbed up through the old quarter by little winding lanes that I had never found on my walks. Up flights of wide stone steps laid into the rock of the hillside. In front of a small flower shop, Magdalena paused.

'If ever you need to get in touch with me urgently, Liski, you can leave a message for me there.'

'Urgently?' I repeated.

'You never know,' she said, turning under an arch into another narrow street. 'Remember it, Liski, just in case.'

We came out at the top of the hill in a quiet spacious street somewhere beyond the castle. There was a small cluster of shops, a tram terminus, the tops of trees in a park over a high wall, and a café. She led me in. We sat at the back, away from the window. Away from the door to the kitchen. Away from the cash desk. Sitting in silence, catching our breath after the long climb. A young girl brought us coffee and went away again. Magdalena unwrapped her sugar lumps and dipped the corner of one into her cup, watching the grains of sugar float off and dissolve.

'Well, Liski?' she said, without looking up.

I had it in mind to dissemble. If she asked. Right up to

the last moment. To talk of Grigor's industry, and my school class. To make a joke about the intransigence of Grigor's mother. Right up to the moment she dipped her sugar lump into the coffee. It must have been the sight of the grains of sugar dissolving and vanishing one by one. It must have been the way the cube suddenly lost cohesiveness and, crumbling between her fingers, fell, and was gone. The words came hesitantly at first. Uncertainly. Circling round and round. Things I had never defined to myself before, let alone spoken of to anyone else. They burst out in short rushes and fell again into silence. They seemed, when I spoke of them, intangible, vague. I wondered whether Magdalena would understand what I meant. The weariness, the emptiness. The lifelessness in which everyone around me moved, like mechanical figures, set on a track and kept there by praise and threat, and beyond which there seemed to be – nothing. And then, once started, I could not stop. Magdalena sat quietly, her elbows on the table, her chin resting in her hands. I laced my fingers together, twisting them knuckle against knuckle. I spoke so low she had to lean across the table sometimes, to hear me. Finally there seemed to be no more to say. I looked up.

'I don't know what to do. There is – nothing – I can do. There is – nothing else.'

Magdalena placed one of her hands over my twisting fingers and everything felt suddenly very still.

'Yes' she said, 'there is.'

I remember the rage that seized me. The fury at having betrayed myself. The fear of having spoken at all. I tried to take it all back. I pulled my hands away roughly. I laughed, a short harsh bark.

'This is just the complaining of all new wives. If Grigor's mother was not always there, Grigor would be – different. If there was not a shortage of housing, we could be by ourselves, we would have started a new life, our own life.' I picked at a fragment of jagged nail on one of my fingers. 'No one knows how a marriage will be beforehand; sometimes it is deliberately hidden from you. And then, afterwards, when you see, when you learn, it is too late. If someone from outside were to look they might see nothing – just a marriage, like any other marriage. I am not cold, I am not hungry, I am not entirely black and blue with bruising.'

'You are all those things,' said Magdalena in a low voice. 'In your eyes and in your face there are the signs of such unhappiness, such strain.'

'That is because I do not sleep well! I hardly sleep at all.' I jerked my chin towards the street outside. 'My face is no different to any other face out there. They are all pale, they are all drawn. No one looks anyone else in the eye. No one smiles. It is the way of life, it is the way we are.'

'Do you think everyone has been this way for ever?'

I would not answer her. I could not see what she meant. I shook my head and snorted in disgust, as though to rid myself of her.

'And Major Jezek?'

My eyes suddenly filled with tears. They welled up and everything swam and coalesced.

'Everyone has their Major Jezek,' I hissed. 'Even you!'

'Hush, Liski,' she nodded towards the kitchen door, 'they will hear you.'

At the back of the room, next to the swing door, the young girl had been replaced by an older woman. Short and stout, she stared out across the room, blank-faced, stony-eyed, as is the way with listeners. I half-rose in panic, in a stumbling against chairs that made the woman turn, sharply. Magdalena caught at my hands.

'Sit down, sit down, Liski. Calm yourself. What can she hear from where she is? What interest, anyway, has she in us?'

But I was not reassured. I moved my chair silently a

fraction to the right so that she could see less of my face. I rounded my shoulders and leant my elbows on the table to enclose and muffle any words I might speak. I brushed away the traces of tears on my cheeks with the tips of my fingers.

'You are right, Liski.' Magdalena had already begun speaking again in a low clear voice. 'We all have our Major Jezeks. Out at Pretin, there is one too, for the Nursery. We get phone calls from him, like you. Like everyone. Visits, sometimes. But – out at Pretin – we are not isolated in the same way that you are, in your school. Your Major Jezek rings and he knows what to say to make you afraid. He knows of Mrs Ostrova and Helena, and the ambition of your husband. He knows that you can speak of his phone calls to no one. He knows what to threaten you with. It is easy to bully someone who has been isolated. You are a perfect target.' She smiled. 'You are like something from a textbook, for him. In Pretin,' she swept her hand across the table, 'things are very different. When our Major Jezek rings, only one of us ever answers him. That one was unanimously elected by all the rest of us to be the contact of our Major Jezek. He was an actor once.' Her voice was very low, but the tone was light, conversational, gossipy almost. I sat rigid in my chair, staring at the small metal salt and pepper shakers that stood on the table, increasingly convinced that they concealed microphones. My neck ached with the effort of keeping my head turned away from the waitress. On Monday, I was sure, Major Jezek would know all about this meeting. 'But he was banned from working. First from the state theatres, then from the fringe theatres.' Under my chin my fingers were locked tight. I had been stupid to tell Magdalena anything. What could she do? What could anyone do; it was just life. 'So he came to us. He is very good, very deft. He talks constantly to the plants. Monologues, whole plays. One day he is the Jew of Malta, the next Soldier Sveik.

His carnation cuttings grow faster than anyone else's. But when his Major Jezek rings – that is his finest hour. He beckons to us to come and listen. To draw out the best performance, you know, the audience must be live.' She grinned. 'We have to stuff rags in our mouths, Liski. Some of us even . . .'

I pushed my chair back hard and stood up.

'I must go.' I tried to speak loudly and clearly to drown out Magdalena. But my words, reverberating in my head, sounded slurred and my fingers shook as I searched for money in my purse.

Outside in the street, Magdalena put her arm round my rigid shoulders.

'I didn't tell you that story to make you afraid, Liski, but to give you comfort. To – to lessen the fear.' She hugged me. 'I don't like to see you unhappy. I want you to come out next Saturday and see Pretin.'

I shook my head violently. She gave my shoulders a little shake.

'How can you judge till you see? I ask you because I think you would like it. Please, for me. It is where I live. Where I work. I want you to see it.'

It snowed heavily the day before I was due to drive out with Magdalena to Pretin. At first I was glad. All day in school, looking out at the grey flakes falling past the window, I felt only relief, rising like liquid in a narrow jar. But that night, lying beside Grigor, staring into the not-quite-darkness, the relief drained away again, leaving me empty. Hollowed. Alone. By morning the snow had already turned to slush in the city. Grigor fretted irritably around the flat till lunch-time, expecting his favourite team's football match to be cancelled. His mother spoke in hushed tones as though a national disaster had occurred. As I gathered up my file of papers after lunch, they scarcely noticed. And when I unhooked my coat from its peg and slid open the latch of the door, they did not even turn their heads from the radio set, which was giving out announcements of sports news for the afternoon.

What was the deception of such people, I wondered as I sat in the library? Did it even count? If Magdalena turned up, I would go with her; if she did not, it would be a sign from fate and I would not contact her again. The time appointed for our meeting came. And went. I could not bend my head to the books and papers I had spread out in front of me. My eyes were fixed on the main door. Above it the ornate hand of the clock slowly jerked its way from minute to minute. And with it an unaccountable, widening sense of loss. When Magdalena's face at last appeared in the doorway, I was already on my feet, stuffing papers into my bag.

The suburbs of Prague through which we drove were grey with the slush of melted snow. It lay about in dwindling heaps. Clung precariously in small sooty patches to roofs. Only when we got out into the country did it lie white and calm. It covered the low sloping hills and stretched along the hollows of furrows between ridges of black earth. We turned off into a side road and the country became flatter. As we emerged from a break of thin trees, across the fields to our right I saw, very low to the ground at first, the huddle of greenhouses. At that distance they were difficult to see against the snow. Then the sun came out from behind a cloud and they glittered and dazzled on their flat field like a heap of broken glass. Behind them and beyond them ran the dark jagged line of a tumbled-down wall. In parts it was still high. In other sections breached, to show a wilderness of undergrowth and the bare arms of trees. On either side the white fields ran level and empty rising again, where they met the horizon, into low hills.

'There is nothing at Pretin,' said Magdalena. 'Except us.'

She slowed the van almost to walking pace, shifting in her seat, peering out of the mud-splashed window. I looked too. At the lines of greenhouses, the cluster of wooden outbuildings, wondering what it was she searched for. Just ahead of us was a long track leading down to the Nursery, a dark muddy streak, like a line drawn unevenly with a finger through the snow. In the desolation of the winter landscape nothing moved. In the silence I could hear the light crunching sound that our wheels made as they rolled slowly forward. I wished I was not there. I wished I had not come. It was . . . it was unwise. I had known that, all along. Inside the van it did not smell of flowers, there was a heavy, milky odour.

'What – what are you looking for?' I demanded.

'Oh, nothing really.' She began to accelerate again and we turned onto the bumpy track. 'Sometimes we get unexpected visitors. We know them and they know all of us and it always follows the same routine. But they would have wanted to know about you. They would have asked you questions. Probably it would have been better, if they had been here, just to drive on.'

We drew up outside a wooden shack stuck onto the end of one of the greenhouses. On its door the word 'office' had been painted in red letters. Narrow cinder tracks led away through muddy snow between rows of glasshouses. We were hemmed in on these narrow tracks. I turned sharply to glance back up to the road. Across the whiteness I expected to see a sinister black car glide from the break of trees.

'Magdalena . . .'

'Here we are! This is the office of the Nursery. Most of these glasshouses are new. Only this one, here, which was the first, was built from the glass of the original hothouses. Most of them were smashed when the big country house just over there beyond the wall was destroyed, in the way such places were, after the war.'

'Magdalena!'

She had already unlatched the van door and bounded out.

'I won't be long. I'll just get clearance for you to come into the greenhouses.'

'I don't want to!'

'What?' Magdalena leant back into the van.

'I don't want to,' I hissed. 'What is this place? What goes on here that – that you are visited?'

'Ohh, "visited".' Magdalena shrugged her shoulders in scorn. '"Visited"! Everyone is "visited"; you in your little school, us. What do you think your staff meetings are? Staff meetings? This place grows carnations, Eliska. It grows the best carnations in the area. We are so good, so reliable, that we have become the main supplier of carnations for government contract in Prague. At every state function in the city and surrounding district the carnations will be ours.' She dropped down into the driver's seat again. 'This place was started ten years ago by a marine biologist who was no longer permitted to work in his profession. He had a half-brother who happened to be Superintendent of Parks in Ludovice. A quiet, careful man, more interested in planting trees than challenging the system. When his half-brother was condemned to a life of manual labour, he came to his rescue. They both had known of Pretin since they were boys – there was some aunt, some grandmother on one side or the other in this area with whom they spent holidays together. They came back, to see what could be salvaged. Everything was done in the name of the Superintendent of Parks, which of course was different to that of the marine biologist. The marine biologist, on paper, was hired merely as a gardener. Gardening is regarded by the authorities as manual labour, Pretin was a collection of dilapidated outhouses miles from Prague: they must have congratulated themselves. Under the tutelage of his brother, he learned quickly. Pretin grew. Every six months another greenhouse. More staff. Carefully selected staff. Manual labourers. From the disenfranchised intellectual stratum of our wretched nation.'

Magdalena's voice was stifled to a whisper. She pounded her fist against the steering wheel and shook her head angrily.

'Take me back!' I demanded.

She shook her head more gently.

'You have nothing to fear here, Liski,' she whispered. 'But if you do not want to go inside the greenhouses you do not have to. Come, we will walk in the abandoned gardens beyond the broken wall and I will show you the remains of the big house. And then we will go back to Prague.'

We walked for some time in silence. Through a thick carpet of ivy that twisted up into the trunks of trees. Among the straggling bushes of holly and yew were other trees, their branches gnarled and spread into unfamiliar, exotic shapes. Along the thin black branches of one, small pink buds were already bursting. Magdalena stopped and put out a finger to touch the delicate petals of an unfurling flower.

'What are you going to do, Eliska?'

I felt all at once like a sulky child. I scuffed one foot in the ivy, snapping small twigs hidden beneath the leaves. I shrugged my shoulders.

'Mmmm?'

I turned on her. 'What can I do? What is there to do?' I was defensive, angry that I had told her anything at all. 'This is how my life is. So are many lives. And many more lives are worse.'

'But your life, Eliska? *Your life?* You accept to live like this? For year after year after year? This is all your life will ever be. You are prepared for that?'

'You think that I should leave Grigor? Where would I go? Home? What is there? You think I should tell Major Jezek to stuff himself? Do you forget how things work in this country? I would be without a job.'

'Yes, Eliska.' She lifted her head so that she looked straight at me. Looked in that particular way Magdalena had, that regard open as clear water. 'Yes, that is what I think. What is the point of living as you do? For some people the point might be that they could still cling to some position within the structure of society. That they were, though not happy, not too unhappy. But you, this is not so for you. It has long passed that stage. You do not live any more as a human being, Eliska. You exist only. You have been deprived of the bare essentials of life: of dignity and free will. Of being true to yourself.'

I remember my arms bludgeoning the air. My feet stumbling in the ivy. I heard my own hiss of rage. And saw the delicate branches shaking violently, pink petals falling in a sudden shower around me. Like snow. But Magdalena had already grabbed hold of my coat sleeve.

'Listen to me, Eliska! No one else will say this to you. No one else cares enough about you to risk speaking of such things. You have nothing, Eliska, nothing. And to this nothing you cling. You do not just endure it, you encourage it. No, listen!' Her fingers dug tightly into my coat sleeve as I tried to pull away from her. 'Just by being there, by staying there, you encourage it because you allow it to go on happening. Your presence is necessary for it to happen. What would happen if you left Grigor? The bullying would stop, you would have removed yourself from it. Grigor makes you feel as nothing but I can assure you, Liski, you would not remain alone for long. And what would happen if you told Major Jezek there would be no more information? What if everyone told their Major Jezeks to get lost. Everyone, Liski, everyone. Everyone in their hearts hates the way that we live. What would these Major Jezeks do, all of them, without informers, without information? They would be useless, they would just dwindle, disappear. If their prey refused to be preyed on . . .'

I snatched my arm away. And stared in front of me into the heart of the wintry copse, away from her glittering eyes. What if we had been followed? 'If everyone told their Major Jezeks . . .' I did not hear what she went on saying, I heard only that which she had said, ringing out among the bare trees. Their branches lifted in the cold wind, the twigs swaying and dipping as though they were dancing. The lifted arms of people, dancing. 'If everyone . . .' But no one, not one person . . . The branches blurred as though suddenly very distant. She was not just mad, she was vicious and cruel.

'No one!' I whispered through clenched teeth, glaring at her, aware all at once of the coldness of tears trickling past my nose. 'No one will *ever* . . .' I whispered vehemently, stamping my foot in the ivy.

She gripped my shoulders, her face glowing.

'One person, Liski, one person. And then another and another. That is all that is necessary for it to begin, and for it to go on.'

We must have begun walking again. I remember pushing branches out of my face, the wet swishing sound of my shoes moving slowly through the under-growth to the rhythm of her words. Of coming out at last on the edge of a vast overgrown lawn.

'It has to do with the self, Liski, with the individual.'

Before us the broken shell of a country mansion. Wide steps led down from a line of gaping doorways and windows onto the frozen grass. Steps littered with rub-ble half-buried under the thin covering of snow that lay undisturbed over everything. The jagged arms of smashed balustrades and toppled urns. Our footprints were black in the whiteness of the lawn.

'It is not political, primarily, Liski. It – it is moral. It is essential. It is the self which must be got right, which must be allowed to be true to itself. Without this it is not possible to function as a human being. And you *do not* function, Eliska. You are not functioning.'

I stared ahead. Silent. Tight-lipped. On one of the lower pediments of the balustrade there seemed to be a figure, seated. All in black, black as the gaping window-less stones. Head bent.

'We do not talk – we do not think – of how we breathe, or how we walk when we are able to do so freely. But when we suddenly find ourselves without air, when we find ourselves crippled, when we have to think of how it was that we put one foot in front of another with such ease, then . . .'

I did not want her to go on. The figure in black had seen us. It lifted its head, stretched stiffly and got to its feet. It was a young man in a long black overcoat, such as students sometimes wear.

'So!' I said, turning on Magdalena, 'the solution is for me to leave Grigor, leave the school and wander home-less in the streets! Major Jezek will make sure I never get another posting.'

'No,' said Magdalena, 'you will come to us. It will seem to the authorities like a labouring job and so there would be no obstacles put in your way. You will appear to have nothing – and you will have nothing, nothing that is precisely your own – but in that way you will have eluded the grasp of the state because it will have nothing to bribe you with, nothing to deprive you of if you do not obey it. But I can assure you, you will for the first time begin to feel happy, to feel . . .'

'Who is this?' I snapped, jerking my chin at the young man. He had slipped a small book into the pocket of his coat and was taking a few tentative steps across the snow to meet us.

'Oh, that's Milos. Hey, Milos!' she shouted.

He grinned and stopped as we approached, lifting his feet up and placing them down again in the snow as though looking for drier ground with the same delicacy as a cat.

'Reading even in the snow, huh!' She turned to me. 'Milos is a walking library, in each pocket there is always a book. What is it today?'

Under the lazy, half-lowered lids his eyes were dark, watchful, missing nothing. He stared at me as if he had already heard my story but was curious to read it for himself in my face. The collar of his coat was worn thin, the stitching of the pockets frayed. He slid a small red book half out of his left pocket.

'This? It is another of the novels of Charles Dickens.'

I could see the soft curl of the worn leather binding, the close head of thin pages. He let it drop back in again, watching me still. 'It is a story – full of hope. Full of optimism. They are all so, the novels of Charles Dickens, even the bleakest ones. Full of hope for a better future. And you,' he held out his hand, 'you are Eliska.'

A slim, strong hand, the fingers very long, very soft. Not the hand of a gardener at all. But I would not smile at him. He grinned over my head at Magdalena as though I was a truculent child.

'She has come to join us?' And then, sensing my anger, the dark eyes fixed themselves on me with the same dancing light. 'It has interest for you – market gardening?'

'It has interest for *you*?'

'You know that there is more involved than that.'

'I don't want to know!'

'No, freedom is not for the weak.' The eyes became hard, glittering points of light. 'You want to go on pretending to believe that the earth is flat, with all the others, don't you. That is the safest thing to do, you think. Anything else is dangerous. Mad. Even though you are all terrified of falling off. And the darkness beyond that edge is commonly thought of as an annihilating nothingness. Yes? Instead of an infinity of possibility. And yet you refuse to believe that things could be otherwise, even when it is demonstrated to you that another system exists. How can that fear be overcome that paralyses our whole society? By starting to believe that the earth is a sphere, by living as though you believed it. By walking towards that supposedly terrifying edge and seeing for yourself how it recedes always before your footsteps. And infinity? What is this ungraspable thing, Eliska? It is the patience of God. Yes, yes . . .' for I had looked angrily away, 'we know only of the patience of men.' He was almost shouting now. 'The patience of men. That runs out . . .'

'Milos . . . !' burst in Magdalena.

But I did not hear any more. I did not run. All I could think of was not running over the endless white expanse of snow whose icy surface crackled into powdery softness beneath my feet. A grey cloud rose swiftly in my mind blotting out everything. A blanket of fear through which first the snapping branches of trees and then the dark broken shadow of the garden wall rose and fell away before me like things that were not real. On the muddy track that led down between the greenhouses Magdalena caught up with me.

'Liski, stop. Wait.'

Through the misted glass panels of the nearest house I caught sight of dim figures moving. These were the professors of logic, the teachers of history, the banned actors and the writers whom the state would not publish, who were allowed to think their thoughts, write their papers, discuss their ideas behind the benevolent security of these glass walls. On the other side of the path to the abandoned mansion there was a line of creosoted wooden huts. That was where the staff lived, Magdalena had said. I had seen a door of one hut open, a cat shooed out into the snow. I had heard the bubbling laughter of a small child and the sound of unfamiliar violin music before the door was slammed shut. I looked hastily away.

We said nothing all the way back to Prague. As we approached the outskirts of the city Magdalena slid a small piece of card along the dashboard to me. It was a badly printed advertisement for the flower shop near the castle, the ink heavy and smudged.

'I'm sorry about Milos, Liski. But do not forget us. Do not forget what I said. Come to us when you are ready.'

I did not pick up the card. She drew up at a bus stop to let me out.

'Please take it, Liski,' she said gently. 'Write the phone number down somewhere and throw away the card if you like, but take it now. And when you want to get in touch you can leave a message for me with the shop.'

So I went back. Because that was what I knew. Back to the small startled beetles that ran fearfully about on the bathroom floor.

I SWIFTLY BECAME A compulsive reader of Dickens. I consumed one book after another, page after closely printed page. I could be torn away from them only to work and sleep. Outside, August ground its way through the city. Days of endless heat. Not even the common remained untouched. It was bleached to a grey-greenness of shrivelled grass and motionless trees. People sat out on benches or on the ground as if stupefied. Nobody even seemed to have the inclination to write letters any more; they were all postcards. I dawdled on my round, reading them, but they rarely had anything interesting to say. Inside, our places had become reversed. Eliska would sit at the open window and I would stretch out on the sofa. I don't remember that she asked permission to use my chair, I just came home one day and found her there, slumped in it, wearing nothing but her nylon slip, the material pulled up almost to her thighs. Strands of damp hair were stuck to her forehead and as she dozed, her mouth, wet at the corners, would loll open. As the afternoon progressed the bubbles in the glass of lemonade beside her on the window sill would rise ever more slowly, scarcely able to summon the energy to burst against its surface, and small stains of sweat would spread out from under her arms.

'Why don't you go and sunbathe properly in a dress out on the common, instead of lying there like that where all the neighbours can look across and see you?' I would snarl at her.

'Out on the common,' she would reply in an irritating drawl, not altering her position in the slightest, not even opening her eyes or turning her head in my direction, 'there are only drunks and tramps lying about on the grass. Do you want me to go and be one of them? Is that what you want?' I didn't answer her when she talked like that. I didn't care where she went, at such times. I thought instead of Marietta; Marietta would never behave in such a way. And I would close my eyes and see again her room. That was an English room, a real English room; next to it this place was unbearable. I had been betrayed by my own eagerness to have this room – if I had seen Marietta's room first. If I had seen Marietta first, I thought, looking across at Eliska with disgust. If my mother had not died, I might have been sent to school in England – she was always talking about it – I might have had friends with sisters like Marietta, with whom I could have stayed in my school holidays. People like the people in Marietta's photographs clustered on her bookshelf in pretty silver frames and curling pieces of faded card. Marietta and her sisters and cousins and aunts, elderly ladies still beautiful and little girls with long hair and grave eyes and perfectly shaped mouths so challenging you had to look away. This was the Englishness I longed for. Between them all there was a sense of continuity and endurance: a belonging that I craved. I could imagine other groups of photographs, Marietta among them, crowding together on the tops of polished tables in vast shadowy rooms staring between half-closed shutters out over deserted parkland. From the lumber rooms of such houses, I was sure, had come her furniture. And it would be back to those houses that eventually Marietta would lead me.

I woke to rain the day of my next meeting with Marietta. When I stumbled into the living room to dress in the early morning there it was, falling against the window pane in tiny, needle-sharp points. I stared at it stupidly as if it was something I was unable to comprehend. I went and made some coffee and when I came back it was still there. It's very light, I said to myself staring out at the rain-distorted street, it'll be over soon. When I arrived at the House, Sid was standing in the hallway looking out.

'Sudden snap,' he observed rubbing his hands together cheerfully. 'Quite a turnaround. Won't last of course.'

It was cold crossing the common. Mr Finch had a knitted cardigan on under his postman's jacket. Wise Mr Finch, free of vanity. I had deliberately chosen a short-sleeved shirt and now I shivered. Light grey clouds were banked over the trees at the far end of the common. Beside the path starlings ran about looking bad-tempered, their feathers blown up into ruffles by little gusting winds. As I entered my streets the rain stopped. The sky will clear soon, I told myself, but it did not. By the time I had finished my second round I was so cold all I could think of was to go home. But it was not possible for me to go home, nor could I go to Marietta's, it was far too early. I hung around for a bit in the Postmen's House.

'Seen Jack?' I asked Vince, who worked on Jack's other side.

'Went down the Nag for a quick one.'

When I opened the door of The Running Nag a warm fug of cigarette smoke and human bodies wrapped itself around me and drew me in. Jack was standing half-way down the bar with Les. He grinned when he saw me and made room for me to join them.

'Well timed, old son, Les is just buying. What's it going to be?'

We stayed at the bar until they threw us out at closing time, us and the middle-aged woman with dyed red hair and chipped red nails, and the retired fireman and his dog. We all stood on the pavement blinking in the light. The dog led the old man unsteadily over the road to peer in at the doors of the fire station, and the woman shuffled off down the street talking to herself. We went next door for egg and chips. I scarcely noticed the rancid smell of frying lard, or the blue haze of smoke that stung my eyes till they watered. I kept peering at my watch wondering why it was that the hands moved so slowly. There was time to eat egg and sausage and chips and a cup of tea. And then another cup of tea. I was surprised how thirsty I was.

'Not going home today, Jan?' asked Les.

I just smiled and squinted through the letters of the menu painted on the café window, at the dusty street which seemed to have been reduced to a blur of grey. No I wasn't going home, not today.

I didn't like having to stand outside Marietta's block on the path and shout my name into the intercom. I didn't like climbing the public stairs. I felt myself exposed, under scrutiny. In my imagination my name crackled out through loudspeakers into fifty hallways alerting every resident to my presence. They watched, unseen, as I climbed the stairs; they listened high up out of sight on other landings, counting my steps to discover which flat it was I visited. Marietta's door was open when I reached it. She was not there but I could hear her voice in another room talking on the telephone. I closed the door behind me loudly and waited in the hall. 'I must *go*,' she kept saying, and giggling. I stared out into the tiled well of the building trying to disentangle the plots of *Little Dorrit* and *Edwin Drood* and the first chapters of *The Old Curiosity Shop* ready for our discussion. But all was not right and I could not keep my mind on them. There was in the flat a strange unsettling undercurrent which had not been there on my last visit. Things did not seem to be happening according to plan – the plan that I had constructed in my imagination. This was to be a serious moment, and she was giggling. The receiver crashed onto the telephone rest.

'Jan, where are you?'

I hesitated in the doorway and she came across the room to meet me.

'Sorry. They wouldn't get off the phone.'

She was wearing a short flowered skirt that looked as if it was one of her big sister's cast-offs and a black jersey in some silky material.

'How are you?' I said; I couldn't ask for her essay straight away. But I looked for it. I looked beyond her to the table where it might have been. The table had been cleared of all its papers and cups and books. There was just a tumbler with red carnations in it, an opened bottle of wine, a glass and a plate of biscuits. As we came close she held out her cheek in an exaggerated way to be kissed and then moved swiftly away to lean against the mantelpiece.

I went on standing in the middle of the room, my arm on the back of a chair for support, my eyes darting from the bookcase to the window ledge, over the sets of chairs and back to the mantelpiece where Marietta leant, chewing the end of a lock of hair that had fallen over her face. Perhaps there were no papers because she had it all in her head. Marietta smiled through the hair. Clearly, to get the information I would have to humour her. But when I moved towards her she skipped away and when I asked her how things had gone she just laughed.

'Hectic,' she said. 'Have some wine. Somebody brought me this the other day; it's quite nice.'

I thought of the egg and the sausage and the tea and the beer and put out my hand to stop her, but she misinterpreted the gesture and before I could speak had thrust a glass into it. She picked up another glass that I had not noticed and clinked it clumsily against mine so that some of the wine spilled over my hand.

'Marietta,' I said slowly. 'Where is your essay?'

The fumes of the wine made my head suddenly heavy, an incipient heaviness, that I found myself on the verge of falling into. I pushed it away but it was like pushing back a snowdrift.

'Have you finished it?'

'Oh that,' she said squirming against the table. 'I just haven't had time. Anyway, I'm not sure I want to go on with that course. It's – it's too . . .'

'You mean you haven't done any of the essay?' I seized her shoulders. 'Nothing?'

She smiled at me from very close to. There was no alarm in her face, no surprise; just the provoking smile of a little girl who has deliberately misbehaved.

I don't remember who it was who kissed whom first. I remember the hard edge of the table and a wine glass being knocked over and doors opening and the brightness of light in another room quickly being turned to dark by heavy curtains. I remember struggling with the zip of her skirt and then the sudden scent of skin and hair like a hayfield opening up before me. Sun and flowers and skin sliding against skin. Fragments of words, like the narcotic drone of bees approaching and receding, lost in the depths of kisses.

I woke to darkness, floating for a moment drowsy-limbed and then, as my eyes blinked, a shadow fell across my face, the scent of an unfamiliar body, unfamiliar sheets; I struggled against a kiss that clamped itself suddenly to my mouth.

'Whattime?' I gasped.

Marietta smiled up at me.

'Five o'clock,' she said soothingly and lifted an arm to

pull me back to her. I let her do it. It was late, but not as late as I had feared.

'Darling,' I murmured. 'I have to go.' I brushed the hair back from her face and kissed her forehead. She twined her legs round me. I shook my head and smiled. 'No, no,' I whispered. 'Very soon, but not now.'

'Tomorrow?'

'Zitka,' I replied and slid out of bed.

She caught me round the waist.

'When's that?'

I unclasped her hands and kissed them. 'Tomorrow,' I whispered into her palms in mock surprise that she had not understood. I curled her fingers quickly over the words, released her hands and laid them crosswise over her breasts.

Out in the hall she clung to me.

'Take care, Jan. Don't . . .' She stopped and bit her lip. I placed my forefinger against her mouth.

'Shhh,' I said.

I was not quite sure what to do about Marietta's misconception of me as a revolutionary, but I sensed that it was central to her passion for me. If I disabused her of the one, I would seriously impair the other. I could see that she hugged the idea of being my mistress to her with a romanticised pride; it stretched her, long-limbed and sensuous against the sheets. It gave her somewhat sallow skin a glow and brought a temporary fullness to her drooping breasts and hollow stomach. She saw herself as an object of adoration, not just my adoration but that of those whom she imagined venerated me as a freedom fighter. She would abandon herself to me with fervour, fastening her mouth on mine and twining her legs and arms about me in a passionate grip. I never knew whether this was just the jagged release of her own desire, or whether it was the way she thought she ought to behave in her imagined role. I thought of the shy glances and hurried rushes of speech of our first meetings, and the dark eyes veiled by hair. Perhaps it had all been intended to be provocative. Perhaps she had been hiding to tease me into seeking her.

At first she wanted to do nothing else but go to bed. Sometimes I even arrived to find her flat door left ajar and Marietta already naked against the pillows, waiting for me. Each time I left she made a token fuss at being so quickly abandoned and once she even cried, but before I had time to think up an excuse to console her she had dried her tears.

'I know you have to go, Jan,' she would say, shutting her eyes and shaking her head. 'I know it's necessary.'

At other times, as she lay and caressed my exhausted body, asking me about my childhood and my life as a student in Prague, she would inevitably turn the conversation to politics and from there slide in a question about my work. I would notice a glitter come into her eyes and a dew of moisture haze her forehead that at first I took to be the consequences of our love-making. She would press and I would evade, but as she saw the agitation in my face increase she would be overcome with remorse at her probing and suddenly drag me to her, stopping my mouth before it could confess its secrets with tiny biting kisses. For the moment it was its own solution: if I really was pledged to a resistance cell then I could not reveal anything to an outsider and my steadfastness was a source of pride to her. But clearly she longed for the day when I would take her into my trust, perhaps even recruit her, and she could be acknowledged as consort in the struggle for freedom.

I used to worry now and then about this day, sitting in Oudenard Road in the evenings gazing out over the rooftops. That day, or the one when she discovered the existence of Eliska. But in the meantime there were more pressing problems.

'We'll have to meet in the evenings for a while, Jan.'

She announced one afternoon. 'I'm working for a couple of weeks.'

My mind went blank and my stomach felt suddenly cold, like the onset of cramp.

'We can't,' I said and stopped. 'I mean – for the moment, we can't.' I stroked her hair. 'It's going to be difficult for a time.' I gazed mournfully at her. And saw it all fall away – Marietta, our afternoons in bed, the shadowy mansions towards which this would all have led, I saw it crumble away like dust under my words.

'I have to work, Jan.'

'I know, I know.'

I held her close to me, holding her angular body tightly against mine to feel the impress of every limb as if I was committing them to memory. I laid my cheek on her head and burrowed my nose into her hair; it had a faint scent of old roses, damask petals drying in a silver bowl. It reminded me of my mother though my mother's scent had been quite different. I remembered the bottle of perfume with the gold top which had stood among the other jars and bottles on her dressing table. After her death I had gone to look for it one day when I was alone in the flat, but it had vanished. I opened the drawer where its white and gold box used to lie, lined inside with peach-coloured satin, but that was missing too. It was only years later that I came across it at the back of a drawer in my father's bureau that was usually locked. I remember I took it out and unscrewed the cap and for a moment my mother's presence had filled the room. Marietta would become like my mother, no more than a memory, a scent in my head. I kissed her.

'I'll think of something,' I said. 'I'll try to rearrange things.'

'At least we'll have the weekends, Jan.' She tried to push away from me to look into my face, but I held her close. 'Jan, let's go away next weekend, all the weekend together.'

'Where?' I asked cautiously; I thought she might name one of the shadowy mansions.

'I don't know. Anywhere – here!'

'I don't think I can; just yet. It's not a very good time right now.'

I gazed out over her head to where the afternoon sunlight crept across the floor between the gap in the hastily-drawn curtains. I had learned to tell the time by this ray of light. Today the light was weak, the sky was overcast and the sun shone only fitfully between breaks in the cloud; I could see I had another twenty minutes left, but the desire to stay had evaporated. When I was dressing to leave she said quite casually:

'I can't see you tomorrow, darling. I've got to – go to the dentist.'

It stayed with me, that little pause before – the dentist. I heard it in my head all the time I was walking back to Oudenard Road and I saw in front of me her grave face and her fingers twisting strands of hair as she spoke. It was the first intimation of a time when she would become bored by our few hours together, when the newness of our passion would begin to subside and she would begin to demand more. But there was no more – no more time; Mr Finch and his injured leg could not be stretched to cover evenings too, or weekends. Eliska could not be left alone any more than she was unless – unless some sort of arrangement could be made. But I could not imagine what arrangement that could be. My imagination could get no further than the truth and there it stuck. Beyond the truth there seemed only disintegration, a half-dark world where fear was the generating energy: fear of the forgotten lie, fear of discovery and fear of loss.

When I let myself into the rooms in Oudenard Road they were empty. They seemed nowadays, after Marietta's flat, more fly-blown and desiccated then ever. Each time

I returned the sight of Eliska lifeless in those lifeless rooms irritated me, stinging me into a sullen silence that could last all evening. But when she was out I liked it even less. Then I felt uneasy, sitting alone. In the silence of the room I heard whispers; in the withdrawn empty look of the unoccupied furniture I sensed disapproval. In my disquiet lurked a worry that she had somehow come to harm or, worse still, found me out. Sometimes I thought of her as she had been in the beginning, when we had come together almost without speaking, without intention, and she had warmed me back to life throughout the bitter cold of that winter and the chill of spring. She had kept my spirits up simply by her presence and caressed me back into a belief in myself, supporting the plans that slowly took fire in my brain and taking risks that I could never have brought myself to ask of her. Then there would come over me the perverse longing to love her, to start afresh. But I could not bring myself to let go of Marietta. That evening as I sat by the window, however, I was thinking intently of where Eliska might have gone: she had been out when I had come home the day before and now she was out again. If only there was a pattern to her being out, if only I could be sure that on a particular day at a particular time . . . But if I asked such a question she would suspect it. She would probably not even answer it. She would just shrug her shoulders and it would hang there between us in the room, swelling with significance in the silence. If I was in her confidence I would know everything. I would know her innermost feelings and the exact extent of her trust and I could plan accordingly, balancing everything perfectly, gauging precisely what she would accept and what she would not. I could even suggest excursions to her, a broadening of her life that would take her further out of my way. If I had encouraged her friendship with Rinka instead of being rude about her, she might have spent more time with her; they might have gone out together more in the evenings or at weekends. Instead I had compounded Eliska's loneliness and had finally withdrawn even myself from her. In the circumstances perhaps it had been a mistake. I crossed to the sofa and, kicking my shoes off, lay down on it in such a position that I could keep my eyes on the door. Not long after I heard footsteps on the stairs and saw the door handle turn. I sat up.

'Hello,' I said and smiled shyly. Immediately Eliska saw me she looked away, but she was not quite quick enough.

'Hello,' she muttered and dropped her handbag on the table.

'I'm glad you're back early. I thought we might go to the cinema.'

She turned towards me, running a hand slowly through her hair.

'I've just been to the cinema,' she said.

'Oh.' I tried to keep the surprise out of my voice. Of all the replies I had anticipated, this one had never occurred to me, but I was determined not to lose the impetus. 'Well, let's go tomorrow.'

'OK.'

'What would you like to see?'

'I don't care.' She shrugged a shoulder and stared at me coldly. 'I don't know what's on.'

'But you've just been. What did you see?'

'"Vorticism and After,"' she said over her shoulder, striding into the bedroom.

I sat on the sofa staring after her, repeating under my breath the sound of the words that I had heard. 'What?' I yelled after her. There was no reply. I went to the door of the bedroom and repeated my question quietly, I was determined not to lose my temper with her. 'What?'

She was sitting on the end of the bed brushing her hair. For a moment she looked up from her reflection in the mirror and I caught something new in her expression. Something minute I could not put my finger on: it flickered in her eyes for a moment and then was gone.

'On Tuesdays and Thursdays in the early evening they show films at the Tate Gallery; sometimes they have lectures. "Vorticism and After" – that was the film today.'

'Oh,' I said, coming up behind her. 'Every Tuesday and Thursday, I never knew that. And you go there every Tuesday and Thursday, Liski?'

She turned round so suddenly, so unexpectedly that she startled me and I stumbled back against the bed.

'No, I don't go every time, Jan. I go only when something interests me.'

My first thought was that she had found out about us. My second that it was impossible for her to have done so.

'Darts, Jan; you play darts?'

'Darts? With small arrows?'

'Yeah, three hundred and one up!'

'No, no I haven't played.'

'Ah, pity. We're getting up a team from the House, directive from Head Office, foster team spirit. Practice nights Wednesdays, matches nights Fridays. You game, Jack?'

I told Eliska that I had been picked for trial in the darts team as we walked home from the cinema that night eating fried chicken out of a box. But she showed no interest.

'The trial is on Wednesday,' I said, 'and if I go through to the team it will mean practising on Wednesday nights and playing matches on Fridays. Travelling all over London, I expect, to play other House teams. Sometimes,' I added, looking across at her, 'it might be quite late.' But her face, clearly visible in the sodium street lamps and the bright lights from the shop windows, showed no attention to what I was saying. She was gazing at the far side of the street, looking up it into the distance.

'All this waste of light,' she murmured, 'and this waste of paper, this endless blowing about.'

I foraged among the batter crumbs at the bottom of the box for a last fragment of chicken.

'What is the difference between heartlessness and soullessness?' she went on.

I did not reply. I don't think she was really speaking to me, anyway. I behaved as if I had not heard her. I closed the lid of the box and tried to squash it into my pocket and we walked the rest of the way back to Oudenard Road in silence.

'Linda's here,' whispered Marietta as we kissed in the hall. 'In her room, doing something.'

'Have dinner with me on Wednesday,' I whispered back. She giggled and squirmed in my embrace, rubbing her ear where my breath had tickled her and shook her head.

'I can't,' she mouthed. 'Tuesday?'

'Wednesday or nothing.'

She pulled me backwards with her into the living room still laughing. With my free hand I closed the door behind us and leant on it linking my arms round her waist so that her body fell against mine.

'If you knew how difficult . . .'

She pillowed her elbows on my shoulders.

'Your wife?'

When the truth is out there is no fear any more. The fear was always the fear of the truth. The fear was always the scurrying round in the brain and the quick piling of armoury upon armoury and the fear of the truth sliding out through a chink, or of the whole falling. Even in interrogation when finally evidence is quietly passed across the desk, evidence of truth denied and truth asserted, even then for a moment in the room there is a calm of such simplicity that you notice the shadow of the light along the edge of the coconut matting beneath the desk and the fact that the shirt cuff of the interrogator is frayed slightly around the button. He too, you realise, is part of the same life which has poorly made shirts, hard water, harsh inadequate soap, light and dark. This is the real life that waits below all our complications. And then the fear closes in again, fear now of the imagined consequences. So it was, in the silence after Marietta spoke. Her words swept away all my barricades and subterfuges. I was suddenly aware of the solidity of the door, the warm Saturday afternoon silence of the street outside, the pleasure of her body pressed against mine, the softness and the heaviness of it, my arms around her stroking her back. It seemed a stretch of unaccountable time before the fear that I was going to lose all this burst in.

'I saw you,' she said, 'last night, coming out of the cinema. But – I knew anyway.'

I cupped her face in my hands and kissed her mouth. I thought it might be the last kiss I would ever have from her. But she flung her arms wildly round my neck, I heard her knuckles bang against the door.

'Jan, Jan it doesn't matter. None of that matters. If we have to love each other in secret for ever – that doesn't matter either.'

'You're so wonderful,' I gasped in between kisses.

We didn't see each other again for nearly a week, not till Friday evening, but I rang her every day at her new office. We embarked on a period of unparalleled happiness, of complete frankness with each other. Frequently we would not even make love during our brief meetings but would lie in each other's arms just talking. She wanted to know all over again in exact detail about my childhood and my aborted studies as an architect and my fall from grace. My shunting round the outlying postal districts of Prague and then my banishment to the wooded town in the depths of Moravia. Most of all she wanted to know about Eliska, about how we had drifted together, almost the only exiles in the small community, and she would shake her head and click her tongue over our misfortune.

'One of those dreadful things,' she said, 'of circumstance; two people, obviously mismatched, just . . .' she waved her fingers in the air, 'drifting together. What had she done?' she wanted to know.

'In her confusion and unhappiness; in her desperation,' I explained, 'to get as far away as possible from her husband whom she had just left, she was prepared to take any posting however unpopular, providing it was sufficiently far from Prague. So she became the local primary school teacher and we . . .'

Marietta shook her head again, solemnly.

'Inescapable,' she agreed. 'Fate is sometimes inescapable.'

And we smiled, knowingly, at each other and twined our arms around each other and kissed each other with soft, small kisses.

'You were "involved" by that time?' she would ask a little later, her eyes suddenly darkening with significance, watching me intently.

'Well . . .'

'No, no!' she rushed in, 'I promised not to ask.'

Eliska's function as wife, she decided, was, like my job as postman, of no more significance than to provide 'cover' for my clandestine activities, and as such both were irrelevant to our relationship. I never tried to find out what she thought my clandestine activities were.

'You are the most wonderful person in the world,' I would murmur, stroking her cheek. And she would smile and twist back a strand of hair.

'You know you could have just as good a cover working at something more in keeping with your intelligence and your ability. My older brother is a designer and he knows lots of architects, perhaps he could do something for you?'

It seemed to be a universal point of discontent, my job in the Postmen's House; my aunt, my uncle, Eliska were all put out by it, even my cousin in Cambridge was sympathetically patronising. And now Marietta. But I did not argue when she mentioned her well-connected brother, I did not become stubborn as I did when Eliska or my uncle nagged me about my apparent lack of ambition. I think I just kissed her. 'Really,' I said, or some such words, 'do you think so?' For I moved, those days, in a haze of love. I loved everything and everyone. Wherever I looked my state of mind seemed to be reflected back at me. I woke to a series of brilliant sunny mornings – day after day a cloudless blue. My life, I thought to myself as I walked down Oudenard Road in the early morning silence, is set, like the sky, into an assured pattern of happiness. I could feel it just beyond my fingertips waiting for me, certain.

'Nice morning,' I would say to Sid as I came up the steps.

'Fine before seven,' he would reply, rubbing his hands, the dry, weatherbeaten skin rustling together like dead leaves. He is too old for love, I would say to myself. It is too late for him, he can only stand now on the sidelines watching others, rubbing his arthritic hands and saying the same thing at the same time every day; words that so far as I could tell made no sense.

'I think Sid's going nuts,' I confided to Jack one morning.

'Losing his marbles, is he? Working in here, mate, that's what does it. You want to get out before it gets you too.'

Leave? Why should I want to leave when all around me was confirmation of progression and order: envelopes thudding with perfect aim into boxes, house following house, street falling after street. The quiet contentment of those early mornings in the House. You cannot fail, they said to me. I did not even notice the way it clouded over every day by mid-morning. It was still hot, it was still light. Even my love for Eliska renewed itself in the love of parting and became a love subtly changed, full, I thought, of understanding. I loved her because she did not have what we had and I saw, in her loveless state, how unhappy she was. We talked, Marietta and I, of how I should leave her, gradually, gently, little by little, or how we should stay friends with her, close friends, loving her, both of us, still; keeping an eye on her so that no harm might befall her till she could establish herself on her own. You must continue to support her, of course, Marietta would say. For a while. There were times, walking home from Marietta's flat and thinking of Eliska, that I would be overwhelmed by emotion. I would see in her deprivation a nobleness that almost brought tears to my eyes. I would stand there on the street, overcome, and then hurry onwards. It was my duty to be with her, to support her through this, it was my spiritual duty as her husband, it was my duty before God. At such moments her suffering appeared to me greater than my love with Marietta. But only for moments. It no longer seemed to me that the answer to life lay in the words painted on the door of the Postmen's House. It was not Dickens, Darwin, Dostoevsky. It was love.

IT IS NOT great events which shape our lives. Such events occur rarely. Frequently it is nothing at all. The petering out of endurance. The over-exposure to fear or threat which numbs the capacity for apprehension. Until you are pushed beyond fear. Into nothingness. Into a white space where all is calm, all is still. I do not know, even now, precisely what it was that one day propelled me forward. Until I was beyond the snatching of fingers. Beyond the gesticulations and empty mouthings of Grigor and his mother. Beyond the murmuring of Mrs Ostrova and Helena. The voice of Major Jezek. And the shrill cries of my schoolchildren. The words of Magdalena floated often into my thoughts in those days: 'You will come when you are ready.' I saw puffs of fine snow erupt from branches. Pink petals drifting in still air past the black criss-crossings of twigs. The address of the flower shop where I could contact her repeated itself over and over again in my brain. Echoing wildly back and forth in the empty hollows of my skull, like a nonsense rhyme. I knew the street. I knew the shop. But – I could not . . . I could not bring myself . . . I . . . It would have been so easy then. But it was too difficult. It was beyond my small provision of courage. I was no braver than anybody else.

It is acknowledged that people may wish to change their lives. That human error may occur. We have provision for people to change their jobs, their wives, their place of residence. Some are easier to achieve than others. But there are regulations concerning all these things. So it was that I found myself in Oslensk. No one came to Oslensk voluntarily. The steelworkers came for the money. The others were enforced postings – troublemakers. The primary school teacher had been trying to retire for almost two years, but no one could be found to take her place. I knew none of this as I queued in the offices of the Department of Education requesting transfer on compassionate grounds. Behind me supplicants shuffled on benches. Beside me at the long counter, the broken-spirited unfolded creased certificates and traced in the splintered wood with stained forefingers the circumstance of their lives. The official dealing with my case leafed through a file of unfilled jobs. She pursed her mouth. She shrugged her shoulders. She raised and lowered her eyebrows as she turned another page. Three-quarters of the way through she stopped and shook her head.

'We have nothing,' she said in a bored voice.

'I will take anything. Anything, so long as it is far from Prague.'

She conferred with her colleague. They looked at me with expressionless faces. They could see by my eyes that I was past caring. She came back.

'*What* were the grounds?'

She tapped a painted fingernail impatiently on the plywood counter.

'Irretrievable breakdown of marriage,' I repeated. 'I – I have a letter. From the lawyer who will prepare my case.'

Irritably, she waved it away and turned to the back of

the file, turning up a page whose existence even I could see she had known of all along.

'There is Oslensk,' she said.

All you see when you look up in Oslensk are pine trees. Dense. Dark. Green. A strip of sky. And slashed into either slope of the ravine, scars of yellow clay out of which grow apartment blocks. Not high. In Oslensk it is always raining. Without trees to hold it the clay slips. It is not wise to build too heavy a structure on such soil. But the effect of height is cumulative. The buildings rise tier upon tier. At the exact point on the slope where one roof ends, the footings of another apartment block begin. They have already reached the ridge of one slope. And begun on the other. In between, along the narrow valley floor, run the road, the river and the railway line. The track of the railway crosses one side of the main square of Oslensk. The only square. The slope of open tarmacadamed ground with the self-service general store on one side and the offices of the steel works on the other. There are no gates guarding the square from the railway line, except where the road crosses the tracks. Perhaps it was thought there was no need. Oslensk is always deserted, apart from the times that the shift changes at the steelworks and the schoolchildren are released. Before the steelworks came, Oslensk was just a hamlet, a string of wooden frame houses straggling along the road where the valley widens. Among these dilapidated houses was the school. Larger than the rest. Two rooms tacked onto it as living quarters. It smelled of damp and in the corners it crumbled with decay. Its back window, angled away from the new settlement, looked across the banks of the river and the overhead cable lines of the railway to the dense cliff of forest. Dark with shadow from the clouds that hung over it constantly. Whitened by frequent squalls of rain.

The forests have always been our comforters. Our

places of absolution and confession. You walk into the forest and the world is left behind you. The ground beneath your feet becomes soft with a dense bed of pine needles. The light is muted. The silence, which is never quite silent, warm. But this not-quite-silence is not alarming. It is the quick rush and scrabble of another world. The twisting and falling of a leaf caught in a shaft of sunlight. The light fluttering of a bird. The echo of its rapid song far above you. You are drawn into this world. And in its calm and in its warmth and its particular quality of not-quite-silence, fear is stilled; melancholy soothed.

I got Jan to take me out to a forest near London. I saw it on my map. It was just on the edge, almost still in the city. I was curious. And I was sad, a lump of sadness that seemed only to solidify rather than dissolve. I had not thought they would have forests here. Perhaps in a forest again . . . We went on Sunday. On the Underground. Right out to the end of the line. We walked down a street of houses. And there it was. I knew at once that it was wrong. I took one step inside it and wanted to burst into tears. I should have known. I had let longing deceive me, lull me into thinking that I might find it all as I remembered it. How could I even have imagined that I would find a Czech forest in an English wood. When nothing else was the same: not the smell of the air, nor the shape of the faces of the people in the streets. A familiar sense of desolation began to descend on me.

'Pretty, isn't it.' Jan remarked.

I looked at him. But he didn't notice. He was too busy gazing up into the canopy of branches. Ahead of us the uneven ground rose into low hills and fell away again into rounded gullies filled with last year's dead leaves in an undulating landscape of trees. I wanted to say to him, 'Remember Oslensk.' But we walked on in silence. I glanced at him scuffling through the beech mast, holding back a brush of leafy twigs barring his way. Oslensk was not so long ago, but he had changed. He was plumper, sleeker. He did his hair in a different parting. He had lost something. A leanness. A sharpness. Pain. He had lost pain. It had been his driving force. And now – it was gone. But I could still see him as he was. As I first met him in Oslensk. We had known each other for some time before we met. It was impossible not to. In Oslensk strangers stood out on the street like sore fingers. You could not hide it: the strangeness, the difference. It was just there, in your eyes. A light, a flash, a depth of looking that gave you away instantly. There were few of us. And we were all suspect, to the inhabitants. They knew no one came to Oslensk by choice. I saw him sometimes after school – in the general store, passing on the road. The teacher and the postman. Our hours of work ended at much the same time. I did not know more of him than that. But he knew about me. He had to. I was on his beat. He delivered my letters. The only letters I ever received, the infrequent progress reports from my lawyer.

'Remember,' I wanted to turn to him, 'how we met? In the crashing of glass, in the early half-light of a summer morning?'

I never knew why I felt no fear in the sudden shattering of sleep, in the string of oaths from the darkness beyond the jagged window. But there was no room for fear in the rage that filled me, in the pounding of my bare feet on wooden floorboards and the flinging back of the front door so that it banged on its hinges.

'What the hell . . . !'

'Your letter – I could not wake you . . .'

I snatched it out of your hands, but I could not stop shouting.

'Please, please.' You kept pushing a small book at me and a pencil. And I kept waving my fists in the air. 'You must sign for it. It is recorded.'

'Sign! I shall write immediately a letter of complaint to the postmaster general of Oslensk.'

'If I had known that the window was cracked, I would not have knocked on it. But you did not hear the door . . .'

You tried to explain. I heard your words but my rage scattered them before I could grasp their meaning. In the end you had to catch my hands between your own to make me listen to you.

'I will mend it for you this evening. I will buy glass and . . .'

I was surprised by the sudden calm of your voice speaking; disconcerted. For a moment I let your hands close round mine. Then I dragged them away.

'I demand a builder. I want it done properly.'

'I know about such things. I was trained to be an architect.'

'An architect!' I growled. 'You are a vandal.' I jerked my chin at the apartment blocks across the valley. 'All architects are vandals!'

And I slammed the door in your face. So hard that in the bedroom there was a light tinkle, as another piece of glass fell to the floor.

That evening you returned. With a bunch of daisies. Red and yellow, pink and yellow – something like that. And a small, shapeless packet rolled loosely in newspaper. You put it into the palm of my hand and it felt like a lump of cold rice.

'This is putty, for the window,' you said solemnly and looked down at the dusty toes of your boots. The sun was just beginning to sink and behind you up on the ridge the tops of the pine trees glowed in a slow blaze, the feathery ends of their branches looking almost as if they curled and flickered. 'But – there was no glass.'

'Hah! What did you expect?

You looked up, dark rings under your eyes, shrugging your shoulders.

'Glass – and no putty?'

It was impossible not to smile then. At each other. At the immense difficulty of such a small thing – the buying of glass – that was our normal life.

I glanced at you, scuffling your feet in the dried husks of beech nuts, but your expression was blank. Memory does not flow in your head as it does in mine. We walked beneath those tall trees whose branches arched so gracefully, bending down to touch us. Up one slope and down another. Between their heavy end-of-summer leaves the sunlight flashed. Light. Dark. Flickering like pictures, moving. Dazzling. Blinding. Even with the eyes closed the images burned onto the retina. One flickering image superimposed upon the next.

You came almost every afternoon to report on the absence of glass. To assure me that you had not forgotten it. I knew you were afraid I would report the damage. You would have had to pay for it. In one way or another. Once you brought a thick sheet of old cardboard and a half-used roll of strong parcel tape that you had slipped into your pocket when no one was looking. You took down the flapping sheets of folded newspaper that I had stuck against the glass. The strips of gummed brown paper had unglued in the heat and curled like fern fronds. In the sunshine the fair hairs on your bare arm glittered as they caught the light. In the heat of the small wooden room, flies buzzed against the window.

Once you arrived as I was setting off for the forest. We climbed through the warm scent of resin with circles of gnats dancing above our heads. You told me about your childhood. After your mother had died.

'We became like two old men, bereft. Widowers, both of us, my father and I.'

You stopped for breath and stared out between the trees at the heavy afternoon silence, the shafts of slow light. The years went by, you said, and the empty rooms of the apartment which had seemed so large and dusty and silent shrank to tiny boxes. The forest seemed always to make you reflective, melancholy. Another time, you stopped suddenly on the path and craning your neck back gazed upwards.

'Look at the trees,' you said, 'like gothic columns going up and up, and then suddenly, when you think they can go no higher, breaking out into arches.' You nudged my arm. 'Go on, Eliska, look up!' And then, lower: '"Look up." My father used to say that to me. "Look up at the little things."' You told me of the long Sunday walks through Prague you used to take together. Of how you learned to look up and discovered another, forgotten world lying behind the grey everyday life that you had fallen into. The stone flowers and cornucopias of fruit, the little chiselled birds that perched among them. The faded paintings on the upper storeys of houses. The faint sense of whispering high in dark corners, of laughter trailing off somewhere behind you that were the echoes of the past still reverberating, you said, because the present was so silent. And then, when we came out onto the ridge of the hill and all around us stretched shoulders of forest – behind and before us nothing but the tops of trees as far as the eye could see – your face crumpled. Your eyes became blank suddenly with unveiled despair.

'This place is the end of the world,' you said, your voice leaden.

And we just stood there, with the evening sunshine all around us. I was unable to bring myself to do anything to comfort you. I could not speak. I could not even put out a finger to touch your limply-hanging hand.

But I remember you laughing, too. You came one afternoon with the shiny cap of a beer bottle winking out of the top of your trouser pocket.

'Come down to the river,' you said.

The day was so hot you unlaced your boots and rolled up your trouser legs. You sat with your feet in the water. I can still see them swaying in the currents and eddies of the stream. I told you about the kingfisher on the river at home and the drifting silver haze of minnows that we used to try to catch in nets made out of our mothers' old stockings. I watched the beer bubbling in the neck of the brown bottle as you tilted back your head. And the soft arch of your throat. And the small damp hairs along your forehead. I told you about Magdalena, and you laid your chin on your upraised knee and watched me smiling, your eyes half-closed against the sun. You wiped the top of your beer bottle with the palm of your hand and offered me a drink. But I would not.

The next time you came there were two beer bottles in your pocket. You made a straw for me out of a stalk of dried grass. But I only laughed and shook my head. You stretched out in the long grass on one elbow and drank from one, while I held the other by its neck in the river to keep cool. I told you about the summer camp on Lake Valcha. When I handed you the second bottle of beer water dripped on your shirt leaving large wet stains, making it stick to your skin.

'Sing me the camp songs,' you insisted. But I pretended to have forgotten them. 'No, no, Eliska,' you lay back in the grass, your eyes shut, shaking your head slowly from side to side, 'you have not. You are required to teach such songs, now, to the children of Oslensk.' You opened one eye. 'You like teaching, Eliska?'

I shrugged. 'You like delivering letters?'

You shook your head again and closed your eyes.

'I wanted to be an architect,' you said. 'But – I had the wrong mother.' You rolled over on one side, suddenly awake, watching my bemused expression as you lifted the bottle to your mouth. 'My mother was English, you know. That's why I'm here. Consorting with foreigners.

My father – consorted, married, procreated, with a foreigner. To begin with it was all right. In the diplomatic service such a thing is necessary, part of the job. Later – for some reason or other – it was not all right. One half of me,' you waved your arms in the air in front of your face staring intently at each of them, 'has foreign blood racing round inside it.' You let your arms fall, heavily. 'You are right not to drink with me. You are right! You should have nothing to do with me. I have been put here, in Oslensk, so that no one can ever have anything to do with me again. I am a destructive element in the community. I go round breaking windows!'

The day that glass was finally expected in Oslensk you turned up in the middle of a squall of rain that swept across the valley darkening the air. I had been out collecting lime flowers to dry for the winter, and was putting a pan of water on the stove to boil for tea, when I heard you. You leant against the wall as I closed the front door, scarcely more than a shadow in the gloom of the narrow hall. Your clothes were soaked, your hair dripping water from dark, jagged points.

'There was no glass. Again. Today, it was promised: a shipment. Today!'

Your voice frightened me, it was tense and low and fast. You would not look at me; you kept your gaze fixed, low down, on the opposite wall.

'You should not have gone out in the rain,' I said quickly. It was all there was to say. 'Just for . . .'

'It was *important* – that someone keep faith.'

You followed me back into the main room with curious, jerky movements. As if you had given up hope so entirely, you had even abandoned your body to make its own way in the world. It carried you with uneven force between the window and the table. Between the rain blowing in thin drifts and the heap of wet flowers. Backwards and forwards. I picked my scarf up from one chair and hung it to dry on the back of another. I shook the small pan on the stove to make it boil. I fiddled with the packets and jars that stood on a nearby shelf. I could not look at you. I stared at the floor, and the toe-caps of your boots entered and re-entered the small circle of my vision. The only sound in the room was the hissing of water in the pan, the drumming of rain on the window; the rasp of your boots against the bare wood floor. And then there was only the rain and the water on the stove. I looked up. You were standing by the table staring at me. Your face was twisted into an intense expression. You shook your head and your voice when it came was thick and heavy, low and distinct.

'This is not life,' you said.

And I knew that it was not. That it had never been. I had known it all along. But I had not been able to bring myself to acknowledge it. Now, when you said it, the pretence, the veil of my life, slipped swiftly past me. Like mists. Like ghosts. I saw it go. I clutched at it. I think I even heard myself gasp. But it was too late. It was gone for good. Your arms knocked over the pan of water. But it fell – somewhere beyond our comprehension. I was surprised by the wetness of your hair against my cheek. The heaviness of your mouth. By the sensation of sinking slowly to the floor the tighter your arms wound about me. And that first gasp, of life lost, becoming a gasp that was not your breath or my breath, the one sounding indrawn in the other's ear as our mouths parted for a second, kissing your neck, my shoulder, as our hands moved stronger and stronger, but the first gasp of life, after so long, found. Everything else dissolved away. The dark, hanging woods, the clamouring children in the crowded schoolroom, the streaming of rain on concrete walls. The general deprivation. The solitude. I only remember from that time the softness of arms. Of being kissed into sleep and woken again by your mouth on mine. And half-sleeping, waking, the ceaseless gliding of limbs. Of the sensation of rolling over and over, weightless, without thought. Of darkness and light being all one through eyes that were half-closed, needing not to see any more, so sure were all the other senses. And then when they opened, seeing only your face, your eyes and the smile of pleasure.

There must have been hours each day when we were separated. Hours of letters. School. But the memory of them does not exist. They were not part of the new world we had created. In the timescale of that existence they telescoped to an infinitesimal part of a second. And the briefest kiss eclipsed them. In the same way the dreariness of Oslensk receded. It was as though the town with all its hills and trees had sunk to the bottom of a river. And we had risen to the surface. There among bubbles and sunlight we broke through water into air so pure that even the intake of breath in a laugh made us dizzy. I saw colour and light and space clearly as if for the first time. I heard the minutest sound break the summer afternoon silence – the scrabbling of a small animal in the undergrowth, the wind through feathers in the wingbeat of a bird high above me. This is love, I thought. But it was more than that that you gave me. When we turned to look back into the river, down at Oslensk, it seemed far away. Blurred slightly with the refraction of water, of new seeing. Its familiar inhabitants moved slowly among its dark buildings and potholed streets, heavy with the weight of water, chilled by lack of air. You put your arms round my shoulders and held me firm against you.

'Look,' you said, 'look closely to understand, now that you are warm and safe. Now that you can see it for what it is. Now that you can stand apart from it.'

The rest of the summer and into the autumn we walked in the forest talking endlessly, returning to the schoolhouse only with the dusk. For talk such as ours it is always safer to be away from rooms and people. Until, as sometimes happens, the pupil overtook the teacher. As winter came so you began to sink down. The sudden shortening of the days affects us all. The prospect of the long darkness, the bite of cold. We have become a scavenging nation. The inadequacies of supply and distribution send us out foraging along the hedgerows and riverbanks, deep into the forest. In the summer there are wild strawberries and raspberries, mushrooms and blackberries. In the winter – nothing. In the winter the small difficulties of daily life become immense. The effort of will required to prevent them from overwhelming you, exhausting. They are unleashed on us almost with deliberateness, like a pack of small dogs. They snap at our heels constantly, goading us, herding us, attempting to scare us. It is then that we feel most deeply our helplessness, our powerlessness. It is then that we are at our weakest. You seemed to – lose heart. You lay in my arms like a sick child, seeking support from the closeness of flesh. You sat on a chair by the stove, while the hail drummed on the window, your chin propped in your hands. Now it was I who had to give you strength. You were truculent, obstinate, given over entirely to melancholy with an almost sensuous pleasure. It was as though you prolonged despair to elicit my caresses, my reassurance. You drank them in and would not allow your hunger to be satisfied.

'It will never be possible for us to change anything,' you would say. 'Never.'

It was towards the middle of winter that you began to talk of escape. It was so wild a dream, so beyond my comprehension I did not consider it seriously. I let you talk. Your words had the harsh rasp of fever. The repetitiveness of obsession. Your arm in mine, dragging me through the snowy forest, was forceful with a brittle tenseness. I humoured you. I listened and nodded. But you did not subside into lucidity. The idea embedded itself. And you grew calm around it.

'It is the only way, Eliska,' you said, stroking loose strands of hair back off my face. And I loved you so much I could not refuse. Besides, I did not know. About how it would be. How can you know, when you have never seen? The land went on beyond the border. You could see it, if you travelled to the frontier. People said it looked just the same. Fields and hills, small houses far off . . . The same, but different. That was how I thought of it. And difference. What is difference? When I thought about it there was just a space in my mind in which confused images swirled. My own country was all I knew, so it became the backcloth against which this – difference – was placed. It was the countryside of my childhood restored – to what I did not know. Dream cities, that were all basically Prague with shining streets and overflowing shops and smiling people. It was the lifting of greyness and fear. It was the possibility to live spontaneously. That was what I thought when I listened to you talk about freedom.

It was as if you had only been waiting for my acquiescence. For with it you became purposeful, certain. You had accumulated knowledge during your years in Oslensk – rumours, whispers. There were foresters, you said, deep in the hinterland beyond Oslensk on contract felling trees for Austria. The Austrians, it was known, had bought up entire standing forests. They were not sent, these felled trees, to the state sawmills but were transported whole on vast, segmented lorries directly over the border. It was possible, it was whispered, among the bodies of these dead giants, for a live body . . . There are always whispers, of one kind or another. We comfort ourselves with little whispering dreams. But we do nothing. Somehow, however, you found the beginning of the chain of contact.

Walking, in London, between those light, spaced English trees, I wanted suddenly to turn to you and say: 'Do you remember that night, Jan?' I even stopped, overcome by the force of thought. But you did not stop. You strode on, immersed in your own world. The world that is not – *my* world, any more. You looked before you at the pattern of sunlight dropping between broad leaves. But I looked back. To the uncertain edge of circles of lamplight on a wet road. Patches of darkness where one circle of weak light faded out, before the next began. And the shadows of our bodies, that came suddenly over our shoulders as we passed below street lamps and flung themselves down on the road in front of us. Lengthening out like a stain running quickly. Like something grotesque and frightening that would rise up and seize us. And the stranger, walking between us, his low voice running on and on. And the splinter-sound of our boots on the road, like the bursting of rifle shots. Like an army marching that would wake the whole town. Until I could hear nothing but our footsteps through the pounding of blood in my ears. Where the forest edged down to the road again and the road itself divided and the street lights petered out, the stranger left us. 'Do not look back,' you whispered, sliding your arm quickly through mine, pulling me close to you, hurrying me on as I faltered there at the crossroads. But behind us there was just silence. Only our footsteps on the road and the gasp of our ragged breathing. Back in the schoolhouse we were afraid to speak. Afraid to turn on lights. We undressed in the dark and lay side by side in the narrow bed. You bent to kiss me and whispered in my ear: 'It has begun, Liski.'

But there was only waiting. Waiting. And knowing. From the waiting – fear. And from the knowing – guilt. Yet all the while it was necessary to behave as if nothing was known and nothing was felt. In my quarters behind the schoolroom I could draw the curtains and, silently sliding open drawers and cupboard doors, pass my hands over the objects kept in readiness. Each object kept separate, unobtrusive, in case of a house search. The second set of clothes that must be worn over the first. The dried raisins, nuts and bars of chocolate that could be stuffed into our pockets. The obsessive rehearsal that did nothing to hasten our departure. I could sit by the stove and twist a strand of hair in my fingers, staring out into a room I no longer saw, with anxious eyes. I could lie awake for hours while the shadow of the moon crept over the rough wooden floor. And fall at last into a sleep pierced by dreams. By the sudden crack of a tarpaulin. The entangling of brambles pulling down, down; while close behind me pursuers crashed through forest. But in my classroom none of this could be evident. I hid it, but I thought always that they saw. That they knew because I knew. I discovered the guilt of the murderer, the petty thief. And fought the longing to confess everything. I forced myself to look into those rows of small bright eyes that before I had met with such ease, searching among their ranks for the mischievous and the lazy. As I made myself look into the faces of the women behind the counter at the general store, the clerks in the post office, the wife of the baker. Their eyes, sharp and begrudging, could see through the mask of my thin, faltering bravery. Oslensk took on a sinister aspect. As though perception had been twisted. Colour seemed almost to fade to monochrome and yet contrast appeared heightened. Objects stood out sharply, so that the third dimension became almost a fourth. Behind the outline of each object and its background there lurked an unaccountable dark space in which – anything – could hide. Below overheard conversations there was a continuous sussuration of indistinguishably elided words. The most ordinary stones, trees, houses and people took on menace. The whole of Oslensk and its surroundings became interlaced with threads of tension. We were the spiders that spun this web. And the flies caught in its sticky substance, also. One puff of air could have blown it away, one word to our contact that we were pulling out. You cannot go back, not in that game. We had been told that. We had been instructed to do nothing that might alert anyone to our departure. To make no leave-takings. To write no letters of farewell to anyone, not even a mother; nor even hint at a change. Not to pay bills before their usual time, nor all together. Not to dispose of any property, nor cancel any subscription. We were instructed to spend our weekends walking in the forest. To set off after breakfast and not return till dusk. We were permitted to talk of these hikes if the occasion presented itself in conversation, or we were asked. Now that spring was full-blown and the days were warmer and longer such a thing was quite natural. It is a recreation many people take. In every forest there are trails marked out for the walker – small coloured arrows painted on the trunks of trees. When the time came, that was how we would leave, walking out of Oslensk on one of these trails, and at some distant point, some point as yet unknown, we would encounter a guide. Then we would leave behind all marked paths.

As the days of silence dragged on we clung to each other more and more, as each other's only support. The time alone together, the only time we could let drop our masks. My divorce came through. From being eagerly awaited, it now seemed inconsequential. A week later, we married. The secretary of the town official and one of your colleagues from the post office were dragged in as witnesses. We even re-used the wedding ring of my former husband. All our money had gone on the escape. We sat at the kitchen table that evening drinking a bottle of slivovitz that we had saved, my head leaning against your shoulder, your left arm round my neck. You told me endless stories of England. Home, you called it. For in your mind you were already there, with your mother.

And I cried frequently, sensing all of a sudden, now that it was too late, how alien it might be. You only smiled at my tears, hugging me tighter, and carried on with your tales. The next morning, when we woke up, there it was, hanging from the school gate, tied to the inside handle of the latch, just as they said it would be. A child's knitted scarf in bands of blue and red. Dangling there in the still morning air. My hand moved instinctively to close the curtain again. To shut it out. To pretend I had not seen it. To cheat time, the time that had come, the hours that must be gone through. But you had already got out of bed and were standing beside me at the window, staring out into the same silence.

I do not want to remember the climb through the forest, the initial dry-mouthed fear of hurrying suspiciously quickly, of walking too slowly. Of being late. Of being early. Of being followed. The irrational bursts of elation. And then, as the day wore on, the exhaustion. The increasing uncertainty, running like will o' the wisps before us, of the way; driving us into panic. Then, with the failing of the light, the man who stepped from behind a tree. Barring our way. Sending our hearts leaping in our chests. Greeting us silently with a handshake. Leading us abruptly off the path. Higher and higher. The pines now, in the dark, straight as sentinels. Unbending. Unflinching. Tall with disapproval. Row after row. Staring down over the land, stiff-backed. While we – we crept away between them. How when the moon rose we rested, ate the last of the sandwiches and buried the empty haversack. And when the clouds came and covered the moon we went on. Stumbling in a raw sleeplessness that was beyond exhaustion. Twigs, leaf drifts, brambles and marshy springs. In the deepest part of the night we were seized suddenly by terror as a dog barked up above in the loggers' camp. We stood for minutes, for hours, for days, still in our tracks. But the dog did not bark again. Dropping down then, down, down, till we came out where the forest track met the main road. Crouching in a clay ditch. Roused suddenly in the violet-coloured darkness that precedes dawn. To silence. That suddenly was not silence anymore, but the hammering of blood against the tense walls of my body and the reverberation, becoming steadily louder, winding slowly down the long slope of the hill, of the lorry. The lorry that had to stop at the junction beside the ditch because the articulation of its segments needed the whole of the road in front of it to clear the bend. The driver who would halt for fifteen seconds longer than he needed to. Who would slip a gear, and roar the engine finding it again to cover any noise of our scrambling onto the tail of the trailer. The car that waited out on the road, engine idling, lights off, to hear the precise approach of the lorry and start forward, headlights blazing to distract the attention of the forestry guard sitting beside the driver, and provide a reason to pause for longer than usual. This was the only pause the lorry was permitted to make during its journey. From here the road was straight, without intersection. At the border, the guard would leave the lorry, certifying that it had been loaded in the forest under his inspection and had driven without stopping to the frontier checkpoint. Our guide had promised us that such lorries were never thoroughly searched. It was not possible, he said. They had at the border no equipment strong enough to lift whole trees. You do not believe such promises. You do not believe anything. Belief is gone, though everything was belief. There is only the wide white space of panic in which, through which, you move blindly. Whispering over and over in your head instructions to a body that has forgotten everything but the necessity of the moment. Has become an automaton of will. That does not know what is running. Or how to jump. Until there is only the stumbling against ruts of mud on the earth road. The scrabbling of finger nails. The slipping backwards and then the lurch forward. The impenetrable heaviness of the tarpaulin. The roaring of the engine bursting in your head. The gasping for breath in the oily darkness.

And then, when it is all over, the warm flatness of afternoon sunlight and the dust on the road that, even though it is a foreign road, is still the same grey. And the flatness of the land stretching away around you, mile after mile. And the knowledge that this is the promised land that you set out to find. And the leaking sense that spreads like a stain in your head that this is all there is.

IT WAS ARRANGED that Marietta's brother would come round one Wednesday evening. I was eager to meet him. He was just the beginning, I told myself. After him would come her other brother, her cousins and aunts and uncles, her godfather and then – her parents. I would be invited to stay in the house she had told me about so many times, the small square house that had once been a farmer's house and stood among acres of wheatfields. It was like a doll's house she said, perfectly symmetrical, with gables and chimneys; the upstairs floors all dipped and the stairs were wide and dark, and creaked. In the summer when you looked out of the windows you felt you were on the sea as the ocean of wheat around you rose higher and higher and the wind blew over it making it ripple and billow in waves. I would see all that. They were six miles from the nearest village and ten miles from the nearest town and so they had had only each other to play with. But there was a shadowy network of other dolls' houses strung out around the countryside in which lived a whole ramification of cousins and acquaintances to whom they were taken sometimes to play. I should be taken there too; paraded, welcomed. The meeting with her brother, however, seemed to cause Marietta anxiety.

'We can't ask him to dinner because he'll think it odd when you leave early, he's used to dinner parties going on till midnight. It's only oldies who like getting to bed early and even they wouldn't dream of leaving till ten-thirty.'

'Well perhaps – just for once – I could . . .'

'And we can't tell him you're married. If you could make lunch there wouldn't be such a problem. But of course you can't. It'll have to be drinks. Then we'll have to have a whole lot of people. At least twenty. Well, twelve, anyway. And if we do that, I mean that would be the best – I just ring up and say I'm having friends in for drinks and I'd love him to come – then he might say "no" because he doesn't really like my friends. He says they're all too young for him. Although I suppose if I said that there was this person I specially wanted him to meet then he'd probably get the message.'

It struck me as odd that she made such a fuss; she was irritable for the rest of the evening. We had met some of her friends once or twice in pubs in far-flung places such as Kensington or Camden Town, not the sort of places where the House darts team would play, but Eliska did not know the significance of one pub against another just by name. I would leave home at the usual time for a darts night and join Marietta and her friends who would have met straight after work. They would have had time for one or two drinks by the time I arrived.

'This is Jan. From Czechoslovakia,' Marietta would say blushing slightly and twisting a thick strand of hair between her fingers.

It was something to talk about. Guardedly. They were sympathetic and friendly. Except that inevitably on discovering that I was a postman they would laugh, a quickly suppressed laugh that burst out of them quite unconsciously. A laugh of amazement and disbelief.

Marietta would smile through small, tight lips glancing rapidly from person to person. She would display on these occasions a curious mixture of pride and agitation, huddling back against the pub settle watching us with a kind of feline contentment and then suddenly darting forward to steer the conversation away from dangerous subjects – like my wife. It was curious because when we were alone she harped much on these things, winding them to her, drawing evident pleasure from them; vaunting herself to herself in particular roles that perhaps she would not admit to her friends. Or maybe that she would not admit to her friends in front of me. But the arranging of such meetings never seemed to cause her the kind of anguish as the one with her brother. She used to announce them casually to me a couple of days beforehand, and she always seemed pleased afterwards. Usually we left before the others were ready to go, but once we stayed later than usual. When we stood up to depart so did everyone else. Usually there were only two or three others, this night there were half a dozen. We straggled through the door of the pub.

'Who's coming round to the Tandoor?'

'Jan, ever had curry?'

'Jan's never had curry. That's it! Everyone round the corner.'

I tried to protest. I tried to point out that it was late, although it was not. I tried to catch Marietta's eye to signal that we should make our excuses, but she did not look at me. I moved close to her to touch her hand. Still laughing at something one of the men had said she linked her arm through mine, squeezing it tightly so that I could not withdraw it, and pulled me down the street with the others. We never linked arms in the street. Never. We never even held hands. We rarely even appeared outside her flat together. These were rules which up to now she had always obeyed. I felt that her arm had turned into steel dragging me forward, biting through the flesh into the bone, but I could not cry out because her friends would hear, I could not struggle because they would stare at me in amazement. The street lamps turned into arc lights and from the shadow behind each one I expected to see Eliska, or worse, Rinka. When we arrived at the restaurant my fear turned into panic. It was not small and dimly lit and deserted as I had hoped, it was a vast emporium of light and noise and heat and we were placed at a table in the centre of it. I don't know what it was that I ate, they ordered for me. All I know was that my stomach twisted against it, my mouth burned, my eyes watered, sweat clung in minute droplets on my forehead and ran down my back. Every time the door opened I choked on my food and in the multiplicity of images that swam in my eyes the faces that entered were all, for a split second, Eliska's. Marietta's friends laughed and suggested another poppadum or more beer. Marietta showed no sign that she had noticed my suffering, she laughed and chattered with them, more animated than I had seen her before. On our journey back we had our first row. And when I got home I was violently sick.

Marietta's brother had a piercing stare and was slow to smile. It was, I could see at once, the point of family resemblance, but on Marietta's face it produced an intriguing gravity which one longed to tease into laughter. He was there when I arrived. We had arranged the drinks party for six-thirty on a darts night, but of course I couldn't get there till just after seven. When I came in he was standing on his own by the fireplace holding a glass of wine.

'You're Jan,' he said, not moving.

I held out my hand. There was a pause and then almost with reluctance he drew his hand out of his pocket and shook mine.

'Can't stay long,' he said.

He kept his hand in his pocket most of the evening. When he was introduced to someone he would just nod his head; sometimes when they had outstared him or his conscience had been stirred, his arm would jerk as though the hand was going to come out. Sometimes he would suddenly laugh shaking his whole body and then the quivering arm would drag the hand almost out of its hiding-place; you would see the wrist and then the tops of his fingers and then it would be pushed firmly back down again. I became so fascinated by this bulging pocket that I found myself staring at it with an embarrassing fixity when my attention was not engaged. And it was not very much engaged. Marietta's brother was an industrial designer who measured life by the bore widths of pipes. Having sparred and foiled, tried each other with morsels of small talk which drifted each time into silence, and retreated to the comforting blur of someone else's chatter, he approached me steadfastly half-way through the party.

'Miv tells me you were an architect in Czecho.'

'Well,' I smiled modestly, 'I was busy training to be an architect.'

'Life moved in, eh? Finding it a bit tricky over here? Can be a bit tricky to start with. Tell me,' the hand wriggled in his pocket and I tried hard not to look at it. 'Tell me, what's the pre-construction industry like these days back home?'

I shrugged. 'OK, I think.'

'They're romping away in Romania.' He took a slurp of his wine. 'Can't get them up quick enough. We've got a very nice little thing set up with them. Been pioneering a new tube' – he called pipes tubes – 'seems it's just what they want, can't turn it to quite the bore we can, on their old machinery.' He stepped back, his face flushed; the hand flew out of his pocket for a second and dived back in again. He bent towards me. 'Who'd be a good man in Czecho to approach?'

The moment the last guest had left I took Marietta to bed. As I unbuttoned her blouse the blue silk furled back over white skin lower and lower.

'I don't want to see anyone but you,' I said, 'for a week.'

'Just a week?'

'A week and then another week,' I mumbled between kisses. But she was abstracted and unresponsive. 'We only have an hour, Marietta,' I said gently.

She propped herself on one elbow.

'Geoffrey's frightfully clever, isn't he? He's meant to be the most brilliant young designer in his firm. Did he say he could help?'

I rolled over onto my back.

'He seemed to be more interested in whether I could help him.'

'He's such a darling. He wouldn't say anything to your face but I'm sure he'll mention you to some people. I did ask him to.'

I pulled back strands of hair from her face and kissed her ears. She shook her head like a dog who has just come out of water, to make her hair fall back over her eyes.

'He says Mummy's been asking why I haven't been down to see anyone and Daddy's breathing's bad again. I sort of promised I'd go down next week; the job with Mathes finishes in two days' time.'

'I wish I could come with you, but it's not possible at the moment with things . . .'

'Come down? Oh no! I mean, not just yet. Soon.' She wrapped her arms round me and pressed herself close. 'When things are more sorted out. Then you must come down and meet everyone.'

She let me kiss her for a while and then drew back again as if she had just remembered something.

'Do you know, the reason why Stephanie didn't come tonight was that she and Richard are divorcing; he just stood there and told me: "Oh, by the way, Steph won't be coming tonight . . .", just as if she had the 'flu. And Livie's having a baby. Already.'

I missed Marietta. I sat out on the common after work and stared at the yellow stems of grass. There was an empty feeling to the city now that she was not in it. On the rare occasions when she had taken a temporary job for a week I used to walk over to the far side of the common, to the corner where there was a telephone box and ring her in her office. Then I would stretch out on the grass for an hour or so and doze. Sometimes I brought a paper with me and read it, sometimes I just gazed up at the sky and the slowly moving branches of trees. But the difference between then and now was that I knew she was there. I had just spoken to her, I had heard her breathing, heard the familiar intonation of her voice which lingered with me so strongly that I could, in my imagination, almost reach out and touch her. She had been diffident about giving me her parents' telephone number, but I had pressed her and in the end she had scribbled it on a piece of paper just as I was leaving, folded it and slid it into my pocket. I took it out again but she took it off me, laughing, pinching the creases of the paper flat again.

'No,' she said. 'It's a message for you for later.'

She was very tender as we parted. The glow of our goodbyes hung on my mouth so long I forgot about the note till I was almost over the common. I took it out and unfolded it. 'I love you' it said, that was all. No number. I rang her flat from a call box, but for some reason there was no answer. So it was that I sat out on the common each day, waiting out the pretended overtime for Mr Finch's round, thinking of her and feeling the year turn. The slight melancholy I felt had pleasure in it as well as pain; the pleasure of knowing that the further the year turned the closer would come the time when we would be together always, Marietta and I.

It was exactly around this time, or perhaps a little before, that Eliska got herself a job. Whether it was ever her intention or whether it was just a whim of the moment, I never knew. She came back late one day, threw some tins and packages on the table and flopped onto the sofa, closing her eyes.

'You can get the supper tonight,' she said, 'I've been out working all day.'

I put down my book, I was on to *Pickwick Papers* now. I closed it very quietly, very slowly. The sullen rage I felt was so violent I could scarcely control the movements of my hands. Working! What would I say in the House? What would I say about my wife, who without my permission had gone off and . . .

'Where?' I demanded.

I could not catch what she said, her voice drawled and slid among the words.

'What?'

She lifted one hand from the sofa in a gesture of irritation, the fingers flickered and then it dropped back again with weariness.

'The big supermarket,' she said.

'The supermarket! What as?'

She raised herself on one elbow.

'Check-out girl.'

I stared at her.

'Check-out girl,' she repeated loudly. 'You get it? Very funny. That's what I am – check-out girl.' She stuck her chin out belligerently. 'I work a money till and you deliver letters. That is our contribution to the great free democracy of the United Kingdom.' She slumped back on the sofa and shut her eyes.

Funny! What was funny? I wanted to hurl *Pickwick Papers* across the room. I wanted to leap at her and shake her by the shoulders; shake her and shake her. Had she thought of the intolerable position she was putting me in? Had she? Colleagues from the House went into that shop. And Marietta! My throat constricted with rage. My wife. Sitting behind a till. Counting out money into the indifferent palms of strangers. Repeating things like 'Forty-two pence change, sir.' 'Thank you, madam' to people who wouldn't even bother to look at her. My breath suddenly rushed out in a hiss. And always, always that jibe about being a postman, at whatever opportunity she could find. No one in the House would have stood for that. I opened my mouth, I drew breath, but I could think of nothing suitably cutting to say. I glared at her, but she just lay there with her eyes closed. The longer I looked at her the clearer it became to me that she was just waiting for me to explode with anger; as if she had calculated all this, gone and got the job specially to get her own back on me. I had the unnerving premonition that if I lost my temper, she would laugh at me. I could even hear it: harsh, derisory. Very well, I said in my head to the closed eyes, I know who's put you up to this. Rinka, isn't it? One of Rinka's cheap tricks. Very well. And with a great effort, forcing calm into my body as its shaking subsided, I made myself look down again at the open pages of *Pickwick Papers*. I would maintain a dignified silence. I would not be drawn. 'Very well' I kept repeating in my head, but I was not convinced or comforted. Things were far from being well. I had the distinct feeling that I had lost. I racked my memory to discover some reference to guide me in such a situation, but I could not recall hearing anything in the House that might help me. Perhaps I should beat her, turn her out of the flat? There was a joke bandied about in the House, a threat: sending her back to her mother, it was called. Why didn't she go, I thought bitterly. But I knew that such a thing was no longer possible for her. None of it was possible. The silence of defeat settled over the room.

We always talk in the House as though we have

complete control over our wives, as though such a condition was our right, the way of ordered life. And when we talk of it we always play it up a bit, flex our muscle. We 'don't have her going there', we 'aren't having her doing that'. I looked across again at my sullen, sleeping wife. I knew already that it was too late, one of them might easily have gone into the supermarket on their way home. I huddled further into my chair. What if any of them had been here, heard her – 'you can get the supper tonight.' It was an insult. There was an accepted way to go about these things; formal preliminaries, if you like. I was not unreasonable if approached properly, if the right forms were used. She could have put her arms around my neck. She could have nibbled my ear, traced little fluttering kisses along my cheek. She could have used the proper words in the right tone of voice, things like 'couldn't you,' 'darling,' 'please.' I might have laid the table, opened tins for her. Now, I eyed the packages she had thrown down, it didn't look as if we were going to have supper at all.

WELL, JAN, I thought to myself as I lay on the sofa with my eyes closed, feeling the ache in my back dissolve and the throbbing in my head of the pop music from the supermarket fade away. Are we going to sit here all night without eating? Without speaking? Without moving? What do you think? That I cannot endure it? That I will break? Do you wait for me to move first, to capitulate? To pick up the food with bowed head, take it into the kitchen. Lay the plates out on the table, the knives, the forks. Your place first, then mine. You first, Jan, that is what you expect, isn't it? That is how it should be, shouldn't it, according to the rules of your Postmen's House. I have not been inside your House, I have not met your friends, but I can guess. You mime their gestures; you graft onto the carefully taught English of your mother turns of speech that even I can see are out of place. They have made you middle-aged, Jan. You have become contented – with nothing! Do you think because we do not speak, because you have said nothing and I have said nothing, I cannot sense your rage? Your injured pride? You are not reading, I know that even though I keep my eyes obstinately closed. You are casting blindly, furiously about in your mind for what might have prompted me to take this job. Your thoughts are running, running, tripping up on themselves. Why? Why did I do it? All you have to do is ask, Jan. Open your mouth. And speak. But that would be a loss of face, too, wouldn't it? And if not 'why', then 'who – who has put me up to it? Your mind always circles back to that, doesn't it? Back and back to one person. Rinka. Well, Jan, you are right – and you are wrong. It wasn't Rinka's idea. It wasn't even mine. It hardly counted as an idea at all. I didn't plan it, it just happened. A piling up of circumstance, one unconnected thing following another and lying together in the mind to form a consequence of thought. But if Rinka had not asked me to go to the cinema with her then probably none of this would have occurred.

I hadn't seen Rinka for some time. She had given up her job and had gone to live in the suburbs with one of the men in the company for which she had worked as receptionist. She had a different hair-cut and new clothes, but she had not changed. She still hated everything English on principle. She complained about the man and the house. She had to go by train now out to where she lived, it was so far. 'The *suburban* line,' she said as we sat in a hamburger restaurant near the cinema, drinking coffee, 'out to the land of the living dead.' She drummed her plum-coloured nails against the top of the plastic table. 'He is so dull.' She ground her teeth. 'So stupid.'

'Why do you stay?'

She pulled a face and shrugged her shoulders. 'It is free. But now,' she leant over the table, her eyes glittering as if at some newly remembered insult, the words hissing out, 'he wants to *marry* me!'

I went with her to Victoria to catch her train. It was on my way home. And besides, I had nothing much else to do. Rinka was still complaining as she went through the ticket barrier.

'Goodbye,' I said, but she scarcely seemed to hear me. Her train pulled out. I watched it telescope to a moving black dot and then vanish beyond sight among the buildings. The train at the next platform drew out. And then the one beyond it. They pulled away in neat, snaking lines. Left behind, the buffers looked forlorn, purposeless, the space between them and the departing end carriage as desolate as a widening stretch of water. There is a finality, sometimes, about departing trains, like the wiping clean of slates. I would not see Rinka again. I was tired of her complaints. You can complain and complain and then there comes a time . . . I turned and began to walk back across the concourse towards the Underground.

It is like a small town, Victoria Station. There are hotels, shops, restaurants, hairdressers. I wandered past the open booths and glanced into shop windows with the disinterested curiosity of strolling through a fairground. It was only at the flower stall that I paused. They had green plastic buckets full of chrysanthemums the colour of autumn leaves, their scent sharp, smoky. They were the tangle of autumn in my grandmother's garden. The sun breaking through the first mists of winter that lay along the river wrapping Prague in silence. In the Old Town, in the small flower shop where Magdalena delivered carnations and collected messages, their piercing scent would fill the shadows of the dark room. Magdalena, coming in, would wrinkle her nose and smile . . . I turned away – and walked into the path of a baggage cart. Its horn bleated at me and I pressed back into a doorway while it trundled past. I found myself standing on a deserted expanse of blue carpet, marked out into sections with low white ropes, like cattle pens, each one leading up to a counter. Near the door, where I stood, was a line of posters advertising foreign travel. Places you could go on the train for holidays – Venice, Paris, Moscow. Prague. It was £195.00 return to Prague.

I had not thought that you could go, just like that, from here. Just get on a train, in London.

'Oh sorry, Miss. You been waiting long?' A man came out of a door set in the wall behind me carrying a pile of brochures and leaflets. 'Just stocking up.' He grinned, opened a hinged gate at the end of the counter nearest me and let himself in. 'Only one on here this evening.' He dumped the armful of papers on a shelf out of sight.

'I want to know . . .' I advanced across the blue carpet. I had not wanted to know anything. I had had nothing in my head except the scent of chrysanthemums. Until he had fumbled for the catch on the door of the counter, until he had smiled. '. . . I want to know the fare to Prague.' I steadied myself with the tips of my fingers against the polished wood of the counter.

'Excursion to Prague, Miss? Hundred and ninety-five pounds return. Leaves Victoria thirteen hundred hours daily.'

'No.' I cleared my throat. 'One way.'

'Not coming back! They won't like that.' He smiled at my confused silence and pulled a battered directory towards him, sliced it open with his thumb and slid his index finger down the densely printed page. 'We can quote you a single, Miss, but it works out dearer than half the excursion.'

'Is it necessary to reserve in advance? To join a waiting list?'

The finger stopped. 'Oh no, Miss, nothing like that. 'Course you'd be more comfortable with a couchette for the night, that's a rackety old journey across Europe, you'd need to reserve for that. When you reserve, you can choose your seat in advance – next to the window, facing the engine, non-smoker – whatever you fancy.' He closed the book with his finger still in it. 'Or you can just come down on the day, people do it, buy your ticket like you was off to Brighton, and hop on the train.'

*

I sat in the Underground compartment like someone in a trance. I stared at the floor so that I could imagine I was on the Prague Metro. That the seats opposite were the familiar curved plastic seats and the people in them Czech. Every time the tube train slowed for a station, I heard in my mind the chime that preceded arrival at a Metro stop. 'Ping-pong'. And the exaggeratedly clear voice that slowly enunciated each syllable of the station's name: 'Staro-mest-ska.' 'Malo-stran-ska.' For the blind and the old women who had never learned to read and the small children who travelled in unfamiliar darkness.

The streets around Clapham Common Underground station looked squat and unreal. I felt dazed and cheated. I had not expected to find myself here, I had expected the portly grandeur of tall nineteenth-century apartment houses. I stood at the crossing lights scowling at the traffic. I felt muzzy-headed, sullen, as though I had slept for too long, for days, for weeks. I marched towards the supermarket and pushed open one of the swing doors. It was there that I saw it. I must have seen it day in, day out and never noticed it before, the printed notice advertising vacancies in all departments. It was right under my hand, taped to the inside of the glass door, torn a little round the edges. I could have bought anything I wanted in that shop, well, almost anything. But I walked past the fresh food counters and the delicatessen. Deliberately. Instead I picked out a tin of stewed meat and a tin of potatoes and a tin of pickled cabbage and a carton of yoghurt. There were more posters advertising vacancies taped to the cash desks and the white-painted pillars behind them. I read them over and over as I waited in the queue.

'Anything else?' sang out the young Chinese cashier.

'What – what are the jobs advertised on the poster?'

'Oh, everything! All staff. Everyone leave all the time.' She giggled. 'Packing staff, cheese counter, meat counter, cash desk. Whatever you like. Very nice place.

Manager very nice man. Mr Fernandez. I call him for you?'

It was as simple as that, Jan. As simple as that. But you will not ask. And I will not tell you. We sit here in our chairs, you and I, in this room and it is as if we were in different countries. A chair space away from each other. As if we had no common language any more. Only silence. In which we have become proficient. Adept. Our conversation has become refined into looking and not looking. We have evolved a whole vocabulary of tensions that build gradually, accumulating like words, forming whole sentences of argument. They are like small electrical storms conjured up by our bodies that hiss and flash in the still air between us. When one of us speaks now, quite often the other is startled. As though such a phenomenon had taken him by surprise. When the other replies the words seem stilted and strange. In such an atmosphere sentences reverberate with a formality that makes them seem empty of sense altogether, or else they echo in the silence, multi-layered with hidden meaning. What shall we do, Jan? What shall we do about this situation? What do you think, Jan, that you cannot say? You want to believe everything is all right, is as it should be. That is the way of the English. They do not like there to be problems and when there are they do not confront them, they look the other way so that they do not have to see them. It exercises you, doesn't it, Jan. It disturbs you. But however hard you try you are not quite English. You can pretend up to a point and then when that point is reached – here I am, your wife. What are you going to do, with this wife? She holds you back, doesn't she. She is like a dog on a leash that is always tugging to go the other way. You have been patient, but you cannot wait for ever for me to catch up with you. You have changed, Jan, like an insect undergoing some subtle metamorphosis. Old habits dropped one by one. New expressions acquired. Even the working of your mind is altered. You will not wait, I see that; it begins now to show in your face, in the covert gestures of your hands and your shoulders. They have increased, these gestures, over the past few weeks. You have become – almost anxious. Your self-containment, your self-assurance have become – fractured – and out leak little silvery trails of uncertainty. Do they escape you however hard you try to contain them? Or do you allow them to escape? Have you laid them, Jan, these trails, on purpose for me to discover them? Am I supposed to find them and, seeing them, melt with tenderness? Am I supposed to take pity on you and say, for you, what you cannot bring yourself to say? I did it once for you, back in Oslensk, when your heart failed you and my heart, full for the first time, proud of its love, gave you its new strength without reserve. Without thought. I brought you here, Jan. Without me you would still be wandering in the forests above Oslensk, watching the mist drift across the narrow valley and the freight trains shunt across the edge of the square. You could not have begun this journey alone. It was not in your nature. Perhaps anyone would have done, as travelling companion. Perhaps. But you chose me. The journey is not over.

I THOUGHT ELISKA WOULD tire of the supermarket in a day or two. But she did not. I thought she would not put up with being ordered around, with such menial work, or the kind of people I imagined she would have to work with. I expected every afternoon to get back and find her in the upstairs front room, heavy with the familiar listlessness that meant she had been home all day alone. But frequently she was not even there. It worried me. It was an unnerving feeling of having lost a battle I did not even know was being waged. And I could not, somehow, regain the advantage. Eliska had slipped my grasp and become – unpredictable. It was the worst blow for someone in my position. The danger was not immediate because Marietta was not due back for another two days. But it was imminent. It preyed on my mind. It seeped into my daydreams of our reunion. The images of Marietta clothed, Marietta naked, Marietta twisting a strand of hair round her fingers in that endearing way she had which drifted constantly across my mind would unaccountably lose animation, dwindle and dissolve away, leaving me staring at the flickering jets of gas in the fire at Mrs Bartholomew's, or the blank squares of the sorting boxes in the Postmen's house. Jack, whose sharp eyes missed nothing, would nudge whoever stood next to him and laugh. 'Here, Jan, what you got on your mind, then?' And everyone round about, who heard, would laugh. I would force a smile to my lips, too, but at that precise moment it would not be Marietta who was on my mind, but Eliska. I could not pin down her working hours at all. I could get no sense of when she might be safely tied to the supermarket till and when she might be free. Each day she came home at an entirely different time. It was so erratic I began to think that she was doing it on purpose. Once she did not come back till nearly nine o'clock at night.

'Where have you been?' I demanded as she dropped onto the sofa and kicked off her shoes. But she did not even bother to open her eyes when she answered me. She just shrugged one shoulder.

'Working,' she said.

The next day I tried to question her nonchalantly about her hours. It was not unreasonable, not unexpected. But she was evasive, offhand in a new kind of way. I felt it instinctively; something in the set of her mouth, the expression behind her eyes.

I became nervous about sitting out my pretended overtime for Mr Finch on the common. What if Eliska decided to go for a walk on the common after work? What if she decided to get a breath of fresh air in her break? After all, the supermarket was only just over the road, it almost faced the common. If she saw me she would know instantly that everything had been a fabrication. She would guess. If she had not already. This anxiety drove me from my accustomed seat on the benches near the fountain. I tried sitting on the far side of the common over near the trees, but it made no difference. Every passer-by I expected to be Eliska. I held my newspaper rigidly in front of my face, staring at the same page, reading and re-reading the lines without taking them in. At the sound of approaching footsteps I would glance anxiously at the section of path or grass beyond the bottom corner of the sheet of newspaper waiting for the toe-caps of shoes to enter my line of vision. I could not bring myself to look up. Besides, there was no need, I would, I knew, recognise at once Eliska's shoes. I tried walking the perimeter of the common to while away the time. I could always pretend, if I met Eliska, that I was just on my way home. But I felt myself hounded. By the time I got back to the Postmen's House with my dangling sack my heart was thudding so heavily in my chest, my whole body seemed to reverberate. I sank down onto the steps of the House, let out my breath in a long stream as if I had reached safe haven, leant back against the door and closed my eyes. I had been sitting exactly here, I thought, when Mr Finch had come hobbling up the path. Mr Finch hadn't limped for weeks now. Today, I decided, it was time Mr Finch got better. It had to stop, the deception. I could not keep it up any longer. Soon, we would not need it any more. The time had almost come. I opened my eyes and felt my body gradually grow calm. It was not so warm here on the steps any more; the sun when it shone was bright, but the heat had already gone out of it. The leggy groundsel at the gate drooped, its stems watery as if frosted. It would probably not be long, I thought, before it became necessary for me to leave the Postmen's House. In my new life with Marietta there would be certain expectations of me, expectations which of course I would be only too eager to fulfil. From her contacts among friends and family would come, no doubt, offers of positions more suitable to my social role. It had been irrational to get so anxious about Eliska finding out about Mr Finch. As soon as Marietta came back, we would have to tell her everything anyway. I pictured myself packing my belongings into carrier bags: my new shirts, my spare pair of jeans. Perhaps as a gesture of magnanimity I should let her keep the transistor radio. 'Well,' I would say finally, 'well, goodbye

Eliska.' It sounded strange in my head, it sent a small cold shiver down my back. I tried it again. 'Good . . .' but it faltered unwillingly and died away half-spoken. Mr Harry's voice cut into my thoughts:

'Still here, Jan, propping up the patron saints? I thought there was somebody about. You seen that stray cat of Sid's? No?' I shook my head and he padded back inside.

I turned to squint up at Dickens, Darwin, Dostoevsky. Their paint had cracked and blistered over the long summer, but they were still there. I had neglected them of late. What had Mr Harry called them? Patron saints? Was that what they were called in the House? Why did nobody tell me that in the beginning, when I had asked about them? Why had nobody said? I had got the impression that nobody cared about them, nobody took any notice of them. Perhaps it had just been protection – you do not tell your secrets to strangers. And I had been a stranger, then, my reactions foreign, unknown. But they had never told me, was I a stranger still? I had thought of the words as mine, that I alone in the House cared about them. Now, it seemed, they belonged to everyone. It was something of a shock, something of a blow, almost. It was, I saw, because of my foreignness that I had given such significance to their existence at all. I kicked at a pebble in the gravel of the path. In my country the door would have been painted over immediately, arrests would have been made. It was because of my foreignness that I had immediately jumped to the conclusion that the words must be a code. That was how we hid statements of importance, truths that might be thought to have a subversive nature. We turned them into unravellable acrostics. We wound them in coded language of unbelievable intricacy, triple-shrouded to preserve their secret, the surface words set, often, as false trails to deflect the enemy and admit only the persistent and the initiated. I would not have guessed at anything of such simplicity, such directness as patron saints. It was so simple it could even be true. And yet Mr Harry's voice had been light, almost joking. It was the habit of the English, I reflected, to joke about something dear to them, their most precious possession. They held it openly on the palm of their hand so that the lightest breath could blow it away, they even turned their gaze the other way as if to provoke loss. To us, who have lost everything, such insouciance dazzles. We long for it. But I am learning, I am learning.

I lifted my fingers to brush against the words, touching them with two fingers together like a benediction, but it felt like sacrilege and I dropped my hand quickly. If they were patron saints, what was their creed? If they were three evangelists, what was the message of their gospels? I had abandoned my quest for understanding for that of love; perhaps I had put myself beyond their protection. But love was central to every religion. And how could these men be saints? – each one of them was flawed, each one had constructed a philosophy of life that they themselves could not sustain. Dostoevsky, who advocated self-knowledge through suffering, loving others more than oneself – and who abandoned his dying wife to travel in Europe, gambling, with his mistress. Darwin, who spent all his life trying to set in order the progress of man from the beginnings of the world, frustrated by strings that would not neatly tie up, links that would not join. And Dickens, the exposer of hypocrisy, the social reformer, the optimist, who increasingly had to hide his private life from public scrutiny. Perhaps flawed men make better saints. They have a common bond with the rest of us. We understand them and they understand us. Perhaps the message on the door of the Postmen's House was that whole philosophies can never be made to work, that instead we should take the best from several beliefs and cobble them together as befits our imperfect world. From somewhere across the common a clock struck; it was time to go home.

That evening when Eliska came in I announced Mr Finch's recovery. But she showed not the slightest interest.

The next morning I woke early, suddenly, as if startled out of sleep, my mind racing and my body tense and alert. I was the first at the House, apart from Mr Harry and Sid. I stood splay-footed in front of my boxes and heard the envelopes thudding one after the other into their slots. The slow stir of the early morning room washed around me, orderly, comforting. Perce, Jack, me, Mr Finch, Little Ted all in a line; the undemanding companionship of comrades. I was surprised, as I took the letters out of their boxes for shuffling and bundling, to find that quite a few were misplaced. Too quick for your own good this morning, Jan, I thought to myself slipping them into their proper place.

'More haste, Jan,' Mr Finch smiled across at me.

I grinned back. 'That's it Mr Finch.' And swung up my sack.

Out on the common the pearl-grey morning had turned to a fine drizzle, but I strode through it almost without noticing it. When I got to the end of my round I was tempted to make a detour back to the House past Marietta's flat. I knew that it was pointless, she wouldn't be back for hours. She probably wouldn't even be awake yet, out in the country. I just wanted to practise, just rehearse how I would see the building again, walk down the path, look up at her window, ring the bell. To look at it and say to myself: 'this afternoon . . . this evening . . .' In the end I went, it didn't make me very late.

At the end of my second shift I called into the Nag. Jack and his cronies were already there.

'Don't often see you down here,' said Jack.

'Got a bit of a thirst on today,' I replied through half-closed eyes, the way we do in the House to look non-committal. The cronies grinned.

'Thirsty work, the post,' said one of them. 'All that paper.' The others nodded. I leant over the bar.

'Half of best, please.'

'Half!' Jack screwed up his face into an expression of pain. 'What you doing with a half?'

'Bit pressed for time, Jack. Anyone else's glass ready?'

Across the street from the pub was a phone box, that was what I had really come for. I knew it was still too early for Marietta to be back but I couldn't resist it. What if she had caught an early train? What if she was there and I was free and . . . The bell of the telephone echoed in her flat in a dull, clipped way, as if the room was hot and airless. I stood in the box for some time just listening to the sound, taking pleasure in the thought of it ringing in her room. I knew the bookshelves that it echoed back from, the silver photograph frames that it got lost among, the shadowy corners in which it circled and the torn velvet of the low chair by the door into which the last sounds were absorbed, leaving the room, as I put down the receiver, deserted and silent once more. Marietta wouldn't be back till four. I had no reason to think that, she had not said, it was just what I had decided was likely. I waited till ten past four and then I tried again. I let it ring for even longer this time, but there was still no answer. I tried again at four-thirty. And then at five. At half-past six Linda answered.

'Oh Jan, it's you.' She sounded surprised. 'No, no Marietta's not here. She rang last night to say she's staying for another couple of days. Well, she wasn't precise, you know how she is. But probably Wednesday because she asked me whether I'd be going out that night. That's our arrangement, that's what we say to each other when we want the flat to ourselves. "Are you going out?" you know, in a particular voice.'

'Wednesday?' I croaked. 'Wednesday?'

'Yes. Well, that's what I assume. Difficult to be sure with Marietta, isn't it?'

I wondered, as I stumbled out of the telephone box, why it suddenly felt so cold. I wondered why it was that the pavement seemed to come up and hit the soles of my shoes in a lopsided, hard way. Why the houses all seemed to be lying back at a strange angle to each other and why they were all so grey. The sun had gone, that was it I told myself. The sun . . . Why could she not have let me know herself? Why couldn't she have telephoned the House, said it was an emergency? Why couldn't she have written? She could even have sent it care of her own address. My name and then hers on the envelope. And her address. As though we were already together. And why was she staying away till Wednesday? Why had she left no message? There must have been a message, there must have been. Linda had forgotten to give it to me, that was all. Marietta should have known better. Linda was stupid, she couldn't remember anything. She was always coming back into the flat, interrupting us as soon as we thought her safely out in the street. 'Forgot my hat,' she would say. 'Forgot my purse.' And Marietta would smile up at me from my shoulder, or the crook of my arm as the door banged behind her and murmur: 'She'll forget her head one of these days.'

'Marietta!' I whispered under my breath. 'Marietta,' I whispered even more softly, 'my darling.' And my arms felt suddenly full of her, a familiar warm heaviness. Two days! How could I sit for two days in those upstairs rooms? With Eliska. How could I contain myself? When my senses were so full of Marietta.

I BOUGHT A COAT this afternoon. I had had it in mind for some days; ever since I had been paid. I knew exactly what I wanted. Something warm. Something that would keep out wind and rain and snow. Something that would last for ever. We used to dream, back home, of being able to buy western clothes. But I didn't want anything smart. Mai Li told me where to go. There was a street market where such things were sold quite cheaply.

'Very good bargains,' Mai Li assured me, solemnly. 'And all new! They have to cut their labels out because they fall off backs of lorries. But they are very nice, not damaged.'

'They fall off in their cardboard boxes?'

'Sometimes.' Mai Li giggled. 'Sometimes they fall off in whole racks.'

'At home we have these bargains too, but they are very expensive bargains.'

'Cheaper than shops, though.' Mai Li studied book-keeping at night-school; when she was a book-keeper she would study accountancy. Economic logic explained every mystery in the world, every human frailty.

'You cannot get these things in the shops.'

'Ah,' Mai Li nodded wisely, 'there you are.'

Mai Li sat at the next till to mine. We used to talk sometimes when it was quiet. Mid-morning or early afternoon. When the aisles of the supermarket were deserted except for one or two people wandering up and down pushing empty trolleys. They were like shadows; you could gaze out from your seat at the till and not even see them. They could place their basket on your counter and you could ring up their things without even notic-ing. Why should we notice – why should we show any interest? We were just hired as robots. To pack shelves, stamp labels, punch buttons on tills. Half of us barely speak English. Most of us drift on after a few weeks. It is nothing for us but a way of making money. We are not asked for papers, working permits, and in return we are not paid a proper wage. We know that. Among ourselves we talked of little else. It was Mai Li who warned me about the pilfering in the supermarket.

'Best to see nothing,' she said, 'and never leave any money in the cloakroom.'

She kept her money in a little felt bag on a ribbon round her neck that hung down inside her blouse. She fingered the ribbon and laughed. 'If anyone ask about it I say it is lucky charm.' She sent all the money that she earned back to her family in Hong Kong, she and her husband. 'Twenty-two people we help,' she said proudly. 'Twenty-two relation.'

'You will go back?'

'I hope.' She sighed and the smile faded for a moment from her face. 'When there is no one else who is sick, no one else to put through school.' She brushed at some grains of flour that had seeped from a bag onto her counter. 'My husband wanted to be lawyer, it is hard for him; but he was eldest, it is his duty to provide. Now he works as waiter.'

They were the sacrifice so that back home life could improve. But they were happy, they were proud to do it; they had a reason to their lives.

When they think, in the supermarket, that we are flagging, that we are more bored, more restless, that the shop is emptier than usual, they turn the loudspeaker music up higher. It works for a while. The girls pricing jars of coffee speed up a bit. The warehouse boys loading shelves bop happily between the shelf and their trolley loaded with packing cases. They have to shout to each other over the noise. They love it. They shut their eyes, cup a hand to their ear and grin. They feign deafness. 'What you say?' I sit, at my till, hunched over, staring down the aisle without blinking. If you stare for long enough at something, eyes wide, the focus begins to blur, the light to dim. I discovered that early on in the supermarket. As the pounding of the pop music crashed rhythmically against my ears, I stared myself out of that place. And into another. Where it was always quiet. Where the only sound was the slow crunching of tyres rolling over snow, the drumming of fingers against a steering wheel. The reflection of light off snow, off sky was a white space in which I floated. I lifted my head and the sudden glitter of sun on glass dazzled me. And the familiar words spoke themselves quite clearly inside my ear with the same lilt always, the same pause between the two phrases: 'There is nothing at Pretin – except us.' And the half-smile ran along my mouth and folded itself into the corners of my eyes at the other smile I did not need to turn my head to see. For this was not the first journey. This was a second. This was the journey Magdalena had predicted – 'You will come when you are ready.'

I have tortured myself with those words in the last few weeks. 'You will come . . .' I whisper and wherever I am I feel my eyes fill with tears. In the shop, in the street. In the unbearable rooms of Mrs Bartholomew. 'You will come . . .' I gasp and beat my fists against the walls. Why did it take so long? In the empty afternoons, imprisoned behind my till, I scowl down the aisles of the supermarket brooding on the cruelty of fate. Why did it take so long for understanding to come? Why did I make things so difficult for myself? Did it take such a journey for fear to be lost? Did I have to be free before I could feel free? What use is this knowledge to me here, here where everyone is free? Where it is nothing, worthless. They only have escape routes one way, Magdalena. We never heard of anyone returning. There are two solutions to living in our country. One is to stay and bury your soul. The other is to leave and bury your heart. You offered me a third way. And I let it go, without even recognising what it was. In my imagination I hear the hard-packed snow beneath our tyres, see the glint of sun on glass. But it might be only the dazzle of light on heaps of smashed glass, the brightness hiding the black skeletons of charred buildings. 'There is no one at Pretin . . .'

'Hey Lizzie, Lizzie-dream!' Always one of the boys would dance up to the cash-desk snatching away my tight-held thought. The chatter of the pricing machine would roll along the top of my till leaving a little white trail of price tags behind it: 1.99, 1.99, 1.99. 'Come on, now!' Or a customer would crash their wire basket down onto my counter and clatter the packages out onto its formica surface. And as I unwillingly punched my fingers into the buttons of the till sometimes they would be overlaid by images of other fingers, raspberry-stained, ink-stained, wine-stained, a line of soil lying below the stubby fingernail. Sometimes they got in the way of my own fingers and I pressed the wrong button, by mistake. Nobody noticed, nobody cared. Nobody bothers about anything much, here.

One day slips into another. I used to wake in the middle of the night, in fright that we had grown old in these same rooms of Mrs Bartholomew's. That Jan was still delivering letters. Now I sleep soundly. I don't care either. It is a blunting-off of sense, this not-caring. I even say to myself that I don't care about Jan. And then all Oslensk rises up and blots out my resolve. But everything else I don't care about. It is a new feeling, this apartness. It generates, now and then, a kind of low bubbling of exhilaration. It was in such a mood that I left work after my first shift and went off to buy my coat. It is strong and tough. Lined with thick fleece. A three-quarters length coat.

'Car coat,' said the stall holder. 'Real bargain. Fifty quid.'

'Car coat?' I laughed. 'I don't have a car.'

'You need a car, darling? You talk to my brother. Get you anything you want, my brother. You want a car?'

I was pulling at the seams of the coat, making sure they weren't weak.

''Ere, you buying that, or you just tearing it to pieces?'

'I want to make sure it will last.'

'It falls to pieces, darling, bring it back and I'll give you a new one. Come on, now; forty-five pound.'

I hoped I would be back before Jan, I didn't want him to see it. But when I opened the door of the flat, he was already there.

I WAS DOZING IN my chair by the window when Eliska came in. I'd been leafing through some of her magazines, I couldn't concentrate on anything stronger, lingering over the adverts. The ones with lovers arm in arm walking through autumn leaves in expensive macintoshes, toasting each other in champagne, throwing each other up in the air and laughing at the purchase of their first home through a particular mortgage company. They were all Marietta and I. I saw our eyes gazing at each other, our mouths kissing, our fingers interlocked. But when Eliska came through the door I woke up at once. I'd decided to make a special effort to be nice, after all things would be much easier if we parted friends. We'd been through a lot, Liski and I; she was a part of me in a way no one else could be, a part of my past. But she wasn't pleased to see me. I could tell by the way she opened the door, by the way she didn't immediately look inside the room as she entered, that she hadn't expected to find me home. The scowl was out before she could hide it.

'Hello,' I said, 'you're back early.' She muttered something and marched towards the bedroom. It was then I saw the wide carrier bag. 'You've been shopping!' I was surprised, Eliska never went shopping for anything but food. 'What did you get?' but she didn't make any attempt to stop. 'Come on, show me.' I stretched out my foot as she went past and managed to get it in front of the bag as a kind of token barrier. She could easily have pushed it aside, but she didn't, she stood there as if trapped, glaring at me. 'Come on, Eliska,' I wheedled. She dropped the bag at my feet and it fell over with a thud. At first I thought it was a rug, by the weight as I pulled it out of the bag and the thick fleece my fingers embedded themselves in. It seemed to be irregular pieces of sheepskin joined together. 'What is it?' But as I held it up I saw exactly what it was. I recognised it with a jolt.

'What do you think it is?' snapped Eliska. 'It's a *coat.*'

She grabbed it and held it up by its arms. The thick segments of sheepskin sewn together by clumsy over-stitched seams swung from Eliska's hands as stiffly as board. We had dreamed of possessing this kind of coat during the long winters in Oslensk. Seeing it was like an accusation. I thought of the elegant camel-hair coat hanging in Marietta's wardrobe.

'Why on earth couldn't you have got something decent?' I exploded. 'Why couldn't you have spent your money on something with style? Why do you have to go round behaving like an impoverished immigrant? You are going backwards instead of forwards, Eliska. For the last three weeks we have been eating only tinned stew and tinned sauerkraut. And now this!' I snatched the coat from her hands and hurled it across the room. 'This is what construction workers back home dream of on windswept building sites, this is what collective farm-workers dream of plodding round icy fields and factory workers struggling to work on dark winter mornings and office workers waiting for hours in tram queues. You are not one of these people any more.'

'I am,' she said quietly.

'You are *here*.' I pounded the arm of the chair. 'You are here. Now! Why don't you act like it, instead of clinging to things that are – ' I turned dismissively from the crumpled heap of sheepskin and strode towards the window – '*inappropriate!*'

'Because I am going back.'

In the sudden silence of the room there was a high-pitched buzzing in my ears, a momentary blurring before my eyes; I turned round so quickly the room seemed to slip.

'What did you say?'

She shrugged one shoulder.

'I am going back.'

'Don't be so stupid. Back!' I spluttered. 'Back – to *that*, to all that?' But she wasn't looking, she had bent to pick up her coat. She smoothed out its sleeves and turned back its collar. 'You can't go back. You can't go back ever. You knew that when you left. It was curtains. Goodbye. Goodbye Oslensk, goodbye Prague – goodbye *everything*! You show your face anywhere near Czechoslovakia – you set one foot inside the embassy here – and you don't need much imagination to guess what will happen to you. If you are lucky, if you are really lucky, you will just be thrown out again. If not – ' I chopped at the air with my hand, but she still had her head meditatively bent towards her stupid coat. She didn't seem to have heard a word I'd said. I took a step closer to her. 'You have forgotten what it was like over there? Uh?' I jerked my chin up, emphasising the words, trying to force her to look at me, but she did not. 'Have you? You want me to remind you?' But she just slowly turned her back on me and walked over to the front door to hang up her coat. It swayed stiffly on its peg like a scarecrow. 'My *uncle*,' I shouted. It was as if she had been suddenly struck deaf, none of my words seemed to reach her. 'My uncle has moved heaven and earth to get you accepted for British citizenship! He has pulled strings, opened doors, given guarantees for you – and all you can do is talk about going back. Do you think that everyone who comes over here is allowed to stay? Thousands of people back home would give everything they have to be where you are. And all you can think of is jeopardising the whole thing. Have you thought about my uncle? Have you thought about *me*!'

'You?' Her voice startled me, the coolness, the matter-of-factness of her tone. 'You? Your heart is here, Jan. And mine is there. It is very sad.'

She stepped forward as if to push past me. But I caught her, I held her by the shoulders and swung her round to face me. So close I could see the dark shadows under her eyes that spread like a stain into the fine pale skin of her cheek. I could see the moist softness of her mouth where her lips parted. And I could breathe in the faint scent of almonds that hung about her. I could have held her tightly; I could have whispered into her hair that she must never, never . . . I wanted to. I remembered in that second how much I had loved her, how much I had forgotten. But at that moment she pulled herself free from my grasp.

'I will give my place to any one of those thousands of people, but this is not the way. This is not the way to free any of us. This way changes nothing.'

'You chose this way of your own free will!'

She shook her head.

'It was not the right one.'

'Well,' I sneered, 'I'm sorry for you, Eliska, because you are stuck with it. You won't ever be allowed back into Czechoslovakia. Never, *ever*!'

She was very quiet all the rest of that evening. My feeling of victory did not last. It was ragged, open-ended, as if I could hardly call it victory at all. It dwindled into a sense of unease. I felt increasingly uncertain that Eliska had been crushed, that she had taken any notice of what I had said, let alone believed it. It made everything unsettled. When I tried to summon up thoughts of Marietta they brought no delight, no comfort. If only it was tomorrow already, I thought. If only I had heard a word from her.

I slept badly that night. I kept waking out of dreams in which Eliska always dogged me. Wherever I went she was constantly at my shoulder, looking lost and wearing her awful coat. In one dream I brought Marietta to meet her, upstairs in Mrs Bartholomew's. I cringed at the sight of the familiar, ugly rooms, the tattered furniture. Eliska stumbled stiffly out of the kitchen, still enclosed in the sheepskin coat. 'This is my wife,' I heard myself say. Eliska held out a hand. The arm of the coat was creased and stained, it gave off a heavy smell like untanned leather. I thought I saw fleas jumping in the wool of the cuff, and woke, my cheeks hot with shame, before I could see the expression on Marietta's face. When I woke to the alarm at dawn, I lay for a couple of minutes staring blearily at the wall. Tomorrow, I said to myself, I will wake in Marietta's arms. No doubt seeped in to cloud the thought. Instead the heavy fog of sleep seemed to roll away. I felt as fresh, suddenly, as if I had slept a day and a night. I slid quietly out of bed, being careful not to disturb Eliska.

WHEN I HEARD the sound of the front door closing, I opened my eyes. The room was still dark. But not as dark as it had been all night. I must have slept. Now and then. But my eyes ached as if they had been open all the time, staring. At what? Shapes in the darkness? The chest of drawers and the chair? The dark line of the shadow of the picture frame? I lay there staring at them, watching the dark grow paler round them. Lighter and lighter. I must have dozed. When Jan woke, I woke. I lay listening to the sound of his footsteps. They ran downstairs hours ago. Hours. I knew it was late. I could tell that by the light and the noises in the street; flat, daytime noises. Now Jan is gone there is nothing to hold me, I said to myself. But I lay there, all the same. Waiting. My mind floating. From time to time I picked up my watch from the bedside table and stared at the tiny gilt hands. When I looked at them they did not move. When I looked away, they jumped minutes.

At exactly one minute past ten I got up. At ten o'clock I was supposed to have been at work, sitting at my till. At ten o'clock I punch out the first bill of the day. They can't phone. They have no telephone number for me. There is no phone in the flat, I told them. They didn't like it at the time. I padded through into the kitchen. I suppose. I remember the pop of gas as I lit the flame under the kettle. But the cold under my feet was the linoleum of the bathroom. And the thunderous drumming was water from the bath taps thudding against the enamel bath. In the raw raggedness of that slow floating morning nothing connected. Everything had the unknown purposefulness of a dream. While the steam twisted into the cold air of the room, I rummaged at the bottom of the linen basket for the little felt bag. The bag like Mai Li's. That is where I kept it when it was not tied round my waist under my clothes. I undid the strings and ran my finger over the tight-packed wad of notes. Two hundred and nineteen pounds. Two hundred . . .

All through my first round, the temptation to phone Marietta was intense. I knew it was too early. Nevertheless, the anticipation of hearing her voice again made my hands tremble so much that I kept dropping letters on people's doorsteps. Envelopes stuck together and were pushed impatiently into other people's letter-boxes. While the wavering form of Marietta danced away before me like a mirage, along the street and up and down area steps, and I hurried after it. The shaking in my hands had spread to my whole body, I could feel its progress through my veins like malarial fever: up my arms, across my shoulders, down into the pit of my stomach. Movement was the only thing that seemed to allay it. As I neared the divide between Mr Finch's territory and mine not only did the feverishness increase, so too did the bursts of anxiety. I kept making sudden darting turns to check there was no one behind me. There was no sense to it. No reason why I should be followed. No reason for Eliska – or anyone else – to suspect anything. After all, I was just walking my round. Doing my job. And the pavement behind me was always empty. The rows of houses lay calm and sunlit, stretching away two by two.

At the beginning of Mr Finch's territory I hesitated, dawdling at the edge of the pavement. Marietta's flat was only two minutes away, down one road and along half of another. I stared longingly across the street; I felt myself leaning forward, one foot poised over the kerb. She could be arriving right now, in a taxi. I imagined the squeal of its brakes, the rattling hum of its idling engine as she fumbled for money in her bag. We do not trespass into each other's territory while on duty; during those hours a man's streets are his and we may only cross them for purposes of legitimate access. I would have no honourable excuse if I were to encounter Mr Finch. And so I turned and headed back across the common. Sunlight came in bursts from behind slowly moving clouds turning the piles of fallen leaves copper and gold. Back in the Postmen's House they were just brewing tea.

Over my old blouse, I put my old jersey. Over one pair of tights I pulled a second. The only thing new I put on was the coat. It was for this purpose, after all, that it was bought. Around my waist over the clothes, but under the jersey, I tied the little felt bag. I walked through the rooms of the upstairs flat of Mrs Bartholomew and they shrank back from me. I slid my toothbrush into one pocket and, as an afterthought, an indulgence, the half-used cake of scented soap into the other. I could hear Mrs Bartholomew moving around in her kitchen. I walked so slowly, so quietly down the stairs, not one of the treads squeaked. I was like a shadow walking. The dog snuffled under the door when I got to the hall. But it did not bark.

I don't know why, but I was reluctant to leave the House on my second round. This is it! I said to myself. I tested the weight of my sack on my foot. 'An hour, Marietta,' I whispered. 'Hour and a half at most.'

'All right Jan?' Perce said, passing me with a bundle of letters. It was the kind of routine thing we said to each other, that didn't always need a reply. I nodded, too breathless to speak. I felt light-headed, as if I had been breathing in and out the same portion of air over and over again. With a numb, mechanical movement I swung my sack onto my shoulder and lurched towards the hall.

'See you,' said Sid as I went past.

'See you,' I mumbled. And then I was outside.

The rush of cool air and bright light raced through my system like an electric current. My lungs were released, my muscles lost their tenseness. 'My darling,' I whispered in my head, and ran down the steps. A milk float wobbled round the corner of the street. A dog trotted, muzzle lifted to the air, from one pavement to the other. And half-way up Oudenard Road a figure turned out of a gate onto the path. For a second I froze but there was nothing familiar about the bulky shape that moved away up the road, and I shook myself and smiled and strode out into the street.

With every envelope that fell through every letter-box I was drawn closer to Marietta. It was as though now, having come through all obstacles, only a set amount of time separated us: seconds measured out by the clicking of letter-box flaps. At last my sack was empty, I folded it up, unbuttoned my jacket and crossed from the last of my streets into the first of Mr Finch's. As I walked up the path of Marietta's building, I glanced up at her windows and saw all the curtains drawn shut. She was there; she was waiting for me. The muscles of my chest were so tight I moved as stiffly as an automaton. I had to bend close to read her nameplate before I could press the right bell; my mind was blank, wiped of all useful memory. The buzzer sounded in what, for a long time, was empty space. And the voice, when it replied, took me by surprise. I had been expecting it so fervently that when it came it was unexpected, distorted into unfamiliarity by the microphone system.

''lo?'

'Postman,' I croaked. I had thought it up as a joke, several days ago. Now I could hardly speak it and it sounded lame. But the door buzzed open. I ran up the stairs. The flat door was ajar. At the sound of my approaching footsteps, it was pulled open wider. But Marietta did not fling herself into my arms. She did not peer, smiling shyly, from behind the door which hid the rest of her naked body. It was a young man who stood there, scowling, with rumpled hair, shirtless, in half-buttoned jeans.

'Marietta in?' I mumbled through thick, suddenly heavy lips.

'I *beg* your . . .'

Then the door was pushed wider, Marietta clutching her dressing gown across her chest appeared at the young man's shoulder.

'I'll deal . . .' He moved back unwillingly. 'Some mistake . . .' she murmured, half-closing the door. Her cheeks were flushed very pink. Her eyes would not look directly at me. 'Ring you . . .' she muttered as the door shut in my face.

I should have hammered on the door, I should have kicked it down. I should have yelled insults through the letter-box. I should have smashed my fist into that creep's clean-cut jaw. I should have refused to leave till the police dragged me off, still shouting. But I had known as soon as the door opened that it was over. As soon as I saw her face. There was nothing to do. I just turned and walked stiffly back down the corridor. The well of the stairs opened up before me like a vast, dark pit that had been waiting for me all along. The uncertainty, the unease had been there all the time, and I had refused to acknowledge them. Outside, the world was very flat. Grey. Without light. I don't know how long I wandered in the surrounding streets, but finally I found myself on the edge of the common, walking over grass. Green and soft. Crushed by my boots that trod, with an increasing purposefulness, over it. One in front of the other. One – two. One – two.

The doors of the train are slamming, now, one by one. From the confusion of noise and pushing of people, we are enclosed. The platform slides past the window. So slowly I cannot believe we are moving. The knuckles of my hands gripping the edge of my seat protrude from my skin as sharply as claws. 'Cologne, Bonn, Koblenz, Mainz, Mannheim, Stuttgart . . .' I cannot believe! I cannot . . .

As my brain cleared, the wisp of an image swept across it and was gone: a bulky figure, hurrying away up a road. Then my boots were running suddenly over the grass, crashing onto tarmacadam. 'Oh my God!' I gasped under my breath.

Tears slip past my nose, but I am smiling really. I shake my head and lick the salt from my lips. I lay my cheek against the cold window. '. . . Prague.' I whisper to my reflection in the glass. I close my eyes, squeezing them tight. *'Prague.'*

Buildings sway towards me and slip lopsidedly past. The Postmen's House rises up. 'Eliska?' I sob. They were there on the door, Dickens, Darwin, Dostoevsky! They saw it all! And let her go.

We have slipped out of the station now. We have crossed the river. To enter the station at Prague you cross the river. You slide in between the backs of buildings, curving round. You pass the white bell tower of a church on your right, grey now with soot. It will be on the border that they stop me.

'Eliska!'
There is no sound only the rasping of my breath and the thudding of my heels on the pavement.

As the platform at Prague slides towards us, I will not look at the men in familiar uniform, who will be waiting.

'Eliska! Eliska!'

I will look up. To where, in the roof of the station, there has for years been a missing pane of glass.

'Eliskaaa!'

Through which you can see . . .

'Eliskaaaaa . . . . . .'

the sky.

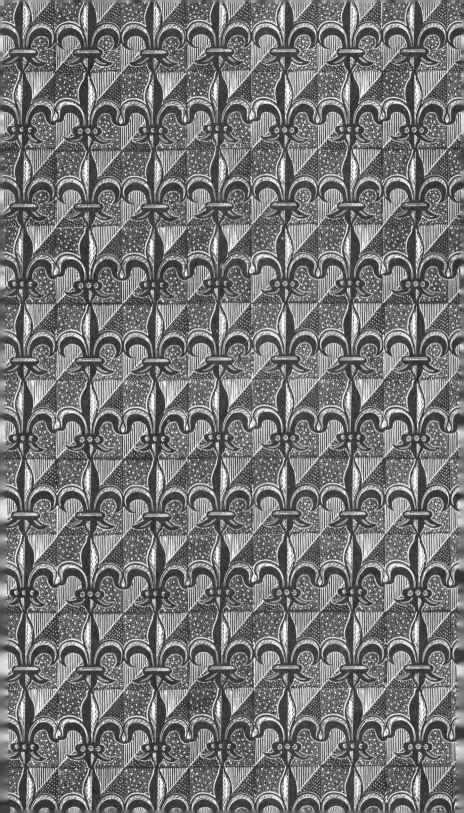